GREAT TELUGU MASTERPIECES

Volume 1 (1910-1947)

A Collection of 25 Great Telugu Short Stories
from the Pre-Independence Period
Written by 16 Masters of Telugu Literature

Translated into English by
Rayasam Srinivas Rao

notionpress.com
INDIA · SINGAPORE · MALAYSIA

ISBN
Paperback 979-8-89363-624-6
Hardcase 979-8-89498-953-2

Contents

Why did I want to Translate Telugu Stories into English?

My fascination with short stories as a literary genre began when I first read KaRa Mastaru's (As Late Sri Kalipatnam Ramarao is fondly known by his admirers and students of Telugu literature) short story collection. Mastaru literally means teacher, a profession he spent his life in. This was when I just passed out of university and started my career. I lost count of the times I reread them. The thought of translating his stories into English came much later when life slowed down a bit from the treadmill that it was. I also went on to read many more short story collections by eminent Telugu writers, and my desire to translate them and introduce them to a wider, English-reading audience only firmed up.

While I never had any illusions about my writing abilities (or lack of them), I was fairly confident I could do a decent job of translation from Telugu to English (and the other way, if needed). The confidence stemmed from my strong foundation in both languages. My school education in Telugu medium combined with constant exposure to English and the 'passion of reading' that remained with me all along. When I saw great Russian and other language stories becoming so popular in English, I asked myself why not give the same opportunity to Telugu. It is true many serious writers had produced translation works from Telugu to English in the past but there was scope to do much more.

When I actually started the translation work, I realised how challenging the task could be. This was when Ka Ra Mastaru's son, a writer and critic in his own right, Sri Kalipatnapu Subbarao, stepped in and offered help by reviewing my preliminary translations and suggesting changes and improvements. He was also kind enough to give me the opportunity to meet Mastaru in person. Mastaru trusted a novice like me and gave me permission to translate all of his stories into English. That meeting with Mastaru in his house in Srikakulam remains etched in my memory forever. During that visit, I also had the opportunity to visit Katha Nilayam, a project initiated by Mastaru to digitise the Telugu story no matter where and when it was published. I was left spellbound by the wealth of Telugu stories made available online now to anyone interested. Katha Nilayam (www.kathanilayam.com) is a one-of-its-kind initiative in global literature, and I urge all Telugu Story lovers to come forward and support the cause generously.

My gratitude is also due to Sri V.V.N. Murthy, author, critic and literary analyst, who gave me an appointment in Bangalore and further introduced me to Sri Dasari Amarendra in Delhi. Sri Amarendra is an accomplished writer and literary critic in his own right. Both of them at that time were on the Katha Nilayam board of trustees, contributing to the noble cause. I have received tremendous support and encouragement from Sri Murthy and Sri Amarendra, including corrections and suggestions on how the translation can be more effective and reflect the original more closely. I remain grateful and indebted to them for this support.

I also want to thank my wife, Anuradha, for her continuous moral support for this passion of mine, including helping to run this latest volume by generative AI engines to get some early feedback. My big thanks to my sons Venu and Raghav for reading some samples of the work and giving their comments. My special thanks are due to Raghav, gifted with an artistic talent, for designing the cover page for my first e-book.

My sincere gratitude is also due to my parents, without whose blessings this effort would not have been possible. My father, Sri RGK Murthy, and mother, Smt. Sarojini Devi inculcated in me a love for literature from a young age, which eventually became the foundation for this effort.

After publishing my first e-book containing eleven of KaRa Mastaru's stories, I took a break for a few years as my work and personal commitments did not permit me to focus on this passion. Again, in 2023, I picked up the thread and decided to do more as I was completely out of the corporate responsibilities.

Introduction to the Current Volume

The first Telugu short story seems to have been published in 1910, penned by the legendary Gurajada Apparao, who is more popular for his epic drama Kanyashulkam. As I kept reading the stories of that time and subsequent decades by multiple authors, I felt it was better to approach the stories starting in 1910 chronologically.

For the sake of convenience and easy understanding—and also to represent the evolution of short stories in Telugu—I divided the period between 1910 and now into four distinct sections.

1910-1947 was the pre-independence period during which writers touched upon topics like freedom struggle, patriotism, human relations, corruption in the government, social reform (selling girls for money, dowry, widow remarriage, eradication of untouchability, etc.), British influence on Indian middle classes, nationalist feelings, oppression of rural population by feudal landlords, etc.

From 1947 to the 1970s, Independent India started as a socialist republic with tight state controls, a license-permit regime, class struggles, fights between landed and landless, Marxism-communism, industrialization-urbanization, poverty, illiteracy, etc.

The 1970s-1991 was when the middle class started emerging as a sizeable section of the population, etc. Socialism, Naxalism, the public sector, government corruption, state controls, and urbanisation were still predominant issues that plagued society and made their way into literature.

1991-now represents a liberalised India, increasingly exposed to the rest of the world, with huge growth in middle-class population, westernisation, technology pervading all aspects of life, etc.

I started my maiden effort with the first period, 1910-1947. I picked authors whose stories were first published during the period. I had read stories that were available to me and picked those that I genuinely liked. I also tried to ensure the anthology touches a wide range of themes such as social reform (untouchability, widow remarriage, etc.), rural life, middle-class psychology, women's issues, satire, corruption, superstitions, pseudo-nationalism, etc. I also showed a deliberate bias towards Gurajada and Sripada as they had been pioneers and my favourites. I picked a total of 25 stories penned by 16 authors. I had to leave out some prominent authors like Chaganti Somayajulu and Gopichand because their stories seem to have been already heavily translated and published. Some of the authors were prolific, and others were sparse in their story-writing. But all of them have a special place in the annals of Telugu literature for the early lead they took, the wide range of topics they touched and the way they popularised short stories as a literary genre. There are many other authors whose stories were published during the same period, and many more stories by the same authors in this book. This is just a sample and purely subjective collection of stories. I sincerely hope discriminating readers would like this book and pave the way for many more such anthologies (either by me or others).

I look forward to sincere feedback after you finish reading this volume.

Sincerely,

Rayasam Srinivas Rao

rsrsrini99@gmail.com

Approach to Translation

Accuracy and Faithfulness

I had to deal with many dialects of Telugu and also many words and expressions that are nearly a century old and no longer in active use. And there are Urdu and Parsi words mixed within Telugu sentences. To stay as close to the original meaning as possible, I relied heavily on Telugu-English and Telugu-Telugu dictionaries. I also referred to publicly available information (thanks to Google) and cross-verified the same wherever possible to ensure accuracy.

Retaining the Cultural Context, Sensitivity and Appropriateness

I had also set a goal to stay close to the original cultural, social and regional context.

Another objective I had set for myself was to directly pass on the beauty of Telugu idioms and figures of speech to English readers wherever possible instead of finding an English alternative. I believe this will give the reader a true flavour of Telugu culture, life in rural, urban, and middle-class settings, and the way people express their feelings in different circumstances. I liberally used footnotes on the same page to explain the terms to make it easier for the reader.

I tried to sincerely portray the complexities of social interactions and interpersonal dynamics within the prevailing cultural setting of the times. I made a conscious effort to convey these themes in a way that is understandable to an English-speaking audience without losing the original Telugu cultural nuances. These include the caste dynamics, the agrarian lifestyle, and the regional backdrop.

The same-page-footnote approach – which I have used extensively - got a favourable nod from the experts who reviewed my draft translations and many friends who were generous enough to review the drafts. This gave me the confidence to stick to this approach

Some examples are a relation like "Vadina (Sister-in-law)" or an animal like "Gangireddu (Decorated Bull)", as well as names and expressions like "Karanam', 'Munsab', 'Madiga', 'Amma', 'Ayya', 'Tambulam', 'Rudraksha', 'Gundam', 'Dora', etc.

I used the words as they were spoken in Telugu when characters address each other or when they speak these words instead of translating them to their English equivalent, like - Sister-in-law for Vadina or Brother-in-law for Bava. I felt this approach exposes the reader to frequently used Telugu terms – both currently and widely prevailing or those that are unique to the time of the story and region.

I tried to translate dialogues in a manner that retained their original flavour, reflecting the characters' personalities and social standings.

My overarching goal was to retain the 'Teluguness' while making the stories easily readable and understandable for English readers.

I welcome scrutiny and critical observations from readers who are familiar with the Telugu version of the stories and who are reading the English version now. This will help me improve the next edition.

Grammar Rules and Principles Followed in this Translation

Most of the stories were told in the past tense, and I have retained this, with occasional deviations into the present tense when the situation or narrative warrants.

To denote what the character is thinking (Inner thoughts), I have used italics, which seems to be a broadly accepted universal standard. I have also used italics in some other cases to highlight a character's surprise or tone, but these are minimal and clearly identifiable.

To denote conversations or something spoken by a character, I have used double quotes, enclosing the conversation or speech in double quotes. I have also followed universally accepted punctuation rules within the double quotes or preceding and succeeding the double quotes.

Regardless of what punctuation was used to end a dialogue, I have taken care to put it inside the closing quotation mark. This includes question marks and exclamation points, as well as periods and commas.

When there are several speakers, I start a new paragraph each time the speaker changes to help the reader understand someone new is speaking. However, it is possible that this rule might not have been followed in some instances based on how the narrative was in the original story.

If a dialogue is extended to multiple paragraphs, I have mostly followed the practice of using opening and closing quotation marks for each paragraph to indicate that the dialogue is continuing.

If a speaker quotes someone else in their dialogue, I use single quotation marks around the phrase being quoted. I have put punctuation inside the single quotes like I did for standard double quotation marks. If the quote is at the end of the dialogue, the punctuation goes inside the single quote, and there is no space between the single and double quotation marks.

About the Original Authors and Their Stories in this Anthology

Gurajada Venkata Apparao (1862-1915), popularly known as 'Gurajada', was the first writer to usher in the modern era of Telugu literature. He started off as an English poet in 1882. His English poem 'Sarangadhara', written in 1882, made him one of the first Indian-English writers in India.

One of the hallmarks of Gurajada's writing was how he represented the complex culture of his time by using Urdu and English words in conversational Telugu. This pattern can be seen in his magnum opus "Kanyashulkam", a play that is a sarcastic yet poignant take on the then-prevailing social practice of selling girls for a price and not letting widows remarry but use them as unpaid servants at home. It also touched upon so many other superstitions and shady practices prevailing in society at that time, especially in Brahmin families. In this play, Gurajada used the vernacular the way it was spoken by different communities. One can also see the liberal use of Urdu words prevalent in society (words like behadbee, kummak, aabroo).

In a literary career of more than three decades (from 1882 to 1915), Gurajada gifted Telugu literature with a path-breaking drama Kanyashulkam (Selling Girls), five short stories, a handful of poems, and critical essays. He emerged as a 'Vaitalika' who awakens a sleeping society with his powerful and fluid style. He created people-centric literature and moved away from the prevailing practice of feudal stories centred around royal courts, palaces, and kingdoms. The vernacular language he championed emerged as the trendsetter for the next generation of writers. That is the long-lasting and glittering accomplishment of Gurajada, which makes him rightfully the "Father of Modern Telugu Literature'.

Many people don't know he was credited with being the first Telugu short story writer in the 1910s. His story "Diddubatu" is officially regarded as the first published Telugu short story, although a few others had already written some short stories by then. While Indian mythology and epics are full of short stories, the story as a literary genre can be said to have been an English influence. I have managed to obtain three of his stories from that decade and translated them. I couldn't get hold of the remaining two. I also felt it is apt to have them as the first three stories in this anthology to honour the great writer.

The three stories in this anthology are very different from each other, yet they are bound by a common thread of Gurajada's people-centric approach and liberal use of spoken language.

In the story 'Matilda', he used Urdu words like "Chaman" (small garden) and "Khaayida" (putting someone to hardship) to truly represent the spoken dialect of those times. Matilda is about a young wife and her old husband and how they are perceived and treated by neighbours.

In 'What is your name', he presents a stark picture, laced with a lot of satire, of the prevailing religious beliefs and how Hindu society was polarised into Shaiva and Vaishnava sects and how people were being taken for a ride by leaders and practitioners of these sects.

In 'Atonement', perhaps the first-published Telugu short story, he touches upon a simple husband-wife relationship and how a straying husband quickly realises his mistake and corrects himself and how his wife gently and cleverly drives him in that direction and then accepts him for what he is.

Sripada Subrahmanya Sastry (1891-1961), popularly known as 'Sripada', was called the emperor of the modern Telugu short story for his phenomenal contribution to this literary form. He was a literary rebel born into an orthodox Brahmin family in Palamuru village of East Godavari district. He studied Vedas, Scriptures, and Astrology.

He struggled to break free from those orthodox shackles and left an indelible mark on Telugu literature with his progressive works. Like his many contemporaries, Sripada also started his writing career with poetry but switched to prose, urged by his guru, who spotted a unique ability in him. He penned nearly 75 stories that touched upon varied social issues and maladies of the day, such as widow remarriage, the plight of women in society, untouchability, the hypocrisy of pseudo-freedom fighters, corruption among government servants and so on. He mastered the short-story literary form, which was alien to Telugu at that time. He expressed himself very naturally and eloquently, at the same time touching upon very relevant subjects of the time. He wrote about what he observed closely, and his stories remain authentic.

His stories can be broadly categorised as Romantic, Message-oriented, Social Reform, Family life, Investigative, History, and Parody. He also wrote many poems, dramas, novels, critical essays, and so on. He opposed Hindi, Khadi, and Gandhi and remained a steadfast Telugu icon.

I picked seven stories of his 75 for this edition and intend to translate more in future editions. My aim was to cover mainly social reform, corruption and hypocrisy in these stories. The common thread among these stories is the fluency of the language, usage of Urdu, Hindi and English words prevalent in those days and sharp messaging that hits the reader hard.

In 'First Attack', the protagonist Janaki (a young widow) – prefers social reform among her own community rather than plunging into politics of the day for fame or recognition. When she is in a dilemma about this decision, the opportunity comes along in the form of an old man trying to marry (rather than buy out) a young girl in lieu of writing off her father's debt. She seizes the opportunity, takes the lead and stops the marriage in the nick of time. She goes on to take all the womenfolk of the village under her wing to educate them.

In 'The Nationalist', we meet a hypocritical young man who claims to have nationalist and patriotic ideals but hates and demeans his own mother tongue (Telugu) and brands his people as second-rate citizens compared to North Indians. He looks to marry a progressive young widow who also happens to be entitled to a substantial inheritance. The story shows us how the lady stands firm for her ideals in the end.

In 'Eradication of Untouchability,' the progressive-thinking king of a province is shocked and frustrated when his attempts to eradicate untouchability in his kingdom fail for reasons he cannot fathom. The story exposes the deep-rooted caste maladies in India, even at the lower caste levels.

In 'Minister's Advice,' Sripada touches upon how a young king—after being coronated and dismissed as an inexperienced novice—takes control of his court affairs and opens the door to well-entrenched ministers until he encounters his match. The story talks about corruption and hypocrisy.

The story 'Weeds' also appears as 'The Dying Telugu Spirit' in another published edition. There are minor variations, and the endings are different. I have taken the liberty of merging the two stories into one because the overlap is almost ninety per cent. In this story, Sripada touches upon deep-rooted corruption among government servants (Weeds), the job-hunger among middle-class Telugu Brahmin families, how that forced them to stray from the traditional path, and finally, how one youngster shows the way forward.

In 'Tahsildar Dream,' Sripada describes how a wife's misplaced ambition (to see her husband as a Tahsildar) misfires and eventually results in a very different outcome.

In 'The Banished' Sripada beautifully takes us through the travails of a young Brahmin scholar who is banished by his own community out of jealousy and how he wins in the end. This story reflects the social situation of those times perfectly.

Chinta Deekshitulu (1891-1960), was born in Dangeru village in East Godavari village in 1891. He completed his B.A. in Rajamahendravaram and L.T. in Chennai and worked as a government school teacher – and also briefly as deputy inspector of schools – in Rajamahendravaram region. Like many of his contemporaries, he started with poetry, moved to detective novels, focused on children's songwriting and eventually penned a lot of stories targeted towards children. He was one of the earliest to take on short stories as a literary form, and he published many short stories with the main focus being humour. Among the nearly forty-odd stories, I have picked up two for this anthology.

His themes and writing style are simple and could easily be attributed to what he observed in daily life and what stirred his thoughts.

In 'Test of Culinary Skills', the writer humorously touches upon the changing times and how age-old, taken-for-granted topics like cooking had become the subject of examinations and certificates.

'First Prize' is part of a set of six stories titled 'Mrs Vati Rao Stories'. These stories are about how the educated and rich of the time were trying to mimic British culture. They touch upon women's clubs, hypocrisy, and the influence of British thinking on the Indian upper class during pre-independence days. The stories are full of humour and satire.

Kanuparti Varalakshmamma (1896-1978) was one of the earliest short story writers in Telugu. She was a freedom fighter and a social worker who fought for women's education. Her writings were mainly focused on women's issues. Sarada Lekhalu was the most well-known of her works. Her stories are simple and touch the heart.

Out of the few stories available to me, I have chosen 'Our Village', which depicts, through the lens of a naïve housewife, how villages have changed and how the old way of life was overtaken by urbanisation even in the 1930s and 1940s.

Gudipati Venkatachalam (1894–1979), popularly known as **Chalam**, remains one of the most influential personalities in modern Telugu literature. He mainly espoused women's causes. Chalam's work discussed how he believed women should face these problems. His writing had a distinctive and bold style which would earn him an enviable place in the Telugu literary world.

In the story 'The Wife', Chalam thinks way ahead of his times when he touches topics such as how a wife is first a woman and how her views should be respected. He touches upon the cruel practices of how girls were married off against their wishes. One such girl's struggle is portrayed in this story in a heart-touching manner.

Kodavatiganti Kutumba Rao (1909 –1980) was one of the foremost names in Telugu Literature. He penned novels, short stories, and critical essays. His literature is known for its critical and reformist tone, which touches human lives directly. He focused on middle-class life and its problems, depicting them in a very realistic way in his stories. His writing style is straight and touches the reader strongly.

The story I have included in this anthology, 'The Bride', is a simple one about how a young girl stands up firmly and bravely against a man her father's age and reforms him.

Munimanikyam Narasimha Rao (**1898-1973**) was known for his gentle humour, mild satire, and flowy language. He is well-known for his Kantham kathalu, in which Kantham is the writer's wife and a typical middle-class Telugu housewife. In many of his stories, he depicts the daily scenes in family life in an inimitable way.

The story in this anthology, 'The Silver Dining Plate', is a classic middle-class story about how Kantham achieves what her husband thought was impossible.

Karuna Kumara (**1901-1956**) was born in West Godavari but settled in the Nellore district and mastered the Nellore accent and dialect in his stories. His real name was Kandukuri Anantham. He started life as a bus conductor, worked as a court clerk and became a

Tehsildar. His stories focused on village lives told in a fluid Nellore accent.

The story in this anthology, 'Polaiah', tells how a hardcore, traditionalist Brahmin – who loves untouchability and despises lower caste people – is outsmarted.

Suravaram Pratapa Reddy (1896-1953) was a Freedom Fighter, Social Historian, Writer, Poet, Scholar, Social Reformer, Lawyer, Journalist, Editor and Founder of various Socio-Cultural & Educational Organisations. At a time when the Telugu language, culture, and identity, especially in the Nizam / Telangana region, was fast disappearing, SPR took it upon himself to revive and rejuvenate it. His stories focused on the lives of common people in the Telangana region. His stories bring to life the times of the Nizam-ruled Telangana region and are replete with Urdu terms used widely in the region.

'Vakil Yenkaiah' is a take on how a daring village lad masquerades as a Vakil. He becomes overambitious and eventually pays the price.

Potlapalli Rama Rao (1917-2001) was prominent among the first-generation writers in Telangana. His stories depict the rural life during the Telangana armed struggle.

His story 'Justice' depicts the brutality of the government officers towards hapless villagers.

Kanchanapalli Chinavenkata Rama Rao (**1921-1992**) was one of the earliest writers in Telangana. He studied law and fought on behalf of Telangana freedom fighters who were convicted by the then-brutal regime. Even as a student, he ran a monthly magazine, wrote stories and essays and encouraged other writers. His stories depict the rural Telangana life of those times.

His story 'In Our Village Too' depicts how the revolution caught up and changed rural folks' mindsets and made them turn against the brutalities of feudal landlords.

Adivi Bapiraju (**1895-1952**) was a novelist, playwright, short story writer, painter, art director, and nationalist. He is mainly known for his literary works, such as Gonaganna Reddy, Narayana Rao, and Himabindu. In his writings, he touched upon historical themes and contemporary social issues.

The story 'Narasanna's Daughter' touches upon untouchability through the eyes of a little girl and how things changed during her lifetime.

Madapati Hanumantha Rao (1885 – 1970) was an Indian statesman, poet, and short-story writer. He was the first Mayor of Hyderabad from 1951 to 1954 and was also a Padma Bhushan recipient.

He was a pioneer who helped revive the Telugu language in Nizam's Dominion and founded the Andhra Mahasabha.

His story 'To Whom' is set in rural Telangana and tells the story of a Zamindar and an honest, straightforward youth.

Kaloji Narayana Rao (1914-2002) was an Indian poet, freedom fighter, anti-fascist, and political activist from Telangana. In 1992, he was awarded the Padma Vibhushan.

Kaloji completed his primary education in Madikonda and his higher education in Warangal and Hyderabad. Although he studied Telugu early on, he also wrote poetry in Marathi, Kannada, Hindi, and Urdu.

His story, 'We are better off', is a satirical take on animal rights, narrated from an animal's angle. It is more of a philosophical dialogue than a story in the true sense.

Nandagiri Indira Devi (1919-2007) was one of the first-generation Telangana writers. She wrote close to ten stories, of which the current story, 'The Bet,' won a lot of critical acclaim for its analysis of human psychology. She wrote mainly about social issues and human relations. Her writing style is simple and uses easy-to-understand language.

Krovvidi Lingaraju (1904-1986) was born in Rajahmundry, East Godavari district. He abandoned his college education to join the national struggle at the age of 16 during the non-cooperation movement of 1921. Lingaraju actively participated in significant national movements, including the Salt Satyagraha and Quit India Movement. Because of his involvement, he faced imprisonment. While in jail, he translated Maxim Gorky's novel "Mother" into Telugu as *Amma*. This is his most notable literary work, apart from the short stories.

His story in this book, 'The Verdict', is a moving narrative about how a father repents when his son strays and how a judge spares no effort to reach the right verdict.

Acknowledgements

I humbly acknowledge that all the copyrights of the original Telugu stories in this volume remain with the original authors. It was not easy for me to reach all the authors' representatives (as none of the authors exist today) for explicit permission to translate. I took the liberty to go ahead with the translation and publishing as I was keen to expose these Telugu treasures to English-speaking readers. And I don't have any monetary motive. Anyone with any questions or concerns in this regard is free to approach me at rsrsrini99@gmail.com.

Rayasam Srinivas Rao

Atonement

Original Author: Gurajada Appa Rao. First published in Telugu in 1910.

"Open the door! Open it!"

The door didn't open. He paused for a minute.

The clock in the room chimed one.

How awfully late I have been! I can only curse myself! I will be careful from tomorrow. All my anti-nautch[1] *principles got drowned in the song of that courtesan. It didn't stop with just one song. Now, I am getting physically drawn towards her presence. If not, where was the need to sit through until the song was complete? Why the craving to find some opportunity to talk a few words with her? I am slapping myself in atonement. From tomorrow I will not attend her singing sessions for sure. If I now call out aloud, I could be waking Kamalini up. If I can gently knock on the door*

---

1 Nautch is an Urdu word meaning dance. Nautch-girls referred to dancing girls and, in many cases, prostitutes. It was common for the rich and privileged to visit these nautch-girls. Some of the reformers who were against the practice called themselves Anti-nautch.

and get Ramudu to open it, I can quietly join her in the bed and pretend to be a gentleman.

As soon as Gopala Rao laid his hand on the door, it opened slightly. Wondering about the same, when he gently pushed the door open, there was no light to be seen in the hall. He crossed over and opened the bedroom door and found the bedroom to be dark, too. He tiptoed to the bed and tried to find out if Kamalini was asleep or awake but could not figure out. Then he took the matchbox out of the pocket and lit a stick. Kamalini was not to be seen on the bed. Stunned, he dropped the matchstick to the floor. Both the room and his mind were blanketed by darkness. Crazy questions and crazier answers manifested and died rapidly, overwhelming him with anguish. Whether it was for his own stupidity or for finding Kamalini missing, he was annoyed and angry. When he reached the centre of the hall and called out to the servants, neither the manservant nor the maidservant could be seen. He was convinced that death by hanging was the only suitable punishment for them.

He went back to the bedroom, lit the lamp, and carefully examined the room. Kamalini was not to be seen. When he went to the main door and opened it, he found Ramudu in the middle of the street, puffing away his cigar and gazing at the stars. With uncontainable rage, Gopala Rao called him, "Rama! Come here!". Caught by surprise, Ramudu hurriedly dropped the cigar and came closer, saying, "Sir!"

"Where is your *Amma*[2]?"

"My mother? She is at home, sir."

"Not your mother! Idiot! My wife!"

"Oh, *Amma*? Where else, sir? She is asleep."

"She is nowhere to be seen in the house!"

Ramudu was suddenly worried. As soon as he crossed the main door, a couple of heavy blows landed on his back. "I am finished, sir," a wailing Ramudu collapsed on the floor.

Gopal was naturally kind-hearted. Even when he committed a wrong, wiser counsel prevailed immediately, anger subsided quickly, and remorse set in. He helped Ramudu get up and gently rubbed his back. Ruing his animal-like conduct, he took Ramudu inside the room.

Sitting on the chair, he asked feebly, "Rama! What happened?"

"It appears to be some kind of mystery, sir!"

"Do you think she went to her parents' house?"

"Of course, she is capable of that, sir! I can't speak freely if it angers you, but what else would happen if women get educated?"

"What do you know about the value of education, Rama? "Saying this, Gopala Rao leaned forward,

---

2 Amma literally means mother but is also used respectfully to refer to a landlady, lady boss, owner of the household, etc., like Madam

resting his elbows on the table and brooding with his head between them. He noticed a letter written by Kamalini and started reading it.

"Ayya[3]!" it started.

"*Dear* is now replaced by *Ayya*? "

"Is the Peyya[4] lost, sir?"

"Idiot! Shut up and keep quiet! "

'Ayya! It has been ten days so far. I have not been aware of your coming home in the nights. You have been telling me that you were attending meetings and spending sleepless nights participating in agitations in the public interest. I have learnt the truth from my friends. Is it not because of my presence here that you were forced to lie? If I go back to my parents' house, you will neither have any restrictions nor will there be any need to lie. Instead of forcing you to lie every day, is it not my duty – as a devoted wife – to stay out of your way? I am heading out tonight to my parents' house. Please be happy and remain kind towards me. '

Gopala Rao finished reading the letter and said, "I am an animal."

"Why are you saying that, sir?"

"I am an absolute animal!"

Ramudu controlled his laughter with great effort.

"Endowed with good character, education and humility, she taught me the right lesson!"

3 Ayya: Sir. Also used to address one's father in colloquial.
4 Refers to a calf. Rhimes with Ayya.

"What did she do, sir?"

"She went to her parents' house! Wait! How did she manage to leave without your knowledge?"

Ramudu took a couple of steps back and said, "I must have been fast asleep, sir! I can't talk about a woman sulking, but if a wife wants to leave for her parents' place without permission, a man should slap her and put her back on the right path. If women get into reading and writing like men, wouldn't it be catastrophic?"

"Idiot! The best object in God's creation is a gem called an educated woman. Lord Shiva accommodated his consort Parvati in half of his body. Englishman called a wife 'better half'. It means she is better than her husband. Do you get it?"

"How can I understand all this, sir!" Ramudu was increasingly finding it tough to hold back his laughter.

"Your daughter is going to school, right? You will soon understand the value of education. Let it be for now. Either you or I must rush to Chandravaram. I cannot leave town for another four days. You have been our servant since my grandfather's time. Go and bring Kamalini back. Do you know what to say to her?"

"Of course, sir! I will say, 'Sir has smashed my back. Please come home, Madam'".

"Forget the blows. I will give you two rupees as compensation. Take it and forget about it. No slip of the tongue on this topic in front of Kamalini! "

"I will not, sir!"

"I am telling you the exact words you should speak out there. Listen carefully. 'Sir has learnt his lesson. He will never again attend courtesans' performances. He will not step out of home at night. This is for sure. Are you following? He asked me to tell you he is pleading meekly, holding your chin, in this regard. He implored you not to reveal his blunders to anyone and to come back within two or three days. In your absence, he is finding days unbearably longer.' Tactfully communicate this message, do you get it?"

"I get it, sir!"

"Repeat to me what you are going to speak there."

Ramudu scratched his head and said, "If you ask me what, I can't say. I don't know. All I am going to say there is, 'Madam! Please listen to me for whatever years of age and experience I have. Women should listen to their husbands and remain compliant. Otherwise, like our senior master, my master will also keep the courtesan. Just for your ears only, one top-class courtesan has just landed in town. My master's mind is no longer in his control. I leave it to your wisdom now.'"

"Oh My God! You Idiot!" Gopala Rao sprang up angrily from the chair.

Ramudu vanished in no time.

Just then, a sweet giggle accompanied by the harmonious sound of armlets could be heard from beneath the bed.

*****

What's Your Name

Original Author: Gurajada Appa Rao. First published in Telugu in 1910.

1

O Humans created by God!

O Gods made by Humans!

What is your name?

When we cast doubts on mythological stories, our Guru used to shut us down, saying, "Your stupid education is making you mindless! You are all utter Buddhists!"

"What kind of people were Buddhists, Sastry Garu[5]?" Rammurthy asked one day.

"I will lecture on this topic next Sunday in Mr Raju's flower garden. All of you be there," Sastry Garu said.

5 Garu is like sir. A respectful reference to someone elder or of higher stature. Sastry Garu and Guru are used interchangeably in this story. Guru refers to a teacher.

About twenty-five of us settled down in the sand under a large mango tree in the flower garden on Sunday around four o'clock in the afternoon. Sastry Garu spread his towel and sat on it, facing us. When we offered him a stool, he refused, saying, "I don't need it, folks. When all of you are squatting on the floor, would I sit on a stool?" After downing the sweet water from a couple of tender coconuts and chewing a Tambulam[6] , Sastry Garu lectured on the Buddhist religion. About ten minutes into the lecture, Rammurthy –quietly reading a book all this while – spoke up, "Sastry Garu, all that you are narrating, is it not from Sarvadarshana Sangraham[7] ? "A surprised Sastry Garu exclaimed, "Oh my goodness! How did you know? Is it a translation by any chance?"

"Yes, sir."

"One must give credit to the Englishman! What is that second book?"

"It is Buddha Charitra,[8] sir."

"I wonder how they manage to get their hands on these rare and priceless books!" Sastry Garu grabbed

6 A betel leaf stuffed with betel nuts and lime, garnished with other ingredients that vary from region to region in India. In North India, it is called Paan. It is typically eaten after a meal but can be consumed anytime. It is also referred to as Killi or Tambulam in Telugu.

7 An ancient, important Hindu book that reviews different systems of Hindu philosophy, written by Madhava Acharya and translated into English by early Englishmen in India.

8 History of Buddha. Charitra in Telugu means history.

the book from Rammurthy and started reciting – in his melodious voice – the slokas from the book, along with the meaning of each sloka[9].

Any narration by Sastry Garu helps the listener to visualise the story easily. Everyone had a great time listening to him that afternoon. When returning home, Sastry Garu said, "I wonder how the Englishman developed this fondness for Sanskrit! They are unearthing hitherto unknown classics. God is surely with them."

After four days, Sastry Garu said in the class, "Folks! To be honest, until I read this book, I did not realise the greatness of Lord Buddha. I am convinced this great man was an incarnation of Lord SriMahaVishnu.[10]"

From that day onwards, Sastry Garu stopped berating us as 'Buddhists'. But he continued to call us Christians. Since it was not possible for us to project Christ as Lord Sri Maha Vishnu's eleventh[11] incarnation, we had no option but to keep quiet.

There was no other Guru like our Guru in this world. He lived in Kashi for many years and studied the

9 A couplet in Sanskrit typically with sixteen syllables in each line.

10 Lord Vishnu is an important God in Hindu Mythology. Vishnu / Maha Vishnu / Sri Maha Vishnu all refer to the same God. Two other major Gods (forming a triumvirate) are Lord Shiva and Lord Brahma.

11 Vishnu was supposed to have had ten incarnations or avatars in mythology (including Buddha, according to some believers).

science of logic. He was famous as a peerless logician. Apart from logic, he could also grasp the subtle nuances of poetry. When it came to naivete, there was no one more naïve than him. It is a wonder how such scholarship and naivete could coexist in one head!

This incident happened ten years ago. Now, Sastry Garu is retired and lives on his pension. He spends time being served by students like us, teaching us from Sanskrit books, making us happy and enjoying the process himself.

I am into business. Rammurthy owns plenty of land. He is into new modes of agriculture. He created a grand garden of flowers. Those flowers are just peerless. And without our Guru tasting the first fruits, Rammurthy doesn't even step into the garden. Strolling in that garden gave our Guru immense pleasure. That is where we frequently hold our meetings. Venkaiah is a schoolteacher who frequently keeps getting scolded for his erratic ways. Six or seven of us from the school batch are still here. Whenever we meet as a group, along with our Guru, it almost feels as if a chunk of heaven has landed on Earth.

Now, let me come to the current story.

Eight miles from our town is a Vishnu holy site called Ramagiri. I will describe it in detail some other time. For now, all you need to know is that this Vishnu holy site is fairly modern. Among the black hills in that town, Buddhist ruins can be found. The locals call them Pandavas' lodgings. In this country, one can't find a cave where Pandavas didn't stay and a water hole where Sita[12] didn't bathe.

The Jangams[13] were treating a Buddha idol in a large cave as Lord Shiva and the adjacent female idol as Gauri[14] and were worshipping them.

As this continued, one day, a British officer arrived with a retinue of clerks and orderlies and camped in the mango orchard west of the hills. He mobilised hundreds of labourers and started digging the mounds between the hills. Locals assumed he was doing it for money, but he started carefully piling up broken idols, statues, sculpted stones, and old pots as if they were more valuable than money. We went there to look.

When we reached there, there was a hubbub in the village over the marble Buddha idol that the Jangams were worshipping. We have seen that idol and it was majestic. The officer told us he had not seen such a grand idol anywhere except in the Gandhara[15] region. On the pedestal of that idol, Buddhist inscriptions like 'Ye Dharma Hetu Prabhava'[16] were engraved very

12 Wife of Lord Rama, hero of Epic Ramayana.

13 Jangams are nomadic Shiva worshippers.

14 Lord Shiva's consort.

15 Kandahar, now part of Afghanistan, was once part of the British empire.

16 Common Buddhist inscriptions that are found on many idols / Buddhist structures. This is the first line of a four-line verse. The verse translates to - Of those things that arise from a cause, The Tathagata has told the cause and what their cessation is: This is the doctrine of the Great Recluse

elegantly. When the officer eyed the idol and asked them whether he could have it, pat came the reply from the elders in the Shaiva sect – "We would part with our lives but not the idol." The reply was polite because the officer had good relations with all. If it were someone else, things would have gone too far. Sensing the mood, the officer didn't pursue the idea any further.

One night, priest Jangam Sarabhaiah—who worships the idol—yanked it out and offered to sell it to the officer for two hundred rupees. The officer refused to buy a stolen item and, further—to avoid being implicated—sent for the town's elders to keep them informed. Sarabhaiah was somewhat surprised at the officer's stupidity, gave him a slip, and bolted towards the hillocks. He was not seen again.

We checked into Sayanna Bhukta's house and stayed there for three days. Sayanna Bhukta studied logic from our Guru for some time. He had good literary taste and was also a small-time poet.

On the third day, we finished dinner and settled on the terrace. Coconut tree fronds in the garden were swaying in a mild wind. The Devudu hillock facing the garden rose in the night sky like a gigantic Lingam[17] piercing the darkness, touching the sky, showing how insignificant man was compared to nature and how the mind was touched by some unknown sorrow and fear. The stars around the peak of the hill glowed like divine flowers offered by Gods in worship. Our minds were occupied with thoughts about the history of that

17 Shiva's symbol – a phallic object.

place. After thinking for a while, I said, "One wonders how this place would have looked then and how the Buddhists of that time lived!"

"Those wretches would have suffered exactly like we do now. In fact, their life would have been worse than ours," Venkaiah screamed, shattering the gentle thoughts with his brittle voice. Enraged, I asked him, "Why don't you stay happy with your own priceless thoughts? Why do you shatter my fantasy Buddhist world that I formed in my head with your harsh words?"

"Tell me, folks," Sastry Garu chipped in, "Buddha was an incarnation of Vishnu, wasn't he? So why are these Jangams worshipping him as Shiva?"

Sayanna Bhukta took out his snuff powder box, inhaled deeply, wiped his nose with the top cloth and said, "There is a story." Sastry Garu loved stories. "Go on," he said. We lent our ears in all earnestness.

Here is the story Sayanna Bhukta narrated:

"The rivalry between Shaiva and Vaishnava faiths in this village is an age-old one. Jangam Sarabhaiah – the priest who fled now - has been the leader of the Shaiva sect. Until the other day, when he removed the idol and fled, he was considered a complete incarnation of Nandikeswara[18]. The Jangams believed he would be grazing the grass opposite the hill in bull form. Even in the current situation, some disciples have floated

18 Nandi (or Nandikeswara —a more respectable way of addressing it) is Lord Shiva's personal bull and vehicle. It can be seen in front of the main sanctum in every Shiva temple.

a theory that the British officer was none other than Lord Shiva in a previous birth. Hence, he desired to have the idol. It is only to obey the instructions of his master, Sarabhaiah removed the idol and while fleeing, he took the form of a bull, bellowed, and fled the officer's tent. Tomorrow or the day after, he will appear meditating in Veerasana[19] posture on top of the hill or some temple tower. The disciples will bring him back in a procession with a canopy over his head. After that, goldsmith Veeraiah (who gets angry unless addressed as Veeranachari) will embellish the story with some fibs and publish a poem in his name. The duo's fame will then spread far and wide."

"Their blind faith and behaviour cannot be found in scholars. Lucky fellows!" Sastry Garu exclaimed. When Venkaiah wanted to interject to say something, I shut his mouth with a wave of my hand. "Who are you to prevent individuals from voicing their opinions?" he snapped. I signalled him to remain quiet.

Sayanna Bhukta continued the story.

"Yes. As you suggested, the learned don't have the deep faith of illiterates, but this blind faith can, at times, become fatal. That is what I am about to narrate now."

"Even I was trying to say the same thing but was not allowed to," whined Venkaiah. "Yes, there isn't anything you don't know. Keep quiet now," I quipped.

---

19 One of the postures in Yoga.

"You know the origin of Shivasthala[20]. Because of Priest Sarabhaiah's publicity skills, Shivasthala attained a lot of prominence and glory during his time. The villagers nearby pay their homage and fulfil their vows made to the deity. Large fairs are common during festival times. The local Devangas[21] are well-to-do. Sarabhaiah's word is law for the villages of Jangampadu and Devapeta. The Vishnusthala[22] in this town was built by a local king two hundred years ago. For the upkeep of the temple, one village was assigned to the Lord. Rangacharya's family members have been the trustees of this place since then. He has employed a couple of Vaishnavas to take care of the daily needs of the deity with a lot of devotion and care. He is a very capable man. You have already seen how proficient he is in Sanskrit literature. The talk is that he is equally good in Dravida[23] languages and Vedas. His son Krishnamacharya is equally cultured but not a very accomplished man. It is Krishnamacharya's wife, Nancharamma, who brought glory to that household. Thanks to the scholarship of her parents, she attained significant knowledge in Telugu and Sanskrit. Her melodious way of reciting mythological stories has no equals. She is endowed with beauty and a matching character. She has one daughter

20 The Shiva temple in the town. Sthala literally means place.

21 Devanga refers to a caste of people in South India who are worshippers of Lord Shiva.

22 Vishnu holy site/temple as opposed to Shiva holy site/temple.

23 Refers to South Indian culture/languages.

and one son. She personally takes care of matters of the household and temple."

"Is it all fiction or reality?" asked Venkaiah.

"We have some dealings with them. Whatever I am narrating is what I heard directly from my wife. I personally heard her recital of Puranas[24]. If you too want to hear, stay till tomorrow. This is the state of Vishnusthala. However, Rangacharya Garu never interfered in religious wrangles. The captain of the Vaishnava side is Satani[25] Manavallaiah. The same fellow who comes for alms every morning and scares the daylights out of everyone with his blaring sloka recitals. One early morning, the collector[26] was riding a horse and came face to face with Manavallaiah on the village outskirts. Manavallaiah took off with a sloka in his customary raucous style. Seeing his bulky figure, the namams[27] on the forehead, the copper banner in his hand and hearing the loud noise, the horse was terrified. The news goes that the irate collector fined him five rupees. Manavallaiah, of course, denies the story vehemently and presents his own version, which says – an impressed collector made him recite the slokas,

24 Puranas are Hindu mythological stories telling God's stories.

25 A sect of Vaishnava Sudras or scheduled class in the old Andhra region.

26 Head of district administration during the British Raj and even now

27 The vertical three-striped symbol that Vaishnavites apply on their forehead to represent their faith.

gifted him five rupees, and he bought a new vessel to collect alms using the money."

2

"Vaishnavas didn't have the same unity that the Shaivas had. Many Satanis are disciples of Manavallaiah, but they don't project him as God's incarnation. Manavallaiah's peeve has always been, 'If Sarabhaiah could be the incarnation of Nandi the Bull, should I not be considered at least a part incarnation of Garuda Alvar,[28] if not full? Because I have the might of Garuda Alvar's talons embedded in me, I am able to tear apart Sarabhaiah.'

"When Rangacharya heard this boast once, he gave Manavallaiah an earful. After being thus scolded, Manavallaiah came out and vented his opinion, 'These Brahmins are neither fully learned nor illiterate. It is only the lower castes who – with their unwavering devotion – became Alvars. Why wouldn't I – who triumphantly slayed the Shaivas and carried Lord Rama's banner all these days – be Garuda Alvar's Talon's avatar? Whenever the talons of Garuda Alvar grow and get chopped off, it is absurd to think that the fragments would go to waste! They are reborn as devotees like me and slay the other religions.' "

---

28 Garuda is the mythological eagle (and a devotee) that Lord Vishnu uses to travel. He is an important element of the Vaishnava religious sect, just as Nandi the Bull is important in the Saiva sect. According to Vaishnavism, twelve alvars are devotees of Lord Vishnu.

"Oh My God! What insolence? What arrogance? Are these ignorant fellows God's avatars? For pronouncing themselves as such, their heads would be blown to pieces! "Our Guru said.

"Sastry Garu, if it were old days, these fellows would be easily considered avatars of God. We would be constructing temples, setting up their idols and worshipping them. Even Buddha was a human, wasn't he!" Venkaiah said.

"You are comparing a washerman's pond with an ocean! "Guru shot back.

"Can't you keep quiet without commenting on every statement? "I asked.

Sayanna Bhukta continued.

"The Nayudus[29] of this village are well-to-do. Among them, Sarathi Nayudu is a millionaire. His brother-in-law, Rami Nayudu, is the Munsab[30] of the village. A little dishonest, alcoholic and foodie, though. The largest arrack[31] shop in this Taluk[32] is right here in this village. So, you can imagine the worthiness of this village."

"Four years ago, a Vaishnava Seer[33] came from the southern part of the country and ceremonially

29 An influential caste in Andhra

30 Village headman/judge/officer of high rank in the village appointed by the Government.

31 Country liquor.

32 An administrative unit comprising multiple villages. Multiple Taluks comprise one district.

33 Vaishnava seer

inducted Sarathi Nayudu and some other leaders into Vaishnavism. That day, Munsab Rami Nayudu imbibed Pulihora[34] and Vaishnavism simultaneously in the Rama temple. From then till now, his commitment to both remained firm. Since then, every Dwadashi[35], Sarathi Nayudu has been organising a lavish feast in the temple. For Rami Nayudu, Dwadashi has become a major festival."

"Sarabhaiah detested – as if his eyes were stuffed with red chillies - the fact that all Nayudus embraced Vaishnavism and were not even glancing towards the Shiva temple. After deep contemplation, he came up with a plan."

"Those days, some wandering Shivacharis[36] came to this area from the Hyderabad kingdom. After a couple of months, they swooped down on this village with a pedestal, lights, drums and all the paraphernalia. Every midnight, they used to worship Shiva. During the worship, the noise generated by the conchs, giant bells and drums used to strike terror in the minds of the illiterate. The sounds used to cause an echo in the black stone hill and further amplify the cacophony. Influenced by this spectacle, one by one the Nayudus started discarding the namams and switching

---

34 Flavoured rice, made by mixing rice with tamarind pulp/ lemon juice seasoning, is a common and popular food in South India. It is also commonly offered to God as an offering to be eaten later by devotees.

35 Twelfth day of the lunar cycle. Important for the Vaishnavites.

36 Shaiva faith priests/preachers.

to Viboodi[37] and Rudrakshas[38]. On the tenth day after their arrival, the Shivacharis conceived large-scale plans to cross the Gundam[39]. Sarathi Nayudu's mind started leaning towards Shaivism. Everyone believed that after witnessing the Gundam demonstration, Sarathi Nayudu would certainly switch to Shaivism. With this aim, the leaders among the Shaivites went door to door with their drums, singing Shiva's praises and forcefully invited the villagers to the show."

"When informed about this, Rangacharya Garu said, 'Whatever is Lord Rama's wish will happen! If a Vaishnava wants to convert to the Shaiva faith, what is the point in blocking the same? In any case, it is Lord Shiva who grants salvation to anyone who dies in Kashi. Would he not grant deliverance in the next birth to someone who is a staunch Shaivite in this birth and liberate him from the birth-death cycle? Someone who is a believer finds his way, whatever his religion. If there is no belief, being a Vaishnava would also not help.' The Satanis didn't like this indifferent attitude of Rangacharya Garu."

---

37 Ash (considered holy) that is taken from a graveyard and smeared on the forehead and arms by Shaivites.

38 Rudraksha refers to a stone fruit, the dried stones of which are used as prayer beads by Hindus (especially Shaivites). Rosary.

39 A Firepit is formed by a rectangular bed of hot and glowing coals, about 10 feet long and 5 feet wide. Faithful devotees step onto the bed and cross it to prove their devotion. If one comes out with feet unburnt, his devotion is considered pure.

"'This brahmin is low in his love for Vaishnavism. Unless we take matters into our own hands, Vaishnava pride will get wounded.' Bragging thus, Manavallaiah organised a large meeting under the pipal tree facing the temple around nine o'clock on the same night when the Shivacharis were planning to cross the Gundam. Hundreds of Satanis and Nayudus assembled. The warriors among them secretly downed some arrack before coming. Then what did Manavallaiah, standing on a flat stone slab and resting his chin on a staff, say? 'Dear staunch devotees! Have you heard? Falling prey to the diabolical illusion created by these Shaivas, many Nayudus have already deserted the royal path of Vaishnavism – that takes them directly to Vaikuntham[40] – and got mired in the darkness of the Shaiva faith. Now, they are making elaborate efforts to convert our dear friend and foremost Vaishnava devotee Sarathi Nayudu to Shaivisim. Tonight, if he goes there and witnesses the horrible acts of the Shaivas, we can no longer hold him back. So, please think of a way how we can save him and how we can propagate the virtue of Sri Maha Vishnu. In my opinion, it is our immediate duty to find a way to prevent Sarathi Nayudu from going there tonight.'"

"When the assembled crowd was deliberating the issue, Ramanujaiah got up and said, 'Why think so much? Why can't we do the same thing that they are doing? If Shiva – who is a devotee of Rama - can have so much power, why can't Rama – who is the lord of the universe – have a thousand times more power?

40 Specifically, the Abode of Lord Vishnu. Heaven.

So, my advice is that Manavallaiah – who is nothing but the avatar of Sri Garuda Alvar – should carry the copper banner and cross the Gundam while reciting Nalayiram[41]. To let the world see the difference between Shaiva and Vaishnava faiths, right now I will create a much larger and grander Gundam under this tree. I wouldn't consider anyone objecting to this idea as a true Vaishnava.'"

"No one could notice in the darkness, but Manavallaiah's mouth went agape. When everyone shouted their approval, life drained out of him. He thought for a minute and said, 'Brothers and devotees! Ramanujaiah is questioning my credibility. Of course, I must face it. I had to portray myself as Garuda only to counter Sarabhaiah, who – in all his arrogance – self-anointed himself as the avatar of Nandi Bull. And I did so because of my devotion towards Vaishnavism. Otherwise, don't I know that, with my heavy frame, I could never be Garuda Alvar? And being the wise men that you are, were you not aware of the same? Ramanujaiah, with his light build, can easily be considered as Garuda Alvar's avatar. Ask him to cross the Gundam. If I step on the coals, I will be mired in the pit a yard deep, and that will be the end of me. Ramanujaiah is very lightly built, and he can easily cross the Gundam in a few strides, with feet barely

41 Nalayiram is a set of four thousand Tamil verses written in the 8th century by twelve alvars, singing the praises of Lord Vishnu. It is widely sung in Vishnu temples.

touching the coals. Brothers! Think fairly!' Hearing this, Ramanujaiah vanished quietly."

"Rami Nayudu intervened at this stage – 'The point we are debating is whether Lord Rama has magical powers or not! Stop the nonsense and cross the Gundam'. Hearing this command, Manavallaiah's face went pale. Being nearly twenty stones in weight, it was not easy for him to do a vanishing act, as Ramanujaiah did. 'Oh My God! If only I could be a true Garuda Alvar for a few minutes, I could fly somewhere and save my life!' he mused."

"'Why are you silent?' Rami Nayudu started needling him. 'Every day, before sunrise, you come to us with all your ear-splitting recitals. Is all that show meant for just extorting some alms, or does it have at least some magical powers?'"

"Manavallaiah sighed, remembered Saint Ramanuja[42] and said, 'Brother Rami Nayudu! We go a long way back as friends. You have been enjoying this powerful Munsab position for a long time representing the Government. You are a discerning man. Let me ask you – To prove the superiority of Vaishnavism, do you want me to ape that lowly act being performed by Sarabhaiah? The sacred saying goes, 'Prithivyapaste jo vayuraakashath' Prithvi means earth. So, one should walk only on earth and not on any other element[43]. One can stretch this further and say water is also acceptable.

42 Great Vaishnava saint who lived in the 11th-12th century.
43 The five elements are Earth (Prithvi), fire (Agni), water (Jal), sky (Aakash) and wind (Vayu).

Jumping into fire is the worst thing a devotee can do. So, all of you accompany me right now. In this darkness, I will take Sri Maha Vishnu's name and jump into SeethaGundam[44]. Then you will understand my powers.'"

"Rami Nayudu came closer, squeezed Manavallaiah's hand hard and said, 'Listen Vaishnava! If my brother-in-law Sarathi Nayudu joins Jangams, the Dwadashi Pulihora and Rice Pudding will vanish. You, too, know this for a fact. Will he accept your powers if you float and swim like a bottle gourd in Seethamma Gundam? Stop these absurd stories and right in front of my man's eyes, walk on the fire reciting your daily prayers!'"

"'Very well, my friend! If that is your wish, so be it. To prove Sri Maha Vishnu's powers, why wouldn't I step on fire? It is very late in the night now. Let us go home and sleep. Same time tomorrow, I will prepare a grand Gundam in this very place, walk on that blazing Gundam and demonstrate the power of Vaishnavism. Garuda Alvar himself will possess me then and make me cross the Gundam in one leap.'"

"'I will have none of it! If my brother-in-law joins the Jangams tonight, it doesn't matter whether you cross the Gundam tomorrow or not. You must cross *their* Gundam, that too tonight itself. Get up, folks! Let us carry this Vaishnava fellow and make him cross the Gundam.' When Rami Nayudu said this, about four Nayudus held Manavallaiah's hands and brought him

44 A lake in the village.

down from the stone slab. Realising things are going out of control, Manavallaiah came up with a ploy. 'Wait! If one must cross the Gundam, should one not go prepared with the right equipment? Or will you just dump me in my current state and burn my body? The way Shivacharis do it is by holding a Veerabhadra[45] idol in hand, chanting hymns, getting pumped up with the sound of the conch, and then crossing the Gundam in that state of hyper-excitement. Likewise, unless you dump one festive idol of Sri Rama on me, how the hell would I be able to do the job? Even Garuda Alvar always moves around carrying his master, Peruma Alvar, on his back! Otherwise, he never flaps even a wing. Don't you know?' Hearing this, Rami Nayudu said, 'He is right! Go wake up Rangacharya Garu and bring him here.' Some Nayudus rushed to Rangacharya's house nearby, carried him without his top cloth, and made him sit on the stone slab under the pipal tree. Observing this commotion, Krishnamacharya climbed onto the loft and hid himself."

"Feigning a lot of humility, Manavallaiah brought Rangacharya up to speed on the goings on and pleaded with him to donate the procession-idol[46] of the Lord. Rangacharya said, 'Fools! Have you lost your mind? This act of crossing the Gundam is a condemnable business. This is prohibited in Vaishnavism. Nowhere

45 Angry Form of Shiva

46 Procession idols are used for processions taken out in temples on festive occasions. These are used as the main idol cannot be moved. These are small replicas of the main idol.

in our sacred books is this process mentioned. There is no method or mantra defined in our scriptures for crossing a Gundam!'"

"'Is there any mantra to burn the whole body with the chakra[47]? Don't talk too much and just hand over the idol to the Satani fellow' Rami Nayudu shot back."

"'Get lost! I am not giving it! Sudras[48] should not be touching these idols. Eyes will explode!' When Rangacharya said this, Manavallaiah sighed in relief and said to Sarathi Nayudu, 'Have you noticed, friend? What he said is true. I should not be touching the idols. So, the next action is for the Master[49] himself to cross the Gundam holding the idol in his hands. He is entitled to that superiority.'"

"Munsab said, 'How can the old man hold the idol and cross the Gundam? Let us go and get the younger master'"[50]."

"'Don't you touch my son! It is fine. I will cross the Gundam holding the festival idols. My son went to the city and is not in town,' Rangacharya said."

---

47 Refers to the metallic wheel with sharp edges (chakra) used by Vishnu as a weapon and a symbol of Vaishnavism.

48 Sudra refers to the lowest class among the four classes in Ancient Hindu society. They were typically treated as untouchables and were denied access to the inside of temples. Common facilities, etc.

49 Refers to Rangacharya, who is the overall boss of Vaishnava sect.

50 Krishnamacharya, son of Rangacharya.

"'Agreed. Everyone! Start moving now!' shouted Manavallaiah."

"Suddenly, a light appeared behind the Pipal tree trunk. All were terrified. From behind the trunk, Nancharamma made an entry. She was holding a torch in one hand and a knife in another. With her curly hair swaying in the wind, she calmly stepped forward, stood beside her father-in-law, pointed the knife to the Nayudus who were holding his hands, and asked, 'Villains! Will you let go of this holy brahmin, or do you want me to make you victims of this knife?'"

"Seeing her sudden appearance, everyone lost heart. The Nayudus holding Rangacharya stepped away from him. Then she kept the torch on the stone slab and asked Manavallaiah, 'What do you want?'"

"Manavallaiah replied, saying he didn't want anything."

"'Just now, were you not saying you wanted the procession idols?'"

"'Why do I need them, Madam! I am an unholy fellow! Even if you want to give me molten gold equal to their size, I don't need them. Rami Nayudu was saying – 'he didn't finish."

"She turned to Rami Nayudu, looked at him without expression and asked him, 'What do you want, Rami Nayudu?'"

"Rami Nayudu lowered his face and said he didn't need anything. And muttered under his breath,

'Who can argue with a woman?' Rami Nayudu's wife is a termagant."

"Nancharamma pressed, 'If no one needed anything, why was this old brahmin woken up in the middle of the night and dragged here without even his upper cloth? Why is everyone silent now?'"

"Rami Nayudu mustered some courage and said, 'One can't win an argument with a woman, but tonight, those Jangams are going to cross the Gundam chanting Shiva's name. If we don't do the same while chanting Rama's name, wouldn't it be a disgrace for us?'"

"Nancharamma: 'Why don't you do it?'"

"Munsab: 'I don't know any mantras and magics. That's why I asked *him* to do it.'"

"Nancharamma asked Manavallaiah, 'why couldn't you do it?'"

"Manavallaiah replied, 'Madam! It was my bad luck that pushed me to arrange today's meeting. My mind was deranged. Look here, I am slapping my own cheeks[51]. If you allow me, I will leave this instant for Srirangam[52]. If I am seen again anywhere near these villages, my head may be hit with a thunderbolt.'"

"Nancharamma told Manavallaiah, 'You have a large heart', then turned to Rami Nayudu and said, 'Munsab Nayudu! Your main worry is that if your brother-in-law Sarathi Nayudu defects to Shaivism,

51 An act of atonement in Indian culture.

52 A famous south Indian town where Lord Vishnu is present in the avatar of Ranganatha.

your regular Dwadashi supplies of Tamarind rice and pudding will stop, right?'"

"Munsab replied, scratching his head, 'It is not just about me, Madam! Wouldn't Lord Rama also be deprived of the tamarind rice?'"

"Manavallaiah interjected, 'Madam! Sugar Pudding and Tamarind rice are not important here. Our main duty is to demonstrate the power and greatness of Vaishnavism and uplift the faith.'"

"Nancharamma: 'Why don't you do that uplifting? Why do you need a procession idol for that purpose? You always carry a sky-high copper banner! Doesn't it have even an iota of power and magic?'"

"Manavallaiah mumbled, 'Things are back to square one' and disappeared in the crowd."

"Nancharamma continued, 'Not just Rama. If we have true faith in any God, we can cross not just one Gundam but any number of difficulties. I will cross the Gundam chanting the name of my father-in-law. If there are any Vaishnavites who can accompany me, come forward!'"

"No one moved."

"Nancharamma smiled wryly and said, 'Are you all warriors enough only to throw the old man into the fire and watch from the ringside?'"

"There was pin-drop silence."

"Nancharamma looked around and asked, 'Is Pir Saib[53] not here?' Pir Saib stepped forward and stood with folded hands, saying, 'Madam, here is your servant.'"

"While Pir Saib was a Dudekula[54] by profession, he was also a staunch devotee of Lord Rama who sang the Lord's songs and practised Hatha Yoga. The Matha[55] in the garden on the banks of the lake, next to the road, belongs to him. He has a strong disciple following."

"'Saib, can you cross the Gundam?' asked Nancharamma."

"'If that is your wish, consider it done, Madam!' replied Pir Saib."

"Nancharamma: 'Where is Manavallaiah? Garuda Avatar has vanished! Rami Nayudu! Despite being staunch devotees, none of you could dare to cross the Gundam, whereas the almighty gave courage to this pure Turk[56] to cross the Gundam! So, tell me, is your Vaishnava faith great or his Turk faith great? Rami

53 Local Muslim leader. Pir is a Muslim term that refers to a banner that Muslims carry in processions. Pir also refers to a Sufi Saint. Saib is a variant of Saheb, which is a respectful term like Sir. It is also used for Muslims in Andhra.

54 Dudi means cotton. Dudekula professionals were local Muslims in Andhra who weaved/cleaned cotton and made mattresses.

55 Monastery where religious leaders live and teach along with their disciples.

56 Muslims were referred to as Turks and Saibs / Sahebs in Andhra in the old days.

Nayudu! Your sole aim is to see Vaishnavas humiliating Shaivas tonight, isn't it? I will suggest a plan to make that happen. Faiths are two types – Gentle and Aggressive. Both types of people can be found in Vaishnavism and Shaivism. Those who perform aggressive acts like crossing Gundams are called Shivacharis in Shaivism. We have similar folks in our Vaishnava faith, too. Do you know who they are?'"

"Manavallaiah's head popped up from the mob with an eager question, 'Who are they, Madam?'"

"When Munsab Nayudu replied, 'Who else? The Satanis', Manavallaiah's head vanished again in the crowd."

"Nancharamma continued, 'You are asking who are those Vaishnavites? Who else? The Turks! What do you think a Pir is? Nothing but the Lord's ThiruNamam[57]. In the town, a Satani – who was our neighbour – used to erect Pirs and cross the Gundam. In the town, many Hindus keep Pirs and cross Gundams. So, I will get a Namam of Lord Rama and create a Pir using the same. Pir Saib will cross the Gundam holding the Pir. You all know Pir Saib's stature. He is as much a devotee as Saint Kabir Das[58] was. So let go of your fears, go with him, and come back victorious. Just in case devotion falls short in saving the day, don't forget to carry your hand sticks.'"

57 Same as Namam. Thiru adds a tone of respect.

58 A 15th-century Indian mystic poet and saint.

"When she paused, Manavallaiah emerged from the crowd, pushing people aside and reciting slokas in full flow. He prostrated in front of Nancharamma and said, 'Madam! You are none other than Sri Maha Lakshmi's[59] avatar. You have saved Vaishnava faith today. Not just faith but our lives, too. Now watch how I will launch into them!'"

"Manavallaiah is a master brain. He drove the rest of the Vaishnava strategy that night."

"When things cooled down, Krishnamacharya got down from the loft. Glowing with the joy of having achieved a difficult task, Nancharamma was walking back home holding the hand torch. When she encountered her husband, she threw a gentle, mischievous glance at him. The next day, Krishnamacharya told me that look made him feel divine, like God's incarnation. And he recited a poem to describe the feeling further. I guess some folks don't get satiated unless they share their darkest romantic secrets with friends."

"That night, I went to see Shivacharis crossing the Gundam. At around four o'clock in the morning, in pitch darkness, the red-hot coals were blazing in the Gundam. A cool morning breeze wafted across the landscape. Suddenly there was a deafening noise from conch shells and drums that felt like it could destroy even foetuses. Even the best English-educated atheists admitted that it numbed them to the bone. "

59 Consort of Lord Maha Vishnu.

"Four Shivacharis – bodies smeared with sandalwood paste - emerged from under the canopy and stood near the Gundam. One held a ferocious-looking copper idol on his head. Another stood opposite him, swinging his sword and belting out words of valour. Another poured Ghee[60] into the Gundam, followed by Pumpkin pieces. Immediately, the Shivacharis jumped into the Gundam and crossed it. They turned around on the other end and were about to retrace the walk in the reverse direction. Suddenly, from the same end, a group of masked men – shouting 'Allah – Ram' at the top of their voices, pierced the band of Shivacharis and crossed the Gundam. Leading that group was one warrior holding a silver Pir in both hands and crossing the Gundam like Bhima. All this took less than half a minute."

"The crowd ran helter-skelter. Some Satanis (and Shivacharis, too) had their feet slightly burnt, which was attributed to a deficiency of devotion. It was believed that after this incident, there was a truce between Sarabhaiah and Manavallaiah. But outwardly, they continued to appear to be bickering.

"Look! The Pir you see opposite our house in that public courtyard is the same Pir used that night. From that day onwards, that Pir is worshipped every year. The entire village—without Shaiva and Vaishnava distinction—pays their respects to the Pir God. Because it is trident-shaped, Sarabhaiah calls it Shaiva Pir. If

60 Clarified butter used in cooking as well as rituals in India

Shiva and Vishnu are Pirs, why can't Buddha be Shiva?" Sayanna Bhukta concluded the long story.

Our Guru was very surprised to hear this saga and said, "Oh my goodness! In Kali Yuga, not just humans but Gods are also getting adulterated. Even if that is so, what is wrong? Whether we call him Shiva, Vishnu, Pir, or Buddha, God is only one. Isn't that so?"

But Venkaiah wouldn't keep quiet. "If all Gods are the same, why not keep all those corpses together, and everyone worship them together?"

Then Guru countered, "Idiot! How can you call Gods as corpses? You are a pure Christian. Wait, even Christians have a God. You are a barbarian. At least these ignorant fellows have some blind faith, whether in Pir, Devil or God. You have conned all the Gods! "

"Except you, Sastry Garu! "Venkaiah quipped.

I nodded and said, "You uttered the most valuable words of your life."

*****

Matilda

Original Author: Gurajada Appa Rao. First Published in Telugu in 1910.

1

During the period when I was preparing for my Botany M.A exams, I used to stay in a two-storied house on Mylapore main road. Another ten or twelve students from our region used to be my housemates.

The third day after my arrival, Ramarao gestured to me and furtively asked, "Have you seen Matilda?" I replied in the negative. "There! Look, but not directly," he pointed.

I looked.

"Enough, come, let's go now," he said.

Without turning my gaze away from Matilda, I said, "How can I come? This is the ultimate fruit of God-given sight! What is wrong in looking at a beautiful woman who is the most bewitching of God's fascinating creation? That too when there is no evil intention in the mind!"

"I have seen many fake moralists like you. You are new here, so I thought it would be good for you to know. That's the reason I have shown her to you. Never look in that direction again." He grabbed my arm and led me away.

"Is she a good person or bad?" I asked.

"How does it matter to us whether she is good or bad? What *good* are *we* doing here, for us to label someone as *not good*? If you ever turn and look at Matilda again, that will be the end of our friendship, "he said.

Being a dear friend, Ramarao left me with no option. I suppressed my urge to look at Matilda and did not even venture towards the house facing her backyard.

The beauty of that golden-hued body—smeared with turmeric and freshly bathed—the tousled hair that spread all over the figure like a peacock's plume, the twinkle in her eyes when she looked up occasionally while drawing water from the well, and the pretty face were etched in my mind and wouldn't let me forget her.

I held myself back for about a week or ten days. After that, unable to control myself when Ramarao was not home, I used to pace the terrace with a book in hand, my gaze fixed towards her backyard.

During that time, she appeared only twice in the backyard and went back inside with lightning speed.

While going to college, I used to crawl slowly like an ant while passing Matilda's house with my eyes firmly focused on it. Occasionally, Matilda would appear through the window like a painting in a frame.

2

I managed to find out Matilda's background by asking whoever I could and from friends without asking.

My friends gave the sobriquet of 'Tiger' and 'Old Tiger' to Matilda's husband. He was not that old but would be about fifty-five or fifty-six. He was slightly fair and of short build. His face was marked by large eyes, a pointed moustache and pockmarks. It had been two years since he arrived in town – no one knew from where or why – and set up residence in the bungalow next to our house. Their house had a large room facing the street and adjoining the front yard. It had three shelves full of books. He could always be seen writing or reading. He used to keep the flower gardens in the front yard and backyards in immaculate condition. Every morning and evening, without fail, he used to dig the basins around all the plants. Matilda used to water them. This was their English way of getting some exercise to the bodies. That was about it! One never saw them stepping out of the house, nor were there any visits by relatives or friends. Tiger used to keep Matilda under strict watch. There was a rule that she shouldn't come to the front door, but she used to make an occasional appearance. One could see a kind of gloom on her face. Not surprising! Husband used to torture her. The husband's elder sister was an old woman who used to indulge in petty quarrels. The remaining person in the household was an old Brahmin cook.

Apart from calling Matilda's husband Tiger, no one knew his real name. It was said that there was an arrangement with the postman not to reveal the address on letters marked to him. The grapevine was that Tiger knew the postmaster well. Probably to guard the secret.

3

One day, after an oil bath, I was heading to school and was walking casually in front of Matilda's house with my hair down, wearing a stylish hat and jasmine-white clothes. When I reached the front door, I froze, looking at her. It was perhaps half a minute. Tiger jumped out of his lair and said, "Hey you! Come here." My initial thought was to flee the place. fearing an assault. But if I did that, I would surely be held guilty but Matilda could also be blamed. I was not worried about myself but wanted to save Matilda. So, I went in.

He took me inside the library. After settling in the chair, he asked me, in English, with a glaring look, "Are you looking at my wife? "

"I was looking at your library visible through the window and was wondering what kind of people you are and what your occupation would be."

"Have you not looked at my wife?"

"Yes, I have. If someone is standing right in front, won't they be visible? Nothing more to it!"

Like thunder, he yelled, "Is that so? Is that so? Hey, come here!"

Matilda didn't come.

"You bitch! Will you come or not?" he was trembling with anger. Matilda came slowly and stood there with her head bowed.

He said again in English to me, "You fool! Look! Look at this bitch's face for as long as you can! Why are you looking at me instead of her? Is my face better than hers? "

I didn't reply. Seeing how the episode was unfolding, I was about to head to the main door when he noticed and said softly, "Stop."

I froze in my tracks.

The fire blazing in the eyes a minute ago had cooled down.

"My dear fellow!" he said.

"Have you ever learnt to speak the truth? Either from your parents or teachers? "I suddenly remembered my parents.

"I never had to learn. I was born with honesty," I said stiffly.

"If that is so, with the born honesty, tell me. Is my wife beautiful or not? "

"I think she is beautiful."

"Is there any doubt?"

"No."

"When you are walking on the street every day, do you try to steal a glimpse of her or not?"

"Since truth is the only option, I must admit I keep looking at her. But I swear on God I never had an iota of wrong intention in my mind!"

"Forget it! Seeing her gives you joy. Yes, or no?"

"Yes."

"Then take this bitch along with you. I am donating her to you. Take her! I will be rid of this nuisance!"

I came out quietly. I was numb and couldn't see any houses or people. Having been humiliated, I cursed myself and went to school.

I decided to shift my residence and vowed never to set foot on that street again.

That image—of a bent head, with tears flowing down and the chest trembling due to the suppressed sighs—was firmly set in my eyes. I was sure even the best poets could not capture that emotion. That matchless beauty and bottomless chasm filled with pity were indescribable.

4

When I reached my house, the old Brahmin, who was residing in Tiger's house, approached sneakily, pushed a note into my hands, and slipped away. Realising the connection this incident had with the previous episode,

I went into my room, latched the door from inside, and read the note. *What did it contain?*

In a neat handwriting, it read like this -

'Will you and your friends not allow me to live in peace? What harm did I do to you? If you go about your business with your head down, I can survive. If not, my fate is doomed.'

What can I do? If I leave that area and go somewhere else, I could rid myself of the trouble. Now, how can I ignore Matilda's request and go? Should I not be saving her from any possible harm from my mates? Can I save her?

If I can't save Matilda, what is the point of living? And what is the point of being a man? Have I become a part of this charming gem of a woman's sorrow-filled story? My life's purpose will be fulfilled if I can alleviate her sorrow and win her approval. Is this beautiful handwriting Matilda's? How fortunate I am to be reading it! What would I not do for her if she ordered me? If I have the three worlds under my command, would I not just give them away and make her the queen, if she demanded?

But what to do right now? I am not that worldly-wise. Will I end up further messing up things? Ramarao is experienced, of good character and adept at these matters. If he scolds me for ignoring his advice, so be it. I will take it. I will fall at his feet and plead with him to help me in my endeavour.

Having thus decided, I narrated the entire story to Ramarao. I also told him about my decision to help her. And implored him not to dissuade me from my path.

Ramarao said, "If I had the confidence that I could dissuade you, I would try. I know you will not change your mind. Did you heed my advice not to look at her? "

"But if I don't candidly tell you what's in my mind and what I know, then I will be guilty of breaching the spirit of our friendship."

"Our elders have clearly forbidden any intervention in marital discords. They are incomprehensible and inscrutable. Middlemen try to repair a marriage but end up breaking it further. Firstly, while we call him 'Tiger, Tiger', we only heard the tiger's roar but never saw it biting. Have we ever heard that he assaulted Matilda even in the slightest manner? No. Secondly, there is no dearth of food and clothing. If she continues to obey him, there is absolutely no problem in leading a peaceful life. Finally, you are strongly smitten by Matilda. That is forbidden. You can always brush it aside, saying 'I have no wrong intention'. But the wrong intention need not come with a prior announcement. It would be hidden in the subconscious mind. We overlook its presence and externally make every effort for it to manifest itself. One always needs an anchor for wrong thoughts – isn't it? If someone is alone in a jungle, he wouldn't have any wrong thoughts about women. If one is looking for the company of attractive women, there is always an opportunity for a wrong thought. Only he is wise who doesn't even give an opportunity for such an opportunity to arise."

5

"You and your friend Ramarao have done a great favour to me. Because of your words and deeds, I have realised that my wife is a good woman. After careful consideration, I had unshackled her from that day onwards. My wife is very obedient. She didn't even use the liberty I had granted her. I told her to go wherever she wanted and meet whomever she wanted. She didn't go anywhere and didn't want to meet anyone. She said, 'You are my world. I don't need anyone else'. That is how she continued to behave..."

"You freed her, and it resulted in my freedom too. By the way, have you studied higher mathematics? No? Let it be."

He rang the bell. Matilda entered like a robot and stayed behind the door.

"Serve coffee."

She served two cups of coffee on the table.

"Serve yourself too."

She looked at her husband with eyes questioning, *'Is it the right thing to do?'*

"No problem. You can also drink. He is our friend, "he said. But she didn't serve coffee for herself. She stood aside.

"Anyway, sit down," he said. She didn't sit. I was impressed by this harmony between wife and husband and congratulated myself, thinking I was partly responsible for this improvement.

While we were having coffee, he kept narrating how he was educating her, how she always read the Ramayana and Mahabharata, how he took her sightseeing, and so on. Some of the talk revolved around my education. I discovered that he was a very learned man.

His final words were, "Now you can leave."

*****

First Attack

Original Author: Sripada Subrahmanya Sastry. First published in Telugu in 1935.

1

"I never imagined you would become such a coward."

"......"

"Are you not ashamed?"

"Do you know what shame is?"

"Don't try to act smart!"

"......"

"If you stopped your education when you failed in school-final, I would have been spared of this torture. Even after qualifying as a B.A., it is sad to see you becoming such a moron."

"Forgive me."

"Don't you say that! No punishment is small enough for you."

"....."

"You always dreamt of a fruitful life like Joan of Arc or Miss Nightingale. You used to accuse me of craving a second marriage. Now, what is it that got into you?"

"......."

"Is the mind drifting towards marriage by any chance?"

"Is it wrong for my age if such a desire crops up?"

"You moron! Will you let a man control your destiny again?"

"What harm did men do to me?"

"Weren't you made a widow?"

"Didn't the same men help me complete my B.A.?"

"Could you escape widowhood?"

"What is the difference between my third, unmarried sister and me?"

"How can you get the same respect she gets?"

"......."

"Your angry stare can't scare me!"

"I had assumed that all who completed B.A. have some self-respect and understand its meaning. But I am wrong!"

"You are going too far with your words."

"I can never compare myself with you in that aspect."

"Oh! Really?"

"......."

"What is your final answer? Mother[61] is beckoning you and me."

"I can hear – a little bit."

"A little bit?"

"Yes. That's all!"

"If you have a heart, even that little bit is enough."

"......"

"Then why don't you come?"

"......."

"Say something!"

"........"

"I don't know how to react to your insolence!"

"Why don't you just let it be?"

"Don't for a second assume I will let you go."

"......"

"Are you scared of jail?"

"Is going to jail the only important thing?"

"That is the only symbol of true patriotism."

"Only if you are in politics, perhaps."

"We don't have any priority other than politics right now."

"I disagree."

61 In this context refers to nation / mother-country / India in freedom struggle.

"Who are you, and what is your stature? No one cares about your opinion!"

"......."

"Even heavyweights in society are being swept away by this tide. Who cares for what you think?"

"Just like you have your tastes, why don't you accept I can have my preferences?"

"You and preferences! Are you serious?"

".........."

"I have reached the limit of my patience. Will you join or not? Will you take the plunge into the fire or not?"

"The fire I want to jump into is different."

"Getting stuck with the kitchen and breeding like animals...."

"Hold your tongue. Don't you dare talk to me like that!"

"Now the ego is getting hurt!"

"Ego is a male quality. On one hand, you are accusing men. Then why mention ego?"

"......."

"......."

"It is my fault. I shouldn't even be talking to you in the first place."

"Go on. Complete the next sentence, too."

"To see your face itself is a sin."

With her teeth clattering, Subhadra took off like a firecracker. Her Rangoon slippers skidded, making her lurch forward as she was going downstairs. She held herself back with great effort and—indignation adding to anger—made her way out rapidly like a snake whose tail had been stepped on.

2

When Janakamma[62] was taking a leisurely walk on the terrace at around six o'clock in the evening—drying her freshly washed, still wet hair—and contemplating her next steps, Subhadra came, got into an argument, and stirred her emotions before leaving.

By nature, Janakamma was steadfast. But it took her nearly fifteen minutes to return to a normal state of mind. In the meantime, it became dark, and there was no light. Her mother called a couple of times, but she was too engrossed in her thoughts to notice. *What next?* was the only thought that occupied her mind.

She knew the clout that politicians enjoyed in society then. Her cousin Subhadra—her younger uncle's daughter—spent three months in prison. After her release, she received royal treatment and tons of respect wherever she went. Even volunteers were treated like heavyweights. If she got into politics, she would receive similar extraordinary respect and acceptance.

62 Also referred to as Janaki in the story. 'amma' at the end of a female name adds respect (with age) or affection (for young) or both.

But she didn't believe, in the prevailing atmosphere, political campaigns would liberate the nation and the public. There were so many castes, sub-castes and branches within the sub-castes. Some people would drift along with the trend; some were pure traditionalists and others leaned towards social reform. Then there were Brahma-samajists[63] and Arya-samajists[64] among the reformists. In short, one could see as many differences and as many selfish motives among Hindus as there were hairs on a Hindu's head. Under these circumstances, neglecting the need to rebuild society and focusing on politics didn't seem right to her. From the beginning, her proclivity was towards social reform. The exposure to English literature and the acquaintances with Western ladies and young girls in college had only enhanced this taste for reform. The fact that she became a widow at nine and was being considered wretched also strengthened her outlook.

This outlook discouraged her from looking for a job. Her mother broached the topic of re-marriage seven or eight times. Every time, she avoided answering and bought more time.

To the question, 'Why not get into social reform?' she was unsure where to begin and what to do. Her dilemma had been that *society is uniformly chaotic. There is no single aspect that can be called worse than*

63 Brahma Samaj was a social reform-oriented organization. Google for more details.

64 Arya Samaj was also a parallel social reform organization. Google for more details.

or better than others. So where to begin the reform process to make maximum impact? For nearly a year – ever since she completed her B.A. – she had been thinking about this conundrum but could not find a way forward. She thought for hours and drew many plans. She patiently assessed the pros and cons. She looked at the cons in pros and pros in cons. But she could not conclude the final approach. All the thinking and planning were wasted every time.

Every day, it was the same experience.

Finally, she came to a conclusion.

I have God's mandate, but I need to work harder. I need more time and effort to achieve complete clarity of thought. Once I reach full clarity on God's directive, there will be no more vacillation, no more dilemmas about possibilities and impossibilities, and no more Do's and Don'ts. When I reach that stage, it will be just execution and nothing else. There is no point in looking at others and losing sleep over their progress.

Even as she was immersed in the same thoughts, a youth came up, saying, "Jaani!" He was carrying a hurricane lantern. His face betrayed a sense of urgency.

"What is it, Bava[65]?"

"Your moment has come now. You must rush without losing a second."

"I am ready."

65 Bava means cousin or brother-in-law in Telugu. Even close friends are sometimes addressed like this out of affection.

"Uncle Dabbanna's Sundari is getting married."

"No one mentioned!"

"It has been kept a secret."

"Who is the groom?"

"Venkata Somayajulu Thatha.[66]"

"What?"

"Uncle Dabbanna owes two thousand rupees to Thatha. The rumour is Thatha returned the promissory note."

"So, he sold Sundari!"

"Absolutely. But Lachchamma Attha[67] doesn't like it one bit." Even daughters didn't approve it. Sundari has not stopped crying. But Uncle Dabbanna took a tough stand because his sons are too young and there is no one to challenge him."

"Where is the wedding?"

"Our town itself. In the temple. Can't you hear the music?"

"………"

"The knot will be tied in half an hour."

66 Thatha is the grandfather (maternal or paternal). It could be any old man who is generally referred to as Thatha.

67 Attha literally means Aunt. It is typically a father's sister. It is also used informally to address slightly elderly ladies in villages and towns.

"Then let us move. You say the knot will be tied? My God! How cheap women's lives have become! Selling human flesh even in this day and age? That too to someone who completed sixty?"

"If you just stay here and get worked up..."

"Here, I have come downstairs."

Keeping the lantern aside, Janaki, followed by the youth, rushed out.

3

"Dabbanna! What you have done is a commendable act of the highest order. In our entire Agraharam, no one is more dutiful than Yajulu. You have fulfilled his one deficit. The sankalpam 'Dasha Purvesham Dasha Paresham[68]' has come true in your case."

"Where is any doubt in this? Despite being younger in age, Dabbanna has shown a lot of foresight. Chayanulu, will there be any obstruction to Dabbanna getting the full fruits of Ashvamedha Yaga[69] for having saved Yajulu's sacred fire[70]?"

68 Part of a larger hymn recited during the wedding – indicates the importance of giving away a virgin in marriage and helping the bridegroom bear children through her to continue his lineage.

69 A major fire ritual performed normally by kings and emperors with the hope of getting eternal glory and permanent residence in heaven. Involves a sacrificial horse (Ashva is a horse)

70 Sacred fire can only be lit and rituals performed only if one's wife is present. A widower (Yajulu, in this case)

"You said it, my man! Didn't his grandfather perform Sarvatomukham[71]? Wouldn't the fruits of that ceremony not reflect in the entire lineage?"

"Moreover, Yajulu is approaching the one lakh[72] mark. He is not some roadside fellow. Both material and spiritual goals will be met! What says you, Ramasastry?"

"What you say is absolutely – do you hear me? Can scholars like you speak otherwise, sir?"

"Also, this will be followed by offspring surely! While the widowed daughter takes care of the family's chores, Yajulu, with his new bride… What else can one ask for, Subbavadhani?"

"Sure. Sure. Even that lone widowed daughter is above forty. She can coach Dabbanna's daughter in all the needed.. are you following me? Isn't this the perfect set-up?"

"Sirs! Chayanulu Garu! Avadhanulu Garu! Sastrulu Garu! Siddhanti[73] Garu has announced that Sumuhurtham[74] is approaching. With your permission----"

---

cannot do this. More so in the Brahmin community.

71 Another important ritual/ceremony

72 Lakh is a hundred thousand. Someone who amassed a wealth of one lakh is similar to a millionaire in the West. A hundred lakhs make a crore.

73 The priest conducting the wedding ceremony.

74 The sacred time slot when the knot is supposed to be tied.

"Where is the need to ask us? Let me see. Have you held the screen[75] properly? Carry on, Deekshitulu!"

When Janaki and the young man reached the venue, this was the situation. The bride was still in the basket[76], grieving over her fate. Lachchamma was wiping her tears from time to time. Even the other women didn't look very enthused. Even when the elders were extolling him, Dabbanna looked pale like a thief caught in the act, ashamed to show his face to anyone.

When the elders granted permission, the priest instructed his assistant to distribute the holy rice grains to all and started chanting the mantras.

When she saw this scene, Janakamma's blood boiled. Her eyebrows took the form of a bow ready to fire an arrow – leaving the youth who accompanied her in awe.

"Yajulu Thatha[77]! What is it that you are doing now?"

"Let us talk later."

"Janaki! Why don't you just keep quiet and observe the proceedings like other women?"

75 In Telugu weddings, a screen separates the groom and bride until the exact muhurtham time and then it is removed. People stand holding the screen in place.

76 The Telugu bride is brought to the wedding stage in a bamboo basket typically carried by her maternal uncles.

77 Thatha literally means grandfather. It is also used to address anyone of that age.

"Is it so Chayanulu Thatha! If I, too, remain quiet, do all of you want to tighten the noose around Sundari's neck? Come to senses now! Yajulu Thatha! This is not a discussion to be postponed. I need an answer now."

"I don't owe an answer to you."

"Very well. You can answer only when needed. There is no hurry. Dabbanna babu[78]! What is your plan for Sundari?"

Hearing this, Lachchamma was relieved, muttering, "Thank God! I am saved." Like a summer vine drenched in water, Sundari looked up. For the first time, all the women could see women's power in action. The half-dead Dabbanna was tongue-tied.

"Why don't you say something?"

"It – is – all – set. Nothing can be done now."

"If you have any sense, there is still opportunity. You, indeed, have the obligation to get Sundari married. But you don't have the right to marry her off to a corpse."

"......."

"Think carefully."

"......."

"If it doesn't occur to you, ask any sensible people."

"......."

---

78 Another way elders/strangers (men) are addressed respectfully.

"Keeping quiet is not an option. This drama must stop now. What do you say?"

"It is not possible to stop it. You stay away."

"Is it you or me who should stay away? Don't rush! What about you, aunt? How could you be around and allow her life to be destroyed?"

"My dear child, with his persistent harassment, what else do you expect me to do?"

"In that case, will you leave the altar and come this way?"

"Now that I have your support, I don't care what happens."

After saying this, Lachchamma set aside the pitcher—meant for washing the groom's feet—and came and stood next to Janaki.

Seeing things unfold like this, everyone remained speechless. But Dabbanna gathered his wits and barked, "Will you come back or not?" Retorting, "I won't," a defiant Lachchamma moved closer to Janaki.

"You stubborn one! Just wait and see what I will do to you! You are perhaps assuming it will stop if you don't come. I will stuff your blouse in my Dhoti and........"

"Well said Dabbanna! You have upheld your family's prestige!"

"Is that so, Subbavadhanulu great-grandpa? Wouldn't he uphold, with all of you cheering him from the sidelines? Will you give away the bride with aunt's blouse stuffed in your clothes?"

"Just one blow!..."

"If that is how it is, you, too, come off the altar, Sundari!"

Even before this command could be completed, Sundari got out of the basket with a new-found energy. Seeing this, Yajulu screamed, "Ah! Ah!" and stretched his hands to stop her. With a trembling voice that was a mix of anguish and outrage, Sundari snubbed him, "You, old corpse!" and, in one leap, joined the women folk and hugged Janaki.

The assembled traditionalists looked at each other. Yajulu looked at Dabbanna, and he lowered his face. All the women—as if possessed by a new energy—maintained a solemn pose.

Breathing fire, Janaki appeared like fiery Lord Shiva, calming Markandeya with one hand and about to throw the raised Trident at Lord Yama with the other.[79]

4

The wedding hall—which was supposed to be buzzing with auspicious music, priests chanting the holy hymns, women folk chatting, and wise men's banter—suddenly

79 The Story of Markandeya and how Shiva saves him from Lord Yama, the God of death, and gives him immortality.

fell so silent that one could even hear the noise made by an ant.[80]

After ten minutes passed like this, Dabbanna – like a beaten snake – got up with great difficulty and settled at the back of the temple. Stung by the insult, the groom went out of the northern door and slumped near the Thulasi[81] plant on the banks of the lake.

Later, some men surrounded Dabbanna, and others approached Yajulu.

Yajulu asked Chayanulu to come closer and asked him for his opinion.

"This is a tricky situation!"

"So, we have to surrender to a woman?"

"Do you call her a woman?"

"From where did this bitch land up to ruin my life, man? Everything was falling in place so nicely – new bride, new family – and now my fully served platter is blown to pieces!"

"......."

"Have you noticed her atrocious ways?"

"Blame it on English! That English education itself comes with these destructive traits. If female devils are also completing B.A., will we have any future?"

"Will this woman and her father have any future after what she has done?"

80 This is a common metaphor used in Telugu literature and conversations to describe pin-drop silence.

81 Holy basil tree worshipped in India by women.

"Don't even mention Mahendra Somayajulu's name. He is a retired deputy collector. If he decides to...."

"You scare me! Do you think that scoundrel will pull the Sharda bill[82] out and apply the same?"

"What do we have to fear? The marriage didn't even take place!"

"........"

"........."

"What is Dabbanna saying?"

"He is broken completely."

"You think the situation is hopeless?"

"It is tough."

"Do you suggest we keep quiet?"

"My advice is to be patient."

"If that is the case, ask him to return my promissory note."

"So, is that true?"

"Principal was thirteen hundred. Interest came to five hundred or so. Total about two thousand."

"If you had told me, wouldn't I have arranged a much better match?"

"This one ended up so well!"

"......."

82 Sharda bill was a bill brought in by the Govt of that time to prevent child marriages.

"Go and talk to him once."

"Can you wait for a couple of days?"

"It is beyond his ability now. In any case, I don't want that miserable girl anymore!"

"........."

"I am still hopeful that he would fear the loss of face in the village and convince his wife. But..."

"If this goes public now, Janaki might become even more aggressive!"

"Oh My God!"

That was when Subbavadhani entered – clearing his throat – and sat next to Yajulu.

"What is he saying?"

"If we can take care of the women folk nuisance, he doesn't have any objection."

"What?"

"No other word from him."

"Can you bring him here for a second?"

"He won't be reachable even with a gunshot now."

5

While the menfolk were deliberating the options, women surrounded Janaki. "Janaki! It is you who saved Sundari from this disaster!" said Venkatasubbamma. "If we resist like this, what can men do?" quipped

Lakshminarasamma, rolling her eyes. "I must say this. Our village has gone to the dogs. Avadhanlu Garu, Sastrulu Garu and Somayajulu Garu consider themselves and their scholarship too high and stoop to any level! Yuck! I feel sick when I think about it!" said Kamasastry's wife, Parvatamma. "I believe he enticed and then arm-twisted Dabbanna with the two thousand rupees note for Sundari's hand. Why does he need marriage at his age? Blame the sick mind! Good or bad, why not spend the rest of his time with that whore who has been his companion anyway..." joined Neelanna's Seetamahalakshmi. Chapalamba interjected and jibed, "I would say this is not bad. At least Grandpa didn't bring his whore's dance troupe to the wedding. Let us be happy about it." Laughter rang out in the room, and the temple premises were lit up.

That's when the groom's daughter Ramalakshmi stepped forward – shy and sad at the same time – and said, "I cried so many times asking him, 'Father, why do you need this marriage now?' I explained the pros and cons in detail to him. If he is so stubborn, what could I do? I told him to drop this idea and adopt a male child instead. 'Unless marriage takes place, how can I adopt a child?' was his argument, and he almost thrashed me. I left him to his fate and kept quiet after that. Why should this come so far but for our fate?" Janaki then took over and addressed the gathering –

"Have you all heard Ramalakshmi? These men have become very arrogant, thinking they are invincible. We are the root cause of this state of affairs. If we remain firm, what can they do? We forgot about our own power. We abdicated our authority and rights. And ended up as self-made slaves. A woman's life is now dictated by a man. In other countries, women are living on par with men. Is this example not enough to illustrate our foolishness? On top of it, look at Ramalakshmi's naivete! She says she advised her father to avoid the marriage and adopt a son instead. When she – his own blood – is around, why bring someone from outside and implant? In England, if a father dies without male heirs, the entire estate is inherited by daughters. Yajulu Grandpa is a millionaire. Why should some outsider inherit his wealth after his death, and then Ramalakshmi should live at his mercy, serving him and his wife for the rest of her life and tolerating their abuses? We have a lot of such malpractices in our society. I will educate you all on these topics daily. I have decided that I will dedicate the rest of my life to the benefit of women. I will not take up any employment. My parents are asking me to get remarried if I wish. But I have decided against the same with this goal in mind. You all know what torture the womenfolk of our village are going through. I will get rid of all that. If you help me in this effort, it will only benefit you."

Hearing this, there were all-around cheers and loud shouts of consent. Chayanulu's third wife, Venkatarathnamma, said, "We will come to your house tomorrow. Please educate us." Venkatasastry's second wife, Krishnaveni, added, "Why just tomorrow? What work do we have at home other than struggling like flies in an ointment doing needless chores? Let us go every day. Dear girl, educate us about all the things that matter," and held Janaki's hand.

"Very well. I will actually give you a proper education, too. From afternoon two until five, no one has any work at home. Even if your men object, you must come home," Janaki exhorted them.

Lachchamma held Janaki's hands and pleaded, "Why don't you stay tonight in our house, my dear?" Sundari joined in, "Please come, sister," in a pleading tone. Janaki pulled Sundari closer affectionately and took a leap forward, saying, "Will you then listen to me always?"

*****

The Nationalist

Original Author: Sripada Subrahmanya Sastry. First published in Telugu in 1935.

1

When Ramachandrudu was lecturing Seethapathi on Khaddar[83] – adding his own fiction to the narrative – and busy packing his suitcase, the mail runner came and delivered a telegram.

It read – 'I am also coming to the Congress. I will meet you in the mail[84] tomorrow in Samarlakota – Sundaramma.'

An ecstatic Ramachandrudu's eyes lit up.

"Is it from Kakinada, my dear fellow?"

"You guessed it absolutely right!"

"What's the matter?"

---

83 Homespun coarse cotton cloth popularised by Mahatma Gandhi during the freedom struggle as a symbol of Indian self-reliance. Also referred to as Khadi.

84 Category of train. Different types during those days were mail, express, passenger etc.

"Sundari says she is coming to the Congress. I should meet her in the mail."

"Great! In that case, I will also come."

"What do you mean?"

"I must come. Otherwise, there is no fun!"

"Why is that?"

"For your wedding, my dear fellow."

"Pointless talk..."

"That *is* the meaning of that telegram. If Sundaramma doesn't have that idea – the wish to marry on the Congress stage – I will create it in her mind. In the presence of many great leaders, in the Mahatma's presence, with a million voices ringing..."

"Bharat Mata[85] ki Jai!"

"What better place for a marriage than Mother India's lap, my dear fellow?"

"What you say makes sense. But without any relatives being present – even her mother not being there – Sundari will not agree. We don't need any secretive marriage."

"Are you serious? Will even emperors have the good fortune of marrying on the Congress stage? Is the Congress stage not the same as a Yagnam[86] venue? Will

---

85 Bharat Mata translates to Mother India. This is a patriotic slogan in the country's praise.

86 A Vedic sacred ritual performed to please Gods.

even Lord Indra's throne – for that matter, even Sesha Talpam[87] – have the same majestic power?"

"Congress is the only saviour..."

"Leave that aside. In the ordinary weddings that take place in our families, just uneducated women show up who haven't seen the wider world and who don't know what class means. In the case of Congress, hundreds of servants of the nation, volunteers, leaders, and delegates – what sight can be more beautiful than that grand stage? Will I not pick the best of the young women from that crowd – in age, education, beauty and singing prowess – and make them sing an ode to your wedding?"

"This sounds too tempting, man!"

"Wait, there is more!"

"What is it?"

"If this is all that it is, where is the fun? Thousands of foot soldiers, deputy leaders above them, senior leaders above them and finally, the supreme commander will be present. Will the couple not receive military honours for a wedding that takes place on Congress stage?"

"Very true! If this auspicious event takes place there, we both will devote the rest of our lives to Congress."

"There is one more thing."

87 Sesha Talpam is considered to be Lord Vishnu's bed. Sesha is the king of serpents, and Talpam means bed.

"I know you. Whatever you plan, you are not the one to keep things simple."

"Therefore, listen to me."

"Go on."

"Hundreds of reporters will attend Congress."

"Wait a second! I will keep a nicely worded pledge ready for that occasion. Or just three poems. Hindi is our national—mother-only—tongue, so one in that. Bengali is the local language, so one in that and one in English for the whole wide world. I will have all three versions ready for the occasion. Directly in the Hindustani Kafi raga for the radio."

"All that is good. First, listen to this."

"Go on."

"I will make arrangements to ensure that those reporters send your wedding news to all newspapers across the whole world through Reuters, especially to newspapers in England, to put fear in the hearts of British cabinet ministers. Your wedding photo will be in papers of all languages…"

"You must also appear in the photos."

"With this, both of you will get all-India fame."

"You have a great imagination. I love it! So, why don't you also go and start packing your suitcase?"

"I don't need much time to pack my bags. I am always travel-ready."

"So, how much money will be needed?"

"How can a wedding be fun without at least a thousand rupees? There is a tea party to be given – at least to the ladies. Then there are round-trip charges – including Sundaramma's that you have to bear – don't you?"

"I will bear your expenses too. You are not allowed to say No. Come on now. Get started."

"Why do you want to bear my expenses, too? There are already enough for you to deal with."

"I don't care! I will spray money around."

"Of course, you are capable of the same, but.."

"What is the problem? Will fifteen hundred not suffice?"

"That will be a glut, of course! I will make sure it is not wasted. I don't have the money, but if I do, there is none to beat me in frugality. If I spend one paisa[88], the return should be one rupee equivalent."

"So, should I go to the Muththa family or the Naalam family for a loan?"

"Your old creditor..."

"I will not see his face again. One week ago, Sivaprasada Rao Garu requested a donation of three hundred to send to his female relative studying at Kashi University. That was when I reached out to him. That rascal not only didn't give the money but apparently made public comments like 'the dues have already crossed twenty thousand.' After returning from

88 Hundred paisas make one rupee.

Calcutta, I will borrow from a Marwari[89] and throw his money on his face. Will I ever borrow from him again?"

"Very well. Go wherever you want to."

A smug Seethapathi and a day-dreaming Ramachandrudu stepped out onto the street and went in their different ways.

2

As soon as he spotted the sugar factory, Ramachandrudu opened the coach door. The moment the train stopped on the Samarlakota platform, he jumped out. He welcomed a smiling Sundaramma—with a thermos flask in her hand—and escorted her into his compartment.

The joy soon turned into depression when he saw her grandfather, Veerappa Yajulu.

Seethapathi – who sold a million dreams to Ramachandrudu by then – was equally taken aback.

Both of them were hoping Sundaramma would come alone or would be accompanied by some seasoned lady-delegate of Congress. But they were unprepared to see Yajulu tagging along like an evil shadow. Since Yajulu was on a two-hundred-fifty-rupee Government pension, they never imagined in their wildest dreams that he would show up for a Congress conference.

Yajulu was no less an achiever. As in a rags-to-riches tale, he amassed plenty of lands and one lakh

89 Money lending/business community from Rajasthan in North India

rupees cash. He also built a palatial bungalow in Kakinada's temple street. When Sundaramma lost her husband in childhood, he helped with her education until Matriculation and Vidwan. He allowed her to attend meetings and conferences and prepared her for a remarriage. And promptly agreed when she proposed to marry Ramachandrudu.

As if this was not enough, he didn't adopt a male child. Without prejudice or causing loss to his daughter-in-law, he wrote his entire estate in Sundaramma's name.

Despite all these good deeds, Ramachandrudu despised Yajulu. Fearing Sundaramma's displeasure and public disapproval—not to mention the risk of Yajulu giving Sundaramma's hand to someone else—he would maintain a friendly attitude towards him in public. But behind the back, he would mutter obscenities under his breath and spit in disgust without Yajulu noticing. In short, he treated Yajulu like a sworn enemy.

The reasons are not difficult to fathom. Yajulu was a government pensioner. He disapproved of smoking. He didn't consider wearing a lungi and kurta as gentlemanly. He never touched Khaddar. He considered English as an eye-opener for Indian society. And he was a regular visitor to the collector.

And there was another hidden reason behind all these.

As soon as the match with Sundaramma was fixed, Yajulu invited Ramachandrudu to come over and stay at his place for a week. Ramachandrudu knew the old man's ploy was to observe his daily routine. So, he took care to behave very carefully. But one evening, when Sundaramma herself brought coffee, he decided to take some liberty and touch her cheek. He hesitated for a few minutes, finally mustered courage and stretched his hand. Even she stood there smiling as if in a trance and as if she, too, was looking forward to the experience. Just then, in the nick of time, Yajulu appeared on the scene.

Unfortunately for Ramachandrudu, the story didn't end there.

Ramachandrudu couldn't let go of his urge to touch her cheek. By sunset, the urge intensified and took the shape of a firm desire to hug her if possible and even plant a kiss.

When he was waiting for Sundaramma's dinner invitation, Yajulu showed up instead. After dinner, when he was hoping to get the betel leaf from her, she sent it through her grandfather. He was waiting for other opportunities to catch her alone, but she never left her mother's company that night.

The wait continued, and finally, it was deep sleep that hugged him instead of Sundaramma.

The next morning, when she brought him coffee, he tried to touch her hand while taking the cup. She pulled herself back reflexively and calmly kept the coffee cup on the table. Then she said, "Please don't touch me until we get married." She added, "Last night my grandfather said it is not proper etiquette."

Ramachandrudu was completely downcast.

He started doubting if the old man would allow Sundaramma to lead a proper conjugal life and if Sundaramma would obey *him* as opposed to her grandfather.

But the thought of losing one and a half lakh worth of estate and a beautiful woman brought him back to his senses and gave him the required patience. The doubts kept coming back now and then, though.

3

The Mail stopped at Howrah[90] station.

Ramachandrudu was hoping that the place would be teeming with lady volunteers eager to welcome Sundaramma. Even after five minutes of waiting, there was no sign of such activity. Just then, a volunteer approached the disappointed Ramachandrudu and asked him in pure English, "Will you go to Madrasi lodging or Marathi lodging? "

This added fuel to an already irritated Ramachandrudu. He gave a cold stare for a second and then replied solemnly, "We will go to the national lodging."

"National Lodging? National Lodging?" the volunteer repeated, biting his nail and completely at a loss. When Ramachandrudu's stare hardened, implying a 'Yes!', he replied, "All the accommodation here is

90 Calcutta's (now called Kolkata) main railway station.

arranged by region." His face betrayed a feeling: 'Oh My God! What kind of nationalism is this?' He quickly moved on to welcome another delegate.

Yajulu, who had been speaking in a very familiar tone with a Bengali old man until then, came up to Ramachandrudu and told him, "We are going to the Atheist Society delegates' lodging. Let us meet later," and started moving. Sundaramma followed her grandfather, saying, "Look, that opposite large building is supposed to be our accommodation. Please drop by after having your meal."

This completely demoralised Ramachandrudu who was already seething with frustration.

"What do you say," asked Seethapathi.

"This is nothing but Bengalis' selfishness. They don't recognise anything other than Bengaliness. When the invitation committee secretary wrote asking, 'Will you stay with Tamils or do you need a separate arrangement?' Sambamurthy Garu and Venkatappaiah Garu - with a lot of foresight – replied strongly, 'Don't make such separate arrangements. Whether it is Hindus or Muslims, please arrange one common accommodation. If needed, provide large rooms that can accommodate bigger groups.' These Bengalis not only didn't reply to that letter but have gone ahead and completely reversed the arrangements. Let us go to the president and fight on this topic. Until this issue is resolved, I will not allow any other topic to be taken up." Ramachandrudu breathed fire.

"You are forgetting our main objective."

"True. But marriage is not more important to me than this task."

"Don't rush. First, find out about our leaders' whereabouts."

"I will have none of that. Let us go straight to the Hindustanis'[91] lodgings and stay there. At least this way we can spend these four days in Hindi ambience and get rid of the rust formed in our ears."

"Listen to me. Right next to Sundaramma's accommodation, there is a southern hotel..."

"Of all the places, do you want us to end up in a Sambar land[92]?"

"Without that, our day might start but will not move forward. So, calm down now."

"How about going to Sundari's lodging?"

"I can't survive even a moment without a cigarette."

"How about Gujaratis' lodging then?"

"Will they let us in?"

"We have the Mahatma on our side, right?"

---

91 Hindi-speaking North Indians in this story's context.

92 South in those days was associated mainly with Tamils / Madrasis. Non-Tamils, especially Telugus, used to joke that it is essentially a place known only for Sambar (a lentil dish Tamils are famous for but equally popular in all of South India and now in North too)

"Yes of course! For our wedding strategy to succeed, we absolutely need Mahatma Gandhi's support. This idea is good. Let us go."

"Call the coolie."

Both followed the coolie. Fifty yards later, they encountered a Telugu delegate.

"Where are you staying?"

"In Sikh lodging."

"Why?"

"Apparently, our folks had written to them saying we didn't need any separate accommodation. That's why everyone has their own lodging, but we don't. Our people are staying in different lodgings—some Maharashtrian, some Tamil, some with Muslims—wherever possible."

"Will we, too, get accommodation in the Sikh lodging?"

"Who cares about Telugus in the Sikh community? They easily devour ten rotis for breakfast, while our Telugus struggle to eat just one. In any case, you folks don't have moustaches and beards, so it is tough to find a place there."

Ramachandrudu's frustration knew no bounds. "Why were we born in Telugu land?" he lamented.

4

Chewing a spicy betel leaf, Ramachandrudu casually came out onto the street. One Maharashtrian old man approached him and asked him in English, "Where are you from?" Ramachandrudu replied in Hindi, "Rajahmundry."

"Which state are you from?"

Ramachandrudu was already irritated listening to the gentleman speaking in English. This question was the limit.

"First, tell me where you are from."

"Poona."

"I know you are a Maharashtrian. I am surprised you don't know where I am from or Rajahmundry belongs to which state. It is these regional sentiments that are harming us."

"What is regional sentiment in this?"

"Where are you from? Which state? These are the first questions we ask when we encounter a new person. Is this not enough? Here we are sacrificing our lives on the Congress stage. Instead of rejoicing at the knowledge that we are all one, it is absurd to ask this question, 'Which state are you from?'"

"Wouldn't states exist if we are all one? Will they not be there?"

"After we win complete freedom, we will decide what to do with Hindustan. But accepting today's divisions - and demanding that the same divisions should continue – is a matter of shame."

"You are talking at a very high level!"

"First, tell me this. Despite knowing Hindi, why are you talking to me in English?"

"My Hindi knowledge is rudimentary. I can't converse well."

"Even after wearing Khaddar! Have you truly come for the Congress?"

"Yes."

"Ramachandrudu closed his ears in disgust, saying, "Oh God!"

The Maharashtrian's eyebrows went up.

"I don't follow you."

"Our country is Hindustan. We all belong to the Hindu race. Our national language is Hindi..."

"National language?"

"Any doubt?"

"....."

"Your question makes me very sad."

"What is your mother tongue?"

"Mine or yours, whether it is mother tongue or national language, it is only Hindi, isn't it?"

"In that case, don't group us with you. Our mother tongue is Marathi, and our national language is Marathi."

"What about Hindi, then?"

"Maybe in the future, Hindi could become a common language."

"Maybe? And, in future?"

"..... Firstly, I am having trouble understanding where you are from. Can you please elaborate?"

"Madras presidency...."

"Oh! You are a Madrasi[93]?"

"We are not Madrasis. I have already said it. All of us are Hindus."

"Aren't there divisions within Hindus?"

"Servants of the country like us should not give importance to such divisions."

".... Well. Tell me the name of a large river in your state."

"Godavari."

"How far is it from your place?"

"Our town is right on the banks of Godavari. We bathe in Godavari, breathe its air and drink its water."

"...... True. The light from the lamp varies by the glass. Goodbye for now." The Maharashtrian left swinging his walking stick. Ramachandrudu was stunned, thinking, *the nation is broken into so many pieces!*

---

93 For all non-south Indians, every South Indian was a Madrasi in those days—for some, even today. Other than Madras, the rest of the southern states didn't have much identity in the north and other parts of India.

5

It was eight-thirty in the morning. The Congress was not due to start until two in the afternoon. Ramachandrudu and Seethapathi headed towards the Atheist Society delegates' lodging.

They could see many women gathered in a spacious room. When Ramachandrudu looked carefully, he found Sundaramma standing in the centre. He was elated to see her gain such prominence among the women delegates. Behind her were Tamil, Kannada, and Malayali ladies. Facing her were Gujarati, Bengali, and Hindustani ladies.

He noticed that Sundaramma looked a little agitated.

"You don't seem to have any decency. Why are you laughing at us?"

"Why is it that none of you is wearing a headscarf?"

"Why are *you* wearing it?"

"It is the custom in our land."

"Not wearing one is our custom."

"In our state, we consider a lady without head-covering a prostitute."

"In our state, a lady covering her head is considered a widow."

The Bengali, Gujarati, and Hindustani ladies were taken aback when they heard this. The Tamil,

Malayali, and Kannada ladies looked at Sundaramma approvingly.

"You are now in our land. So, you must wear the scarves."

"When you come to our land, will you move around without it?"

"Haven't we mentioned? Lady with no scarf is a whore."

"Haven't we replied? Lady with a scarf is a widow."

Both groups' eyes were breathing fire. Just then, the bugle sounded, signalling the start of the conference.

Everyone started for the meeting.

When she saw Ramachandrudu and Seethapathi, Sundaramma stopped.

"Why do you want to argue with them, Madam?" Seethapathi asked.

"Wearing the headscarf is the right thing. Arguing against it is not a very clever thing to do," Ramachandrudu said, feeling awkward about Sundaramma's assertive behaviour.

"If that is true, why do we not have the custom of wearing a scarf in our state?" Sundaramma glared at him.

"Do you call our state also a state? The best customs and culture in entire Hindustan belong to Gujaratis, Hindustanis and Bengalis. In social matters, they are the role models for the country."

"Perhaps that is the reason there are plenty of Muslims in the states you mentioned."

"Hindustan's history has been distorted. We were all misled reading that wrong version."

When Ramachandrudu was speaking, Yajulu appeared on the scene and gently chided Sundaramma, "The conference is about to begin. Why are you still here, my dear?" Sundaramma looked around and realised she was the only woman there, and all the others were gone. She vanished from the place immediately.

"Sundaramma Garu's English is so good!"

"True. This is just a small sample. But I am very sad at how she differed from the North Indians, especially in how she forcefully argued. She almost looked ready for a fight on the topic."

"Leave it. Why couldn't the North Indians accept it as a local custom in the South and keep quiet?"

"My friend! You have been my companion for so long now. But you haven't grasped the essentials of the nationalist outlook," retorted Ramachandrudu, leaving Seethapathi with a hung face.

6

Ramachandrudu and Seethapathi slowly started heading toward the delegates' lodgings.

"Do you know Congress ends tomorrow night? The day after, we begin the return travel."

"I know. I am not getting a chance to talk to Sundaramma Garu in private. The old man is shadowing her like a personal secretary."

"Even in future, this devil will continue the same way. I am at my wits' end."

"I spoke to Rajendra[94] babu. I reminded him about your one-thousand-one-hundred-sixteen donation for the Bihar cyclone and his return telegram praising your action. I also reminded him about the Mahatma's exhortation to the youth to marry widows. I have taken the liberty of adding that, in response to that appeal, you have decided to marry a widow. "

"Great! What was his reply?"

"He said he would discuss with the Mahatma and get back."

"Oh yes! The job is done in that case! But how can we make all the arrangements without knowing if Sundari will accept it or not?"

"You need not worry about it. If the Mahatma is insisting that your wedding must take place here, then..."

"Very good! But, will the old man agree without the mother's presence?"

"With Mahatma's blessings on our side, won't an aeroplane be at our disposal in no time? Will I not go to Kakinada and get your mother-in-law instantly?"

---

94 Senior congress leader/freedom fighter and first president of independent India.

"Now, this is what I call a plan! Splendid! Get on with it now!"

"By dusk today, all arrangements will be done, all materials will be in place, and your mother-in-law will have arrived. Tonight, just before the start of the final resolution meeting, the wedding will take place. Does it sound good?"

"It sounds great! But to avoid last minute rush, go to the handloom society and get a nice khaddar saree, blouse and a shawl and keep them in the lodging. Give a hundred or one-fifty as advance to the garland folks. Otherwise, how will all those items be ready by the time you return from Kakinada? The conference will start in another half hour. In the meantime, I will take a stroll around this place. You go and be on the job."

Seethapathi left.

7

As Ramachandrudu started walking, he first encountered the Tamil lodging. When he went inside, he noticed Rajagopalachari, Satyamurti,[95] and Sambamurthy[96] conversing in English. A miffed Ramachandrudu stood there uneasily. Noticing his presence, Sambamurthy invited him, "Come! Take a seat," in English.

"All three of you have sacrificed a lot for the country. When leaders like you ignore our national language and talk in English at the national conference,

95 S Satyamurti. Freedom Fighter in the Madras Presidency

96 B Sambamurthy – freedom fighter

it is a huge letdown for ordinary volunteers like us," Ramachandrudu said. Sambamurthy Garu first smiled, followed by a glare and said, "Is this relevant now? Should we focus on the total freedom resolution or discuss these petty matters?"

Then Satyamurti Garu inquired as to what was going on and, having got the point, replied, "Hindi is our national language. Anyone denying the same is not an Indian. Our liberation is also tied to the same. In South India, in one generation, Hindi will push back the other languages and settle as the only language. There is no doubt about it. But, in the interim, if our programs have to jolt the British, we have no option but to use English. This is a minor issue. Just keep listening to us, and don't create any obstacles now. We have the task of blocking the Justice Party's rise. That is our life's goal. Look, if all of you don't come together to oppose Malaviya's[97] stand regarding the social resolution, how can we win? Rajaji and I have been discussing the same matter. Also, the Mahatma is convinced that Malaviya Garu cannot help the movement in any manner. On the contrary, he thinks his ideas could cause monumental damage. So, he rests all his hopes and trust on me alone in the Assembly matter. Thanks to Rajaji's genius, the Assembly fortress is in our control now. How can we show our oratory skills in the Assembly if we boycott English? In all the meetings in the country, the literates would be in tens and the illiterates in thousands. What

97 Pandit Madan Mohan Malaviya, a contemporary of Mahatma Gandhi and a freedom fighter.

is the use of demonstrating our oratory skills in front of the illiterates? Assembly is home to the elite and heavyweights of the society. Do you even realise the advantages of showing our oratory brilliance there? You are ignorant of these matters. So, please don't think too much about it. Just focus on following our instructions. Sambamurthy Garu will meet you separately in a minute," he spoke non-stop.

On his way back, Ramachandrudu encountered a Tamil Iyengar youth holding three plates of Idly-Sambar and coming inside saying, "Vothungo, Vothungo.[98]"

8

As he took barely a few steps, Sundaramma and four Maharashtrian young ladies met him. During the conversation, it became evident that both sides had ventured out to explore the delegates' lodgings.

Accompanied by the ladies, he went to the Bengali lodging. When he tried to enter, a youth at the door blocked him and denied entry. When he peeped inside, he found only middle-aged folks, young men and women, but no one older. The discussion was going on in a low tone in Bengali.

He was disappointed that he and his fellow delegates—despite being an integral part of the Congress—were blocked. More disappointing was that, despite being very progressive in all matters, they were conversing in Bengali instead of Hindi.

98 Coming...

The fact that some young men kept staring continuously at Sundaramma - who was not wearing a head scarf – further irked him.

But he laid the entire blame in this episode at the feet of the Telugu race. He thought *this was the result of staying close to the Tamils.* Then he went closer to Sundaramma and whispered, "Without the headscarf, we cannot win here."

Sundaramma gave him a nasty look and moved on without replying.

Next, they reached the Hindustani lodging. Ramachandrudu was elated and started conversing with a young man.

"I am congratulating you on behalf of my region on the fact that your language has been declared the national language of the entire country. In our region, many youths are striving tirelessly to ensure that Hindi emerges as the sole language for all matters."

"It is the right thing to do. We are rotting because of too many languages. Hindi is the most melodious among all world languages. Without Hindi, there is no Hinduness. I congratulate you for this progressive effort towards learning Hindi by your people. Recently, many of your folks were fortunate enough to have come to this part of the country and share the details of their Hindi services. Very good. I am convinced you are also doing your bit to spread Hindi. Your salvation depends on how well you can give prominence to Hindi in all matters in South India."

"Sure. Sure. Recently there was some upsurge among the regional languages. But the Hindi evangelists quickly stepped in, taught Hindi to even uneducated folks and quelled the upsurge. Our leaders have been preaching that, 'Only when all languages, other than Hindi, die, that's when we would be completely successful,' and attracting people towards Hindi."

"Absolutely the right thing to do. What are the newspapers saying?"

"Some are publishing multi-page Hindi articles. Some large ones are considering the idea of completely abandoning Telugu."

"Nice. It is time to go to the conference. Come later. I will introduce you to our leaders. I hope even women are learning Hindi among your people!"

"Yes, sir. They are."

"If women learn Hindi, then they will teach Hindi to children and ensure regional languages are not even taught. This is the reason for us asking women to learn Hindi. Why learn regional languages first, then forget them and learn Hindi? What do you say?"

"You are absolutely right, sir. This logic is very good. I will spread your thoughts far and wide."

"No. No. There would be anti-development folks among your people. They might spread canards among people and damage the movement."

"Yes, sir. This is also true. Our people are cowards. They lack courage. I will take your leave now."

"Please go."

Ramachandrudu felt as if God himself appeared and granted him a boon. He then gathered the women and went to the conference.

The conference was in full flow. Pattabhi Sitaramaiah[99] Garu was delivering an eloquent speech in Hindi. Seeing that, Ramachandrudu felt relieved and congratulated himself with folded hands and closed eyes and muttered, *Thank you, sir! You have upheld our prestige.*

After a few minutes, noises could be heard from all corners of the hall. Ramachandrudu assumed others were also expressing their gratitude like him. But when he listened carefully, the voices were very clearly saying, "We are not able to understand your Hindi. Speak in English."

Ramachandrudu's blood boiled. And his vision became blurred. In that pandemonium, even he started shouting incoherently.

After five minutes of effort, the seniors managed to nudge Sitaramaiah Garu to speak in English. Ramachandrudu collapsed, saying, "Shame! Shame!"

At precisely that time, Seethapathi arrived—shivering from head to toe—and said, "Our luggage is stolen."

"What?"

---

99 Another freedom fighter from Andhra, Gandhi's contemporary and senior Congress party leader.

"Even towels were not spared."

"......"

"Despite my repeated reminders, you had kept the money in the luggage but did not carry it on your person. Fourteen hundred rupees after accounting for what has already been spent. Let us go and report to the police."

"No way. That would be highly inappropriate."

"......."

"If we report to the police about a theft - right in a Congress conference and in the delegates' lodging – will it save our honour? What is gone is gone. If police arrive on the scene, they will examine all the lodgings. That will be nice fodder for the foreign newspapers. Forget about it and keep quiet."

"To go back home..."

"One telegram and hundred rupees will land in one hour. Don't underestimate me!"

"What about the marriage then?"

"Not now. Let us handle it when we return home."

Seethapathi's shivering reduced slightly.

As a stunned Ramachandrudu was watching, Seethapathi vanished, saying, "Let me see if I can find some trace of the thief," without listening to the shouts from behind.

9

The conference was over. Despite searching the place thoroughly and checking with several people, there was no trace of Sundaramma. Even the Atheist Society organisers could not provide any information.

The third day after Ramachandrudu returned home, he received a letter in the morning at nine. When he opened it, it felt like the letter had sharp needles instead of words. He remained stunned, and when Seethapathi asked him, “Is it from Kakinada?”—he came to his senses and threw the letter towards him.

Seethapathi read it aloud.

“My grandfather and I returned home four days ago. I am writing this letter trusting that you would have also reached Rajahmundry by now.”

“It is my good fortune that I could completely understand your opinions and intentions during the Conference. I am offering millions of salutes to the almighty for saving me from being the victim of an unimaginable catastrophe.”

“I am born in the Telugu race. Being a Telugu is my life and my breath.”

“I can forgive those who don’t understand Telugu culture. I can even pardon those who don’t make any effort to understand. But I cannot see, talk to or even think of a Telugu person who insults Telugu and doesn’t embody the Telugu culture.”

"In the name of Congress, you are deceiving yourself. There is no worse pest for the Telugu race than people like you."

"Our marriage will never happen. Stop having any such hopes in future. I have already half-erased your image from my heart. Unless I completely wipe out any remaining traces, I can neither sleep nor eat."

"I am feeling ashamed that I had a few sweet dreams in the past thinking about you -Sundaramma"

Ramachandrudu was stunned. After Seethapathi consoled him for a few minutes, he recovered, got angry and said, "Even I escaped from a great disaster. Thanks to Mother India's blessings, I managed to avoid the trap of this devil. If that stupid woman comes back, falls on my feet and begs me, even then, I will not marry her. I will not allow her to stand in my presence for even a second. I will not see her face. Not only that, I will not marry a Telugu girl at all. I will sell all my assets, go to Allahabad, seek blessings from the leaders there and marry a Hindustani girl. I will put in whatever effort is required to break my Telugu blood. I will not only forget the Telugu language but ensure that my children will never hear one word of Telugu. "He grabbed the letter from Seethapathi's hand, tore it into pieces, threw them into the street, staggered inside the house and collapsed on the bed.

Seethapathi quietly left the place, shaking his head.

*****

Eradicating Untouchability

Original Author: Sripada Subrahmanya Sastry. First published in Telugu in 1925.

Some key events of the reign of the great king, His Majesty Pullamraju, are being retold here.

Once, the king visited Bombay and stayed there for ten days to witness horse races and take care of some other business. Ideally, he was supposed to be—and deserved to be—there for at least a month. Having adopted societal reform as his prime goal in life, he did not waste any time during his stay.

The ten days he was in Bombay saw hugely successful meetings. Whether it was conferences, people's societies or what have you, patriotism was overflowing in full display during that time.

The one meeting he liked the most and that touched his heart was the one on untouchability. He got all the speeches in that meeting carefully preserved. He also went out and bought any available book on the topic in the market. He then returned to his capital with lightning speed with only one thought on his mind: *when can I solve this problem in my kingdom?*

Even when he was in Bombay, this news reached his inner circle in Duppalapudi. All the Bombay newspapers showered praises on his keen attention in the untouchability meeting. Seeing that, the local Englishmen and Bengalis made all arrangements to let the flow continue when the king returned.

As soon as he returned, the king called for a closed-door meeting with his inner circle. Ideas were exchanged. Bengalis leapt forward, and the British took the teacher's seat.

Immediately, Congress[100] organised many meetings in the British Indian territory surrounding the Duppalapudi kingdom. Two meetings happened in Anaparti, followed by four in Dwarapudi, three in Bikkavolu, and four and a half in Rajanagaram. Half because the last meeting did not attract the kind of audience Congress leaders were hoping for. Even the chief guest and the Swaraj newspaper reporter did not show up. Many more meetings happened this way. All these developments intensified the king's feelings. He decided not to wait any further.

Do such things remain a secret for long? Matters leaked and spread far and wide. It became the talk of the town. Sensing the opportunity, all the untouchables in the capital organised a meeting. The meeting witnessed two or three key speeches whose summary ran like this. 'We are also human beings. You will find the same flesh and blood if you cut open our bodies. Our present plight is a direct result of your actions but

100 The political party that led the Indian freedom fight.

not God-made. Our future is bright in British India. Even Brahmins are ready to uplift us. As subjects of a native king, we expect to be liberated much sooner. Our demands are not unreasonable. Tell us how you are superior to us. We are the same kind of Hindus as you are. Just as Rama and Krishna are your Gods, they are our Gods, too. There is a lot of good in us, too. Your ancestors realised this good and even worshipped some people born in our caste. However, you have now degenerated a lot, hence not being able to recognise the good in us. Each devotee among us is a sage. Show us such great souls in your communities. Even now, if you mend your ways, we are ready to forget your old sins. What we are asking for are not any special privileges or things that will upset any societal equilibrium. We are just asking for the same rights that everyone born as a human deserves. Why can't we have our houses amidst yours? Why can't we draw the water from your wells and lakes? Why can't we stay in the same lodges where you stay? Why can't our children study in the same schools where your children study? Why can't we enter the temples that you visit? 'It continued on these lines. Finally, they wrote to the king, appealing to end this untouchability.

The king replied, saying he was on the job. Hearing this, the city went into a huge uproar. Some nobles fell at the feet of Ramachandraiah. "Brahminism will get destroyed before anything else. Please spare our generation from this calamity," some old Brahmin scholars appealed. "Please ensure that the caste order is not disturbed," kshatriyas requested. "How can malas[101], madigas and us be the same? We have never heard of such an absurd argument! Please don't let it happen," The vaishyas argued with Ramachandraiah. Some said, "Let us cultivate our own fields if things go too far."

Ramachandraiah contemplated deeply. He pored over the scriptures and analysed the present conditions. His thoughts ran like this. *When told to do something, our folks refuse even if it is good. They argue it would destroy the religion. But they do the same without complaint under the pretext of 'changing times. Scriptures don't work. Tricks don't work. Just blind following works. We never understand, on our own, what is good for our society. Just following other societies is the royal path. We don't know how and where to reform. Just do it whimsically. This is the reason for social reform making stumbling progress. Even this episode is starting in the wrong order. Anyway, let us wait until the right time.* He kept quiet.

One day, there was a huge meeting in the capital. It was presided over by an Englishman. The king attended the meeting. One Bengali gentleman delivered a lecture,

101 Mala and Madiga were considered fourth and lowest in the Indian caste hierarchy (Shudras) in old times. They remained untouchable for several generations. According to scriptures, Brahmins are the highest caste, followed by Kshatriyas (warriors), Vaishyas (Merchants and farmers), and Shudras under the four-tier caste system. Today, India is completely free from this evil practice of untouchability, by law and in practice, too.

stroking his long beard. While he spoke on behalf of the untouchables, a Brahmin delivered a sermon to Brahmins in the audience. "No doubt we are great. Our scholarship is infinite. Our structure, too, is strong, but over the years, it got ruined. Our Brahminism is no longer sufficient."

"It might look good if we run the society like before. But it is no longer possible. We have come into contact with many divergent societies now. Tastes have changed. Points of view have changed. Brahmins themselves are not able to appreciate Brahmin rituals. The conditions and future of untouchables are uncertain. Owing to our apathy, they are converting to other religions. While our society is rotting on one side, it is shrinking on the other. This is a very dangerous development. It is better for us to be proactive. Otherwise, if the untouchables rebel, what can we do?" Saying this, the brahmin stopped. Then, the Englishman got up and tore Hindu society into shreds.

The king's natural leanings were already clear. This meeting further ignited the fire and gave him a sleepless night. As soon as he finished coffee the next morning, he called for Ramachandraiah.

The old man, who believed his society was the best, and the young man, who believed there was nothing worse than his society, sat down face to face.

"Have you heard?"

"What are my orders?"

"There is no use saying later you were not told. Ideally the orders should have gone out to all villages yesterday itself. But I held back because I wanted to respect your seniority and inform you before acting. Do you think untouchability – treating a human worse than the worst of animals – is good?"

"Not sure why our ancestors created this arrangement...."

"All that is irrelevant now."

"Changing with the times is, of course, good. So, how do you want the orders to be drafted?"

"Have you heard the demands of malas and madigas?"

"Entry to temples, schools, lodges, allowing them to live among us, draw water from the same wells as we do, and some more on these lines..."

"Yes. What do you have to say?"

"Do we have any option?"

"Why can't the orders go out then? Every second is like an eternity to me!"

"Bengalis and Englishmen...."

"Why do you care about what they say? You never saw eye to eye with them!"

"There is nothing for me to say if you talk like that. You know well that my mind always looks at the negative side first."

"We don't need this sermon now. This is not like the prostitute topic of the past."

"Yes, sir. How can there be any objection to your orders? Reform is necessary in this case. But my difference of opinion is about where to begin. All the happenings in British India are targeting just one goal – that is to adulterate our higher castes. People like me desire that whatever happens under your rule is focused and comprehensive. I am happy with whatever orders you want to send out. However, you sought my opinion. So, once, you should accompany me in disguise. Get the Bengalis and Englishmen, too. No one should take the lead and speak. Everyone should go by what I say."

"What do you want me to do?"

"Let us get started. I will explain everything."

The king was worried that the old man was up to some trick. But he calmed himself, thinking he could not go against royal orders. Everyone started out as planned.

Ramachandraiah's followers made announcements saying, "As per the king's orders, a team of royal officers have set out to eradicate malas' and madigas' untouchability." Hearing that and seeing the presence of Ramachandraiah in the team, citizens were perplexed. On the other side, untouchables were ready to welcome the team with garlands.

Eventually, both sides met. Numerous citizens were there to witness this wonder and—if required—to plead against it. As the Englishmen and Bengalis were puzzled, not knowing where this was leading, Ramachandraiah stepped forward.

"Our king has decided that untouchability has no place in our Duppalapudi kingdom. Brahmins, kshatriyas, vaishyas, shudras, barbers, malas, and madigas can all touch each other if needed. There is no mention of eating together and building relationships for now. The main purpose is to say there should be no one who cannot be touched. It doesn't mean people previously considered untouchable should leave the kingdom. No one can ask another to stay at a distance. All humans are equal. Owing to these reasons, the following is the message his majesty has sent across through us. From this moment, malas and madigas and others like them in this kingdom can start using public and common facilities like pubic lodges, temples, schools and lakes without any problem. Those who want to and can afford to can come into towns and villages and set up their households amongst others."

The king thought, *what is new in this?* It seemed to him that Ramachandraiah's ploy was to directly communicate the message and earn some respect for himself. When translated and informed, Bengalis felt *the idiot communicated it himself and lowered the value of the king's order*. The Englishmen, malas and madigas were overjoyed. Other citizens were bewildered. At this point, Ramachandraiah continued, "There is another small point." This put a check on the overflowing joy among untouchables. There was silence. "We all must thoroughly understand the king's orders. We should not misuse the same. While enjoying the benefits of this boon, you – I mean the untouchables – must earn the right to ask for even greater boons. When we say all public facilities and organisations, there are no exceptions. There are so many castes, races and sects in this kingdom. His Majesty has created special schools and so on for them. All those organisations will now form part of this order. Before we implement this order, there is another important task that must be done. Both malas and madigas are equally untouchable to all of us. However, there are differences among yourselves. To start with, madigas must share malas' wells and other facilities while malas continue to use them as before. After one week of such practice, malas and madigas can start using other common facilities." He stopped here. For those who could perceive, there was a certain profoundness in his face.

Bengalis dismissed it, saying, "These are small matters." Englishmen shrugged.

When the king looked at him, Ramachandraiah said, "Madigas! What are you waiting for? Go and get your buckets to draw the water from the malas' wells."

There was a stunned silence for a second. The next moment, the venue was filled with whispers and confused faces. Ramachandraiah's voice rang again, "You must come forward quickly!"

The general public began enjoying this with the comment, "He pulled a good trick." Just then, one madiga came forward with a bucket. Immediately, an old mala stepped forward. "Hey! Hold it there!"

"No one can say how long ago our castes were born, but since birth, we have never had any relation or contact with madigas. In many ways, our caste is superior. It is not fair on his majesty's part to contaminate our caste today. If you insist, we would rather leave this kingdom and go elsewhere, but we cannot have madigas touching our wells. So, please convey our position to his majesty and get this order annulled," the old man pleaded.

Ramachandraiah looked at the king. King looked at Bengalis and Englishmen. When they lowered their faces, Ramachandraiah began again.

"Ever since thousands of years ago, when this royal dynasty started, no royal decree has been withdrawn. Our present king is a very kind-hearted man. Just as you objected to madigas drawing water from your wells now, other higher castes might object to your drawing water from their wells. Hence, his majesty ordered that military force be used to remove those not obeying and strictly implement the orders. It is better for you to fall in line; otherwise, I will be forced to call for soldiers. "

Saying this, Ramachandraiah prodded madigas, "What are you waiting for?" When madigas started to move forward, malas came forward with heavy sticks.

Ramachandraiah asked the king, "What are your orders?" and the reply was, "I am at a loss to understand what is happening."

"What is there to understand in this? A war will break out. Your orders, please?"

"Why?"

"Malas are not ready to let madigas touch their wells. They want their wells to be uncontaminated, but they want permission to use higher castes' wells."

"What do you say?"

"What can I say? It would glorify your majesty if I said, 'You are kindness personified.' There should be no resistance to your order."

"What do the malas say?"

"Nothing. They are ready for war."

"What if we call for the force?"

"Mala-Madiga war will then turn into a war between malas and our soldiers."

"You see no other way out?"

"I can't. In any case, I think it is better for you to remove the disguise now and speak as your true self."

The king immediately appeared in his own true form. Malas instantly threw the sticks aside and fell at his feet.

"Your majesty! For several generations, we have been living as your loyal subjects. Please don't contaminate our caste, sir. Don't humiliate us," one mala said.

"Your order is unchallengeable. But if your orders are weird, then we will have to say no. Madigas are inferior to us in many ways. Don't humiliate us, Your Majesty!" another mala chipped in.

"Have we ever seen madigas and malas sharing water from the same well? Our lives are at your disposal. We will be happy to die in your service but don't allow this contamination, O King! "Another pleaded.

"It seems this is all happening as a result of madigas' pleading with Ramachandraiah Garu. Your Majesty should intervene and save us. We are ready to lose our and madigas' heads, but we will not let them come anywhere close to our wells," another mala warned.

When the king looked at the Englishmen, they mumbled something. Bengalis said, "This is a small matter." When he looked at Ramachandraiah, he said, "This is how it is."

The king got angry. "We are putting off this untouchability eradication program for now. Only when malas come to me and agree to take madigas to their wells voluntarily, that is when I will rethink this subject." Saying this, he turned back.

The crowd dispersed. Ramachandraiah left quietly. People were happy that a calamity was averted.

This happened in the Duppalapudi kingdom a long time ago. Will find out the latest situation there and present it to you separately.

*****

The Minister's Advice

Original Author: Sripada Subrahmanya Sastry. First Published in Telugu in late 1940s.

1

"Diwanji Venkatappaiah stands dismissed from service," Rayani Garu announced. The grapevine was that he started as a clerk in the court. Rayani Garu was well aware of his rise through the ranks to the Diwanji status.

As a matter of fact, Venkatappaiah was a witness to Rayani Garu's birth.

Rayani Garu's upbringing and education were also overseen by Venkatappaiah.

After the king's untimely demise, Venkatappaiah also handled Rayani Garu's marriage and coronation. It was all done according to his will, without consulting anyone else—sometimes even the queen.

After the coronation was done, Rayani Garu started taking care of all the court matters.

But it was Venkatappaiah's word that carried weight on the ground.

He was a terror to people.

This was when Rayani Garu suddenly announced the removal of Venkatappaiah from the position.

Venkatappaiah went home smiling.

But the whole town was stunned.

The royal court came to a standstill, too.

Consternation spread through the villages.

Some called Rayani Garu, an ungrateful man.

Others spread the word that Venkatappaiah cheated the king.

The old clerk Appalanarasaiah, who initially worked as a peer and later as a subordinate to Venkatappaiah, proved with reasonable evidence that Venkatappaiah's wealth crossed a million rupees.

Ramasubbaiah, who was working as Venkatappaiah's personal clerk and suddenly became the Diwanji after his boss's fall from grace, demonstrated with numbers that the treasury balance was always in just hundreds during Venkatappaiah's term.

The royal family was small. Rayani Garu lived frugally. His annual income exceeded three lakhs. Those in the know were amazed at Venkatappaiah's audacity.

2

Rayani Garu started worrying about why no farmer had been approaching him of late.

"Venkatappaiah Garu crushed them under his boots. And made it clear that he would see their end if they showed up anywhere closer to the court. That's why they could not appear before your majesty during his term. After I took charge, I changed the system completely. Now, they don't have any grievances that need Your Majesty's attention. That's why you don't see them now," was Ramasubbaiah's response.

Rayani Garu was not convinced.

Rayani's intuition told him Ramasubbaiah, trained under Venkatappaiah, would have mastered all the dirty tricks.

He contemplated deep and hard.

Ramasubbaiah mentally dismissed Rayani Garu as a 'Greenhorn.'

He unleashed his talent.

Exactly at that moment, Ramasubbaiah's personal secretary, Chenchupunnaiah, sensed the opportunity. He understood that was the moment to be careful if he wanted the Diwanji's position.

He gave up sleep and food.

One year passed.

"Please check the safe your majesty," saying this, Ramasubbaiah presented the accounts ledger to Rayani Garu.

The amount in the ledger matched exactly with the cash in the safe.

The treasury that never saw more than a few hundred rupees was glowing with more than a lakh now.

Ramasubbaiah's eyes twinkled with pride, and the message 'Look at my loyalty!' But Rayani Garu remained poker-faced.

This is all fake stiffness, dismissed Ramasubbaiah in his mind. But one day, when he reached the office and was about to keep his turban on the table, he got wind of the news that his majesty had been regularly summoning four clerks to his presence.

He then remembered other recent happenings. Head servant Bhairanna had been frequenting his street and loitering around. One afternoon, the payroll clerk's wife came to his house and pleaded desperately, saying to his wife, 'We are starving for food. You must recommend our case to Diwanji and take care of us. ' He then toured the entire house on the pretext of helping his wife with chores.

And he suddenly suspected all his movements were being watched by his personal clerk from the corner of the eye.

He collapsed in the chair.

Occupied with these thoughts, he could not work anymore that day.

He sent back every clerk who came for signatures, saying, "Let us see tomorrow."

That was it.

When he was about to grab his turban to go home, a clerk came and handed a piece of paper that said, 'You are dismissed with immediate effect', then made a face at him and left.

The next instant, Chenchupunnaiah, with the airs of a to-be-Diwanji, approached the table and extended his hand for the keys with a scowl.

Ramasubbaiah sighed and limped out of the office.

The gate watchman stepped aside as if an untouchable was passing by.

"On a full moon day, sunset and moonrise happen at the same time," a clerk commented.

"This analogy is not good. Only after Ramasubbaiah's safe was filled with one lakh rupees did the treasury safe get one lakh," another clerk said, raising his eyebrows.

3

"Be careful!" warned Rayani Garu and then installed Chenchupunnaiah in the Diwanji chair.

"Yes, of course, Your Majesty," Chenchupunnaiah bowed in reverence. As soon as Rayani Garu left, he flexed his back.

All the clerks gathered around Chenchupunnaiah. They took care not to use the singular tone they were used to addressing him in. Everyone heaped praise on him. "It is not as if we are extolling your virtues on your face. The truth is, after a long time, the Diwanji position has gone to an honest man."

When he heard the word honest, Chenchupunnaiah suddenly got inspired by the scriptures he read and started off excitedly.

"Look here. Let us agree, for argument's sake, that Venkatappaiah amassed huge wealth. Hence, even after losing his job, he is in a position to live a rich life. But the shame he had to endure, was it any smaller? Is earning millions the only goal in life? Wouldn't one be able to live just by begging? Is death not better than humiliation? Even after watching the plight of Venkatappaiah, Ramasubbaiah couldn't remain honest. If the king could remove a four-decade-old Diwan, does he care about someone who held the seat for just one year? Is there any depravity worse than a hundred-rupee salaried employee stashing one lakh rupees in one year? Not just stealing the king's money but fleecing the general public for bribes is also a barbaric act. Scriptures say, 'Rajyanthe Narakam Dhruvam, ' meaning, at the end of his reign, a king is certainly destined for hell. But it is not right on the scriptures' part to say this and stop. The saying is not complete, in my opinion. What

I want to add is – Not just the king but his servants are also destined for hell if they stray from the path of honesty. So, we must be careful. Speaking for myself, I am accepting this position not because I don't have any other means of livelihood. I will prove that the minister position is a noble position and not some low position. I have vowed to demonstrate to the world that every person who has risen from clerk to a high rank is not corrupt. To prove to the farmers that everyone who becomes a Diwanji doesn't have to be evil, I am accepting this position. My resolution is sacred. I know that my ancestors' blessings will be with me. We are all eating out of the king's hand. If what we get is not sufficient, let us go and inform him. Let us melt his heart by sweating it out and then take an extra pie. Understood? No devious paths for us. If anyone strays, consider him dead in my hands."

As soon as he finished speaking, he sat down and immediately grabbed a pen and wrote as he uttered the words, "I am hereby writing my resignation letter. There is no other proof of a service-focused person's sincerity than this. This will always remain in my pocket. Not just that. It will always wait for the moment when it can adorn his majesty's hands. His Majesty trusted me and elevated me to this position. Keeping my faith in almighty, I will serve my king and people." Saying this, he signed the letter, folded it, and kept it inside a nice envelope and in his pocket.

When the bewildered clerks didn't know what to say, Appalanarasaiah took the lead and said, "Very glad to see you starting a new era, sir. Could anybody who held the Diwanji position in this court speak as assertively as you did today? Did it even occur to anyone that, at the time of assuming the role, they should preach dharma to their subordinates like this, give a message to the world and bare their heart? Forget writing a resignation letter and keeping it in their pocket; did they even manage to understand the sanctity of such a letter? I am speaking the truth. For them, the *position* was important. For you, your *honour* is important. For you, this Diwanji position is worthless. It is like a toothpick for you. An old man like me uses a toothpick to clean his teeth after having food. You have accepted the toothpick to rid the world of corruption. That's why his majesty has chosen you when there are so many contenders. You are blessed. Even we are blessed for this opportunity to work under your command. Our province will now flourish without any doubt." All this while he was repeatedly touching his folded hands to his forehead in reverence.

Even when so much was being spoken, not a single clerk clapped. Initially, Chenchupunnaiah was upset but consoled himself, thinking, *these fellows are frogs in a well. What do they understand?* Finally, to make them see the sense, he thumped the table twice and assumed the Diwanji status.

Rayani Garu came to know about the entire episode.

That evening, Chenchupunnaiah went home, finished dinner, and, in his new status, sat outside on a coarse cotton cot with his wife and young daughter. By the time they finished the small talk, Chenchupunnaiah had a divine inspiration. *Venkatappaiah, who spent all his life as a Diwan, vanished overnight. Ramasubbaiah was washed away in the flow after only one year in the role. Who am I to expect any better? So, I must be careful.*

By the time he understood the nuances of the job, one month had passed.

Word reached him that all the clerks were getting regular summons from Rayani Garu. Nobles of the town, who until now never visited the court, were getting frequent, unsolicited audience with Rayani Garu.

He started preparing one statement of accounts every day.

Another month passed.

He started observing some frequent practices in and around his office by his colleagues, who were not trying to hide them.

Whenever he summoned a clerk, the standard response from another clerk would be, 'He went to see His Majesty on summons.' Most of the time, he wouldn't find anyone besides the servant outside his office door. Even if he saw one, that fellow would go away quickly, quoting summons from Rayani Garu.

The third month passed like this.

The treasurer came and delivered the third month's salary.

Appalanarasaiah entered, closely following the treasurer and asked, "Sir, have you come with the resignation letter in the pocket today?" He stepped aside when Bhairanna approached.

Bhairanna quietly kept a piece of paper on the table and left without uttering a word.

When he opened it, it read, 'You are dismissed with immediate effect.'

Chenchupunnaiah collapsed in the chair with eyes popping out.

He came to his senses only when Kamanna, the junior of all the clerks, entered the room and barked, "Keys!".

4

As soon as he took charge, Kamanna, too, called for a meeting of the clerks.

Everyone assumed he, too, would deliver a lecture. But Kamanna had a blunt message. "None of you need to keep coming to me. There are servants. Just keep sending files regularly. If any specific document is needed, I will ask for it. Any document that comes in on any day must immediately be addressed and dispatched the same day. If any documents are due from the stations, send reminders. I expect everyone to be promptly in the office by eleven in the morning. When it is five in the evening, everyone must leave, and the office must be locked. I will not tolerate even one minute delay."

He appointed Appalanarasaiah as his personal assistant.

Not one clerk could fathom the logic behind Kamanna's moves.

Only Appalanarasaiah nodded his head as if he understood and approved the move.

Rayani Garu came to know of the developments.

He was startled but couldn't comprehend what was going on.

"Whatever the workload and urgency, only documents must be sent to the office, and no one is supposed to come in person. Except for clerks and servants, no one else is authorised to enter the office," Kamanna passed a second order.

Notices went out the same day to Munsabs[102], Karanams[103], station officers and staff of neighbouring villages, clearly instructing them not to visit the head office and not to visit the capital without explicit approval. All matters must be handled through papers and mail. Any delay won't be tolerated.

Orders went out to temple management staff, telling them any inconvenience caused to devotees or any lapses in regular worship and services would lead to stringent punishment. Similar orders went out to public lodge keepers saying any funds mismanagement, pilferages and inconveniences caused to travellers would not be tolerated. If any file that came to him was small,

102 Munsab: The village administrative head/magistrate

103 Karanam: The village accounts and revenue officer

he would get his doubts cleared, and Appalanarasaiah would write an endorsement. If it was big, he would read it himself and write the endorsement. Finally, every document would have Kamanna's signature, and immediately, it would leave the office. This process had been going on without any interruption.

Soon Rayani Garu himself started experiencing a new set of controls and restrictions. If any file requiring his signature was stuck with him, he would get reminders and deadline warnings. If he wanted to see any clerk during office hours, he was forced to write a note to Kamanna – and there was no guarantee that the desired clerk would show up.

All the employees heard rumours that Kamanna's trusted agents have been hovering around their homes incognito.

It took everyone's breath away.

The first month passed like this.

When employees entered the office on the first of the month, they promptly received their salaries.

But they were in a quandary whether to rejoice at the prompt salary payment – which otherwise never came before the tenth of the month – or to grieve over the loss of additional income that has now been cut off.

Clerks were distraught. Servants started feeling beleaguered.

The second month passed.

It was as if Kritayuga[104] passed.

Again, salaries arrived on the first of the month.

But what use? They were like cleanly wiped notes!

Even if people wanted to somehow live with that, those rupees felt like leeches that sucked the blood completely.

Staff started feeling the pinch.

Groups were being formed, and whispers started gaining momentum.

They concluded – dejectedly so – that as long as Kamanna remained Diwan, their fate would not improve.

They put their collective brains to work. They launched campaigns.

As soon as the clock struck five in the evening, Kamanna would personally ensure that the office is locked and then go home in his horse carriage.

Appalanarasaiah would follow on his old bicycle.

The clerks and servants would pretend they were also leaving but would turn back as soon as Kamanna was gone.

That was the only time they had to vent their frustrations and imaginations with Rayani Garu.

---

104 Hindu mythology divides time into four ages or yugas. Krita Yuga, Treta Yuga, Dwapara Yuga and Kali Yuga.

But that time was also meant for Rayani Garu to visit the flower garden in the palace accompanying the queen. Knowing the queen's evil temper, Rayani Garu couldn't risk even one second's delay.

Yet, Rayani Garu took some time one day because the new Diwanji's actions were a constant riddle to him, too. So, he wanted to listen to the woes of the clerks and servants.

Everyone fell on his feet.

There were different expressions and versions, but the message was common.

The summary was, 'Your Majesty! Kamanna is no different from his predecessors.' Some colour was appropriately added to this message. Ordinarily, it was tough not to believe such versions.

Even Rayani Garu had great faith in the clerks until Kamanna took over. But Kamanna's ingenuity won Rayani Garu's heart while it didn't touch others.

While it was possible to believe that clerks and servants might be having issues with Kamanna, Rayani Garu couldn't convince himself that Kamanna was a traitor.

The clerks then changed the tune and said, "Our travails don't matter. Serving someone itself is a hardship. Once we treat service as dear, other difficulties don't matter. We are not talking about our issues, Your Majesty! Kamanna is a traitor under the garb of a loyal servant."

Not just clerks and servants but even cooks who never had interaction with Kamanna sang the same tune.

Rayani Garu was so disgusted that he couldn't speak to anyone other than the queen.

5

The third month was over after lasting an eternity.

Everyone received their salaries.

Rayani Garu received a fresh burst of protests.

He couldn't take it anymore.

One fine day, he went directly to Kamanna's office.

Appalanarasaiah, sitting in Kamanna's office studying some files carefully, stood up, "Your Majesty! "

When Kamanna looked up, he saw Rayani Garu standing in the doorway, holding the door, slightly bent and peeping inside.

Kamanna stopped writing, kept the paper on the table, holding the pen still in his hand, and stood up quietly.

"Kamanna!"

"Yes, Your Majesty. What are my orders?"

"What should one do to those who constantly indulge in slander?"

"Simple, Your Majesty. Just slash the ears of the person who believes in them."

Appalanarasaiah was startled.

Rayani Garu slowly exhaled, took his hands off the door frame and made a quiet exit.

*****

The Banished

Original Author: Sripada Subrahmanya Sastry. First published in Telugu in 1935.

1

It was the month of Aashaadha[105]. The skies were overcast, and the threat of rain was lingering in the air. When it was not a heavy downpour, there were frequent drizzles without any let-up, and the skies remained dark. It was difficult for folks wearing white clothes to leave home and venture out. But the farmers busy with field work were an exception. The paddy transplantation work was in full swing. The rain didn't deter them. At times, they abandoned their palm-leaf umbrellas and were working in the rain. Any delay would mean the loss of saplings. What was more pressing than agriculture for a farmer?

It was already past full-moon day. Farmers were in a hurry. And the rain kept intensifying. Godavari was in a spate, with the water breaching the canal banks

105 The fourth month in the Indian calendar. The beginning of the rainy season coincides with June-July.

and overflowing. Water was entering some of the fields without any effort. All the farmers were in a state of urgency at the same time. The daily wages were up but it was still tough to find labour. Some women were taking along their unmarried daughters to do the fieldwork. Good or bad, the three-kilos-grain-per-day earning was tough to resist for the poor.

The cloudy sky made it appear like evening. A strong wind was blowing. It was already nine in the morning. All the women from Malapalle[106] boarded the canoe with their children. Everyone was scared, but no one backed off. Even as the farmers behind them were cautioning them not to push each other, the canoe moved. The helmsman was steering the boat with great difficulty. When the canoe reached the middle of the canal, it started moving slightly faster. One minute passed, and the very next minute, the canoe overturned. Heart-rending cries pierced the sky. The canal was filled with women and young girls who were rapidly drowning.

The farmers who were at the banks of the canal were stunned. Some of them rushed into the water. Along with them, Viswanatha Sastry –bathing in the jetty nearby – also jumped into the water. But what use was the effort? It was like an army of ants jumping into a fire. Some eight or nine women who could swim saved themselves. Viswanatha Sastry and the farmers rescued

106 The separate residential quarters outside the core village, designated for the Malas or Dalits, who were treated as untouchable by higher caste people those days.

another ten. The number of dead was considerably higher than the survivors.

By the time Seetharamaiah Naidu rushed there, Viswanatha Sastry managed to bring an eighteen-year-old girl to the shore with great difficulty. And then collapsed struggling to catch his breath.

Naidu observed everything. "You saved the bride, Brahmin. God bless you," saying this he helped Viswanatha Sastry recover.

That young woman was Naidu's head-farming-partner's wife. It was just fifteen days since their marriage took place. And Naidu was the one who organized it. The turmeric traces on her body were still visible.

The next moment, the entire village arrived on the scene. Whoever witnessed that mass death praised the farmers and Sastry.

2

The Brahmins stood afar and heard the talk. "Vissanna[107] touched the malas. He cannot be readmitted into our community. Be careful! "Saying this aloud, Padmanabha Sastry walked away. Other Brahmins followed him. Not one approached Viswanatha Sastry.

Naidu – who was watching all this - turned towards Sastry. He shrugged and said, "Let them leave. Why worry about humans' anger and affection? If the almighty is happy with what I did, that's enough for

107 Nickname for Viswanatha Sastry. Easy to pronounce.

me." Before anyone could say anything, Naidu took Sastry to his house. Hearing this, the landlord's family – where Sastry was staying – sent his clothes and other personal effects to Naidu's house on Padmanabha Sastry's orders.

"What is the use of staying here now? Allow me to go to my village, " Sastry pleaded. Naidu refused. You have nothing to fear. As long as I am around, even Lord Rudra cannot harm you." Saying this, Naidu made arrangements for Sastry's stay and provided facilities to cook and sleep in his granary yard. Apart from the lack of contact with the Brahmin community, there was no dearth of comfort for Sastry.

3

There used to be many scholars in Chintapalli. It was famous as the abode of the science of logic and the science of literary aesthetics. Even today, it retains its fame. But the scholarship dwindled. There were many pseudo-scholars. Padmanabha Sastry was their leader.

Having heard about the fame of the place, Viswanatha Sastry arrived there three years ago to complete his education. Initially, it was difficult for him even to get admission. The main reason was the differences among the multiple Brahmin sects. Among Brahmins, Padmanabha Sastry's sect was the one that had some unity among its members when any issues cropped up with other sects. Viswanatha belonged to a different sect of the Brahmin caste.

Believing education to be the primary goal, he somehow managed to find a place there. His keen intellect, determination and fearless attitude helped him to become successful. In two years, he surpassed all the other scholars in the village. His teacher passed away six months ago. Even then, one factor held him back in that village.

It is better to describe Viswanatha Sastry as a good mythology expert than someone good at literature. He studied Mahabharata, Ramayana and Bhagavatam very critically. He had a good voice and sang melodiously. He was also endowed with handsome looks. With the holy ash smeared on his broad forehead, his radiance would make people imagine him as Lord Shiva himself.

Two or three of the villagers' children were his students. They didn't like to let him go. That was the public reason the Brahmins knew for Viswanatha's staying back. There was another hidden and important reason, though.

Seetharamaiah Naidu was a rich landlord and of the same age as Sastry. He was also known to be intelligent, brave and generous. His mother loved listening to mythology readings. He told his wife, "Mother is getting old. Her desires must be fulfilled." The old lady asked Sastry to remain in the village until the Mahabharata, Ramayana and Bhagavatam reading was completed. Sastry hoped to get a good reward and complied with her request. No one other than Naidu, his mother and Sastry knew *this* reason.

Ten days after Sastry's teacher died, Naidu's father passed away. When Naidu performed the last rites and the religious rituals that followed, he decided to do Kanyadanam[108] along with other donations. A lot of villagers had high expectations on account of this and also the land donation that Naidu planned. Eventually, both donations went to outsiders. Land was donated to a doctor. "At least make sure you donate the Kanyadanam amount within the village," insisted Padmanabha Sastry. He pushed his brother-in-law's son forward and recommended his name, saying, "This fellow lost his parents. He is poor and deserves it. Donate to him." But a discerning Naidu didn't oblige. He said, "It is important to see merit rather than relationships and nativity in such matters." He went ahead and donated the amount to Viswanatha Sastry and told him, "Find a suitable girl. I will give you one thousand rupees for the marriage." The neighbouring village folks were happy. Locals were left fuming. Padmanabha Sastry abused Naidu, the donor, and Sastry, the receiver. But Naidu was not the one to take things lying down. He roared like a lion and asked Padmanabha Sastry to get lost.

---

108 It literally means donating a virgin. Normally, the process of giving away a bride in marriage by her father (or some relative if the father is not alive) is called Kanyadanam, and the donor is supposed to get a lot of divine benefits. Scriptures prescribe that those who don't have girl children can donate a substantial amount of money to a deserving Brahmin to get the same benefit.

4

"The matter crossed even district boundaries! Where is Godavari, and Where is Guntur? Without verifying his caste and antecedents, how dare Naidu donate to him? Just because he applies the holy ash on his face and sings melodiously, does it make him eligible? This is a huge humiliation for our villagers!" Saying this to the Brahmin youth who trusted him, Padmanabha Sastry left the place. "The local villagers were expecting this donation. Due to some previous incidents Padmanabha Sastry Garu was already upset with me. If I accept this now, I could end up....." when Viswanatha Sastry hesitated, Naidu was firm. "I don't care. If you accept it, I will give it to you. Otherwise, I will completely drop the idea itself." Even at such a delicate moment, Naidu's mother called Sastry aside and whispered, "Please accept it. I have told him to give it to you." Left with no other option and unable to forgo one thousand rupees, Sastry accepted the Kanyadanam.

When Sastry's Guru was alive, during a wedding event, a debate was set up. Viswanatha Sastry was alone. But the opponents were ten. This group was led by the tiger-faced and sharp-tongued Padmanabha Sastry. The Guru, who was supposed to adjudicate, was in a dilemma. On one side, he had Padmanabha Sastry from his own sect, and on the other side, he had Viswanatha Sastry, who was his beloved protégé and who could uphold his prestige. Unable to be impartial, the Guru recused himself and walked away.

The entertainment program was going on. A renowned dancing girl was performing the sequence from Manucharitramu[109]. She was singing poems that depict the conversation between Varudhini and Pravarakhya and acting to them. Following established protocols, she asked the audience for feedback on her performance. Immediately, Viswanatha Sastry responded. The jealousy stemming from Viswanatha's first move, the ego that prodded him, 'Why should I remain silent?' and the expectation of getting a large reward from the hosts in recognition of his scholarship – these three reasons forced Padmanabha Sastry to start his counter-argument. His large frame, severe countenance and loud voice scared the gentle dancing girl. She began to worry that Viswanatha Sastry – that handsome and melodious young man – who was leaning towards her, would lose. A severe debate ensued for two hours. The audience concluded that Padmanabha Sastry's argument lacked any substance other than shouting. The dancing girl and Viswanatha Sastry sensed that the opponents were moving away from the main subject and became indifferent. This riled Padmanabha Sastry. This defeat in argument and loss of face in an open court – in the presence of dancing girls – against a dancing girl and a youth from another sect – became difficult to stomach. The sense of shame was unbearable.

A hurt and spiteful Padmanabha Sastry vowed revenge. The insult in Naidu's house added fuel to the fire. It culminated in Viswanatha Sastry's excommunication

---

109 An old Telugu poetic composition

with the words, "He touched a mala. He cannot be admitted back into our Brahmin community!"

Poor Viswanatha Sastry came from Guntur. All he could call his own was an old mother. He kept her at his maternal uncle's place and came here for an education foundation for a better future.

5

"To humiliate us, Naidu is apparently forcing Sastry to find a local girl to marry. Folks! We must be careful." When Padmanabha Sastry cautioned thus, the villagers agreed. After he was banished, Sastry's disciples abandoned him. Sastry took Naidu as a pupil and started teaching him with the advice, "Your sharp intellect will further be embellished if you learn Sanskrit."

As days passed, there was news of one of Naidu's relatives marrying a widow. Naidu's mother asked Sastry, "Sastry Garu, do scriptures approve of such a wedding?" A debate ensued between Naidu and Sastry. Naidu tried to fill the void left by Veereshalingam Pantulu[110] in the debate. Sastry concluded, "Times have changed. One cannot argue that old customs must continue to prevail. Leaving the scriptures aside, one can't help but take pity on the plight of young widows. I think Veereshalingam Garu was very kind-hearted. Perhaps that's why he started this practice of widow-remarriage."

110 Renowned social reformer who strongly advocated widow remarriage and actively supported the same, including providing financial legal assistance.

"Women are of stronger morality than men. Ideally it would be nice if women don't remarry. But times have changed. For today's young widows, remarriage could be a correct option for many reasons." The old lady chipped in with her views. Naidu and Sastry were astounded by her broadness of mind and liberal thinking.

Over time, Sastry's repute spread to the relatives of Naidu in neighbouring villages and there was a steady flow of visitors to listen to his mythology discourses. Viswanatha Sastry became a persona non grata to the local Brahmins who were under Padmanabha Sastry's grip. Even others limited themselves to a mild greeting when they publicly encountered Sastry. Adding to these woes was the need to do his own cooking. Bringing his mother over was not a viable option as he was unsure if he would permanently live in that village. Even if permanent residency was to be considered, what use was it to stay in a place where one was banished from one's own community? Sastry was mired in these conflicting thoughts all the time without being able to figure a way out.

Apart from the bother of having to cook himself, his food supply was adequate. Naidu made it amply clear that he would not tolerate any shortcomings in Sastry's food arrangements. Added to his decree was his mother's supervision. Naidu's wife would frequently depute her maid to see if everything was alright. In short, Sastry's meal arrangement was nothing short of that of a wealthy landlord.

As days passed, Naidu's wife went to her maternal place in Kakinada for her delivery. Unable to bear her absence, Naidu followed suit. Soon there was news that delivery was due anytime. This made Naidu's mother also depart for Kakinada. Sastry was home alone. Naidu's absence and the consequent shutdown of the mythology reading sessions made Sastry uncomfortable.

6

The second half of Phalguna[111] month arrived. Winter started receding, giving way to the advent of summer. At around six in the evening – when the sun was about to set – Sastry was sitting on the stone bench in the granary yard and was deep in some thought. At that time one young widow – perhaps twenty years of age, not very fair complexioned but beautiful nonetheless – was heading towards the canal and cast her long glance towards Sastry.

What is this? Why is canal-bound Narasamma acting very strange today? wondered Sastry. But he couldn't decipher. *For the past month, I could sense her side glances. Was it anger? Or something else? If it is anger, it is understandable. Could it be something else? By chance, could it be?* his thoughts ran in many directions. *Let her come again.* Thinking thus, he waited at the same place even though it was nearing the time to cook dinner.

---

111 Last month in Telugu calendar. Coincides with Feb-March.

It was dark. He could hear Narasamma's voice near the canal shore. When another lady asked, "I will wait. Will you come with me?" her reply - "My clothes are dirty. I will have a bath and come. It will be late. You carry on" - was clearly audible to Sastry. Sastry's heart started racing. In the meantime, an old lady came from the shore and walked past. Sastry's heart beat faster. Suddenly, Narasamma appeared. Instinctively, Sastry whistled, and Narasamma quickly entered the house. An entranced Sastry followed her inside.

After staying for about twenty minutes, Narasamma went back to the canal, bathed again, and left. Sastry cooked and ate his meal but couldn't stop wondering at her audacity.

A week passed. After secretly conferring with Naidu for a long time, Sastry saw him off and went to bed. But the train of thoughts pursued him and denied him sleep. His mind was overwhelmed with wild imaginations, expectations, and anxiety. He kept tossing in the bed.

It was midnight. The howls of jackals in the fields also stopped. The entire world was immersed in darkness. At that time, someone quietly pulled the door. Sastry asked a couple of times who it was, and when there was no response, opened the door. Someone entered and immediately held Sastry's hand. When a stunned Sastry asked, "What's this?" the person replied, "When I was leaving this place in the evening, someone noticed and informed my father. We had a fight tonight. My father thrashed me and also threatened to poison me. The fight went on for nearly six hours. After repeatedly scolding me, my father went to bed. Let us leave immediately and go somewhere." Sastry paused for a second and then said, "Stay here. I will be back shortly. Keep the door bolted from inside." He stepped out into the street.

Around eight o'clock the next morning – near the bathing ghat - the Brahmin women were heard gossiping, "It seems Padmanabha Sastry's daughter Narasamma eloped with Viswanatha."

7

The news and the accompanying chaos engulfed the entire village. Padmanabha Sastry was livid, and why not? She was the lone daughter. He had no sons. Despite being widowed, she stayed at home and was cooking for him. He didn't worry so much, even when he lost his wife four years ago. His daughter's transgression, followed by her elopement with her lover-the lover being none other than Viswanatha Sastry-all added up to his extreme embarrassment and frustration. His enemy has now become his daughter's lover. There could be no worse humiliation than this for an egoistic man like Padmanabha Sastry.

Soon, the crowd gathered. Karanam was ready with paper and pen. Munsab also arrived but delegated the writing duty to Karanam, who was taking the help of Seetharamaiah Naidu.

After two hours of deliberations and considering the villagers' advice, Karanam drafted a complaint that said Viswanatha Sastry eloped with Narasamma and took jewellery worth a thousand rupees. Before signing the paper, Munsab questioned the witnesses again to make sure. Padmanabha Sastry barked, "Do you think they are scared? They will, of course, give thumping evidence! Fellows, go ahead and speak!" Munsab replied, "In that case, there is no need for further speaking." He noted Sastry's comments in the paper and then signed it.

Karanam and Munsab then had a private conversation. Munsab didn't seem to be coming around. Karanam approached Sastry's party and told them, "Talk to Munsab and get him around to your side." But no one came forward. The complaint was dispatched.

The future was uncertain. Sastry didn't have anyone who could cook for him. It was already late morning when he remembered this. When he set out towards the canal with a pot to fetch water, his neighbours and relatives stopped him. After lunch, four or five young men went out in search of Viswanatha Sastry and Narasamma.

8

One week passed. One early morning, when the crows were cawing, a boat arrived from Rajahmundry and stopped in the jetty. By the time the sun was fully up, a motor car had arrived from Kakinada and parked near the boat. When the police deputy superintendent disembarked from the boat in official uniform, Naidu approached him and greeted him with folded hands. A few constables also alighted from the boat. As this scene was unfolding, Naidu's workers - who till his farm - came and stood there. Music from a band could be heard from Naidu's granary yard. As the Dudekula Saib[112] was playing the trumpet, Viswanatha Sastry and Narasamma – in bridal attire – alighted from the boat and got into the car. The police officer took the seat next to the driver. As the constables led the way, the procession started. Naidu's head partner – the husband of the eighteen-year-old young woman rescued by Viswanatha Sastry from the canal – was ardently dancing with a banner at the head of the procession.

The word spread across the village quickly. Whoever had eyes watched it, and whoever had a heart enjoyed it. Many were surprised. Many Brahmins locked themselves and stayed indoors. Padmanabha Sastry's plight was like that of a man who was being burnt alive on a pyre.

Everyone had their own interpretation as to what was happening. Around twelve noon, the police superintendent conducted an enquiry in the village court and made it amply clear to Padmanabha Sastry that he would be registering a case against Sastry for filing a false complaint. "Your daughter is much wiser than you. She has a heart. Love –the beauty of human

112 Muslims who are into cleaning cotton and making mattresses

life – is abundant in her. It is better for you to mend your ways at least now. While you banished that young scholar due to jealousy, she respected him with love. The one whom you banished is now your son-in-law. Be careful. If any harm befalls him or your daughter, you will lose your head." Giving this stiff warning, the officer left with his staff.

After one week – upon his mother's instructions – Naidu gave the promised thousand rupees and some more, along with new clothes, and sent off Viswanatha Sastry and Narasamma to Guntur.

*****

The Tahsildar Dream

Original Author: Sripada Subrahmanya Sastry. First published in Telugu in the 1930s.

1

Venkatasubbaiah was an obedient youth. He never went against his parents' wishes. When he was studying for the B.A. exam, Sundaramma joined the household. Succumbing to his mother's nagging, he took Sundaramma to Chennapatnam, kept her with him for four months and sent her back.

In due course, he passed the exam and returned home. "It is good to take up a lecturer job in a college. There is no risk of transfers and no major responsibility or hard work involved. You can make nothing less than a hundred per month," his father reasoned. "A magistrate job is what gives high status. There is no need to sweat things out. It comes with money as well as rank," was his mother's advice. "Tahsildar[113] is better. One can tour

113 Tahsildar was a revenue/admin head role when one district had many Taluks. Tahsildars used to report to the district collector.

the entire Taluk[114]. And all the Karanams[115], Munsabs[116] and servants will be under your command. And there is the 'extra' income to be considered," Sundaramma suggested. Venkatasubbaiah weighed all the options. "Your idea is better. At present, there is no vacancy in the collector's office. At the right time, I will get in there." Saying this, he convinced Sundaramma and his mother and joined the King's College as a lecturer.

My son heeded my advice, rejoiced the happy father. "Why sit idle? And why let a hundred rupees go?" mused the happy mother. "For the time being, this arrangement is fine. But it will be good to be in regular touch with the collector's office." Sundaramma convinced herself.

2

One year passed. The college management dismissed Venkatasubbaiah, citing his lack of teaching ability. Luckily, there was a vacancy in the collector's office. The one-hundred-rupee salaried man now joined for thirty. Father was downcast, saying, "It is very low, my boy!" Mother took a slightly positive view, saying, "It may be low now, but it will increase. No need to worry." "You used to get two sovereigns every month. Now, what will you get, and how will it be enough for

114 Taluk: Administrative sub-division within a district, headed by a Tahsildar.

115 Karanam: Village accountant. Normally a brahmin.

116 Munsab: Village administrative head/judge. Always a higher caste / landed person.

household expenses? At least take care to be in the good books of the collector," Sundaramma advised. Every time he handed over his monthly salary, his father used to grumble, "What's the use my dear? In your greed for Tahsildar and Magistrate posts, you neglected the lecturer duties and lost a hundred-rupee job." Venkatasubbaiah had no answer.

Around this time, the son of the neighbour in the opposite house started practising law.

Another year passed. The workload increased, but the salary didn't. The European officer was replaced by a Tamil Pillai officer. Before he got down to his main duties, Pillai examined the profiles of the clerks in his office. Very soon, the Brahmins lost hope. Pillai downgraded the Brahmin names in the priority list and brought some non-brahmins forward. This meant the revenue inspector job that was guaranteed to Venkatasubbaiah had gone to a clerk belonging to the barber caste. Sundaramma and her mother-in-law were completely dejected.

Another year passed. Pillai was transferred by the government to the revenue board. In his place, a Saheb[117] came.

The priorities changed again. The number of Muslims in the office has increased. If Hindu clerks wanted leave, it had to be recommended by the Muslims even if they were lower in rank. Every vacancy

117 Muslims used to be referred to as Sahebs, Saibs and Turakas / Turks in the olden days in Andhra.

was being filled with Muslims. The Dafedar[118] Meera Saheb's stature grew higher than the personal assistant. "Turks must be taken care of," was the verbal notice that went to all the Taluk offices.

After one year, Saheb received orders transferring him as an assistant collector to the Guntur district. The grapevine among the Hindu clerks was that government confidential reports said, 'Saheb Garu did not show the same alacrity in his office responsibilities as much as he had shown in promoting his community folks.'

The Turk was replaced by a Christian. Priorities changed, and the screening started again. All the vacancies went to Christians. After a few days, due to poor health – the Christian collector got himself transferred to Thanjavur. Having closely observed the drama that happened during the past three years, the higher-ups, this time, sent a European as a collector. The boasts of 'Collector is our man' stopped. Brahmins took solace, saying, 'No matter who comes, we are the last ones in priority.' After two years, Venkatasubbaiah finally became a revenue inspector.

3

Venkatasubbaiah's father passed away before he could witness his son's career progression. To pay for his father's final rites, Venkatasubbaiah had to borrow one

118 In military terms, it refers to a non-commissioned officer who is junior to a sergeant. But in government offices, it means a peon or bellboy.

hundred rupees from Narasaiah, the lawyer who started practising in the opposite house.

Watching Narasaiah's wife buying new jewellery every year and Narasaiah replacing his old house with a new two-storied building agitated Sundaramma. She calmed herself with the thought, '*There is no problem. We have reached till the inspector rank. Tahsildar won't be too long.*' And accompanied him on an official visit to Tapeswaram. Someone used to being called Venkatasubbaiah's wife so far has now acquired a new sobriquet, Revenue inspector's wife. Her imagination grew wings. "I am going to inspect the first harvest. I will not be back for one week. Do you want to come along?" When Venkatasubbaiah made the offer, she didn't oblige. '*If I travel with him, that will be only as a Tahsildar's wife. Two palanquins must go in tandem, one behind the other. If he is received by the Karanam, I must be received by the Karanam's wife.*' Driven by this logic, Sundaramma stopped accompanying her husband on official tours.

For someone who had been starved for a new income for four years, Sundaramma started feeling better. "I don't have too many pocket expenses. Run the household with the salary. Whatever we get as 'extra' is completely yours to spend," Venkatasubbaiah told her. Small supplies started flowing in. Honey, new jaggery, sugarcane, pumpkins, and bottle gourd were plentiful. From time to time, milk and curd were also in supply. There were many times when there was no need to buy ghee.

As a revenue inspector, Venkatasubbaiah was transferred to seven or eight villages. Thanks to Sundaramma's smart handling, the household was in good shape. The jewellery craving mostly eased. But there were no offspring yet. One night, Sundaramma asked, "My dear, it has been three years since you became revenue inspector. When will the promotion to tahsildar happen?" "Can't say. The English officer considers only merit. He is impartial and fair. And a good man. God willing, this year or next, I will become at least deputy tahsildar, if not tahsildar," her husband replied. '*Even this is fine. There will be no dearth of opportunities to go on tours. It certainly counts as a higher job. If we manage the affairs carefully, building a two-storied house will not be a problem,*' Sundaramma mused. Immersed in her thoughts, she missed giving the betel leaf to her husband that night and slept.

4

Summons arrived from the collector the next day, asking him to report to the camp office in Ramachandrapuram. When Venkatasubbaiah went there, the collector handed over a paper. It claimed that he took bribes and assigned government lands in some villages to some farmers, thereby acting against the public interest. "This is a lie. You can investigate. My detractors have given this complaint. When working in villages, there are many challenges. Because we have direct contact with every farmer, they approach us seeking favours. Those who are denied favours indulge in such complaints," pleaded Venkatasubbaiah. The collector then handed over another paper.

Tahsildar had written in that note confirming the allegations against Venkatasubbaiah to be true. Venkatasubbaiah was stunned. "What do you have to say now?" When the collector asked, he replied, "Sir, there are instances when the tahsildar is known to have taken bribes. I can prove it. Be it eggs, tobacco, castor oil for his little daughter or green grass, the grapevine has it that the tahsildar is actively taking bribes. You must get it investigated, sir." "As a first step, I am demoting you from revenue inspector to clerk position again. If you do well, I will think of promoting again. If I get petitions against tahsildar's bribery, I will take action against him." With this firm message, the collector issued an order for him to report to the Kakinada office immediately.

5

Sundaramma was devastated. She grieved for nearly a month as if her half-built house had collapsed. Another month went by in deep contemplation. "How about this? If you become a lawyer, you don't have to fear anyone. You can earn freely. Study for the law exam, my dear!" she prodded him. Venkatasubbaiah agreed. But a shortage of funds made him hesitate. An emotional Sundaramma told him, "Sell the gold necklace and waist belt. We can get them done again in good times."

When he failed the first-year F.L. exam, he considered his options. *With some luck, even first-grade passing should be good enough to practice in district courts. It is not as if all the B.L.-passed folks are practising in the high court. Many prospered with just second-grade qualifications. Having thus decided, he studied for the first-grade exam and passed.* Immediately, he started his practice in Kakinada.

His neighbour Narasaiah passed on some spillover cases when he was overwhelmed with work. While Venkatasubbaiah was sitting on the veranda, studying the clients' papers and drawing up plans inside the house, Sundaramma was fantasizing about a bright future. Venkatasubbaiah used many tactics to mobilise clients. He started addressing people – whom he had never previously cared for – with a lot of respect. He was buying tiffin for agents. He was providing free services to Munsab and Karanam whenever they needed some paper work to be done in the collector's office. In many meetings, he started tabling resolutions and pushing for debate regarding the need for legal cases to protect temple funds.

6

None of the tactics yielded any result. Narasaiah started pulling back his work offers. He adjusted the money due to Venkatasubbaiah against the previous outstanding loan. Parties stopped visiting Venkatasubbaiah. The practice was heading southwards. And Sundaramma's questions increased about the state of affairs.

"What do you expect me to do? No one knows the law better than me in Kakinada. But I am not good at speaking. I can write notes, but I cannot argue face to face," Venkatasubbaiah bemoaned. "Then try for Munsab post," Sundaramma said.

Just when Venkatasubbaiah sold his law books and went to Madras to seek the patronage of some senior government officials, a resolution was passed in the legislative assembly denying district Munsab jobs to Brahmins for the next five years. A crestfallen Venkatasubbaiah returned home.

Then, one fine day, his brother-in-law from Rajahmundry arrived. Heeding his advice, Venkatasubbaiah decided to move to Rajahmundry and join his brother-in-law as a partner in his clothes business. "Brother, are you saying he should stop looking for a job? Don't you see any hope at all? We have lost the necklace and waistbelt as well. He couldn't get to become tahsildar even for a month! Will business suit us?" When a dejected Sundaramma posed so many questions, her brother calmed her down and convinced her that this was the right thing to do.

At an appropriate time, Venkatasubbaiah sold his house in Kakinada and moved to Rajahmundry. Fortune favoured him soon. The dedication and hard work of the brothers-in-law made their shop the largest in Rajahmundry. Even when profits were flowing in, Sundaramma remained upset for quite some time with the fact that her husband couldn't become tahsildar. Finally, she turned around and convinced herself thinking

This is actually better. Tahsildar's wife would always be looked at as the wife of a servant. I am independent now. With the early profits, she recouped the necklace and waistbelt. Venkatasubbaiah started detesting the days when he was an employee under someone. He started advising the young men who visited him not to hanker after jobs but to get into business.

*****

The Weeds or The Dying Telugu Pride

Original Author: Sripada Subrahmanya Sastry. First published in 1935.

1

"Yes, sir! With one pen stroke, you can feed a Brahmin family for life!"

"Whether feeding or starving, only the district board president can do. What can I do?"

"Of course, it will be in his name. Please let me explain myself. If there is a lodge, two people are involved: the donor who established the lodge and the clerk who takes care of daily administration. Isn't it the clerk's duty to honour the donor's orders, sir?"

"But I am not a donor! And the president is not a clerk!"

"If that's how you see things, what can I say? Which district president can ignore a sub-collector's orders and survive?"

"That was in the old times. Those days, some well-deserving pleaders used to get appointed as district board presidents. They knew how to deal with higher officials. In today's generation—I am talking about most, not all—they don't even have to pass the school final exam. Everything is driven by the magic of the vote. Many are asking the attender whether it is a big signature or a small signature, and only then....."

"Since you broached the topic, let me submit my thoughts. Our president – I am sure you see my point – not counting his other vices - spends day and night in the company of prostitutes..."

"How can you say that about a fellow Brahmin?"

"Because he is a fellow Brahmin, we are forced to go through all these travails. If it is some Nayudu Garu or Chowdary Garu[119]...."

"Your brahmin trickery seems to be on full display! "

"Your Excellency! Other than the cries of a hungry soul, what tricks are there in what I am saying?"

"Since you know the matter fully, why not get hold of a Nayakuralu[120]?"

"That will be needed only if you can't make it happen."

---

119 Brahmins, Nayudus and Chowdarys, are three higher caste people in a village. Brahmins are supposed to be the learned ones and scholars. The other two are in farming / business / administration, etc.

120 Prostitute and typical resident of Meraka Street.

"If things can be done easily, where is the need to take a complicated route?"

"What can be worse than approaching a prostitute or dancing girl? If needed, our entire family will fast for a month, but we will manage to supply..."

"Now you are talking! If it is the district board president, folks like you don't spare any effort in supplying..."

"Understood, sir. It is my mistake. By this time tomorrow..."

"Why are you misinterpreting what I casually said? Will I take a bribe for this small recommendation?"

"Bribe! How dare I use that word in Your Excellency's presence? Do I even have the stature to bribe you? Just because you are gifting us a livelihood, one manugu[121] ghee for your upma[122] – of course you will not even smell it, I know – one basketful of jaggery that could be useful for some pulusu, and of course, one boxful of honey syrup..."

"Are you suggesting you will supply these and similar items to me? You are a smart fellow!"

"I hope you will not get angry.."

"Why would I get angry with a poor Brahmin? By the way, my eldest daughter, son-in-law and grandchildren are coming in two days. I was anyway planning to buy these items myself..."

121 Old unit of weight in Andhra. 25 LBs

122 A breakfast dish in South India

"Please don't. I will deposit them here by tomorrow morning. I, too, have girls. I know how many expectations daughters have from their parental home and how parents should take care of such matters. In any case, if you are taking care of my son's livelihood, arranging a little upma and coffee for your daughter..."

"Yes of course. Forget jaggery. Even flies don't land on jaggery in our house. It suddenly occurred to me when you said coffee. I heard you own a cow that recently delivered..."

"Of course, your majesty. I have it. It slipped my mind. I will personally bring it."

"Are you assuming I will take it as Godanam[123] or what?"

"Am I a fool? Why does his excellency need a donation?"

"If given to Brahmins, it becomes a donation no matter what name you use. But what is given to us – are you following me? – becomes a supply or gift, also called najarana[124]. "

"Yes, sir, of course."

"As a matter of fact, isn't it you brahmins who designated us as only the donors and robbed us of our right to accept gifts?"

123 Godanam: Donating a cow. Normally, Brahmins accept cow donations as part of rituals. 'Go' refers to cow (Govu in Telugu). Danam is a donation.

124 Urdu word for gift

"I shouldn't be saying this. But old timers didn't know anything except sitting on a high moral ground".

"You brahmins never sat on any moral high ground. In fact, you corrupted and weakened the entire society with your actions."

"Meaning?"

"It means dividing people and promoting jealousy... Oh! That's a long story. Leave it for now. Coming to the point, I was planning to send jawans to Dwarapudi market[125] tomorrow morning. Are you suggesting I drop the plan?"

"Why do you need to do it anymore sir?"

"Are you sure?"

"Absolutely. I Swear on Gayatri[126]!"

"I don't believe in things that we don't follow. Anyway, this is only while our daughter stays with us. After that, we don't need your cow, do you get it?"

"As the saying goes, a dry cow is like an albatross around the neck. Will I not come and take it away after the job is done, my lord?"

"Good. Even for this reason, giving a cow to me will not count as a Godanam."

"I don't understand why you keep getting this doubt..."

---

125 A nearby weekly market where cows are bought and sold apart from many other items.

126 Gayatri is the sacred mantra for Brahmins.

"There is no doubt, but another point needs to be considered..."

"What is it, sir?"

"If it is really considered a donation, then taking it back will be considered stealing a donated item. Since that sin can't be attached to you, this cannot be considered a donation. Understood?"

"Yes, sir"

"Good. You may go now. You will be here in the morning, won't you?"

"Will I not come and wake you up by the time crows caw?"

"That's what I call as being smart! If the sun comes up, the tongues will start wagging..."

"How about another idea?"

"What is it?"

"By midnight twelve..."

"Sounds great! It means you will bring the cow by the time we return from the cinema."

"Yes, sir."

"I will write a strong letter to the president tonight. Later, you can carry the letter."

"Yes, Your Excellency!"

"Go now."

"May God bless the donor of livelihood!"

2

"Manugu ghee?"

"We have no option"

"Have you already committed?"

"What choice did I have?"

"I have delivered so many kids and have been managing this household for so many years. Never did we have more than a small spoon of ghee..."

"Did even that scoundrel have when he was not in this job? His time is good now."

"I hope nothing else!"

"C o w too"

"What?"

"I don't need this talent of sitting at home and shouting! We need to deliver our cow, too."

"You have ruined us!"

"We need to manage somehow. Do you think getting a job is some child's play? In any case, it was gifted to our son by his in-laws, right?"

"Do you have any sense of right and wrong at all?"

"Why? What is wrong with my sense?"

"Haven't his in-laws gifted it for our granddaughter's milk needs?"

"Now we need to give it away to help her father land a job."

"Will this not put us to shame in public?"

"What is more important? The public shame or the livelihood being granted by that officer?"

"Anyway, why should I care? The cow belongs to our daughter-in-law. It is up to her and her husband and your needs. Do whatever you want to do."

"Our son himself will take it along and deliver it. None of my business."

"Stealing milk from the child... Does that sub-collector have children?"

"His daughter, son-in-law and grandchildren are coming in two days. This is for their coffee.."

"So, he has a daughter. How did he have the heart to...?"

"Power. Power. They can get away with anything."

"Three-month-old infant. Will that fiend not suffer her curse?"

"Shh! Don't talk. A stick that catches fire will eventually burn fully. Do you know who those fellows who come begging at sunset time now are? These were the same officers in previous lives. Calm down now. After taking the pension, who will care for them?"

"I don't know who cares for him later. Right now, our granddaughter will starve. We have to feed her powdered milk."

"One month. Just bear for a month. While our son has to take the main responsibility, I suggest you also explain the situation to the daughter-in-law. After just one month, fifty rupees will land in our hands. With the first month's salary, I will buy a grand cow that equals Kamadhenu[127]. The entire family can then have curd. With the second month's salary, let us buy one Benares saree – do you hear me? – because she is fair complexioned – let us go for violet colour, that too with a flower pattern. With that, her face will start beaming again. With the third month's salary, let us buy jewellery for the little one. That will compensate for stealing her food. After that, the family will run smoothly like a..."

"Enough of your colourful imagination! Stop it now, and don't go around talking this nonsense to others. Neighbours will mock us"

"They can go to hell. Once our son gets the job, will I talk to those idiots?"

3

"....If you say like that...."

"What is there for me to say in this? I have told you the facts. It is up to you now."

"Please. If you get angry, I can't take it. I am a poor Brahmin and a family man. I shouldn't be singing my own praises, but I am a Ghanapaathi[128]. I am seeking your kindness."

127 The mythological cow from heaven

128 An expert in reciting Vedas

"As soon as he comes home, I have no problem arranging an audience. What do you say?"

"What can I say if you talk so stiffly?"

"What about the way you are talking?"

"....."

"My services are much needed, but...."

"....Need your kindness"

"What is this? Oh!"

"Please accept!"

"You throw a five rupee note and want to move mountains. Great optimist!"

"My Lord! Treat these as legs and not hands[129]. I had to pawn my rosary to get these five rupees. I can't manage anything more, even if you cut me into pieces. I need your kindness now."

"Fine then. This greed is the hallmark of you, Brahmins, not us. Today, it is too late. Tomorrow. Got it? If you come by eight thirty in the morning, I will arrange the audience when he is having his coffee. But keep one rupee ready for the jawan.[130]"

"One more rupee?"

"Jawan is the key fellow."

129 It is a standard expression in India to hold someone's hands and ask the person to treat them as legs. This amounts to unconditional surrender/begging / pleading

130 The doorman.

"All I am left with now is my head to mortgage. I will do that and get the rupee. Do I have a choice?"

"You have to manage somehow."

"Struggling for daily survival, what can we manage, my lord?"

"Just because you have given me one note and will give the jawan another, don't assume that the entire responsibility becomes ours!"

"Of course, I understand that! What about the letter?"

"Letter!"

"Why do you sound cynical?"

"Don't panic. But let me make one thing very clear: I am not the type to indulge in cheating and dishonesty. Your pleading is making my heart melt—it has already melted. Listen to me."

"Please go on."

"In the current situation, my job is to give you sufficient time with the President and plead your case with him. The entire job should get done with that letter only. But..."

"Please tell me the facts..."

"President Garu doesn't like the sub-collector."

"I am finished! Why?"

"The reason could be whatever. It is a fact. That letter is not good for even cleaning the tongue."

"This is a disaster!"

"How much did he squeeze there?"

"Rama! Rama[131]! Collector Garu is favourable to Brahmins. I have approached him, and he blessed me."

"Is that so? Fine. What happened there is not my concern. But remember my words. That letter and a blank paper have the same value."

"So, what do I do now?"

"There is a great way forward. If you want to hear it, I can share the details."

"Please go ahead"

"If you approach this way, you don't need to meet him. By morning, the order will be in your hands."

"Please spell it out without further suspense!"

"That's what I am trying to do. But I need one more fiver when the job is done. Got it? Unless you commit, I will not reveal."

"One more note?"

"Good then. Why do I care? Come tomorrow and I will arrange the audience with the president as agreed. Since I took your money, I will keep my word."

"Is it fair?"

"If you find it unfair, take your note and leave."

"Please tell me the plan."

---

131 Telugu and Indian equivalent expressing exasperation (similar to Jesus Christ!)

"Of course, I will. First, say yes."

"Where will I get it from?"

"Back to the beginning again? Should I tell you where to get it from and how to get it? What about manugu ghee and…"

"…."

"Why do you look shaken?"

"I don't know what you are talking about. Have you, by any chance, discovered the value of my head? And then…"

"The cow itself reveals your head's value."

"….."

"Why are you shaken?"

"……"

"Say something!"

"Please tell me the plan."

"That's better. You will certainly pay the fiver, won't you? If not, the order will be cancelled by the following morning"

"……."

"Remember carefully, and now listen. Meraka street. Duggirala Seshachalam. Have you heard the name?"

"No. Who is he?"

"Not he. She. Prostitute."

"…."

"Why? Hearing the word itself made you impure now? Do you need to take a bath?"

".... Oh. Please go on."

"She is very beautiful and in prime age. Once someone sees her, it is difficult for him to get out of her spell. Already, four or five fellows have become paupers."

"No need for a detailed description. Please come to the point."

"If she recommends...."

"Recommends?"

"Yes. It means if she agrees to romance."

"....."

"Now, use your brains and get things done."

"I have studied Vedas..."

"If you had taught the same Vedas to your son, then there would have been no need for this job hunt. Vedas and scriptures should remain your forte, and jobs should also go to you folks, right?"

"......."

"While your ancestors ruined us fully, they at least allowed us to have servant jobs. Now, your ambition is to deny us even that job. Right?"

"......so, this letter..."

"Castor oil. Pure Ambajipet[132] variety. Cleans intestines very well and has already done so in this case."

"You are rubbing salt into the wound."

"It will heal quickly without getting infected. Isn't that good?"

"......."

"Now get going, poor Brahmin! Will things get done if you stand there looking puzzled?"

"Are you saying I have no other option?"

"Of course, you have an option. No one is forcing this on you. My advice is to drop the idea. That is the best course of action. But before pursuing that, if you can get rid of the itch for the job—that desire is the filthy force driving all your actions right now—then there is no need to visit either prostitutes or Gods. You can sit peacefully weaving jandhyams and reciting scriptures. Please move now. I don't have the whole day."

4

"Who are you?"

"We are Brahmins."

"Please accept my greetings. What brings you here?"

"May God bless you. I have come on a big task."

"Do you need a dance performance?"

132 A town in Andhra famous for its castor oil

"I can neither afford one nor do I need one now. I have a large family to take care. Only work can feed us. I have come with the hope that you will help feed us."

"What is your native village?"

"Actually, it is Duppalapudi. But we have been living here for the past four years."

"I will be back shortly. Please have a seat."

"......"

"I have neither the stature nor the means to honour people like you. However, as Lord Srikrishna said, 'leaf, flower, fruit and water'. Please accept and bless me."

"You have all the wealth. What more can I bless you with? You have given me ten rupees and are saying you don't have the means and stature...."

"I am ashamed that I could not give you at least a month's wages. Please consider this as annual gift and please bless me with your noble visit once a year. Just like today, by the time I finish my morning worship and come out."

"Madam! I heard about your nobility. And now I am seeing the proof of what I heard. But, please consider one point. I have not come here for money. So, please take these rupees back."

"Please keep them and use them as needed. I will not take it back. Let me know how I can help."

"May I?"

"Why the hesitation?"

"Because I have come with a lot of hopes."

"If there is something that deserves to be done and I can do, I will not say no."

"With your kindness, you can feed our entire family. That's why I came looking for you."

"Understood."

"This is the first time for me in a prostitute's house. I was half dead when I came here. But after seeing you, I feel there is no need to be ashamed."

"Now tell me what help you need from me."

"Unless you promise, I will not reveal."

"I can never make such promises. Normally, there are no great tasks that get accomplished through prostitutes. Even if there are – I have already mentioned this – it depends on how deserving the task is and whether it is within my ability."

"I have six daughters. Three are already married and living with their husbands. All of them have children and the eldest has a grandchild too. Two daughters are waiting to be married off. The marriage consummation for the fourth one is due. And I have just one son. He has one daughter, a three months infant."

"One look at your family in the morning washes away all the sins!"

"It is my good fortune you feel like that. With great difficulty, I have got my son past matriculation and LT. Now the struggle for employment – a teacher job – has started."

"... Oh."

"I came to know that your recommendation will get things done. Why don't you be a nice woman and bless us with your generosity?"

"Who? Me?"

"Yes, Madam. That is the information I gathered. Why don't you do this good deed and help us?"

"Who is supposed to give the employment letter?"

"District board...."

"Don't you say it!"

"President Garu."

"....."

"What's wrong, my dear? Why are you so shaken? And why the sweating? Why don't you speak?"

".... Who told you that he will give the letter on my word?"

"The clerk who is always with him."

"Srihari! Srihari[133]!"

"Why? What happened, madam?"

"....."

"Your reaction worries me. Please speak up."

133 Similar to Rama Rama (Taking God's name in exasperation)

"Don't worry. This has come like an acid test for me. So, is it that thin and wily fellow, that scoundrel who told you this?"

"Yes. That toothless tiger."

"..... Does God exist, Sastry Garu?"

"Why do you say that, madam?"

"What else can I say? There is no God. Only devils exist. There is no righteousness. Only evil. Good is not to be seen even with a searchlight. Evil is omnipresent. Not just our community but the entire country is without morals. People speak only lies but not the truth. Wherever you turn, only violence and blood can be seen. God doesn't exist at all, sir!"

"What caused this disbelief in God, my dear?"

"... Don't get angry and don't blame me. Do you agree when I say there are absolute outcasts, even among Brahmins?"

"I can't entirely deny the fact..."

"Then let me tell you, the president you mentioned is the head of that outcast community."

"...."

"Do you find it difficult to digest?"

"No. No. But there are some tasks that even these outcasts' control"

"True! But don't blame the outcast community. Cleaning toilets is their profession. Is there a correlation between profession and behaviour?

"No."

"An outcast should do toilet cleaning work. If not, he should show higher abilities."

"You are right."

"So, what about a Brahmin?"

"He should embody Godliness."

"Your president doesn't have even an iota of Godliness. As a matter of fact, he is a demon in human form."

"I have heard about some shortcomings in his character. But I didn't know he was such an evil fellow. What harm did he do to you, my dear?"

"He didn't harm me directly. But he showed his true barbaric nature."

"Meaning?"

"Even tribals respect and venerate dance customs."

"I don't get it."

"Once, I went to a Brahmin house to perform at a wedding."

"Please go on."

"Your president happened to be a close relative on the groom's side. He was in attendance. One night, I was invited to come to his lodging. The street dog who told you about me was the emissary."

"I am asking out of ignorance. Didn't you and the president have a prior relationship?"

"I had received invitations, but I never agreed. My younger aunt's daughter was in a relationship with him. Considering that sensitivity, I declined. Once, when I mentioned this to her, there was some discussion. This eventually led to them breaking up after two months."

"Oh! There is a lot of background to this!"

"I conveyed a message saying I don't visit anyone's lodging. And I maintain celibacy when I go to perform in an event."

"You did the right thing, my dear!"

"He showed me a hundred rupee note. I ignored it and went my way."

"You should have been born in a higher caste, my dear."

"Why do you say that, sir? What is so great about today's higher castes? Do women get respect in these higher castes? Isn't she treated like a slave even in those castes?"

"....."

"Sorry if my words have hurt your feelings. Please forget and forgive."

"No need, my dear! What you said is what is prevalent in society today. No need for apologies. Please continue."

"I don't know what that street dog communicated or whether he lost his mind. The next afternoon, when I was about to perform in the main event, he made me step down and made some other second-rate dancers perform. He asked me to perform in that night's procession."

"Understood. Vengeance was at play."

"That was more of barbarism than vengeance. Is he a human who makes a senior dancer step down from the main event and forces her to perform in the procession?"

"What do today's generation know about our arts, culture and customs, my dear?"

"They don't know arts but they want women who learnt those arts. That's why I call them barbarians and animals. Let it be. I made discreet enquiries. Your president is just a worshipper of money. This conspiracy was hatched by the street dog."

"To get into the president's good books?"

"To eat money underhand whenever possible."

"......"

"Now you see his true colours? Normally, we entertain anyone who comes with money. But true connoisseurs among them are rare. Rest are...."

"Why? I am getting the point."

"So, now you understand what value my recommendation carries?"

"Understood, madam."

"Suppose I agree. Will that mean your son will get the job for sure?"

"That's how the clerk had put it."

"It means the betrayal of my soul – combined with the president's barbarism - will ensure livelihood for a Brahmin family. Am I right?"

"......"

"So, Sastry Garu, please tell the dog to bring the president tonight to me."

"Madam...."

"Tell him I won't be charging a single rupee."

"Madam.."

"Why are you leaving? Please sit down."

"Nothing. I will go away quietly. Please don't betray your soul for my sake."

"Why?"

"Such an evil conspiracy? So much deceit? He is, anyway, a pimp. How dare he convert me into one? I assumed and hoped that you and the president already had a past relationship, and all I had to do was request you and get your recommendation. I didn't know you were such a virtuous person. I am a Brahmin. I have learnt and recited Vedas. Seeking alms is my profession. I can always approach a few more to meet my family's needs. But I cannot dare to bring down the stature of a prostitute – who is as proud and virtuous as a family woman – and throw her to a wolf just for my selfish ends. Madam! Please forgive me. Forget my request and allow me to leave."

"No way! Sastry Garu, please sit down. I must do this. It is my good fortune that I am able to help a poor Brahmin family today. This is a noble incident in my life. In any case I am neither a married woman nor a chaste woman. So, there is nothing to lose and no chastity to gain. I am not worried, and you don't worry either."

"Madam..."

"Not a word more. I am not going to listen. This must happen this way only. Haven't I said before? We are used to the company of these animals. Sastry Garu. Stop worrying about this matter. Just tell that dog what I have told you."

"Please.."

"I won't let you say one more word. I swear on the Vedas you have learnt."

"You have tightened a noose around my neck!"

"Please don't say that and leave now. Please bless me with your audience once in a while. Convey my respect to your wife."

"My dear! You have sewn my lips and tied my hands and feet. You have turned me into a corpse even when alive. What a nobility! What a birth! You are born in this prostitute clan by mistake."

"Why? Has the prostitute clan degenerated so much? Are all the higher caste women spotless in their character? There are many like me – even much better than me – in my clan. But this world is blind... All this is irrelevant talk now. Please leave. Let me touch your feet once.."

"God bless you! How much he is making me suffer! Is there no God? Is he not watching all this? This scoundrel – will he now deliver?"

5

".. sixteen, seventeen, eighteen, nineteen, twenty."

"What? The full amount – two hundred – is there?"

"Yes, of course. But delivering just plain cash..."

"....."

"You Brahmins don't know the etiquette in these matters. The market is overflowing with sweet limes. Couldn't you have packed a hundred? Or four banana bunches, a dozen apples or three kilos of grapes..."

"It didn't occur to me. Don't get angry. When the first month's salary comes..."

"Six hundred per year, sir! For two years, it will be twelve hundred!"

"Why harp on that? Haven't I agreed to deliver them?"

"Don't forget another item."

"What is it?"

"One piece of cloth for a frock. Just four yards is enough. One yard must cost around two or two and a quarter. Just hand the cash to me, and I will take the trouble of buying it myself."

"....."

"Why are you silent?"

"....."

"I have just one daughter. She was born after four sons when we gave up hope. She turned nine recently. We named her after our mother-in-law. And she is the light of my life!"

"I will get it."

"That's the spirit. Now please leave. Come back in the morning."

"I will. But please make sure it will be a one-time order for the entire two-year period."

"Do you think this is a tongue or palm leaf? My word is final!"

"Goodbye then."

"Bye."

".... One minute, sir. I believe the 'Mala Pilla' film has been released. Shall we go?"

"If I start, my entire family will also want to join, do you know?"

"That is not a problem. I will organise a horse cart and have all of them join."

"Awesome! You are a daring brahmin! Look here. The district board is like my private empire, and the president is firmly in my grip. So, don't you forget me, and I will not forget you."

"Agreed."

"After two years, I will pull you up to a hundred-rupee grade. Watch me."

"Fine. Goodbye then."

"......"

6

"....President Garu...."

"Is he coming, or has he asked me to come?"

"I believe he will come."

"Good. You leave now. Before leaving, take these five rupees—the road contract connection. These two pertain to the school teacher postings. Take them and leave."

"Thanks. Thanks."

7

".....Any contractors to be seen today?"

"No, sir."

"Any applicants?"

"No."

"I need money immediately. How can we manage?"

"If it is tomorrow, there is some hope..."

"Can't wait until tomorrow. Unless I carry a minimum of a hundred rupees, Ammanni[134] will not let me enter her house."

"Why? Is she upset with you?"

"Yesterday was bad."

"I will ensue today will be doubly better. Forget Ammanni."

"Forget and then?"

"Let us go to someone who beats her hands down."

"What?"

"Today, your long-time wish is going to be fulfilled."

"Who is that?"

"I will tell you."

"Rajamani?"

"No!"

"Neelam.."

"Forget her!"

"Veerabhadram?"

"Yuck!"

"So, who is it then?"

"You will soon see. We will be starting after dinner, in another two hours."

---

134 Prostitute frequented by the president.

"Forget dinner. Let us leave right away."

"......"

"Drop that expression! Call the driver."

"Not that way. I will tell you. Please sit down."

"Quickly!"

"Seshachalam."

"Duggirala?"

"Yes. It is her."

"Oh yes! You are the ultimate definition of a clerk! You deserve to be the private secretary to emperors!"

"Just words and hand-shakes?"

"Of course not! You have brought around a hooker who snubbed me. How can I repay your debt? Ask what you want. It shall be done this moment."

"Then please sign on this."

"What is this? Road metaling contract? How much was your cut?"

"Rama! Rama! He is my mother-in-law's relative, sir!"

"The quote seems to be higher than Venkataiah's quote!"

"Don't worry. I will get it corrected."

"Should be done quickly and quietly..."

"One signature on this paper too..."

"What is this?"

"The high school vacancy."

"There are two, right? Oh, this is the fifty-rupee one. How much cut in this?

"Terrible fellow! And my mother-in-law's priest's only son-in-law. Despite my turning down, he offered a frock cloth for my daughter...."

"I don't care. Leave it."

"....."

"What is this?"

"Two months' vacancy."

"Twenty-five rupees?"

"Yes."

"At least some cut in this?"

"Seshachalam's services are for this recommendation only."

"Oh!"

"I have unleashed the Brahmin onto her."

"Smart fellow. Why can't I release the order in her presence?"

"Why do you want to waste your precious time doing this dirty work instead of enjoying her company?"

"Super! There is no better organiser than you!"

"As long as you take a little care of me, would I not sacrifice my life for you?"

"In the future, I will sign wherever you ask me to without asking a question. Keep an eye on the board funds, too..."

"One house in your name..."

"Say 'Bungalow'. I will get the prime minister himself to lay the foundation stone."

"Well. I will go, organise everything, have my dinner and come back. Be ready by eight thirty."

"Alright, my dear Premier!"

8

"Have they given the order, my son?"

"They have given and immediately taken it back."

"Oh my God? Why?"

"What can I say, mother? The whole effort went down the drain. We are where we started."

"Our back is broken. Sit down. Tell me what happened."

"If you hear, you will lament. Forget it. I will do something that I like, and I will feed the family. You keep reciting "Rama! Krishna" and relax in a corner."

"......"

"When I protested, saying I didn't want to be a teacher, you forced me to attend teacher training. Now, to get this job, you used every conceivable dirty means. Finally, you pushed an honest Seshachalam to do an immoral thing. Despite all these efforts, I don't have a job now. If you ask me why, I can't even explain properly."

"What happened, my son?"

"What can I say? He gave a job – that was vacant for two years – to a Krishna district fellow after taking a bribe of three hundred. When one teacher took a three-month leave, he gave me that temporary post."

"Salary..."

"Twenty-five per month."

"Just three months?"

"Even that was not to be. In less than one week of going on leave, that teacher returned to work saying he didn't need the leave then."

"So, how did the president give the job to you?"

"Last night, he wrote the order letter. Today, when I was there, his rejoining letter came by post."

"What is the final result, my son?"

"My coming home, scratching my head."

"May he go to hell! Will this president survive after doing such a thing?"

"A lot of money was wasted. The cow was gone. And finally, this is the result. When I asked you to let him take up work at the moneylender, did you listen? Job, Job. This is all your father's doing."

"How could I guess it would turn out like this? When every eligible and ineligible fellow was doing a job and living in style, I thought even my son should be like them, and I put him through an English education. But God is not with us. What can I do?"

"You don't have to do anything now. You have done your best and educated me, and you always had my best interests in mind when doing so. But you did not listen to me when I said the job was not suited to my temperament. Whatever happened has happened. Our generations are different. My generation's hopes and aspirations are different. You don't know this, and you will not be able to understand. That's the problem with you."

"So, what are you suggesting you will do now?"

"Mother! Times have changed. Attitudes have changed. We are living in times of dignity of labour. Any profession that is useful for others is a good profession. It is our behaviour that can be classified as good or bad, not the profession itself."

"Stop the oblique talk and come to the point."

"Don't get angry, father!"

"Why are you giving this long lecture when we have already lost our mind?"

"Then listen to me carefully. I will open a coffee hotel and restaurant to serve meals."

"Oh My God!"

"May you go to hell!"

"Please don't curse the boy."

"Mother! You don't intervene. Let him curse me. Father! Have our ancestors ever worked under someone else? Is it good for our lineage? Is English meant to be our family education?"

"So?"

"When there was respect for jobs, and they were easily available, you started putting me through the English education. By the time I passed out, times have worsened."

"Your horoscope is that of a loser. That's why my entire effort went down the drain."

"You are always into cursing. Please stop now."

"You shut up! Do you expect me to dance with joy hearing this fellow's plans to open a restaurant?"

"The kind of things you did for my job – were they any better, father?"

"Shame on you! You outcast!"

"I know you will curse me. But I will not do anything other than this."

"Why limit ourselves to just this town, my son? Isn't there another president to help in this world? Why this idea of an eatery that will make us a laughing stock in the community?"

"Mother! You don't know this world. It is tough to explain and convince you. But let me try. When a Telugu fellow leaves home, he is not getting Telugu food even in his own land. And he is not even worried about the fact that he is not getting food that suits his taste.

Here and there, some of our folks are running hotels. But many of them lack the practical skills to run a good business. And the customers lack loyalty too. That's why I will start an eatery that works in a new model. And a coffee hotel would make it more viable. When so many outsiders can come here, set up coffee hotels and eateries, and become millionaires, our Telugu youth is lacking vision and running after petty jobs. Moreover, eating the bland non-Telugu food is killing the hot Telugu spirit!"

"Why do you care about what happens to the country, my son?"

"In that case, why care about which profession we pursue, mother?"

*****

Test of Culinary Skills

Original Author: Chinta Deekshitulu. First published in Telugu in 1931.

1

"Sister is crying. Take care of her, my dear!" I called out to my elder daughter. She was in her room, completely immersed in her study, and didn't reply. I tried to listen carefully to understand what she was studying. This is what I heard.

"Brinjal[135] curry has four types: one with tamarind paste, the second with the dry variety, the third with lentils, and the fourth with chilli paste. For the chilli variety, dry chilis or green chillis can be used."

I called her again.

"I am busy, father. Today is my exam," she said.

"Which exam, my dear?" I asked.

"Culinary exam. I am preparing hard, Father," she replied.

135 Eggplant, Aubergine

In our time, we didn't have culinary exams. When I dug deeper, I found out that the culinary exam has not just a theory part but also a practical section. I felt happy to see this new development and the possible benefits of the same. I started thinking about how I could use my daughter's culinary skills. When the older generation women – those who didn't have formal culinary education in schools – cooked food at home, it would be unwise to even talk about the travails we had to endure. Should one need to say how the cooking of today's women (if they cook, that is) – who have passed the culinary exam – would put to shame Nala and Bheema's cooking? Another interesting point. Until now, just about anyone was getting into the cooking business. Women believed cooking to be as natural as marrying. No one paid attention to the fact that cooking is a fine art.

Now, if certificates are given to those who pass culinary exams and laws are passed saying, 'only such certificate holders are allowed to cook. If non-certificate holders cook, they are liable for punishment under the penal code (new edition),' culinary science will get its due respect and place alongside other sciences.

Similarly, if exams are conducted in other areas like Rangoli, floor mopping and so on, and if it is clearly stated that only those who pass the exams are allowed to draw rangolis and mop floors, the nation would benefit greatly. If the white man wrote the books – just as he did for culinary science – for Rangoli and mopping, it would be even better.

Getting back to my daughter's current challenge,

She studied until early morning and the entire day without touching any other work and went for the culinary exam.

I am not sure how she fared in the exam, but she came home with a beaming face.

"How did the exam go, my dear?" I asked.

"Very well, Father," she replied.

"Did you answer all the questions in the paper?"

"I did, except for one question that was about the place of coriander seeds in culinary science. I didn't know the answer."

"What about the practical exam?" I asked.

"They asked me to make a ginger pesarattu[136] , Dad. It was burnt a little, but I am sure I will get the minimum pass marks," she replied.

"Was pesarattu the only item, or were there more?" I asked.

"They gave us a choice between ginger pesarattu and raw banana fritters, Dad."

Saying this, my daughter handed the question paper to me.

Since the readers would be curious, I am reproducing the paper here:

Section 1: Theory of Culinary Science: Three Hours

136 A pancake made using green gram batter. A speciality of Andhra.

1. What is the difference between Brinjal tamarind paste curry and Brinjal dry curry? What other vegetables and green leaves can be combined with brinjal when making a curry?

2. (a) Among the frequently used ones, which normal vegetables, which roots and which green vegetables are suitable for making chutney?

   (b) Describe in detail the process of making veldt grape fryums?

3. (a) What implements can be used to hold the cooked rice vessel when draining out the water?

   (b) Can the seasoning used for pulusu[137] also be used for charu[138]?

   (c) List the similarities and differences between chili gaares[139] and vadas.

4. (a) In which curries can we add curry leaves, and where are they not supposed to be added?

   (b) Mention the role of the following in culinary science: asafoetida, mustard seeds, fenugreek, black pepper, coriander seeds, and cumin seeds.

5. (a) List the differences between South Indian charu and Andhra charu.

---

137 A soup / thick liquid gravy made with tamarind juice and other spices/seasoning.

138 Similar to pulusu but lighter and with less gravy/lentils / vegetables

139 Gaare is a deep-fried cake made of gram paste. Vada is very similar.

(b) Explain (with reasons) which, in your opinion, is the best lentil-based curry.

6. How are the following creatures enhancing the art of cooking? Chicken, deer, goat, quail and pigeon.

7. (a) What causes indigestion and what are the ways to prevent the same?

   (b) List the names of three Andhra poets, two judges, ten Andhra doctors, and fifteen lawyers who suffer from indigestion.

8. (a) From which region are the following most tasty? Gongura[140], Cucumber, Jackfruit and Mango.

   (b) List the advantages and disadvantages of cooking by stove, pressure cooker and normal cooking.

Section 2: Culinary Science – Practical. Three Hours

Note: Read carefully the questions below and attempt only one question. If spice or salt is high or low, marks will be reduced.

1. Prepare five ginger pesarattus. (Describe the measure of green gram and other ingredients used.) The pesarattus must be roasted just about right to a golden-brown colour.

   OR

2. Prepare raw banana fritters enough for five people. (list the ingredients and their measures)

I read the question paper and was delighted.

140 A leafy vegetable rich in iron used to make dal and also chutney.

Over the next few days, my daughter spent time visiting the evaluators' houses. The final result was an 'Overall Pass'—with a 'Fail' in practical and good marks in theory.

"Why did you fail in the practical, my dear?" I asked my daughter.

"The five judges got one pesarattu made for each of them."

"What do you mean, five judges?"

"Dad, don't we need someone to evaluate the responses, taste the items, and decide which is best?"

"So, the result is decided after these five judges taste the items and assign marks?"

"The marks given by the five judges are averaged out, and the final result is decided."

"Good. What happened then?"

"The five sat down and began eating the pesarattus."

"Go on. What happened next?"

"They couldn't apparently eat."

"Why?"

My daughter answered hesitantly. "With the overdose of chillis, apparently, they couldn't get their tongues back in condition for half an hour."

"Why did you add so much chilli, my dear?"

"There was a problem with the measurement, Dad. I was supposed to add one ounce of green chillies and a quarter ounce of red chillies. Instead, I used the wrong measure, and more chillies were added."

"How many ounces did you add?"

"I used eight ounces of green chillis and two ounces of red chillis."

"Never mind. What matters is that you somehow cleared the exam. "I said consolingly.

"I made only this one mistake. Otherwise, I cook very well, Dad," said my daughter.

"Very well then. Show me your culinary skills once," I said.

"When, Father? When?"

"I will tell you," I replied.

I had assumed that my daughter would cook the normal way using the tools available at home. But she said that was not how she was trained and made me spend twenty-five rupees to buy the tools that were part of her training.

I ended up buying one sensitive weighing scale to weigh chilis, salt, mustard seeds, curry leaves and so on. I also bought a box with 'one gram' measures and two or three types of glass measuring cups to measure the water that needs to be added to lentils, rice, curries, chutneys, upma and so on.

I bought a small-ounce glass to measure oil and ghee for seasoning.

I bought four or five types of tongs to hold rice and lentil vessels and pans.

I bought two or three types of thermometers to measure the temperature.

And I bought other assorted items that my daughter asked for.

After acquiring all this equipment, my daughter started waiting for the right occasion to demonstrate her culinary skills to me.

That time arrived soon.

2

My son-in-law arrived with the hope of getting funding from me for his B.L. exam. I could see through his strategy of initially trying the peaceful methods and – if that fails – adopting more aggressive tactics.

Not to waste the opportunity of my son-in-law's presence at home, I asked my daughter to do the cooking that day. I asked my wife only to observe. I asked my daughter to make Gaares (my son-in-law's favourite) as a special item on the lunch menu. My daughter got down to the task right away.

She turned on two noisy stoves and measured rice and water using the equipment she had. After measuring the black gram lentil separately, she soaked it and asked her mother to grind it. She asked me to weigh two grams each of mustard, cumin, and fenugreek seeds.

When her mother complained, "My dear, the water is not sufficient for the lentil paste," she dismissed her, saying, "You don't know, Mom, I have added a ratio of 200 cc of water to 250 grams of lentils. It is enough."

When her mother cautioned about excess water in rice, too much fenugreek in curry and no need for coriander seeds in pulusu, she got into a confrontation with her. I intervened and chided my wife telling her to give a free hand to my daughter. Ater five or six hours on the job and after breaking one glass cup and two thermometers, my daughter completed the cooking. Huffing and puffing, she retired to her room and started referring to the cookbook to verify whether her cooking came out well. My wife served me and my son-in-law.

My son-in-law, who until that very moment was in a jovial mood, suddenly started fuming after having the first bite. And remained in the same mood till the end.

Even when I explained to him that his wife passed the culinary exam and she was the one who cooked that day, he didn't relax.

He got up with a half-empty stomach and, without even asking for the B.L. money, took the evening train home.

"Not sure why he was so upset. He didn't even touch the Gaares," my wife wondered.

"Why should he be upset?" I asked.

"Rice ended up like a paste. Lentils were half-cooked. Curry was bitter. Some Gaares were burnt. Some were not cooked fully. Not sure what the poor soul thought!" my wife said.

"If he cannot appreciate his own wife's cooking – a wife who has also cleared the culinary exam – whose cooking would he like?" I asked.

My daughter overheard the conversation. She felt we were attributing words that her husband never said. Angrily, she retorted, "If I had cooked like this in the exam, I would have passed in first class. In spite of such best cooking effort, you folks are criticising it. It's not fair." She was in tears. While she didn't explicitly say so, it was clear she was blaming us for her husband's abrupt departure without completing his meal.

*****

First Prize

Original Author: Chinta Deekshitulu. First published in Telugu in the 1920s.

1

Swamiji asked me to wake up well before sunrise and sing hymns in God's praise while going around the town during Dhanurmasam. He also reminded me that the morning meal must be completed prior to this.

To make it sound attractive, he narrated a few more points. Apparently, people living in the Himalayan region get up at night, finish their meal, put on warm wool clothing, climb onto their terraces, and wait for sunrise. The appearance of the red sphere in the east fills them with boundless energy and happiness.

And some others from the same region put on Lord Shiva attire, blow conches and do outdoor hymn-singing uttering, "Shivoham" in loud voices.

It is Swamiji's desire to see Telugu people singing hymns in God's praise in the same manner. The desire of a person who was supposed to have conquered all desires! Perhaps it is his hope that the ancient dharma would get revived this way.

"Why can't we let everyone sing hymns in their own houses? It may not be easy to mobilise people outdoors these days for such a task," I said hesitantly. The large-hearted Swamiji immediately accepted the proposal.

He further elaborated on the main purpose of hymn-singing. It is for Shiva to wake Vishnu up. It means knowledge should rouse action. The husband should wake the wife up.

I laughed at the last part. Swamiji understood the hidden meaning of my laugh and said, "The main dharma of household life is for the husband to wake the wife up. It is not the wife waking up earlier, making coffee, and waiting for the husband to get up. If a wife gets to see her sleeping husband, she will go directly to heaven. Today's householders have forgotten this secret."

Swamiji narrated another key point. In the Himalayan region, ascetics are believed to get their alms before sunrise. After sunrise, getting alms for mendicants is nearly impossible. He was speaking from his experience in Kashmir.

After satiating the body's hunger with food, it is a great thing for children to assemble on the terrace and await sunrise to delight the mind. The appearance of the sun god fulfils the human mind's hunger for beauty. It also causes devotion and wisdom to sprout.

Keeping Swamiji's advice in mind, I was very excited about starting hymn-singing in our own house. The thought of donning Shiva's attire—applying holy ash all over the body, wearing a rosary, applying vermillion on the forehead in lieu of the third eye (I don't think we need leather garments, spear, and drum), with a conch in the hand and crying out 'Shivoham' while blowing the conch—would be such a grand idea, but....

2

A few months ago, all the ladies in our town formed a club. The funds for the same were sourced from higher government officers who have been tirelessly persevering for the upliftment of women. The money helped fund a building for the club, chairs, tables and equipment for indoor and outdoor games. Newspapers and shelves for an English library were also provided.

Wives of senior officers, those who could ride a bicycle at the minimum, wives of other rich men in the same social strata, those who didn't need to do any work at home, and all such women joined as members, paying a monthly subscription. There was no rule barring anyone without English knowledge as such. But all those who joined were good in English. It is not wrong to say that many only know English. Since Telugu happened to be the mother tongue of many members, one can't say they didn't know Telugu. However, the club did not have any Telugu magazines or books that could promote the language. Also, speaking in Telugu was considered an inferior practice in the club.

The club's most important rule restricted membership only to women. Not even a male fly could enter the premises.

It was named 'Ladies Culture Club', or, in other words, a society of knowledgeable women. Culture translates to the inner awakening and reform that comes from reading many books, travelling widely, and being in the company of good people. In today's times, the presence of this 'culture' is restricted only to English-educated men and women. If one were to elaborate on its external manifestations, one should list playing tennis, wearing sweaters, smoking cigarettes, always speaking in English, reading second-rate English novels, and regularly changing hair and dress styles to look trendy. The internal quality of the culture is the loathing towards one's own native dress and language.

To be honest, this culture is what we have inherited from the English government, apart from the other 'good things.'

Now, coming to the main point, my wife joined this club as a member. How many men are lucky enough to call an M.A. degree holder as their wife? Both of us have been speaking English at home, wearing English clothes, reading English magazines, and filling the house with 'culture'. In the initial days of marriage, we were even under the impression that our kids would be born with English cries and laughs and full of 'culture'. But I am sad to report that they were very normal with runny noses and so on. We admitted them to a convent school. Our initially colourful, love-filled married life started losing its sheen as the years passed. I became more of a traditionalist. My wife remained a cultured lady. That's why she joined the club.

While I can't say this put our marriage at risk, it certainly led to some discord. When I say I want to perform religious worship at home, my wife organises tea parties. When I hang Gods' portraits on the walls, she brings them down and hangs cheap art prints and cinema stars' pictures. When I apply tilak on children's foreheads, she wipes it, washes their faces with soap and applies white talcum powder. Once when I advised her to apply traditional turmeric on her face, it almost led to a European war. Another time, when I – in a lighter vein – asked her and the kids to apply holy ash instead of face powder, it became tough to get a proper meal for the next two days.

Suddenly, against the flow of things, one day, my wife began to admire my traditionalism and rituals. I racked my brain but couldn't understand why. It is possible that one tends to mature with age and take a turn towards a better path in life. I assumed my wife was going through a similar experience.

I told her about my decision to go ahead with hymn-singing as Swamiji advised. I had decided to don Shiva's attire and sing the hymns within the house while blowing the conch and uttering "Shivoham". I requested her to join me – as my life partner – in Parvathi's attire.

This immediately irked her. She said she had never played such roles. I wanted to remind her about the plays she has been part of in the club but refrained from doing so, as this would have further needled her. She ranted about why such an ask is unfair and why she should not be ill-treated like this. She went on to add how sad her parents would be—for having got such a disgusting son-in-law—if they came to know about this request.

I told her there was no need to apply holy ash as part of the Parvathi avatar. It is enough to apply some turmeric to the face along with some vermillion. She faked fear and mockingly asked me if it would involve wearing snakes around the neck, too. I felt sad at this comparison of applying vermillion with wearing snakes. I told her no one needed to wear snakes, neither me nor her. She mocked again, asking if she could get me rubber snakes.

I was upset and turned my face away. As if to soothe my anger, she agreed to don Parvathi's attire.

From that day onwards, the tormenting started. Which saree would look good? Can she wear a sleeveless blouse with a low neck? Are hair pins allowed? Is a braid better or a bun for the hairdo? Are slippers allowed? The questioning went on like this. Still, there was reason to believe she was keen to play Parvathi's role. When I showed her Ravi Verma's Parvathi painting and asked her to dress up the same way, she hesitated a little, saying it was uncivilised, but finally agreed.

I was very happy when she converted to my ways and agreed to play Parvathi's role. Then, I believed that my wife was a truly cultured lady.

3

One fine day in Dhanurmasam, I got up before sunrise and took a cold-water bath. I dried myself and smeared holy ash all over my body. I wore the tiger-striped cloth my wife gifted me. I applied vermilion on my forehead. When I was about to squat on the wooden low stool, she arrived. She pushed my hair up and tied it into a bun. She inserted a thin, moon-shaped metal sheet into the bun. Ignoring my protests, she tied two rubber snakes on both hands. She hung a garland of bones around my neck. She tied the small drum - that she bought from a beggar – to my fingers. She laid the tiger skin, which she managed to procure from somewhere, on the low stool and asked me to sit on that. She kept the conch next to me and asked me to blow it from time to time.

I fought back, saying I didn't need the rubber snakes and bone garland. I asked to be allowed to wear the garland of Rudrakshas[141]. She didn't agree. I was about to throw the stuff off in anger. She then laughed, came closer, patted my cheeks and kissed me on the lips. I didn't fail to notice that she went into the adjacent room and washed her hands, face and lips with soap. She returned and kept a petromax light in front of me, the light falling entirely on my face.

141 Rosary. Rudrakshas are stone-fruits that are then stitched into a prayer garland and also as ornaments.

I was elated that she helped me with humility and enthusiasm and kissed me. I asked her to put on the Parvathi attire quickly.

She stood facing me, gave me a close look, nodded in appreciation and laughingly asked me to blow the conch. I loudly uttered "Shivoham" twice and blew the conch. She clapped, saying, "Great! Splendid! Keep it up!"

Then she went away, telling me she would return in Parvathi's attire, and asked me if a green saree would look good. My ears could catch some muttering about a prize, too.

My planned hymn-singing started for all practical purposes. If my wife also joined me in Parvathi attire, I was confident we could do a grand joint hymn singing. Half an hour passed.

She didn't come back. I knew she had her own compulsions – being a woman - like taking a bath, applying turmeric, wearing a saree, putting on jewels, wearing flowers in her hair and so on. To create a sense of urgency, I started uttering "Shivoham" at the top of my voice and blowing the conch. One hour and still she didn't show up. Regardless of their education and culture, women are women! So much delay in donning a Parvathi attire? I repeated the "Shivoham" and conch-blowing again. Before I could complete it, she entered the room. I was shocked. She was not in Parvathi attire. When I was about to ask her if one hour was not enough to get ready, five women entered my room one after the other. I felt embarrassed. I observed that they were feeling more awkward than me. They took a close look at me. “What is this called?” one of them asked. I wondered if she was not able to identify me and why she was using the term ‘this’ or if it was their ‘culture’. My wife responded in English, “This is Shiva attire. I am pleased to inform you that he is my dear husband.”

The five ladies broke into giggles. They came closer to me and started examining me in more detail. They were impressed by the moon figure shining brightly under the lights. They voiced suspicion, claiming the holy ash to be face powder and thereby insulting me. They were taken aback when looking at the garland of bones. One lady almost fainted, saying, “Horrid!”. They took the rubber snakes to be real – despite my wife’s entreaties – and one of them tried to poke a snake with the umbrella to make sure, ending up actually poking my arm. I was furious and wanted to drive them away. But I controlled myself, looking at my wife’s smiling face and the flying kiss she blew towards me. “This… this person… I am sorry to ask.. is he really your husband?” one lady asked my wife in a sympathetic tone. They stood stunned, feeling very sorry for my wife’s misfortune. But my wife stood there smiling and with a proud expression. Not to tolerate this insult anymore, I considered how to drive them away. Then I played the drums with a frenzy and uttered “Shivoham, Shivoham” at the top of my voice and blew the conch – just as Bheema blew it in the war of Kurukshetra. It is said that blowing a conch would cause a lot of damage to the women of enemy kings, especially pregnant ones. As soon as the conch was blown, all the five women were scattered away. I don't know if any subsequent damage happened to them. My wife followed them.

Ten minutes later, I heard the sound of a car leaving. I checked if my wife was at home but she wasn't. Apparently, she joined them in the car.

I didn't understand what happened. Instead of coming back in Parvathi's attire, why did she bring the five ladies along? Why did they examine me so closely, not bothering about the fact that it was a man they were looking at? Why did my wife join them in the car and leave me? Is this how my hymn-singing fated to end?

How can I face Swamiji now, and what update can I give him?

I decided not to take the insult lying down. My wife will have to answer when she gets home. I was almost certain this was a conspiracy to humiliate me. I started pondering what could be the apt punishment for this insult. Several ideas started taking shape in my mind, and I was filled with embarrassment. Strangulating her was one option. Hanging her from the rafters was another. Or locking her up in a room and starving her was one more possibility. So many such ideas started swirling in my mind.

My wife returned home after a few hours. By then, I had changed back into my normal attire. As soon as she entered, she hugged me and started kissing me non-stop. She said I was the pupil of her eye, I was the peach of her life, I was her dearest husband, I was the pimple on her face, I was her darling, her saree, her blouse, and it went on. For every word, she would pull my moustache and kiss me again on the lips.

I feared she lost her mind and suspected her actions to be hysteria symptoms. But it turned out to be none of that. She told me I caused her boundless joy. She also said she owed her status in the club to being my wife. She also said she got a prize because of me.

When one's own wife was behaving this way – regardless of the thoughts of hanging her to death – does a husband have any other option but to cool down? I had cooled down. There was another reason for my cooling down. After the hugging and kissing spree was over, she went into the adjacent room and brought out four cardboard boxes that she had hidden when she entered the house. She said those were the gifts she – and I – jointly received. The glittering toilet set comprising a perfumed hair oil, talc, perfume, comb and so on was something she got.

The shaving set was something I had received.

The gold-coated brooch was what she got, and the five-inch-tall Nataraja idol was for me.

While I was irked by the shaving set, I was very impressed with the Nataraja idol. To show my happiness, I picked up the brooch and pinned it to my wife's saree border.

Then it struck me. What were those gifts for? She was a member of the club, so one could understand if she got some gifts. But why for me? My mind smelt something fishy, and I asked for an explanation. I asked her to explain why those ladies came home.

My wife tried to hoodwink me into accepting the gifts and keeping quiet instead of raising unnecessary doubts. But I didn't give up. Then she asked me to promise not to get angry if she revealed the truth. I refused. She pointed to the Nataraja idol and praised its beauty again. I didn't fall for the trick. I insisted on an explanation. She said there were many like me, but none of them received any gifts. This made me even more suspicious and I insisted on an answer.

This was what I finally managed to extract from her:

One day there was a meeting in the ladies' culture club. The club's primary goal was entertainment, and so was the goal of the meeting. After discussing some items on the agenda, the entertainment topic came up for discussion. The discussion was about how to decide the annual prize that goes to one of the members of the club every year.

Some suggested running races and some swimming. One lady who returned from England proposed that the best-dressed woman receive the prize. This idea was shot down by some cigarette-smoking and not-so-rich members.

Several ideas, like the best hairdo and best jewellery, were floated. One lady with several children made a side comment about why can't the prize be given with the number of children as the criterion. While this debate was going on, one lady apparently mooted an idea. My wife didn't reveal her name. I suspected it was her idea. When the group heard this idea, everyone was speechless. When they recovered, the idea was unanimously passed (except for the lady with the maximum children, of course).

The meeting considered the following:

Just like men, women, too, need individual liberty. So far, men have been treating women as slaves. It is time now to give it back to men. This can be done in many ways. He can be beaten up, scolded, harassed, made to cry, made to starve, made to do household chores and in many other ways.

After considering all the options, the meeting resolved that willing members must try to fool their husbands. Whoever did it most impressively and convincingly would win the year's first prize. Both wife and husband would be eligible for the prize, so the prize must be useful to both.

After this resolution was passed, five members were selected for the jury. Their job was to visit every participating member's house, observe the husband closely, determine how much of a fool he had become, and finally, decide the winner. The members were busy for a week. Each one considered several ideas. They kept the ideas close to themselves without revealing them to others. By the deadline, everyone was ready.

The jury members visited all the houses and decided my wife to be the winner.

My blood was boiling. The only solace was the fact that I had the company of other unfortunate husbands. I asked my wife how other wives fooled their husbands.

One lady made her husband – who always wore western dresses – wear a Dhoti.

Another lady made her husband cook while she relaxed, smoking a cigarette and reading a novel.

Another lady tricked her husband into wearing a saree, blouse, and bangles. She had put on trousers and a shirt. When the jury members visited their house, the couple was in a conversation.

I asked my wife why that couple didn't get the first prize. "Ideally, they should have got it. But the husband, who was in female attire, got furious when he saw the jury members and almost ended up thrashing them. The wife and husband got into a spat. The judges ran away and denied them the prize."

Another lady made her husband put on a loincloth and climb into the attic to bring down the pickle jar. After he got into the loft, she removed the ladder and made him sit there until the jury showed up.

When I heard all these episodes, my irritation knew no bounds. I asked her to stop and started scolding her.

"What is my fault in this? You were anyway keen to don this attire! Are you upset because I went out of my way to procure the drum, moon, snakes and garlands? Is there nothing called gratitude? Did I ask you to put on the Shiva attire? Did I make you wear a blouse or climb a loft? The other husbands are better. They never complained despite what they had to go through. Why should you get angry with me when the decision to don Shiva attire was yours?"

"But why did you bring those devils – those ladies – home?" I asked with my teeth clattering.

"Because I brought them home, we got this prize. Otherwise, who would have cared to appreciate your attire? Enough! Don't talk to me!" She barged out of the room, accusing me of being ungrateful.

True! How can I blame my wife? Those who asked me to put on this garb must be held responsible. Yes, Swamiji caused this.

After a few days, I encountered the Swamiji. I bowed to him.

"Have you done the hymn-singing?" Swamiji asked.

"Yes, sir. I have received the fruits of it, too," I replied.

"Didn't I say?" said Swamiji without even bothering to know what the fruits were.

*****

Our Village

Original Author: Kanuparti Varalakshmamma. First Published in Telugu in 1930's / 1940's.

1

Soon after Venkata Ramanaiah Pantulu retired, he faced the dilemma of where to spend his post-retirement life and broached the topic with his wife, Buchilakshmamma.

"Where else? Let us go to Ramavaram and live there," Buchilakshmamma was quick to reply.

"Ramavaram? Come on! Even after living in a city for twenty-five years, why do you love that village?" Ramanaiah Pantulu ridiculed.

"I don't know. My village feels like heaven to me," Buchilakshmamma said.

"You must be joking! There is not even a railway station in that village!" Pantulu said.

"What if there is no railway station? I believe buses are running every hour," Buchilakshmamma shot back.

"There is no newspaper and no radio. One must travel eight miles to the nearest town to buy even the simplest item. In any case, who do you have there? Your parents passed away. You don't have any brothers. Your only sister lives somewhere else. What do you have in that village for us to go and live there?" Pantulu asked.

"Don't we have the house that I inherited from my father? Let us go and live in that house," Buchilakshmamma argued.

"Very true! That decrepit house is a big attraction for us to go there!" Pantulu mocked.

"Not just the house! I have been told that the village now has everything one needs. Didn't my uncle's grandson Ramakoti say the other day?" Buchilakshmamma said.

"What facilities was he talking about?"

"They now have a radio that runs on battery. And even newspapers are being delivered," Buchilakshmamma said.

"Of course! The village has everything!" Pantulu sneered.

Tears rolled down Buchilakshmamma's cheeks at this repeated mocking.

"The palatial house is in ruins with no one to maintain it and light a lamp daily. You are interested in only paying forty and fifty as rent and staying in this city. You never consider the option of living in that large house inherited from your father-in-law and taking care of it. How grand that house used to be when my father was alive?" Buchilakshmamma was in tears again.

"Shh! Don't cry. Unless we move there, you will not understand the practical difficulties. In this city, if we turn the tap, water – as thick as an elephant's trunk - flows instantly. What do you have there? We must draw water from the well until our hands fall off."

"How much do we need, and how tough would that be? Just a few feet long rope is enough."

"After sunset, the village is blanketed in darkness. Here, we have twenty-four-hour lighting. There, wherever you need to go, you have no other option but to walk. Here, we have city buses, rikshaws and jatkas[142] at your beck and call. Your feet don't even have to touch the ground. The city is a junction for five railway lines. We can go to any place just like that," Pantulu argued.

"True. You call it 'living in the city' regardless of where one lives. Tell me, how far away do we live from the railway station?" asked Buchilakshmamma.

"So what? Are you walking to the station? How can you get the city conveniences in the village?" challenged Pantulu.

"Don't tell me about conveniences! Milled rice! Water from the machine! Electric lights! Without any sense of the time, blaring songs day and night! We are living a very happy life! Even the people who live in this city are machines! Just as the parts keep moving in

142 Jatka: Cart with a hood and drawn by a horse or pony.

those machines, these people are always on the move, looking at their watches!" scoffed Buchilakshmamma.

Pantulu guffawed. Without controlling his laughter, he said, "Goddess Saraswati seems to have blessed you with literary powers today! You are dishing out poetry like Kalidas."

"Enough of your mocking! The only thing missing among my talents is poetry now! Say whatever you want. This city can never give us the village comfort. Fresh milk, thick curd, pure ghee, freshly picked vegetables, grain from our farm, hand-pounded rice, and I can go on listing. Every item there will be so delicious that we can't compare it with the city food. Do we even have anything called fresh in this city? Everything is stored and processed. We used to eat freshly picked guavas when we were young! I still remember their taste! My mother used to get paddy ears fresh from the farm and get flat rice made from them. The sweetness of that rice is still fresh in my memory!" Buchilakshmamma slipped into nostalgia.

"Motherland where one was born is always sweet!" said Pantulu in jest.

"Laugh if you want to. My love for my Ramavaram hasn't diminished even a little bit. And I haven't seen anything in this city that could make it happen." Said Buchilakshmamma.

Their neighbour Saradamba, who was overhearing the conversation, suddenly appeared and said, "Our aunt's love for her village hasn't been dented despite the years of enjoying city comforts, uncle!"

"That's what surprises me, my dear!" said Pantulu.

"I can't spend one day in my village. I don't know how she plans to spend her time there. My maternal uncle's place is a tiny village. If we ever visited it - out of sheer bad luck - it used to be a maddening experience. The villagers don't spare any newcomers from their stares and interrogation—'Where are you coming from? Who are you visiting here?' - it gets under my skin. They don't have any sense of urgency. Even in late morning, one could see men sauntering lazily with a neem stick or a cigar in their mouth. Women have nothing to do except carry a basket and collect cow dung or carry a pitcher to fetch water from the tank. You are lucky to have a backyard with vegetables and a cow or buffalo that gives milk. Otherwise, there is nothing available to buy there. If one wanted to escape from the village, that was entirely at the mercy of my uncle, who had to arrange a cart. That's why I hate villages," Saradamba finished her monologue with a hearty laugh.

"Count me in," said Pantulu.

"Tell me this, aunt! Do you have Brahmin families in your village? We didn't have any in our uncle's village," Saradamba asked.

"There is no dearth of Brahmin families. Our house, my uncle, priest Punnaiah Sastry Garu, Vishnu Priest Rangacharyulu Garu, Shiva Priest Bhadraiah

Garu, School teacher Gopalam Garu, total I can think of six houses," said Buchilakshmamma.

"There was no brahmin in my uncle's village. If my aunt had to perform Nandikesha Vratham[143], she was forced to come to our village," Saradamba said.

"We don't have such a problem. We used to have a large army of friends and relatives. All we had to do was to paint the threshold yellow for any festival, and loads of relatives used to land up," Buchilakshmamma said.

"If she gets into narrating these stories, your aunt loses sense of time." Saying this, Ramanaiah Pantulu draped his uttariyam[144] on the shoulder and quietly slipped out.

"Saradamba! Your uncle can say whatever he wants. My mother never limited any event at home to just the family members. The entire village used to join for every major occasion. It was like one large family where each celebrated the others' successes and lent support in times of difficulty. Occasionally, my aunt's family used to come from Guntur. Just like you are laughing now, they used to mock our village customs. I remember clearly when my younger aunt was with us. One day, when a boy from a weavers' family was going on the road, my father told me to call him. I shouted, 'Brother Narayana! Brother Narayana! My father is

143 A form of Lord Shiva's worship.

144 A top cloth, normally worn when people stepped out.

calling you.' Seeing that, my aunt laughed derisively, 'How is that weaver's boy your brother?' I got angry and complained to my father. He was dismissive about my aunt and said, 'Ignore her. What do these city folks – who live amidst synthetic relationships – know about true affection and village customs?'"

Buchilakshmamma's voice choked with emotion, and tears swelled in her eyes.

A sympathetic Saradamba said, "Leave it Aunt. Because you enjoyed such a comfortable life, you still have the affection for that village."

2

Egged on by Buchilakshmamma, Ramanaiah Pantulu admitted son Chalapati Rao – studying intermediate – in a hostel. They took their young daughter Subbulu and went to Ramavaram. After she lost her parents, Buchilakshmamma never visited the village in the past twenty-five years. The farm she and her sister inherited from her father was leased out. The tenant farmers used to come every year and pay the lease amount. If there was some other pressing need, Ramanaiah Pantulu or his co-brother[145] used to visit the village, but the women never had a reason to go. When Buchilakshmamma entered the village, it looked completely new to her. They reached her father's house.

145 A typical Indian or Telugu-English term used to refer to one's wife's sister's husband.

The first look at that house made her miserable. The house—which saw the peak of its glory during their childhood—stood dilapidated. She remembered her childhood looking at the nooks and corners of that house. She slumped in a corner and sat still.

"Why are you sitting there so downcast? You nagged me and brought me here. Now get up and get the house back in condition," Ramanaiah Pantulu rushed her.

A school teacher was staying without rent in one corner of that rundown house. They repaired another corner and made it suitable for cooking and living.

Buchilakshmamma's list of woes was endless: lack of a maid, having to do all the chores herself, drawing water from the well, and the non-availability of milk and curd were only some of them.

Everyone in the village appeared to be a stranger to her. No one talked to her. She couldn't experience any of the sweet memories with which she came there. The village itself seemed alien to her. When she enquired about Karanam[146] Ramakoti Garu, she learned he had been living with family in the city due to his children's education and came only occasionally to the village. Oh God! *How much has our Ramavaram changed in twenty-five years?* sighed Buchilakshmamma.

146 Karanam: Village accountant/record keeper.

3

Ramavaram is no longer the old Ramavaram.

The village has grown. It now has a panchayat board. Street lamps can be seen here and there. Roads—though unpaved—were laid. Thatched huts are now being charged tax. The evening news is on the radio near the Mahalakshmamma tree. Main Bazar now boasts a barber shop, a laundry shop, and a coffee hotel. Newspapers are arriving from the town on bicycles every day for those who are subscribing. A library and a reading room have become key attractions in the village. The town vibes could be seen all over the village. The innocence, friendliness and simplicity –the defining qualities of the villagers in the olden days – are not to be seen now.

People used to address each other as 'sister', 'brother', 'sister-in-law', 'cousin', 'uncle', or 'aunt' even if they were unrelated. Now, a lot of artificial decorum is visible when people talk to each other. People also got divided along political lines—Congress, Communists, Socialists, etc.

On the third evening after their arrival, Karanam Ramakoti came from the city and visited Ramanaiah Pantulu and Buchilakshmamma. Pantulu treated him with much respect and asked him to stay for dinner.

Karanam Ramakoti politely declined, saying he had his arrangements in place.

Buchilakshmamma insisted that he stay back for dinner and, finally, had her way.

After dinner, when they were engaged in small talk, sitting on the stone bench outside the house, Ramanaiah Pantulu commented, "What, my dear! Your village has completely changed!"

"You are right, uncle! The village now has all the city's flavours," Ramakoti replied.

"All the political parties seem to have set up a base in your village," Pantulu said.

"Uncle seems to have grasped the village details in just three days!" Karanam said.

"What else? Yesterday, agents from three parties came to me with application forms asking me to join as a member. Of course, I didn't join any party. But that told me about the divisions in the village," Pantulu said.

"Which village doesn't have divisions now, Uncle? The advent of elections has killed the camaraderie and bonhomie among villagers," said Karanam.

"You are right! People are rejoicing in this democracy, but the downside is that two people in any household cannot agree on one point."

Buchilakshmamma cleaned the kitchen and joined them. "Ramakoti! Who is the Munsab[147] of the village now? Are Brother Ramaswamy and Kotamma Vadina[148] doing fine?" she asked.

---

147 Munsab: Village administrative head.

148 Vadina: Elder brother's wife.

"Ramaswamy Garu is very old now. His son is the Munsab. Kotamma Garu passed away four years ago. Her death weakened him further. He still loves us so much! You should visit him once, aunt!" Karanam said.

"How about Uncle Perisetty?" asked Buchilakshmamma.

"He passed away long ago. His wife is bedridden and not able to move around. Sons are into business. The daughter is at her in-laws' place," replied Karanam.

"So much change in twenty years!" exclaimed Buchilakshmamma.

"Why twenty years? The world is changing every second," Ramanaiah Pantulu said.

"My aunt is old-fashioned," Ramakoti said.

"You are right, my dear. I am not familiar with the current trends," Buchilakshmamma agreed.

"If you were, you wouldn't have insisted on coming to this village," Pantulu said laughingly.

Ramakoti joined him in his laughter.

"Laugh as much as you want to! How would I know Ramavaram has changed so much? When you got one Sunday off, you used to crave a visit to your Guntur. Wouldn't I have similar affection towards my village?" Buchilakshmamma protested.

"You love your village. But it would have been nice if your village loved you too," Pantulu laughed again.

"Don't treat me as so dumb! A village never loves anyone. It is the people of the village who love each other," said Buchilakshmamma.

"Not bad! My aunt has given it back!" Said a laughing Ramakoti.

"True. We city folks can never match the villagers' smartness." All three had a hearty laugh.

4

The next day, after lunch, Buchilakshmamma, accompanied by an escort provided by Ramakoti, went to see Ramaswamy. Ramaswamy's son, Gopalaswamy Naidu, was pacing up and down in the veranda. He saw the escort and asked him about the identity of the lady accompanying him.

"I don't know, sir. Karanam Garu asked me to take her to your father," replied the Escort.

The grandsons and granddaughters – surprised to see a Brahmin lady visiting to see their grandfather – gathered around soon.

Buchilakshmamma went straight to Ramaswamy's room. The bedridden Ramaswamy looked frail. His hair was white, his face wrinkled, and his eyesight weak. The picture Buchilakshmamma had in her mind was that of a young Ramaswamy with curly hair, a thick moustache, and a youthful swagger. She couldn't reconcile to seeing this old and frail Ramaswamy with her mental image. Unless someone explicitly pointed out, it was impossible to recognise Ramaswamy.

A stunned Buchilakshmamma said, "My brother Ramaswamy! Is that you?"

That gentle voice instantly brought back decades-old memories to Ramaswamy.

He got up in his bed and peered into Buchilakshmamma's face closely.

"Is it you, my dear? It has been so long! When did you arrive, sister?" he asked in a choking voice and offered her the three-legged stool nearby to sit.

Buchilakshmamma sat on the stool and gave the sugar candy she brought, to Ramaswamy.

"My dear girl! You still have so much love for this old brother, don't you?" A tearful Ramaswamy said.

The next few minutes were spent getting to know where they had been staying, why they returned to the village, the children's well-being and occupation, about her younger sister Ramalakshmamma, etc. And he shared his helpless condition with her.

"When your Vadina was gone, my good times vanished with her. She would have been overjoyed to see you and give you the royal treatment if she had been alive today. I have become alone and helpless." Ramaswamy cried like a small child.

A teary-eyed Buchilakshmamma said, "Calm down, brother. Vadina was lucky to have passed away as a Sumangali[149]. How many women could be so lucky as her?"

"You are right, sister! She was certainly lucky. As long as she lived, she lived like a queen, and she departed like one. It is I who am now stranded in this helpless state. I don't know when I will be relieved from this empty life!" Ramaswamy said, tears swelling in his eyes.

"Brother, just keep thinking of God. What more do you need? Your son has grown up and is as capable as you. He will handle everything,' said Buchilakshmamma.

"True. I don't need anything. It is just that my inner feelings came out when I saw you after a long time. Tell me, has your husband also come with you? Is he retired now or still working?" asked Ramaswamy.

"He retired this month. He, our daughter and I have come to the village," replied Buchilakshmamma.

"When can I see them?" asked Ramaswamy.

"I will send them over to you tomorrow. Now I will take leave," Buchilakshmamma got up to go.

"Why do you want to leave so soon? When I see you, I am reminded of your mother and father and the old times. Stay back for some more time," Ramaswamy implored.

149 Sumangali: A woman whose husband is alive. It was considered fortunate for a Hindu woman to pass away as a Sumangali while her husband was still alive.

Buchilakshmamma sat down. Gopalaswamy Naidu arranged for some bananas and a coconut and asked his wife to give her Tambulam[150] and see her off. His wife applied bottu[151] on Buchilakshmamma's forehead and handed her the Tambulam and fruits.

"My dear, I am not in a position to even gift you a saree and blouse piece. If your Vadina were alive, she would never let you go back without a saree."

"Forget it, brother! Why are you being so formal? I have come on a casual visit," said Buchilakshmamma.

From there, Buchilakshmamma went to Perisetty's house. Perisetty's wife, Mahalakshmi, was lying on a stone bench in a thatched room in her second son's house. Buchilakshmamma called out, "Shahukar[152] Attha[153]!" While Mahalakshmi was physically weak, her eyesight and hearing were perfect. She immediately sat up, saying,

"My dear! I am seeing you after so many years!" and hugged Buchilakshmamma.

---

150 Tambulam: Means pan/killi made of betel leaves. As per traditional Telugu custom, a Tambulam is given as a parting gift to a woman who visits one's house. This is a courtesy extended to a married woman whose husband is still alive. It comprises betel leaves, betel nuts and fruits.

151 Bottu: Thilak/Bindi. A dot applied on the forehead of a married woman whose husband is alive or an unmarried woman.

152 Shahukar: Merchant/Moneylender.

153 Attha: Aunt.

Buchilakshmamma offered the sugar candy.

"You love me so much! You have come all the way to see this old aunt!"

"Don't say it, Attha! How could I come to this village and leave without seeing you? My very purpose in coming back to the village was to see all of you. Tell me about your sons' families. Where is your daughter Nagaratnam now?" Asked Buchilakshmamma.

"What can I say? The elder son has no children. His wife is a termagant and doesn't get along well with anyone. That elder one is a meek fellow and can't go against her word. The younger one is tough, but his wife is not bad. That's why I am staying with them. Nagaratnam is doing very well. My sons' wealth pales in comparison to what she has. Her husband is in business in Bombay. I am not sure if you have seen it, but they have a three-story bungalow in Tenali. But, regardless of how much a girl has, she always has expectations from her parents' family. After your uncle passed away, neither brother called her even once and gifted her something! All the gifting and family customs vanished with your uncle," Mahalakshmamma vented her frustration with teary eyes.

"Don't worry, Attha! Whatever you have anyway goes eventually to Nagaratnam, doesn't it?"

"Of course, it will. Why would I give my wealth to others instead of my only daughter? I am staying here because staying with a married daughter is not the right thing to do. My daughters-in-law expect me to divide my jewellery and give it to them. The elder one is more vocal, but the younger one doesn't explicitly ask. Finally, I will give some part to the younger one, her children, and the rest to Nagaratnam. Not a penny will go to the elder one. As long as there is life in this body, this jewellery must stay on my body! If I let it go, will these folks give me even a drop of water?" Mahalakshmamma ranted.

Buchilakshmamma got up to leave.

"Wait, my girl. Let me see you out. I don't know when I will see you again." A stooping Mahalakshmamma walked along with Buchilakshmamma with the help of her walking stick, and they turned the street corner. She took out the small purse from her saree fold, handed four rupees to Mahalakshmamma and told her, "My dear! Get a blouse stitched with this money and treat it as a gift from this aunt."

"You don't have to do this, Attha! I came for a casual visit," Buchilakshmamma protested.

"If you don't take it, I will feel insulted," Mahalakshmamma replied strongly.

Buchilakshmamma didn't have any option. Her mind briefly wandered about the old-time affections and human relations.

5

It had been one week since Ramanaiah Pantulu came to Ramavaram. When they were sitting in the front veranda after lunch, a letter came by post. While he was reading it, Buchilakshmamma asked him, "Where is it from?"

"From Chalapati. It says he had been down with fever from the third day after we left the city," replied Pantulu.

"Oh God! I very much feared this! Hotel food doesn't suit him. I hope it is not a serious ailment!" Sadness engulfed Buchilakshmamma.

"Alright. I will ask him to take ten days of leave and come here," said Pantulu.

"Why should we ask *him* to come? Let us go to the city," said Buchilakshmamma with a finality in her tone.

Pantulu remained quiet as if silence was half-agreement.

*****

Wife

Original Author: Chalam (Gudipati Venkata Chalam). First Published in Telugu in 1924.

My friendship with Rukmini goes back to our childhood. We studied in the same school. And our houses were close by. There was no other girl naughtier than Rukmini. Even boys would fear her presence. And we girls were ready to do anything for her. Without her, there would be no playing, singing, festivals, or religious rites. Even if there were, it would be lacklustre. How many new games she would invent? How many new songs she would sing? When it was Atlathaddi[154] time, she would wake us up by two in the morning. Then, our racket would wake up the entire town. We would swing on the rope as if we were possessed. Rukmini would swing so high - she would vanish into the tree branches and reappear in a flash. When infants heard Rukmini's name, they would leap from their mothers' arms towards her. Just seeing her face alone would induce merry laughter. The joy in the babies would rise like waves of an ocean. When Rukmini tossed them up and

154 A festival in Andhra celebrated by women and includes making pancakes and distributing them.

caught them again, they would be spellbound. Twenty babies would surround her legs, pleading, "Me, me, me." Mothers would soothe the babies crying at night, saying, "Go to sleep now. Rukmini will come tomorrow and hold you." She would use flowers and colourful cloth pieces to make the kids up. After she was done making them up, they used to look so beautiful. After a shower, if Rukmini were untangling their hair, even the most obstinate kids wouldn't cry even once. Whether it was youngsters, adults, or the very old, everyone loved Rukmini. The old ladies would make Rukmini sit beside them and narrate stories about their younger days. Rukmini seemed to be the personification of all the kindness, gentleness, happiness, and laughter in this creation.

She was no less intelligent! One reading, and she would remember any book. While in third grade, she would help solve the sums for the neighbouring student in the first form. One day, she learned the English alphabet from that boy. Immediately, she started reading names. How melodiously she would sing regular songs, god's wave-offering songs and lullabies! Her voice was so enchanting that any random song would sound like great classical music! Even the awe-struck passers-by would stop and listen to her singing. One thing she didn't like was stitching. She tried her hand at it many times, but her fingers could never master even one thread twist.

Rukmini was fearless. She would go anywhere, even at midnight. And she was never scared of anyone.

On one occasion, she slapped her cousin – who was a police inspector – when she was upset with him. If she believed someone to be doing wrong, she would say it on their face. She would go to a mother-in-law and say, "Madam! Why are you harassing your daughter-in-law this way? Don't you have any pity? Are you even human?" Another time, she would taunt a skinflint, "Will you carry all this money to heaven? Why don't you spend it?" Once, unable to bear her husband's torture, a wife jumped into the well and died. Rukmini went to that fellow and bluntly told him, "It was you who killed her! Because she was your wife, no one is pointing a finger at you. If it were someone else, you would have been hung by now." That man wanted to marry a second time. Rukmini spread the word about his wife and ensured no one would offer their girl in marriage to him. When there was an enquiry from another town, she met them and implored them, "Don't give your girl to this fellow in marriage. He will kill her, too." That was Rukmini.

Rukmini was a beautiful lass. Slightly short and plump. She was two years younger than me. But appeared older. Everyone was charmed by her. But she never allowed men to touch her. She was very fond of her body. She could always be seen freshly bathed and neat. She wouldn't tolerate one speck of dirt. Even when it came to infants, she wouldn't hold them without first wiping them clean. We both got married. Rukmini was married to a thirty-year-old man who had lost his first wife. Her in-laws gifted her a lot of jewellery.

Immediately after the marriage, she was forced to discontinue school. Rukmini was into games, as always.

As she grew older, Rukmini morphed into a beautiful girl. It was tough for anyone not to stare at her. One morning, Rukmini was standing in our front yard. One of our school teachers – fond of Rukmini from her school days – was leaving our house after speaking to my brother. He noticed Rukmini and approached her. "Rukmini! How much have you grown!" he touched her on the shoulder very familiarly. "Don't touch me. I don't like it," an angry Rukmini shook his hand off. I am older than her, but I would never have said that. He laughed and touched her cheek. Do you know what she did next? She spanked him hard on his back to leave a trace of all five fingers. He was bewildered and walked off, cursing and stroking his back, "Are you crazy?" That was how proud and dignified Rukmini was.

Two months before I was due to go to my in-laws' place, something happened. Rukmini was eleven then. Her husband came for Deepavali and stayed for two days. We couldn't see Rukmini for those two days. She showed up the same day afternoon when he left. My sister, brother and I teased her a lot. We loved teasing Rukmini. She would never get angry. She always had a witty reply ready when teased. Our teasing was aimed at listening to her wisecracks. But that day, she was quiet. She turned her head away. Tears swelled in her eyes and – brushing her kajal[155] – fell as dark drops. She suddenly got up, went to the adjacent room – we used

155 Dark eye liner used by Indian women.

it as our bedroom – and closed the door. We looked at each other's puzzled faces. Rukmini had never behaved like that before. No one had seen her crying before. We were concerned. We thought she must have been going through significant agony.

After waiting for a while, I opened the door and went inside. She was lying face down on the rolled mattresses and crying inconsolably. When I sat near her, she pushed me away, saying, "Don't touch me. Go away!" Despite my repeated pleas, she wouldn't speak up. She was violently shaking her limbs, pulling her hair and holding her breath as if to die. When I was terrified and tried to call others, she wouldn't let me. After several minutes, she calmed down, freshened herself, combed her hair and left. That was it! From that day, we never saw Rukmini laughing, playing, or visiting anyone's house. She wouldn't even talk to small children. The entire town was downcast. People were just not themselves. Children forgot games. But no one knew the reason for what was happening.

Two months passed. I went to my in-laws' house. Within six months of my going, I started hearing strange things about Rukmini. Initially, I didn't believe what I heard. Then, when I started hearing the same story from people who knew Rukmini very well and people who adored her and her relatives, I had no option but to believe it. I was flummoxed. I never imagined Rukmini would turn out that way. In the beginning, there was sadness. Then I felt ashamed, as if I did all those things myself. When I heard more details, I began detesting her.

One day, when I was back at my mother's place, I saw Rukmini. She had just returned from her husband's house. There was a lot of talk in the town. Women gathered in groups and were discussing Rukmini. One afternoon, she approached me when I was standing near the front door.

Wait! Was it Rukmini? How much change! She looked emaciated. Her eyes were withdrawn deep inside. She appeared as if she had lost all interest in living. Her face was wrinkled like an old lady's. White hair could be seen in small patches. She came closer and held my hand. I quickly went inside and closed the door. Later, when I recalled her face, I felt sorry. She looked utterly devastated. *Why did she come to me? Because of our friendship? But she deserved what she got! The terrible things she did! Disgusting! She is not worth talking to! But could I have spoken a few words?...* That was the last time I saw Rukmini.

These are the things I heard about Rukmini. Not just me. This is what the entire world heard. No one suspected them to be untrue. There was no need to seek confirmation from anyone as to their veracity. Those who loved her, those who trusted her, everyone spoke unanimously the same thing. Some people claimed to be eyewitnesses, too.

When her husband came to consummate the marriage, she was believed to have told him, "I don't need this consummation. I can't live with just one husband. I have a friend in this town, Mani. Like her, I too want to become a prostitute." She told her husband not to touch him that night unless he paid her a lot of money. When her in-laws were pained by this shameful behaviour and wanted to take her back with them, she refused. They had to eventually take her back forcibly. Her mother-in-law was a nice lady, and so was her husband. When she tried to escape mid-way, he somehow got hold of her and took her back. But eventually, she escaped and returned to her parents' town alone. Her grandfather and mother scolded her. Then she rebuked them, went to prostitute Mani's house and stayed with her. That noble soul - her husband - returned and pleaded with her to go back with him. Then Mani and Rukmini gathered a few rowdies and were prepared to assault him. Left with no option and with a lot of anguish, they complained to the police. Police tried all the tactics to convince her. When they were finally about to put a lot of pressure on her to go back with her husband, she jumped into the canal and died.

This was the story in circulation. How reprehensible! Indeed, she must have suffered from some poor fate or wrong planetary position. These people are attributing it to her own volition. When I heard that she died, I didn't feel sad.

One month after this incident, I went to my town. My sister-in-law was unwell one evening, so I went to the canal to fetch water. One woman approached me in the darkness, stuffed some papers in my hand and quickly vanished. I came home and started reading. What emotions I went through while reading that note, you will know if you read it. The dead Rukmini wrote it.

"To Sita Ramamma: I know you are very angry with me. You spit if you hear my name. The spit of virtuous people like you should not land on my body. I am unsure if you would even read this note, which was contaminated by my touch. Even if you don't read it, there is no harm. But I was consumed by the desire to write to you. Although you forgot about our childhood friendship, I haven't. You are all chaste women. You have erased my tainted name from your pure minds. But the memories of your virtuous lives remained in my pure mind. You managed to take away your faces, words and kindness, but you could not erase your memories from me."

"I know, to some extent, what the world has been talking about me. When people – regardless of how evil they are – put on a respectable façade, no one dares to indulge in loose talk with them. But with someone like me – who gave up all pretensions of virtue, sin, chastity and morality – who is afraid to talk freely? Moneylender gentlemen who destroy families with their unscrupulous interest rates, police officials who are habituated to bribes, pious women who abetted the suicides of their daughters-in-law, chaste women who cheat on their husbands – everyone is out to attack me! I want at least one person to know the truth. When I look back, I feel amazed. Many friends and relatives were keen on my friendship and company two years ago. Today, I don't have anyone willing to look at me or talk to me! Except for this prostitute, who is considered a blot on society. Not one had asked me, 'What is the truth? Why did you become like this?' This is friendship! My husband knows the truth partly. He is not capable of knowing more. I pity him."

"While there are thousands of animals in human form like him, only he had to endure all this hardship. That too because he married a shameless devil like me. He doesn't have the nerve to reveal even the little truth he is privy to. He is a respectable gentleman. Would he discuss such topics, especially the truth, with others? Respectable people never reveal the truth in such matters. If they do, they are boycotted by civil society."

"I am giving this letter to my trusted well-wisher and the famous prostitute of this town, Mani. She will give it to you. She will never hold it back. If she were respectable, she would say one thing and do another. And hide the letters to promote morality!"

"If this letter lands in the hands of any honourable people, they would fear damage to societal morality. They would promise me that they would keep the letter safe but they would burn it behind me. I can't, of course, come back after being dead and question them! By the way, these honourable people don't believe in heaven. They believed that we would never meet again. In any case, I would be going to hell! And they would go to heaven! If I cross over and ask them, they will have me thrown out. Your anger may not subside even after reading this letter. But give it a try and read it."

"Tonight, I am leaving your world. I am not yet sixteen. But I have managed to gather a hundred years of experience. Enough of this world! This earth cannot tolerate a sinful person like me anymore. I don't know if the water would be kind enough tonight to accept me! Many will rejoice when they hear the news of my death. Mainly my husband. I am certain he would get another obedient wife within a week. There is no wonder that my husband would marry again if an immoral person like me died. Are we not seeing so many husbands marrying again, even when their chaste wives die?"

"Already, other offers were coming his way, with the talk of our discord going around the town. Next, my poor grandfather and mother! There was so much that respectable family had to endure on my account! They tried their best to disown me, but to no avail. The whole world consoled them for the calamity they had to endure. But they doubted how such a girl was born in that family. I think they were bundling us together. Isn't that what respectable people are supposed to do? Praise on your face and laugh on your back! There is nothing wrong with saying, 'Mahalakshmamma's daughter eloped.' Poor mother. So much she had to endure! She must have been wondering why she ever gave birth to me. When I was young, she was proud that no one else had such a child. She had shed tears of joy looking at my playing and singing. She forgot about the days when she made me sit in her lap and kiss me, remembering Dad.

Also, all my friends would be happy if I died. If anyone asked about me, they could neither give the details nor deny our friendship. That would be a pain for them."

"' We don't know. Ours was not that close a friendship.'

'Thinking about it, she had this arrogance even when she was young.'

'We allowed her to be one among us all these days!'

'Yes, we did. But she had these qualities even then.'

'Thankfully, she is gone before our kids learned from her.'

'Good riddance! If she is around, can we hold our heads high?'

'With so much burden in that heart, how could she live anyway?'"

"I can hear all these comments already."

"Before you went to your in-laws' house, I cried in your house one day, do you remember? Two days before that, my husband came to our town. That was the onset of my sorrow, my hell, my pain and my death. Trust me when I say this. Before that, I didn't know what marriage was. But I loathed men touching me. I used to be very angry. It was not just our teacher who touched me that day; I used to hit anyone if they touched me. I could sense the difference between normal touch and *that* touch. I used to feel as if my body was insulted. When my grandfather's brother-in-law kissed me with saliva all over my face, I scratched his whole face. Despite seeing my revulsion, my mother never said anything. After I grew up a bit, he used to find me alone and touch my breasts. His touch used to sting my body. But I never told anyone. My diffidence used to outweigh the pain. I used to scratch him, bite him and even spit on him. But he was shameless. One day, I old mom. She smiled with some difficulty and kept quiet. That day, I cried like never before. I wanted to run away. One night, I felt like killing him. I used to wash ten times, every spot where he touched me. Later on, he stopped bothering me that much. But never completely."

"The worst part of the ordeal was mother's silence - with a smile. I used to believe that she would solve any of my problems. I don't know why she remained quiet. I'm unsure whether it was diffidence or she didn't understand my agony! Or perhaps she was happy with the treatment I was getting. Or was she jealous of me? Would any mother keep quiet when her child is suffering? A few more such incidents happened. But I never knew what was meant by marriage until that afternoon."

"It was two o'clock in the afternoon. As always, my mother asked me to carry coffee to my husband. As usual, I took the coffee and went to his room. He asked me to shut the door. I didn't move. He then got up, closed the door, held me tightly and pushed me onto the bed. There was no talking, no cajoling, and no gentle fondling. I didn't know then what it was and why it was happening. Even a bird caught by the cat wouldn't be more scared. I struggled. I remember the pain even today, and it sends shivers down my spine. I screamed and cried. I yelled so loud that the entire town could hear. I hoped my folks would bang the door open and throw him out of the house. No one came. They knew in advance. I think they were perhaps salivating and enjoying my screams. I concluded that this was a ploy to kill me. I cried. I held his hands and begged to be let off. I was terrified. But there was no use. Even a butcher would perhaps take pity on a sheep. I fought hard for my life. I dodged him. Frustrated, he finally got up and angrily kicked me out, saying, 'Go. Get lost!' I landed outside. When I saw the rest of the house, I felt somewhat relieved. Crying loudly, I went and hugged my mother. Mother used to say – even as a young girl - I never cried aloud when in pain. That day, I cried my heart out. And that was the only time I cried. I never cried again. I wish I could. My sorrow had frozen completely. This is the last time I am crying through this letter."

"Whenever I was in pain, whenever someone offended me, I always believed mother would punish them and comfort me. My aunt and mother looked at me and laughed aloud. They didn't have a clue as to what I was going through. My aunt touched me and asked, 'Did he bite you? Where?' Their imagination was dead. Were they assuming I knew it all previously? How would I when they never told me? For them, it was perhaps as common as eating and sleeping. But aunt! I could simultaneously notice so much envy, joy, and salivation in her eyes! If someone spoiled her Tulsi[156] tree, she would land a thousand blows and curses on the person! When he spoiled me that way, not a single curse came out of her mouth. Instead, there was a beautiful, vulgar laugh as if he did a favour to her."

"I ran into my room. I didn't even try to look at my own body. That disgust and hatred and filth! Even now, I feel like tearing my muscles apart if I think about that day. If it were someone else, I would have torn him apart! This fellow caught me alone and suddenly threw me onto the bed and.... Oh My God! How did I remain alive?"

"That was why I cried so much in your house that day. To whom do I narrate my ordeal? I lost interest in life. I was ashamed to look at anyone else's face. The same thought haunted me day and night. How should I treat someone who forced himself upon me that way? The joy in my heart, the love for this world and the faith in humanity – I lost it all that day."

"He went back. And a barrage of letters followed immediately after. 'How long should we wait? Why hasn't your girl reached puberty yet? You claimed she was eleven at the time of marriage! Had we known she wouldn't reach puberty for so long, we would have found another girl!" Every week, a letter on these lines used to arrive. After three or four months, one letter said, 'Even if she hasn't reached puberty, it is alright. Just prepare her well and send her. There are

156 Holy basil tree worshipped by women

good muhurthams[157] next month.' My grandfather disagreed. That enraged them. 'We don't need your girl. We are looking for other matches,' said the following letter. That letter created a furore at home. There were arguments and fights among my grandfather, mother, and aunt. Aunt wanted me sent immediately. She was widowed when she was eight. Perhaps that was why she wanted to see me with my husband. But grandfather wouldn't budge. He and mother fought and cried, too. What if they find another girl? Would I remain at home forever like an added burden? If the household already has two burdens – my aunt and mother – would I be too much to bear alone? Unable to argue beyond a point, my aunt started rebuking me. What did I do? When she was giving me an oil bath, she would curse me using filthy language. My joy was boundless when I heard he would marry another girl and leave me. Irrespective of how much my folks scolded me, I couldn't stop being happy. I used to go around the house singing merrily. I wanted to remain young forever."

"But grandfather suddenly changed his mind, I don't know why, and wrote to them saying I had attained puberty. Immediately, they replied, saying there was a good muhurtham in one week, and they would be arriving for the consummation. My family was surprised knowing there was no good muhurtham around that time. But they remained quiet, not wanting to annoy them further. My grandfather was also very

157 Auspicious time for any event like wedding and even consummation of a marriage.

tired of this entire episode. I also heard that some middlemen approached and coerced him to agree."

"He somehow wanted to get rid of this nuisance. No one spared a minute to think about how the nuisance would engulf me. I started trembling. Now I knew what marriage meant. I couldn't sleep and eat with the fear haunting me. They didn't care. It was me who had to undergo the torture. How long? Perhaps until he dies or I die. Is everyone living their marital lives bearing such torture? I have not seen anyone crying! I cried again with mother. First, she laughed, and then she severely rebuked me. She said it is natural, just like a tree grows and bears fruits; a girl is born, grows, marries and then the marriage is consummated. If this cycle is broken for any reason, it is as if the creation itself facing a huge hurdle! How could a girl, a small girl like me, say no to living with my husband? Did anyone say no before? Even if they did, would the world appreciate their actions? They wait if a tree doesn't flower. They can do nothing if an animal doesn't become pregnant. But when it comes to me! How could they shut my mouth, beat me up and force me to do something that I didn't want to? How could they do this to someone who can think on her own, who can speak, who can experience pain, shame and pride? And who is already afraid? And who is a free being? They gave birth to me, and they fed me. So, I have become their property, their animal now. They sold me to this animal. Did I ask them to give birth to me? They fed me because they were the reason for my birth. Because they brought me into this world, they fed me. So, even animals are being fed. Am I just another animal? Can they do this to my aunt? Just because I am young and powerless, they are doing this to me!"

"Alright, she is my mother! Let us agree for a moment that she has the right over me. But did she ever explain to me what marriage was, how future life would unfold for a woman, and how difficult that could be? No. That is forbidden. Such topics must not be discussed with children. But children can suddenly be sent into rooms where men are waiting for them! When my mother's gentle tongue could utter so many curses, couldn't a few words of knowledge and comfort come out of the same tongue?"

"They arrived on the muhurtham day. When my mother started preparing me, I felt like an animal being readied for sacrifice. To my husband, I was just a machine. I think that's how all men see a woman! All my years of growing up, eating food, playing games, and studying are supposed to culminate in my being offered to him. I wonder why half the people in the world must become slaves to the other half! If a woman has beauty, she should please a man. If she had strength, she should do chores for the man. If she was educated, she should maintain his accounts. If she knew music, she should entertain him. How is this world tolerating so much injustice? People's hearts got mired in tradition, rotted and died. Wouldn't Lord Rama take birth again to kill these male demons and rescue the helpless?"

"I cried a lot that evening. I pleaded desperately. But who cares? It was not my grandfather who had to endure that night's pain. My husband's eyes were gleaming like those of a snake about to catch the frog. I could see them mocking me, 'Your time is up!' All escape routes were shut for me. What crime did I commit for me to be punished like this? A death row convict also has some hope of escape. But I didn't have any! Who gave them the right to throw my body, my heart, my honour and my desires at his feet to be looted in one night? Who cares to listen to the cries of this orphan, whose kin are sacrificing her like an animal? With each passing minute, it was like the hideous lizard creeping closer to the beautiful insect."

"The dreaded night arrived. They asked me to go inside the room. I cried and fought for my life and my honour. They dragged me, pushed me in and locked the door. He was pacing the room like a hungry tiger waiting for its prey. Trembling from head to toe, I tried to hide in a corner. He grabbed my hand, pulled me onto the bed and started cracking vulgar jokes. And he was reeking of snuff powder. He would wipe his nose with his fingers and rub the fingers on the bed. And he would touch my neck with the same hand. He would break a piece of the sweet on the table and push it into my mouth with the same fingers. Moreover, he would ask, 'Why do you hate me?' After this continued for five minutes, he got into the actual act. For those eyes, I didn't appear like a human being with likes, pain and a heart. I was just a machine with which he could fulfil his lust."

"The next day, Grandfather nearly thrashed me for the nuisance I had created the previous night. Apparently, I was not supposed to cry even if the pain was unbearable. He would scream and be ready to thrash the barber if he got even a slight nick during the shave. I was vainly hoping that if he could admonish me, he would also admonish my husband for his crudeness. But this is what he said to him during mealtime. 'Initially, all are like this. Slowly, they get used to it. Don't worry and don't hesitate. Just keep at it.' I was so furious, I felt like killing my mother and grandfather."

"The next night, my husband started off with a sermon. It started with chastity and a woman's duty towards her husband. Then he read some Telugu poems and Sanskrit slokas. He narrated the stories of Sita, Mandodari and Arundhati from mythology, who were devoted to their husbands regardless of what they had to endure. Then he compared me with his first wife!"

"' You are complaining about this little pain. Those days, I was in the prime of my youth. She used to be thin and weak. Her eyes had some sickness, and she always used to complain about headaches. Even then, she used to consent. Is there any other option for a wife?'"

"Perhaps it was the same suffering that eventually killed the poor soul. I started wondering if I would meet the same fate."

"' That woman fell sick without cause but never said no, even when sick. She was very obedient and chaste. After she passed away, I didn't want to marry. Whenever I wanted, I could buy nightly pleasure. This continued for fifteen years. But my mother persisted. She argued that no one would look after me in old age. She was right. Would these bitches take care of me in my old age? Only a properly wed wife would do! Age is catching up with me. I am no longer able to run around the whores' houses. Even I felt it was time to settle down.'"

"Three nights were over. They said they would take me along immediately. I cried my heart out with mother and grandfather. They didn't show any pity. The same people who used to be so concerned, even if a small thorn got stuck in my flesh, have now completely abandoned me. My whole body felt tainted, as if a thousand worms were crawling. Why doesn't my pain move them? I was not ready to leave the house I grew up in and the plants and trees I grew up with. But with whom can I share my agony? When mom went to Shivaganga, she couldn't leave the cat home for just three days! No one bothered to understand my pain when it came to leaving that house and going somewhere!"

"I went to my in-laws' place. It was a large house. Except for my mother-in-law, there was nobody there. She was very kind and took good care of me. She used to do all the household chores herself, including cooking. She used to scold me if I tried to lend a hand anywhere. He used to chide his mother if he saw me getting to any household work. It was as if he wanted my entire energy to be conserved for only one activity. I had no work other than resting from morning to evening and again from night to morning and be always ready when he wanted me. He threw Ramayana, Mahabharata and Bhagavatam at me to read. Most of the time, he used to be at home. But he never talked to me much. He didn't have much to do either. And I was indifferent to whatever happened in that house. He used to be angry and irritated with me for not showing gratitude, happiness and love. I never understood why and how I should show love towards him. I knew how to love my friends, but how could I show the same love towards him? He used to rebuke me. He used to say, 'The first one was obedient even if she was in pain. She used to show happiness, even if it was fake. This one is stubborn.' I used to pity him. Perhaps I could love and respect him if he was not my husband. His friends treated him with a lot of affection, and he used to reciprocate. The beggars who received alms from him used to bless him wholeheartedly, calling him 'noble', 'kind' and so on. He had a good name in that town. But that didn't help me. Everyone tasted his goodness. But, by virtue of being his wife, I had to endure his bad qualities."

"One day, my mother-in-law handed me a postcard and asked me to write to my grandfather to come and take me home for a few days. I wrote the letter. My grandfather promptly arrived. *He* refused to send me. When I pleaded with my grandfather to take me home anyway, he didn't oblige. 'Grandpa! If you too stop being kind to me, to whom I can turn to?' I cried. Tears flowed down from his eyes."

"' After handing you over to a man, what say do we have? Convince him,' he said."

"Why would he fight with my husband for my cause? Why would he let go of juicy mangos, tasty savouries, and silk panches[158] for my sake? He left quietly without even informing me."

"My fights with my husband increased. For some time, I tried showing fake love towards him to make him feel good. I tried imitating other chaste women in my behaviour, killing my natural instincts in the process. I tried to shadow him. I did dirty and unimaginable things. I started hating myself. These things didn't come to me naturally. It was like torturing my body and soul. According to him, it was not enough to bear the pain and hand over my body. I must look happy and appear desirous towards him. Disgusting! The kind of things he used to force me to do made me feel like burning my body. It was not enough to wash it with water, but it required cleaning with fire."

"After a week, I started feeling pain, but no one called for a doctor. I became very ill and was bedridden. Finally, the doctor visited. 'I am not sure. Call a lady doctor,' was what we had to say. They called the missionary lady doctor in the town. She and the male doctor talked something between them and then spoke sternly to my husband in English. He

158 Panche = Dhoti (Bottom cloth worn by men)

replied nonchalantly, 'She is my wife. My wife.' They asked him about my age. I heard the words 'Police' and 'Magistrate'. My husband asked them to leave. He never called that doctor again. They used some crude medicines. It led to fits. I suffered a lot. I used the pretext of fits to avoid him and tried all possible stunts. My grandfather came again. He refused to send me. Grandfather went back."

"I decided not to stay in that house any longer. I didn't enjoy one minute of my stay there. The pain and disgust were unbearable. I gathered courage and spoke to him one night. I told him I didn't want to live with him as his wife. I told him about my suffering and told him I would go back to my mother's place. I promised I would never return, and he would be free to marry again. I also offered to return all the sarees and jewellery he had gifted me. I told him I would remain indebted for the rest of my life if he did this small favour. He refused bluntly. He listed the difficulties I would face if I pursued this course. He told me it would be tough to live without a husband. Society would treat such women with scorn. And call them 'women-abandoned-by-husband'. He tried to scare me by saying my folks would not treat me well. I said I would tolerate all these difficulties. He said that I would stray and become immoral in the years to come. I said, so be it. He said it would be a disgrace for him in society, and he would be forced to remarry, and that would cost money. I replied, saying that was none of my business. He refused. I was enraged. Why did I deserve this prison sentence? For what crime? Every crime has a release date from prison. This crime called marriage seemed like a life sentence. I told him I would run away. I cautioned him about my serious intention to flee and told him he could not stop me and that I was not joking. He said He would catch hold of me and bring me back. I told him I would leave anyway. He got the message finally. He wept and opened up."

"' I will be disgraced if you run away. Already, there are doubts about my first wife's death. If you run away, how will I be able to lead a normal life in society? Who will respect a man whose wife had deserted him? Don't do this. What harm am I causing you?' Disgusted, I kept quiet."

"There was an old washerman in that house. He had been staying in that house for a long time. Previously, he never spoke to me even once. One fine day, he approached me when I was alone and talked to me. He told me to leave immediately and go to my maternal home. He warned that I would meet the same fate as the first wife if I remained there. He offered to help me escape. Everything happened secretly, and I reached my town the following afternoon. My folks were pleased to see me. My grandfather hugged me, and my mother cried. I felt so relieved when I saw my house and my family. I forgot all my travails, and my trust in this world started returning. I started wondering why I left them in the first place. Everything seemed normal. The plants in the backyard were flowering, and the cow was giving milk as usual. I repented at my anger towards my mother and aunt."

"The next day, all my hopes were dashed. He came running. Everyone knew I came without permission. My grandfather cold-shouldered me. Aunt took to her customary scolding. Mother swore and said, 'It would have been better if you died during the major fever during your childhood. You are a disgrace to this family.' He asked me to accompany him. I told him I would rather die. There was a major fracas. The whole town knew. Whatever the case, I decided not to go with him. Nights turned out to be a nightmare again. He took out all the frustration and anger on me during the night. My grandfather was again ready to thrash me. *Why are you so angry with me, Grandpa? What did I do to you? Is my behaviour discrediting you? You used to take bribes in the office! I remember you bearing all the insults the white officer threw at you and you falling on his feet! Is my presence in your house causing you disgrace? I have never seen you eating food without worshipping God. Have you ever considered what God would think? You are more concerned about your neighbours! He is asking me to be virtuous and saying a wife has no other option than to serve her husband! Can't you think independently instead of blindly following the so-called scriptures? Where in the scriptures was it written that falling at the feet of a white officer is the right thing to do? Grandpa! Is it the right thing for a Hindu man to do? I am leaving! You will not have to deal with this tainted person anymore! At least now, will you shed a drop of tears for me? Or will you consider this as a well-deserved punishment for me? Will you ever ponder whether there was any fault on your side?*"

"I couldn't stay there any longer. They stopped feeding me properly. I felt humiliated and wanted to end my life. What other choice did a destitute woman like me have? I had set out to die that night. When I reached the canal, I was scared. The water was cold and dark. I didn't feel like sacrificing my warm life to that cold water. I did not feel like going back home, nor did I have the courage to jump into the canal. I sat there crying, and after some time, I returned to the town. Prostitute Nagamani was going that way, and she started a conversation with me. She already had an inkling of what I was going through. When she spoke, there was no anger or hatred in her tone. She appeared to me like God's envoy. She asked me to stay with her. I obliged and happily stayed for four days. No one had ever showered so much compassion on me. I felt like touching her feet and paying my respect. Finally, they traced me. My husband and grandfather arrived to take me home. Mani kept me hidden inside. Some of her male friends took an aggressive stance and prevented them from entering the house. I remained comfortably in that house for another week. After a week, police arrived. Poor Mani cried. She looked at me and said, 'Why weren't you born in our community, my dear? You would have been spared of this slavery!' Let my husband try to treat Mani the way he treated me! Would she tolerate it? We consider their community inferior and don't let them enter our homes. The reality is they should be treating us as inferior beings. They took me to the police inspector's house. Mani also accompanied me. Grandpa and my husband were present there.

Everyone severely admonished Mani. Mani tried driving some sense into their heads. But would they listen? The inspector asked me to go with my husband. I told him I would go only if he promised not to touch me."

"'Then why did you marry him?' asked the inspector. 'I didn't marry. It was my folks who married me off to him. Moreover, I never knew that marriage meant this atrocity. No one told me,' I replied."

"'I don't care. Once you have become his wife, you must stay with him, no matter what he does to you,' the inspector said."

"I cried loudly. All he could do was hand over a helpless woman like me to my husband. Don't I have any right over my body? Can't I say 'No' to someone when they want to touch my body? A prostitute could say that with so much freedom! Why can't a legally wedded wife say that? In the olden days, they used to sell slaves. Even then, did the owners have the same power over the bodies of the slaves? If a cartman makes an injured bull draw the cart, police arrest him. But if a wife refuses to undergo the torture in her husband's hands, they tie her hands and feet and throw her to the husband and give him the freedom to do whatever he wants! And we call ourselves a civilised society!"

"They sent me with him again. My mother-in-law didn't say anything. She remained as loving as she was before. But my struggles had increased. Previously, he had at least some notional love towards me, if not compassion. Now that was gone. Mocking and scolding had become a daily affair. I didn't have any motivation to live any longer. I knew that, as long he was alive, I wouldn't be happy even for a day. Why should that poor soul die? I decided to go instead. He would marry again. There would be no dishonour for anyone. Everyone can live proudly with their heads held high. Tonight, the water won't be able to scare me. I have written my complete story in these papers."

"I am assuming you are living happily with your husband. But I lost faith in this society. Everyone in our town used to love me. Now, no one is willing to even talk to me. No one asked me for facts. They made up their minds about me without even asking me. And they believed – that it is the woman's fault that always causes marital discord. I was hoping you would at least talk to me. That afternoon, I lost that one hope. It was not your fault. Why would anyone pollute their life by talking to a tainted woman like me? How much misery it would lead to? What would the husband say? Why should you forgo your happiness by uttering my name? When society comes together to give you a husband, would that society accept if you denigrate that husband? It would accuse you instead. Women are embodiments of patience and virtue! A wife should tolerate whatever hardship she is put through! Instead, how could she shamelessly go public with her problems?"

"I don't love anyone anymore except Mani. If I said this openly, they would burn my tongue. How dare I say I don't love my husband! Once the marriage is done, the love for the husband should sprout instantly and unconditionally! If it doesn't, one should pretend to be in love. Otherwise, the society would not approve. Will they – by any chance – hand over my dead body to my husband? My body is not mine. Would they accept it as God's? Where will he catch hold of me again? In heaven? Why would I go to heaven? He would surely be in heaven. If I go to hell, I can escape him. No hell can be worse than this hell I am going through. Perhaps the clean water will wash my body of all the hatred, disgust and the terrible things I did to please him! If that happens, will I end up in heaven? No! I don't want to ever go to heaven. I will walk into him again there. I don't want a husband in any future life! Oh God! Bless me to remain a single woman in all my future births! This is my only wish."

"I am handing over this note to the washerman. He will give it to Mani, and she will give it to you. Good Bye."

*****

Bride

Original Author: Kodavatiganti Kutumba Rao. First Published in Telugu in 1933.

"How shocking! Perhaps a third marriage is in your fate," Raghavaiah said, trying to sound sorry.

Venkateswarlu Garu suppressed his smile, increased the lamp intensity and kept looking at his childhood friend.

It has been ten years since Raghavaiah looked straight into Venkateswarlu Garu's eyes. Before that, Raghavaiah acted as if Venkateswarlu Garu was almost his peer in status. But ten years ago, Raghavaiah went bankrupt due to some peculiar circumstances, and Venkateswarlu Garu bought – in one go – twenty more acres of fertile farmland. Raghavaiah was upset with God for this unfairness. But he concluded that it was important to let everyone know Venkateswarlu was his childhood friend. He also realised there was no harm in not being able to look Venkateswarlu in the eye. He averted his eyes from Venkateswarlu's gaze, looked around the house and said, "No wonder the house looks colourless when the light of the house is no more. For some time, this...."

"After some time, what?" Asked Venkateswarlu Garu.

When he had to respond to Venkateswarlu Garu's question – and the response was what he originally wanted to say – Raghavaiah was tongue-tied. It was like asking someone to sing when he was about to start singing. Since he was an experienced hand in such matters, he retained his composure.

"After that? Marriage! Will it wait?"

"It didn't occur to me yet!" Venkateswarlu Garu said.

Raghavaiah didn't notice the sarcasm in his voice.

"Didn't it occur to you? Has no one approached you yet? Already, four or five people have broached the topic with me. I have recommended saying, 'He is young, zamindar, competent, and is in a good position.'"

"Who is young?"

"You, of course! Would a thirty-five-year-old be called old?"

"We both started our education at the same time. Do you remember? What is your age?"

Raghavaiah feigned surprise. He was certainly north of forty-five but not less.

"So what? I know men who remarried at seventy."

"If there are people who can give their girls..."

"Who wouldn't give their girl to you? You will get eighty girls. I am guaranteeing that! But the most suitable among whom I have seen..."

"Those who are giving, will they see *me* or my wealth?"

"That's a tough question. Surely, some will see *you* and give."

"Name one."

"Myself," Raghavaiah smiled.

Venkateswarlu Garu looked at Raghavaiah with an expressionless face. He never had any doubt about Raghavaiah's ulterior intentions.

"Venkateswarlu! Even I have been searching for a suitable match for our Saradamba. If it were someone else, I wouldn't have rushed you into marrying her. But you don't need to doubt my credentials. You know the girl from childhood. You know her beauty. I don't like giving her to someone else."

Venkateswarlu Garu didn't speak. Raghavaiah was slightly disheartened. But he didn't back down. He considered a couple of more blows while the iron was hot.

"Anyway, you need to remarry, and my girl needs to marry, too. I hope you will be equally heartened by this union as I am. Think about it. Instead of marrying a girl from a strange family and struggling, a relationship with a known friend..."

Venkateswarlu Garu kept pondering without saying a word.

Finally, he said, "I must speak to your girl once."

"Of course! Let us go home right now!" Raghavaiah couldn't conceal his joy.

"I will come tomorrow morning exactly at eight."

Raghavaiah considered his daughter's marriage as done. His financial woes will vanish now. He will be the manager of the entire estate. His daughter's kin will inherit Venkateswarlu's wealth and property. Venkateswarlu Garu had a son – Lakshmi Kantham - by his first wife. Sarada and that boy had been friends from the beginning. Raghavaiah initially eyed Lakshmi Kantham as his son-in-law. When his daughter was very young, he encouraged her to be close to the boy with words like, "There is Bava[159], my dear! Will you marry Bava?" All that changed. Three years ago, Venkateswarlu Garu banished his son from home. Father and son didn't see each other's faces after that. Apart from a vague detail that Lakshmi Kantham had some relationship with his stepmother, no one knew the real reason for this falling out between father and son. Father and son did not discuss it with anyone. There has been a lot of negative news about Lakshmi Kantham in the past three years that prevented him from being presumed innocent.

159 Bava: Cousin/Brother-in-law. Potential bridegroom in this case. It is normal to call someone very close as Bava in Telugu states, even if not related.

When he noticed that Venkateswarlu Garu didn't reconcile with his son even after his second wife passed away, Raghavaiah concluded Sarada had no choice but to have the old man as the groom. Lakshmi Kantham was ruled out as the heir to his father's wealth. But Raghavaiah didn't have a smooth time with his efforts to make this match work. When he went to see Venkateswarlu, he was unsure if he would remarry. Thanks to God's will...

Raghavaiah made his friend sit in the front room and brought Sarada, already bedecked for the occasion.

"We need to talk in private for some time. You carry on with any other business you may have," Venkateswarlu Garu said.

An elated Raghavaiah exited the room.

"Keep the door open," Venkateswarlu said, leaving no room for Raghavaiah to eavesdrop from behind the closed door. A disappointed Raghavaiah kept the door open and left.

Venkateswarlu looked at Sarada and said to himself, *if my Lakshmi were alive, she would be the same age. Perhaps equally beautiful.* Sarada ignored him, paced across the room for some time and finally went to the cupboard. She removed the two or three ornaments from her person, kept them in the cupboard, and leisurely started untying her braid.

"Hey girl, how old are you?" Venkateswarlu Garu asked.

Sarada said with knitted eyebrows, "Younger than you by forty years."

Venkateswarlu Garu laughed. "Ah! It can't be that bad. Wouldn't you be at least ten years old?"

"Two years more than that!"

"Even with your hair down, you look beautiful. If they deck you up as a bride, you will look even better. Do you know the purpose of my visit?"

"Yes! To cut my throat. But that's easier said than done."

"Why did you say such a harsh thing? I was planning to arrange your wedding!"

Sarada confidently approached Venkateswarlu Garu and kept staring at him. *The only thing missing was keeping her hands on her waist*, he felt. He had already started fearing that girl.

"If my father makes me marry you, I will jump into a well and take my life. Remember, I am not like other girls. My mother calls me Shakti." The breeze coming through the window was causing her hair to flutter.

"You almost seem like one. What is the reason for this great opinion you formed about me?"

"You are inhuman. If you were a normal human, you wouldn't have exiled Kantham from home, trusting your wife's words."

Venkateswarlu Garu didn't reply immediately.

"Is this how you talk to everyone?"

"No."

"Is it only with me?"

"Yes."

They remained quiet for a while.

"Why do you believe Kantham was not at fault?"

"I know. I have known Kantham from childhood."

"Don't I know him?"

"No. You don't."

"Do you know whom Kantham is befriending now?"

"I do."

"Rowdies and Prostitutes."

"They are better than you and your wife."

Venkateswarlu Garu smiled weakly.

"How do you know?"

"If not, Kantham wouldn't remain friends with them for so long."

"Is there no evil where Kantham is present?"

"No."

"Who taught you to speak so boldly?"

"Your son."

So, it was not just friendship but she was his pupil too.

"Does Kantham come here every day?"

"Yes."

"Does he say anything about me?"

"No. He told me to stop talking to him if one word slips from his tongue about you."

A surprised Venkateswarlu Garu asked, "Why?"

"Because he is clever."

"So, if such a thing happens, will you stop talking to him?"

"No. I will not."

"Why?"

"I am not against abusing you."

"Do you like it if all the women talk like you?"

"Do you like it if all the sons end up like Kantham?"

"No."

"Even I don't like."

"Perhaps it was Kantham's mistake!"

"No. If it was, then even I am in the wrong."

"So, have you changed for his sake?"

"Yes."

Venkateswarlu Garu chuckled and said – almost loud enough for her to hear – "How long do I test you?"

"I have not formally invited you to test me for a specific time. Perhaps you should ask my father how much longer to test me."

"I have discovered long ago that Kantham was not at fault."

"Are you not embarrassed to say that? Why didn't you go to him and touch his feet the instant you knew the truth?"

"It was beyond me. I have been waiting for the right time."

"If it were your son who wronged, he would have fallen at your feet the moment he realised the truth."

"True. He inherited the good qualities of his mother."

"When such a wife passes away, no one would remarry unless he is a beast."

"Say what you want to. My heart became a stone long ago. It can only erode, but it cannot melt."

Even as he was saying those words, tears swelled in his eyes.

Sarada realised she started losing this argument.

"Come closer, my dear!" Venkateswarlu Garu said. Without protest, Sarada went closer and stood by his side.

"Get ready and braid your hair, my dear! I will give you in marriage to Kantham. One woman separated us. Now, it is your job to unite us." Sarada lowered her head. Venkateswarlu Garu didn't notice the teardrops that rolled out from her eyes. But Sarada sensed the tears from his eyes falling on her head and accepted them as blessings.

*****

Silver Dining Plate

Original Author: Munimanikyam Narasimha Rao. First Published in Telugu in the 1940s.

1

Just one vistari[160] for a kaani[161]!

I need two vistaris per day, and my wife needs two. That makes it four per day, costing one anna. At this rate, my monthly expense on vistaris works out to nearly two rupees.

I wish I could buy a silver kancham[162]. With one, I could save twenty-four rupees per year.

A silver kancham costs eighty rupees, lasts forever, and pays for itself in four years with the savings on vistaris. After that, the kancham is practically free. And

160 Vistari: A disposable dining plate built using a special type of broad leaves and stitched together with small twigs. About 12 to 14 inches in diameter.

161 Old currency. The old rupee during the British period consisted of 16 annas. One anna consisted of four kaanis, and one kaani had three dammidis.

162 Kancham: Dining Plate.

twenty-four rupees savings per year after the initial four years!

Buying a kancham is like buying a half-acre farm!

A half-acre farm does not fetch more income than the savings on the kancham!

Even if four out of the twenty-four rupees are spent on other expenses, there will be a net saving of twenty rupees!

In twenty years, it will add up to four hundred! It is not a small amount!

There is more! If the annual savings of twenty rupees can be invested for interest every year, they will become a thousand rupees after twenty years.

If I can add another thousand to this thousand, I can build a house.

The more I consider it, this one purchase of a silver kancham looked like a life-transforming idea.

2

However,

With a fifty-rupee salary per month, running a large household is turning out to be a challenge. How do you spend eighty rupees to buy a silver kancham? The silver rate is skyrocketing! I ran out of ideas.

It has been my long-cherished dream to eat from a gleaming white silver dining plate! Who doesn't dream of beautiful things in life? Who is against enriching one's life with objects of beauty?

But I couldn't think of a way to source money to buy the silver kancham. After thinking hard, I came up with one idea.

How about buying a silver-plated fake plate?

Great! It is my good fortune that I got this idea on a Sunday morning. I got up quickly, draped the uttariyam[163] on my shoulder, and walked long strides to Hebbar's shop. Such items are only available in his shop.

There was a brightly shining fake silver kancham in the glass showcase. I got it out and examined it. Oh! What a bright white shine! I didn't perceive any difference between this plate and a silver one.

I felt buying this was enough for my standing in society.

But the price – twenty rupees – seemed slightly on the higher side.

But what did Hebbar say? "This is a very good kancham. We got this before the war started. Nowadays, we don't get this type of material. It is fake only for the namesake. But it is better than a pure silver kancham."

I asked him anxiously, "Will this colour fade away?"

---

163 Uttariyam: Upper cloth (formal) men wear when stepping outside the house.

"For the present-day material, we can't guarantee. But this one? This will never fade. It will remain bright forever."

"Then what is the extra benefit people get when they buy a silver kancham?" I asked.

"Nothing. If they have more money, they buy silver kancham. Normal people like us buy this variety only. Does every household have a silver kancham?" Hebbar said.

"Are you sure?" I asked a little sceptically.

"Are you still doubting? Even rich families have these kanchams, sir," Hebbar said assuredly. He revealed a huge secret to me at that moment—intentionally or inadvertently. I was very satisfied. I decided to buy the item and told him, "I will be back tomorrow," and was about to leave. Hebbar called back and said, "Many people have been asking for this kancham. C.C. Rao Garu visited yesterday and took a look. If you are serious about buying, let me know. I will keep this aside for you. I have only one piece of this kind. No use regretting later!"

"I will let you know tomorrow. Until then, don't sell it to anyone else," I said. Hebbar nodded and kept the plate back in the showcase. I came home and pondered deeply. He said everyone has a similar plate in their house. It must be true. The kancham was shining brightly. No one would take it as a fake silver item.

Eating off that white plate would give the same joy as eating off a pure silver kancham. Why not buy it?

The only dilemma bothering me was the longevity of the colour.

Hebbar says it will remain. Why should he lie? And it didn't appear as if he was lying.

If that kancham is not good, why would C.C. Rao Garu ask for it? He is a rich man. He would never think of buying a fake, colour-fading kancham. Why would anyone buy, for that matter? It is not a fading type.

Another point must be considered. Will the colour not remain for at least four years? Three? Is that not enough? The cost of vistaris for three years works out to seventy-two rupees. I am getting this kancham for just twenty!

All my trains of thought led me to just one conclusion. Buying that plate will be a prudent decision.

My wife usually agrees with me in matters of saving money. When I wanted to buy a wooden chair, she advised me against it, saying a wooden chair gets damaged in four years, while an iron one would last forever. I approached her confidently and shared my plan with her.

She gave a weird look, shook her head disapprovingly and said, "How can you be so foolish? Why do you want to buy a fake kancham? We are not in such a poor state!"

Her words riled me. Why is she talking as if we could afford genuine silver kanchams? Managing the regular monthly expenses within the salary itself is challenging for us!

I controlled my anger and asked, "Aren't the others buying?"

"Who is buying such items, my dear?" she asked.

That question was innocuous, but it was sufficiently insulting. I forgot to ask Hebbar about who bought such kanchams in the town. I didn't give up, though. I listed some well-to-do names.

She laughed and said, "Why would they buy fake kanchams when they could afford much better?"

"So, who do you think is buying all the fake kanchams sold by Hebbar?" I asked peevishly.

"Why should we care? Some useless fellows must be buying," she said dismissively with a glint in her eye.

If I get angry, it will turn into a fight I was not ready for.

I spoke in a conciliating tone. "That kancham was shining as brightly as a genuine silver kancham."

"Of course, it shines! That shine is also a fake shine!" she said contemptuously.

"If I can't afford a genuine silver kancham, I will at least buy this look-alike and be happy," I pleaded.

"If you can't afford it, so be it. You can buy it when you have the money. But why buy a fake kancham?"

"What is wrong? It is in bright white colour..."

"White? How long will that last? It will be gone in a day. Also, will it be useful for any other purpose? If it is a silver plate, it will remain as an asset. We can sell and make money whenever we need it. Or we can mortgage it and take a loan. What use is a fake plate?" She said with disdain.

After that, all my pleas fell on deaf ears. She remained stubborn. I realised it would not be possible to convince her to buy the item.

My sadness at the lack of respect for my opinion slowly turned into rage, and my ego was badly hurt. I decided to do something to redeem my lost ego.

I will buy the kancham without informing her. Yes, I will certainly do it! I loved it so much! I tried to swear mentally about what would happen if I didn't buy that kancham. But I stopped myself.

3

I consider myself to be a tenacious man. I went to Hebbar that evening, showed him the plate and told him, "I want to buy this. As soon as I get my salary, I will pay cash and take it. Keep this for me."

Hebbar felt sorry for me. "Alright, sir. Take it when you have the money. I will hold it for you."

"Please do. Even if there is a slight delay from my side, don't give it to others," I urged him.

Hebbar laughed and said, "Once I have committed to you, why would I give it to others? Consider that kancham as yours. Come whenever you want. It will remain here."

I happily returned home.

From that day, I made it a practice to visit Hebbar's store every day and ensure the kancham remained in its place. As far as I was concerned, it was my kancham, but temporarily stored there. This thought pleased me immensely.

I was firm in my decision to buy it by the end of that month. However, the reconciliation of the month-end accounts told me that the entire salary was spent on household expenses.

My wife claimed she had to borrow twenty-five rupees from Mrs Naidu a long time ago to buy a frock cloth for my elder daughter and an orange saree for herself. I vaguely remembered giving money for these purchases, but I was unsure. She presented some complex accounts and insisted that the loan must be repaid this month.

I had no choice but to take two private tuitions. Both of them paid a total of twenty-five rupees. I gave the amount to my wife and asked to repay Mrs. Naidu.

Because of this episode, my kancham purchase was postponed. Next month, the tuition kids will pay twenty-five again. With that amount, I decided I must buy the plate.

My yearning for the plate became stronger. Eating off the vistari seemed the worst thing to do. The small twig pieces were getting stuck in the mouth. Banana leaves would have been better, but they were very expensive. And not available every day. Life seemed miserable.

When can I experience the divine pleasure of eating jasmine-like white rice on that white plate?

Every human has a longing for beauty. Man is never happy with just some food and clothing. The human heart keeps desiring objects of beauty.

In my eagerness to buy the plate, I made sure to visit Hebbar's shop every day, indulge in some small talk and check whether my kancham was in its place or not. The kancham used to shine brightly next to some glasses in the glass showcase. The sunlight during the day and the electric lights during the night amplified its brightness. All I could do was to take a good look, swallow and come back.

August's salary arrived. My wife and I sat down to reconcile the accounts. The cost of milk and curd was five rupees more than last month. There was another snag. My wife claimed that she occasionally borrowed small amounts from Mrs Naidu, totalling twenty rupees. Mrs Naidu is now insisting on prompt repayment this month. Again, I had no choice but to hand over the salary and the tuition amount of twenty-five rupees to my wife and empty my pockets.

Not having a single penny in my pocket made daily life miserable. I needed money for cigarettes and killis[164]. Every two days, I had no choice but to ask her for a half-rupee.

164 Killi: Betel leaf and Betel nuts. Also called Pan and more formally Tambulam.

"This is too much! Where do I have the money?" she used to protest.

I must admit she was right. It was not as if she had tons of money hoarded away somewhere. She meticulously paid all the vendors from my salary and ensured all essential items were purchased. What else would remain with her? So, I used to ask, "Why don't you approach Mrs Naidu and borrow a couple of rupees?"

"You say this now, but you get upset at the end of the month," she complained.

"I will not. Please get it!" I used to plead. Finally, she used to give me a rupee or half. The month passed like this.

Life was tough. Taking tuition was not an easy business. It is not easy to teach during the day in school and again teach two dumb kids at home. No one other than a teacher can understand the pain.

Moreover, tuition is illegal. If authorities find out, the punishment could be severe. How long can I continue this surreptitiously? I decided to end the tuition as soon as I purchased the plate.

The September salary arrived. My wife showed expenses matching the salary and the extra twenty-five and said we needed to borrow ten rupees more to manage the month.

"I can't raise any loan. You borrow from Mrs Naidu again," I said and walked away in a huff.

My wife was proud of her smartness. She always claimed it was her ingenuity that helped manage the family expenses month after month. I am giving her the salary and the additional income every month! Instead of managing within that limit, she was showing a loan of a minimum of twenty-five every month!

October and November also passed like this. I didn't lose hope in the plate. I used to visit the store every day. The plate remained in its place. My only happiness stemmed from the thought that the plate was mine and I would one day own it.

This monthly ritual by my wife - of stealing my salary, the extra income and leaving me penniless and my inability to buy the plate – became unbearable.

One day, I said sadly, "I trusted your intelligence and hoped you would run the household within our means. I have been giving you the salary to manage expenses. You have not saved anything. Moreover, every month, you have been showing a loan. This is no good! From this month, I will run the household expenses."

My wife gave me a cold stare and replied sarcastically, "You running the household expenses is what we are missing now! Thanks to my effort, we are somehow navigating the household waters. If money stays with you, it will be nothing but fasting for me and my children! Look at your friend Srinivasa Rao! How he is struggling! His wife has been constantly complaining to me! They have a one-acre farm and he is planning to sell even that to manage the household affairs!"

"What are you trying to say exactly?"

"What else? If you spend the money, we will be ruined!"

"Nothing of the sort will happen. We will never be forced to sell any property."

Kantham looked at me strangely and mockingly, gesturing dramatically with her hands, "Even if we want to sell, we have nothing, right?" I was hurt. Indeed, I don't own any property, but a blunt comment always hurts.

"Such comments annoy me!" I said angrily.

"Why are you getting angry when I speak the truth? We don't have any, so I said we don't." She was not afraid in the least.

I was enraged. I said loudly, "Yes. We don't have any property. So, what?" I was at a loss for words. I waited a while and said, "Is everyone selling because they have it? If we seriously want to sell, we can sell anything!"

I spoke out of anger, but there was nothing to sell—not even jewellery. The old household items were just enough to run the family.

Instead of ignoring my outburst and remaining quiet, she pressed further, "Tell me what you can sell!"

Now, it became a matter of my ego. So, I shouted loudly, "I will sell the house in Arandalpet in Guntur."

My wife was a tough nut who stood her ground despite my outburst. Anyone else would have got scared thinking, 'This crazy Brahmin – out of sheer anger towards his wife – would sell his house.' That was the effect I managed to create. Without flinching, my wife asked calmly, "Do we have a house in Guntur?"

Analysing how she spoke, I could sense ten per cent doubt and ninety per cent dismay.

I replied haughtily, "What do you know whether we have a house or not?"

"Why did you never mention it?" she sounded perplexed.

"There is no rule that every detail needs to be informed to the lady of the house."

"Alright. You didn't tell me before. Tell me now. Do we have a house there?"

"Yes!" I said as if to erase any remaining doubts from her mind.

She was still not convinced. "When did you buy it?" she asked.

Now you are coming around, I thought. "I never said I bought it!"

"If you did not buy, how can that house be ours?"

"I never said it is ours."

"If it is not ours, how can you sell it?"

"Because I have the right to sell."

"What are you saying? How can we have a right to sell if it is not ours?"

"Nothing. I have my in-laws' house there. I will sell it."

Kantham laughed heartily and asked, "Will they let you sell it?"

"Doesn't a son-in-law have that much right on in-laws' property?"

"If people hear what you are saying, you will become a laughing stock."

"No one will laugh. On the contrary, people will congratulate me for being very clever."

The conversation ended there. But I could not convince her to hand over the money management to me.

She was convinced that thanks to her money management skills, the family remained afloat despite the meagre income. If I started managing the money, I would be forced to sell a neighbour's house to survive. That's why she never lets me touch the money—even I know that! There was never an occasion when I went out with a rupee in my pocket and returned with any change. It is better for our family's survival if she runs the household expenses. But, with December passing, I could still not buy the plate. It remained in Hebbar's shop.

The poor plate didn't have a voice. Otherwise, it would have asked me with teary eyes, "How long do I have to remain imprisoned here? Why don't you take me with you?" I almost imagined the plate saying those words and felt sorry.

In January, ten rupees landed in my pocket. I decided to buy the plate without informing anyone and set out to the shop.

The cost of the kancham was twenty. I have only ten. I came up with a plan. Hebbar would agree if I told him I would pay ten now and the balance next month.

I rushed to the shop. Today, I can boldly look at the glass showcase. Previously, I had the hidden fear that Hebbar could snub me, saying, 'You come every day to take a look, but you are not the buying type. Stop this nuisance.'

I went confidently to the showcase to take out the kancham. To my horror, it was missing! Where has it gone?

It used to be there brightly shining. Today, it is gone! My heart skipped a beat. I scanned the showcase fully.

No doubt. This is the job of some thief.

Hebbar was not present in the store. A youth was manning it. He asked me, "What are you looking for, Pantulu[165] Garu? Can I help?"

"My kancham must be here," I said.

The surprised youth asked, "Why did you keep *your* kancham here?"

How can I answer him? "When I say mine, almost! I was planning to buy it," I replied awkwardly.

---

165 Pantulu: Teachers/Brahmins are normally addressed as Pantulu. Garu is like Sir.

"Couldn't you have told Hebbar sir to hold it for you?"

"I did."

"When?"

"Six months ago."

The young man chuckled and said, "Sir, would it remain if you told him six months ago?"

"He promised to keep it. And he did, until a few days ago."

"Then I am certain he must have lost his patience after waiting so long and must have sold it to someone else. How long can he hold?"

I was overwhelmed with anger and frustration. This was atrocious. Hebbar cheated me!

Whoever that buyer was, he turned out to be an opportunistic predator who snatched my bright white kancham. What can be more unjust?

What do I do now? Should I reconcile to my loss? Or should I chase the thief and recover my plate?

"How much did he pay?" I asked.

"I don't know, sir. When I last heard Hebbar sir, he was quoting twenty-five," the youth replied.

Hmm. Things are becoming clearer. He sold it at a better price.

Forget twenty-five; even fifty rupees will not get such a beautiful piece for any buyer. There is no other piece like it in the market. It is just my bad luck! I stood there downcast.

In the meantime, Hebbar arrived and asked me, "Pantulu Garu, what are you looking for? Why do you look so dispirited?"

"I understand someone bought my kancham. Didn't you promise to keep it for me?" I asked weakly.

"That was long ago, right? In any case, why do you need that iron piece?"

His words scorched me. The same fellow sang the praises of the plate and now he is calling it an 'iron sheet'. That too after making extra money!"

"When I asked earlier, you said it was a great piece!" I countered.

"That was then. I was just testing your resolve. When you were serious about buying that item, I was amused at your naivete."

These lies further irritated me. "Why are you spinning new stories? Why don't you admit you sold it for a higher price?" I asked without hiding my annoyance.

"Oh! Is that what you suspect? Here! Take a look." Hebbar took out the plate from under a bunch of trash papers.

Yes. It was, without a doubt, my plate. While the border looked white, the bottom was completely rusted, and holes could be seen. It was of no use anymore. Tears swelled in my ears when I saw that. That plate waited for me for so long. The long wait and the agony at my not keeping the promise destroyed its body. I felt I committed a great sin towards that plate.

I realised there was no point in continuing the conversation. I delayed it by six months. In the meantime, the plate reached the end of its life. In hindsight, it turned out better that I delayed the purchase. But how would my dream of eating on a bright white plate be fulfilled now?

I returned home. I wept at my shattered dream. I could never afford a silver kancham. And I couldn't own even the fake one.

When I returned home, it was nine. I went to my room and lay down. My wife came up and invited me to dinner, but I refused.

"Why?" she asked.

"I am not feeling well," I replied.

"Tell me the reason," she pressed. Then she came closer and laid her hand on me.

I told her. Kantham laughed and said, "Just for this small setback? If you love a white plate so much, why go for a fake one? Let us buy a genuine silver one, come," she said. *I don't have so much luxury*, I told myself, got up, washed my feet and entered the dining room.

What did I see there? A large low stool, and in front of it—a brightly shining silver kancham! I couldn't believe my eyes!

"What! Where did this kancham come from?"

"It is ours," She chuckled.

"Ours? How did we get it?"

"I bought it."

"Where did you get the money to buy?"

"Is everyone buying things because they have money? You like it, so I bought it for you. It cost eighty-eight rupees."

"First, tell me where you got the money from. I am scared."

"You eat first. I will tell you later."

"Unless you tell me, I will not eat."

"I borrowed."

I was speechless. "You borrowed? Can I ever repay this loan? I will not even be able to eat with this weight on my mind now!" Until then, I remained standing. Kantham held my hand and forced me to sit down. "Why do you worry so much? I didn't take any loan. I bought it with my money."

This sounded even more weird. Her money! Where did she get money from? I asked the question.

"I sold my house in Ramannapet."

"Do you have a house in Ramannapet?"

"Do I need to have one? Is everybody selling houses because they have them?" These words sounded familiar.

"This is not funny. Tell me the source of the money."

"I earned it."

"How?"

"That was easy. My husband earns seventy-five per month, which he hands me. I somehow worked hard, saved money and bought this plate," she said with a drawl.

I chuckled. "So, it is as if you earned it!"

"Is there any doubt about it? This is my hard-earned money. This is what is called women's earnings. This is my kancham. I will have my name engraved on it," she told me bluntly.

With happiness difficult to hide, I asked her, "Will you let me eat on this plate?"

"Sure. As long as you remain nice to me and don't indulge in funny acts, you must eat in this kancham. After you finish your meal, I will eat from the same plate," she said affectionately.

Without another word, I ate to my heart's content on that plate.

Later, she ate from the same plate and washed and wiped it. Carrying betel nuts and leaves on the same plate, she walked into the bedroom. The plate was shining proudly in the electric light.

Chewing the betel leaves, I asked her, "So, come clean now. How did you earn so much money? Every month, you used to give me an expense account. Were you lying to me then?"

"Why would I lie? Every bit of it was true. I worked hard and saved money."

"I still don't get it. Throw some light on the 'hard work'."

"I did it in my own way. Why do you want to poke your nose into ladies' secrets?"

"Please! Be a nice girl and tell me" I pulled her towards me.

"No way! I will not reveal my secret," she pulled herself away and said, "By the way, I owe ten rupees to Mrs Naidu. She is rushing me to repay the same. I think you have some cash with you. Give it to me!"

I was puzzled. *How did she know I had ten rupees with me?* I asked her the same question.

"How tough is it to know such a small matter?" she asked, brushing aside my surprise. She then started taking money out of my pocket.

I received that money from Madras. The postman delivered it in the school. How did she know? Unable to hide my surprise, I persisted with my question, "Tell me, how did you come to know?" She remained stubborn in her refusal to answer. Then she went on to say, "If it remains with you, it will get spent easily. Let me have it."

"What will you do with the ten rupees?"

"Didn't I say already? I need to repay Mrs Naidu."

"Enough of your games! I know the secret now. I will meet Mrs Naidu and find out how much you owe her." I was unable to control my laughter.

Kantham pretended to be angry and said, "Oh! This is too much! You can't do that! Mrs Naidu doesn't talk to strange men. She might even get angry."

I laughed heartily.

Kantham took the money out of the purse and said, "It is better to repay her promptly. I will send it to her first thing tomorrow morning. If any small balance is left, we can repay later."

Thanks to Mrs Naidu, we now have a silver kancham. *If only every wife had a Mrs Naidu to borrow from, households would run smoothly*. I slept happily.

*****

Polaiah

Original Author: Karuna Kumara. First Published in Telugu in 1937.

Vithala Puram Agraharam[166] was a stronghold for Vaidiki[167] Brahmins. Venkata Sastry was the undisputed leader of the two hundred Brahmin families in the Agraharam. He was renowned for his scholarship in the science of logic and grammar and was also very orthodox. Without doing Sandhya Vandanam[168] three times a day, he wouldn't even touch water. He would give his right arm for tradition and the Varnashrama-Dharma[169]. He had been to Kashi in his childhood

166 Brahmin street/locality/village, typically gifted by kings to Brahmin scholars.

167 A sect among Brahmins who are into conducting rituals and teaching Vedas. The other sect is Niyogi who are more into worldly jobs.

168 Sandhya Vandanam is a ritual that involves praying to the Sun God. Very orthodox Brahmins followed them.

169 Varna broadly translates to caste. Ancient Hindu scriptures prescribed four castes – Brahmin, Kshatriya, Vaishya and Shudra. People outside the four castes are also known as Panchama, Chandala, or Dalits. They were treated as untouchables by upper castes.

leaving his parents behind and lived in a Gurukul there for ten years to learn scriptures.

It was not surprising that he never liked Panchamas. There were many Brahmin scholars he despised who were worse than Panchamas. But he had put in special efforts when it came to dealing with the issue of Panchamas. Ever since Mahatma Gandhi started his movement to eradicate untouchability, Sastry pored over several ancient books and scriptures and did a lot of research regarding the ancestry of Panchamas. Our hero brought out a new theory that said Panchamas were not even related to the Hindu religion.

As he grew older, and thanks to the research he did, his opinions about the Panchamas took deeper roots. He began getting more joy and confidence in the exercise he undertook. Ever since he returned to his village from Kashi and married, for the past thirty years, he had been teaching Brahmin students in his village.

Whenever he heard about legislative bills, lectures and movements that demanded untouchables be renamed as Harijans, that they should be granted access to temples and so on, his frustration knew no bounds. He decided it was not right for people like him to sit back and allow such an attack on traditionalism to continue. He took a vow to protect the traditional dharma and as part of the effort, decided to tour North India to blunt the untouchability eradication movement.

Varnashrama Dharma is the practice of strictly believing and practising this hierarchy.

He handed all the responsibilities of running the household to his twenty-year-old son and departed for North India about two years ago. His sole aim was not to let Malas and Madigas[170] come up in society. He toured Kashi, Gaya, Prayag, Delhi, Punjab, Baroda and so on. He discussed all the matters related to Panchamas with the local scholars and kept strengthening his theories. When he heard the rumour that Panchamas decided to leave the Hindu religion and join other religions, he was overjoyed.

Twenty-two months after he left home, he received a barrage of letters and telegrams that broke the news of the birth of a son to his son and the planned naming ceremony (Barasala) for the newborn. The ceremony was planned for Magha Shuddha Panchami – The fifth day of the lunar calendar - on Tuesday morning at nine o'clock. And the presence of the grandfather was a must. Just four days before the muhurtam[171] day, Venkata Sastry started in Kashi and on Monday night at eleven, he reached Punjur railway station close to his village.

Punjur was the third station south of Nellore. It was a reasonably large station but that night not more than four or five people alighted from the train other than Venkata Sastry. As soon as he got off the train, Sastry handed the ticket at the exit gate. He held one

170 Mala and Madiga were part of the Panchama castes and were treated as untouchables by upper castes.

171 Auspicious time when the ritual is scheduled to take place.

bag containing his clothes and Kashi Ganga water pitcher in one hand and in the other, he held a copper water pitcher and exited the gate.

Punjur station was eighteen miles from Vithala Puram. The journey entailed sixteen miles on a paved metal road and two miles on an unpaved road. Normally that road used to be busy day and night with traffic that was bound for Someswaram via Ganga Patnam, a distance of thirty miles. Assuming he would reach home by the time the crows would be cawing on Tuesday morning, Sastry reached on Monday night. Usually, the cartmen would mob the passengers as soon as they got off the train and take away their luggage and load it into the carts any time of the day. But – as Sastry's luck would have it – not a single bullock cart was to be seen.

It was approaching eleven thirty and almost twelve. The train that brought Venkata Sastry departed long ago. All the co-passengers who alighted went their way. The railway employee on night duty locked the gate and settled down on a bench with the lone porter occupying another bench. There was complete silence in the station. The lamp – that was already dimmed – was just flickering.

Venkata Sastry climbed down the stairs and looked at the open ground on the western side of the station. Not a single soul could be seen. Compared to the place he left two years ago, this looked like an abandoned and dilapidated house. Being a Shuddha Panchami day, the moon was hardly to be seen. Darkness was spreading fast and dew drops started falling. The cold was bone-chilling. He couldn't even open his fists for fear of letting the cold get to his entire body and eat away the bones. Venkata Sastry was not very old but he crossed his fifties and entered the sixties. Hence, he was not able to tolerate too much cold or hot weather anymore. In any case, he had no option but to cover the eighteen miles and reach home by morning. Unless he started immediately, he wouldn't be able to reach home in time for the muhurtam. If he didn't reach, apart from the entire effort being wasted, his non-arrival could alarm the family members too. He travelled trusting bullock carts to be available for hire. How would he know the changes caused by time? *I should have written asking them to send a cart from home. What a slip!* rued Sastry. After a while, he began doubting if he got down at Punjur station or if it was some other town. He went back to the platform and read the station name again. When he saw "Punjur" clearly written, he was a little relieved and also felt reassured.

But to what avail? There was no solution in sight to his problem. He couldn't fathom why not a single cart was available. To ask someone, not a soul was to be seen anywhere around. In that eerie silence, he could hear nothing except some distant dogs barking or crickets chirping. He considered going into the village to find a cart. But that was one mile away. He didn't feel up to it in that darkness and cold with a bag on his shoulder. A nonplussed Sastry – unable to bear the cold - then decided to get back into the station waiting room and started moving. Just as he took a few steps, an approaching cart could be heard from the west. Sastry quickly turned around to take a look. A cart, driven by a single ox, arrived and was parked near the neem tree. Hope kindled in Sastry's mind. *Things are not all that bad* he felt. As he took rapid strides toward the cart, the cartman untied the bull, lowered the yoke, took out some fodder and laid it in front of the bull. The bull was busy shooing away the stinging flies with its tail and ears and had not yet started eating. When the cartman was about to pull out the mat made with the wild date leaves to get some sleep, Venkata Sastry approached him and asked, "Hey You! Will you give me a ride to Vithalapuram?"

"Forget Vithalapuram and get lost!" the cartman scoffed.

"My dear! You will be doing me a huge favour. I am in a hurry. If I don't leave right now, a lot of plans will go awry at home. Please take this trouble for an old man and a good man's sake!" Sastry pleaded.

"I am feeling sleepy and I don't intend to do anything other than sleep right now." The cartman settled down on the mat.

The next few minutes saw the Brahmin pleading on one side and the cartman turning down his pleas. Finally, Sastry said temptingly, "I will pay you one and a half rupee! I am not getting any other cart. This is way over the normal fare for this route. Don't lose it."

In a world driven by money, this offer of an extra half rupee was irresistible for the cartman. He got up, rolled the mat, tossed it inside the cart and asked, "How many people?"

"I am the only one," Sastry replied.

The cartman spread the hay under the mat and readied the cart with the bull in place, the yoke on its neck and rein tied to the bull.

Venkata Sastry took the pitcher of water, relieved himself in a corner and then brought the bag and kept it in the cart. He pushed the slippers under the mat and cautioned the cartman to hold the cart steady and hopped into the cart and settled down. For the next ten yards, until they reached the road, the cartman walked holding the yoke. After getting on to the road, he settled down in the saddle. Even as he was looking for the whip, the bull settled into a gentle trot.

It was approaching one o'clock in the night. The Brahmin was exhausted with two days of continuous travel. He wanted to catch some sleep and pulled the bag under his head. When the cartman warned, "Overweight in the back sir!" he moved forward with the bag. The bag and his head resting on the bag touched the backside of the cartman. "Please move back a little. Now the load is high in the front," cautioned the cartman. Sastry pulled the bag back, and when the cartman nodded, settled down into a figure of three, folding his legs.

The cart covered two miles. It was a cart old enough to be in a museum rather than on the road. The wild date leaf mat on the roof was dilapidated. One could see the stars in the sky when lying down face up in the cart. The wood used for the wheels was of poor quality and was warped, having been exposed to heat and cold. The nuts and bolts of the axle were loose and making a lot of noise as the cart was moving. The wheels – being warped – were giving the cart a huge wobble as it was moving. The wobble was more intense whenever the cart hit a pothole. Every time the cart wobbled Sastry's body was also shuddering. Whenever the cart lurched forward, his knees were getting smashed. It was the spine's turn when the cart jerked backwards. With his right hand supporting the head, he had to use his left hand to rub the injured spot. And sleep eluded him. In all his travels across the country, he had never experienced this kind of travel comfort. When he couldn't take the knee pain anymore, he would scream Shankara, Mahadeva, and look at his legs. When he stretched his legs, his calves extended out of the cart. With each jerk, he was further slipping out of the cart. When he was slipping, the head and the bag – being used as the pillow – were getting separated. In the meantime, the yoke lifted upwards and bruised the bull's neck. The cartman warned again, "Watch the rear load, sir! Watch it!" "Stop your nonsense! Here I am almost dying!" Sastry retorted. He let the bag remain where it was and held a couple of wooden side bars to remain stable. This stopped the sliding but sleep continued to elude him. With his entire energy being spent in keeping his body inside the cart, where was the chance of grabbing some sleep?

The bull was a perfect match for the cart. The cartman never fed it any green grass or proper fodder. When he was hitting it with the whip - with no sign of flesh except bones and skin – the sound was that of a wooden stick hitting another wooden stick. With nothing other than water in its stomach, every time the bull tried to run harder, the intestines were getting shaken and a loose discharge followed. Unable to bear the stench, Sastry got up and covered his nose with a cloth. He yelled at the cartman, "What a mess in the name of a cart you have got here! This cart's only purpose seems to be to snuff my life out! Disgusting! One should light a match and burn this down completely!"

The cartman chuckled.

"What is wrong with my cart sir?" he asked.

"Everything! Every bone in my body is getting broken!"

"Nowadays, not many cart rentals are to be had. Not being in use, and with no repairs, the cart ended up in this state. What do you want me to do sir?"

"I have travelled across so many places. Nowhere did I have to suffer like this. Every road is getting motor vehicles except this godforsaken road. Shameful! What a horrible journey this is turning out to be! Without knowing what was in store, I got into your cart!" Sastry ranted.

"Why Sir? There are two motor vehicles – that run up and down – on this road."

"Why didn't you tell me about it earlier?"

"The first trip towards the east doesn't start until after the eleven o'clock morning train arrives. You told me you had to reach home early morning."

"Why can't these fellows run one vehicle in the night too?"

"If they could, of course they would. After he had jailed every single cartman, what would stop that great soul from running vehicles day and night?"

"What do you mean jailing the cartmen?"

"That's a long story. Narrating the story wouldn't ease our agony." The cartman prodded the bull.

The bull picked up speed.

"Who brought motor vehicles to this route?"

"There is a nobleman. Turned out to be a curse for our lives!"

"His name?"

"Chenchu Naidu."

"Which Chenchu Naidu?"

"Bolla Chenchu Naidu."

"From which village?"

"He is from Gangapatnam."

Gangapatnam and Vithalapuram are separated by one mile. Chenchu Naidu was a close friend of Venkata Sastry. When he heard his name in the context of cartmen and prison terms, Sastry was anxious if his friend Chenchu Naidu was in some kind of danger.

He wanted to pretend as a stranger to those parts and extract more information from the cartman. He asked, "So, it has been how long since motor vehicles started operating on these roads?"

"About a year. Where are you from sir?" the cartman asked.

"I am from further south. I am visiting some relatives in Vithalapuram."

The cartman kept driving silently. Sastry didn't like his silence. He was eager to get more details out of that fellow.

"Do you know why the cartmen were jailed?"

"Ever since motor vehicles came to this road, they snatched away the cartmen's livelihood. That nobleman competed with the cartmen and killed their rentals completely. If they asked for half a rupee, the motor fellow would take only six annas. If a cart quoted six annas, they would charge only four. This went on until cartmen's business was completely destroyed by the motor operators."

"So? Did that make them come to blows?"

"They never came to any blows. How can the poor ever take on the powerful? When they were completely ruined and their families had nothing to eat, one fine day a hundred souls landed at Naidu's house, broke open his grain stores and took whatever grain they could lay their hands on."

"Oh My God!"

"What other choice did they have? How long can anyone bear the hunger pangs? They were forced to sell their carts and bulls too. Besides, all the Gangapatnam cartmen were Turks. Women in their families are not supposed to come out of the house even for any labour work. The man is the sole breadwinner. Do you expect them to starve to death? Finally, the Turks mobilized people from other castes too and raided Naidu's house."

"What do you mean by other caste folks?"

"These motors ruined so many other lives, sir! Be it the carpenters who make the carts, the bull traders, the vendors selling the yokes and wooden beams, the basket weavers who make the cart roofs, even the Mala and Madiga women who earned a rupee or two by supplying grass to the bulls. Everyone was ruined! I believe it was the Turks who mobilized the others in Gangapatnam. If they are serious, they are capable of doing anything sir!"

"Good for them. So, they taught a lesson to Naidu!"

"I can't say that. It is the rich and powerful who have their way these days."

"True."

"Naidu and the police didn't rest until they slapped cases on all the hundred or so raiders and ensured everyone got at least a two or three-year jail term. Let it be. God is watching all the goings-on." He spat out the tobacco and prodded the bull again.

When he heard that Chenchu Naidu prevailed in the end, Sastry was relieved. He guessed that some major conflict had happened between the cartmen and Naidu. Sastry knew Naidu's stubborn attitude. He wanted to gather more details and asked, "That was one hell of a conflict! How long ago was it?"

"The case was filed six months ago. The trial was over recently and only last week the judge announced the verdict."

"Is Naidu doing fine?"

"Of course he is! What wrong can happen to him? That noble soul will live another hundred years to ruin the lives of the poor!"

"Is he well to do?"

"Of course, sir! He is a major landowner in these parts. He bought half of Gangapatnam. And he has so many other businesses. The rumour has it he earns twenty thousand annually."

"Hmm! Why should such a rich man stoop to the level of harassing poor folks?"

"They claim that the motor vehicles were brought in for public convenience. Does he even understand the public and what their convenience is?"

"The rich always bother about their profits."

"Even filing a case is understandable. But where was the need to drag poor Mala women who survive on selling grass? Our caste has become the butt of insults for everyone sir."

When the cartman said "Our caste", Sastry initially didn't get it. He was unsure whether he was talking about Malas in general or if he meant *he* was a Mala. Seeds of doubt were sown in Sastry's mind.

The cartman continued his rant. He didn't know his customer was a Brahmin. In any case, he had Brahmin customers before. He started again. "Do our Malas have anything that can be robbed? Just because those Mala women were selling grass to the cartmen, a vengeful Naidu made sure to drag them into the case. I believe those ten women were mothers of infant children. And those infants are now starving at home. The thought itself is heart-breaking sir!" As an emotional cartman continued venting his anguish, Sastry suddenly understood he was a Mala. He was completely shaken and paralyzed. Consumed with rage, his first instinct was to jump out of the cart. But he couldn't do it and didn't know how to react. All his life-long efforts to weed out Panchamas and keep them at a distance went down the drain. The pitchers holding the holy Ganga water were in the cart. His entire endeavour came to nought. He felt like smashing the cartman's head into pieces but couldn't muster the courage. He was alone in that darkness with no other help. The cartman could be in his twenties and looked well-built. If he counter-attacked, he could thrash ten Brahmins like him. Sastry felt it was not the time for impulsive actions. He decided to wait till he reached the village and then handle the matter. He pulled back his bag that was touching the cartman. He wanted to know more about the cartman and asked, “Which village are you from?”

“I am from the north sir. Tenali.”

“What brought you here?”

“I married my maternal uncle’s daughter in Punjur and stayed back here. My uncle owns this cart.”

“Your name?”

“Polaiah.”

“Do you know the Gangapatnam cartmen?”

“I know some of them.”

“Being a Mala, are you getting enough customers hiring your cart?”

“These days no one cares about caste sir. When they needed, many Brahmins also hired my cart.”

“Did you ever visit Vithalapuram in the past?’

“Not Vithalapuram but I had been to Gangapatnam.”

“Do you have any relatives there?”

“No sir.”

“Alright. Go faster. Daylight is almost here.” Sastry said.

It was still pre-dawn and another five miles needed to be covered. Venkata Sastry lost his peace of mind completely. He was upset with himself that a scholar like him got stuck with a Mala. He was frustrated at his powerlessness to punish a lowly Mala who committed such a grave crime against an upper-caste man like himself. The fire of anger warmed up his body and dispelled the winter cold. He removed the shawl that was covering his body and threw it into a corner of the cart. He was desperate to get home.

Around five-thirty in the morning, the cart got off the paved road and entered the village road. The sun was up in the east and the cartman's face was visible. He loathed seeing a Panchama's face first thing in the morning. In that early sunshine, even the cartman could see Sastry's face. He appeared to be a Brahmin but there was no life in his face. He seemed to be in some deep thought, with a red face and blazing eyes. The cartman attributed this to the sleeplessness of last night.

When it was six o'clock, the cart reached Vithalapuram and parked in front of Sastry's house. The naming ceremony of his grandson was due that day. The main door was decorated with a garland of mango leaves. The entire family was eagerly waiting for Sastry's arrival. Sastry got down from the cart, kept his bag on the stone bench outside the house and stood there. His wife brought water for him to wash his feet. He asked for a neem twig to brush his teeth and finished brushing and then washed his face. He still didn't step inside. His wife and son asked him to come inside. Sastry replied, "I can't bring the clothes I used on the journey inside. I will enter only after taking a bath."

The cartman asked for his rent. Sastry asked him to wait, quietly called his son to a side and sent him to fetch Chenchu Naidu urgently.

Chenchu Naidu held Sastry in very high esteem. Out of this respect for a scholar, he gifted a house to Sastry. And four acres of paddy fields too. He also provided monetary help for Sastry's son's wedding. Naidu's affection and love for Sastry's family was well known and it was an enduring relationship from his ancestors' days. It was customary for Naidu to visit Sastry whether it was his work or Sastry's requirement. When he heard that Sastry asked to see him, he rushed out of bed, tied a flannel cloth to the head, put on his slippers and – with a stick in his hand – rushed to Vithalapuram.

The sun was fully up by then. Many neighbours and folks from the Agraharam gathered around Sastry's house and started greeting him. "After a long time, Sastry Garu." "You have completely forgotten us and the Agraharam Sastry Garu." "Trust all is well. Long time." While these greetings were pouring in, Naidu arrived on the scene and greeted Sastry with folded hands.

"God bless you with a long life and may your family grow and prosper," Sastry blessed Naidu. He asked for a mat, got it laid on the stone bench and asked Naidu to sit down.

"Sastry Garu has blessed us with his presence after a long time…" Even as Naidu was about to complete his sentence, an impatient Sastry started his outburst. "I heard about the entire episode. It has come to my knowledge how these lowly drunkards had treated you. A major calamity was averted, Naidu! Your life was at needless risk! You never bothered to write a small letter when so much happened here. Even my son here didn't bother to update me." He poured out his sympathy and support for whatever Naidu had to undergo.

"I wanted to write to you but neglected it. Anyway, God is with us. What harm can these scoundrels do?"

"True. Why did you spare them without cutting them to pieces?"

"I almost did as much. I managed a three-year term for each one and sent all one hundred of them to Nellore jail. Haven't you heard?"

"All your efforts have come to nought now! Things are back to square one. Have you heard? If these Malas and Madigas didn't care for a landowner like you, do they even bother about folks like us? I have toured the entire country but have never been humiliated like this before."

"Why? What happened?"

"Look there! The cartman standing there is a pure Mala. It is only the other day that you sent nearly a hundred of them to jail, right? This fellow – without any fear or respect – dared to give me a ride in his cart from Punjur to Vithalapuram. No punishment is small enough for him!"

"Is he a Mala?"

The Cartman didn't speak.

Sastry glared at him. "Disgusting! Why are you silent? I will have that tongue scalded! You hurled the choicest abuses at Naidu the entire night! What happened to that tongue now?"

The cartman was trembling.

"Who did you think I was when you offered me the ride? You assumed me to be a Madiga or Mala? Don't you have the responsibility to identify the person before committing the ride?"

"How would I know you are a Brahmin sir?" asked the cartman.

"So, you are blinded enough not to distinguish between a Brahmin and a Mala." Naidu fumed.

"I could not identify in the darkness Sir."

"Who asked you to ply a rental cart to start with? Did your grandfather do it or did your great-grandfather do it? Tell me where is it written that an untouchable can ignore his caste's vocation and get into something else? Even if someone like me asked you to give me a ride out of ignorance, how dare you agree? How dare you destroy the caste hierarchy? Shouldn't you have immediately said 'Sir, I am an untouchable?' Venkata Sastry's teeth were clattering by now.

"Smack the scoundrel with a slipper. That's the way to kill his arrogance." Naidu said.

"I did it out of ignorance Sir," the cartman replied.

"Don't you dare repeat the same story! Would I believe you? The years I had spent studying scriptures have all been now laid to waste. I brought Ganga water from Kashi for the ritual here. Everything is ruined now!"

"This fellow did it deliberately. The way to teach him a lesson would be to squeeze his eyes with a pair of pincers. Sastry Garu! You can't imagine how much I had to endure in that case with Turks and these Malas! I had to spend a fortune to prove the case and send them to jail. That money could have been spent on better things. At least if I had donated it to a Brahmin like you, you would have been grateful and blessed me. Credit goes to that righteous judge who believed our argument – despite all the lies uttered by these fellows – and convicted them," Naidu said.

In the meantime, all the Agrahara residents who gathered there picked up sticks and joined the verbal abuse.

Naidu was fully heated up. Ever since the legal wrangle, he was furious with the cartmen. In that heat, he asked Sastry, "So, what punishment do you suggest for this fellow Sastry Garu?"

"The only way a Brahmin - who touched a Chandala – can atone for his sin is to burn his skin. Otherwise, the sin wouldn't be forgiven for fourteen rebirths. My atonement must become his punishment," Sastry said.

Naidu immediately summoned two men and made them tie the cartman to a pole in the animal yard. He further arranged for a basketful of dried cow dung cakes, created a fire with them and started heating an iron rod that was as thick as a thumb.

The cartman suddenly found himself in a precarious situation. The matter had gone too far and was getting out of control. He never imagined it would come to this. It was like a solo deer in the company of a thousand tigers! How could he counter so many Agrahara residents? And to whom could he complain? He couldn't fathom what his mistake was. His end seemed certain. His throat was parched and he desperately needed to relieve himself. But he couldn't move even an inch. He could see the iron rod being heated and turning red in front of his eyes. He despaired at the thought of what was to follow next. *O God! What sin have I committed in my previous life? Why are you making me go through this torture?* He wept silently and closed his eyes.

Suddenly, Sastry pulled Naidu to a corner and whispered, "Naidu! If word gets out about what we are doing, will there be any trouble from the police? Think about it."

"Do you think I am a fool, Sastry Garu? Police dance to my tune here. Don't worry," assured Naidu.

"Then hurry up," Sastry ordered.

Naidu asked the men to check if the rod was sufficiently heated up.

Polaiah had some character and was also educated a little. He was a town-bred man. He was aware of current affairs and where things were heading in the society. Sometime after closing his eyes, an idea occurred to him. *If my death is inevitable, it will happen anyway. Even if it is a lie, let me try one trick. Won't God be with me?* Finding courage from within, he addressed Sastry and Naidu.

"You are torturing me like this. Whether I live or die, this matter will get leaked to the outside world. If our English father comes to know about this, you will suffer the consequences. Don't think you are the only powerful people. Even after we renounced your religion and converted to Christianity, you are putting me through such torture. Lord Jesus is watching this," saying this Polaiah let out a huge scream.

When they heard these words from the cartman, Sastry and Naidu were taken aback. "This fellow is claiming that he converted. Could this be true?" they hesitated.

"Are you a Christian?" asked Sastry.

"Yes. My grandfather converted during his time." Polaiah replied with a poker face.

"Your name?"

"Paulaiah."

"When we were riding in the cart, didn't you say Polaiah?"

"No. I said Paulaiah."

"Your father's name?"

"Jakaraiah."

Naidu immediately ordered the cartman to be untied and joined Sastry behind the haystack to confabulate.

Sastry: "He told me his name was Polaiah in the cart. I think he is playing a game."

Naidu: "It is possible that you heard him wrongly. Look at his head. He has cropped hair. No doubt he is a Christian!"

Sastry: "Forget the cropping of the hair, but if he is truly a Christian then we must think twice."

Naidu: "You said it! These missionaries are very close to the Government. If needed, they can go all the way to England and fight the case. If things go that far, even the police will turn the other way no matter how much we grease their hands. So, we must be careful."

Sastry: "Alright. Do as you wish. Even scriptures prescribe shunning excessive methods. Moreover, if he is truly a Christian, then we have nothing to worry about. If his religion is the same as our rulers' religion, then we are bound not to criticize the same. God always exists in the king's religion. Also, it is only *our* religion that has Chandalas and there is no such provision in their religion. But the only doubt is – if this fellow is truly a Christian or not?"

Naidu: Whether he is or not, we can't take any risk now. We should back off now. He also claimed he was from Tenali in the north. Who knows how much clout he has there?"

Sastry: "True. It is his good nature that restrained him so far."

Sastry satisfied himself with this logic and, avoiding Polaiah's eyes, he slipped away from the back side of the house. Naidu untied Polaiah, took him home, handed him three rupees, fed him and sent him off.

*****

Vakil Yenkaiah

Original Author: Suravaram Pratapa Reddy. First Published in Telugu in the late 1920s or early 1930s.

1

This story goes back nearly forty years. In those days, vakils were considered as high-ranking officials. They didn't have to read many books either. Anyone who could speak a few Urdu words and go around the village carrying a couple of bulky volumes was considered a vakil. Our Yenkaiah's real name was Venkata Reddy Dora. He was born in Singaram village in Palamur (now Mahbubnagar) district in 1277 Fasli[172] calendar (1867 Gregorian). His parents were poor. Their simple life consisted of tending to the small farm, and they remained debt-free. Yenkaiah went to Nambi Rangaiah's school, where he learnt reading Bharatam, Bhagavatam, some writing, decoding complex letters, interest calculations, and writing promissory notes by age fifteen.

---

172 Islamic calendar. Fasli + 590 gives us the Gregorian calendar (Source: Google)

One day, Venkata Reddy and his father had an argument. The father, known for his temper, asked the son to leave home. The following morning, Venkata Reddy was not to be seen. The father didn't care, though his mother shed tears.

2

In those days, people practising law travelled in palanquins in Hyderabad. Khaja Kamaluddin Dehlavi had a long beard resembling maize fibre because he used to colour it. He had a large turban, and his pot belly suited his stature. His long sherwani almost touched the ground. He was dark brown complexioned, tall and had cat eyes. He used to earn two thousand rupees per month. His reputation was mainly in criminal cases. The rumour was – that he could get even the most hardcore criminals released. His proximity with the judge was well known. He never used to argue much, but if he stood up to argue, the case was almost considered won. One evening, Venkata Reddy somehow landed at his feet after fleeing home. He bravely covered the sixty-mile distance from his village to Hyderabad. The Maulvi Saheb asked him the purpose of his visit. "I want to serve you," replied Venkata Reddy. "Very good," said the Maulvi. Venkata Reddy's daily chores included carrying Vakil Saheb's books to the court, organising the papers at home, and getting vegetables and meat from the market. Five years passed. Venkata Reddy mastered spoken Urdu. And he also learned to read and write a little. He bought five or six large law books. One day, when some merchants were travelling to Palamur, he joined them in a cart.

The news of Venkata Reddy's return caused a lot of buzz in the village. Several rumours about Venkata Reddy's whereabouts were floating around. Some said he became a mendicant. Some said they spotted him in a group of vagabonds heading to Rameswaram. Others said he converted to Islam in Janampet (now Farookh Nagar). One version said he married a Madiga woman. Another version was that he jumped into the river Krishna and died. His parents waited for a long time and then gave up any hopes of his return and believed that he was dead. Now Venkata Reddy arrived with five large books, a bunch of papers, a sherwani, a Turkish cap, Turkish clothes and shoes. The whole village went crazy. The man had transformed a lot. There was the cropped hair and a thin moustache. He wore a sherwani and pants and topped them with a foot-long Turkish cap. He talked in Turkish. The rumour quickly spread that he returned after becoming a vakil in town. He drew much respect from the villagers. Parents were elated. The entire village soon started calling him Vakil Yenkaiah. While the government didn't do anything, the village folks took the lead and made him a Vakil.

3

Two years passed. Vakil Yenkaiah became twenty-three years old. He routinely threatens the village folk. Every argument ends with a warning about going to court and handcuffing and chaining his opponents. He talks nonstop in Turkish. Unable to handle his aggression, the village police Patel[173] gave Yenkaiah a power of attorney and asked him to do the police Patel's job. But the Patwari[174] and Mali Patel[175] joined hands. This led to two groups being formed in the village now. Initially, the power was equally balanced between the two groups. While things were like this, a murder took place in the village. Someone killed a ten-year-old boy and threw the body into a well. It happened during the night, and the perpetrators were unknown. Vakil Yenkaiah immediately sent a report to Amin[176] Saheb. The Amin arrived by the same evening. In anticipation of Amin's arrival, Vakil Yenkaiah kept a dozen labourers ready to receive him and care for his needs. A cartful of logs, fifty eggs, five chickens, two goats, ten kilos of scented rice (for pulao), one box of ghee and assorted masala and spices were kept ready. He tied up ten of Mali Patel's strongmen. Amin Saheb, two jawans, one cook, his wife in a zenana cart and a servant woman arrived. Curtains were tied in the veranda. Accommodation was arranged for the zenana. There was no dearth of soft pillows and mattresses. A grand smoke indicated that the Bawarchi (cook) had started cooking.

173 Police Patel was the headman responsible for village security and law and order in Telangana areas (the erstwhile Hyderabad state), similar to Munsif or Munsab in Andhra.

174 Patwari maintained the land records in the village in Telangana. Same as Karanam in Andhra.

175 Mali Patel was the village administrative head. Also responsible for land records in the Telangana area.

176 Amin – Police Inspector.

Amin Saheb arranged for the corpse to be removed and conducted a panchnama[177]. He asked the victim's mother if she suspected anyone. The sobbing lady replied, "Sir, what can I say? The Mali Patel was after me for nearly a month. I did not oblige. Last night, he came home with these ten fellows. I closed the door, but my boy remained outside. 'Will you come out, or do you want the boy to be killed?' he asked. I didn't move. He dragged the crying boy away. I came to know in the morning that he was killed and dumped in the well." Amin Saheb looked at Yenkaiah. Both of them disappeared to a corner and talked in Turkish. Amin Saheb could sense a heavy bag touching his hand. Both came back haughtily. Amin barked, "Catch hold of the Mali Patel and bring him here." When his name came up during the panchnama, one of his men reported the matter to Mali Patel. Mali Patel was sure this was all Vakil Yenkaiah's doing. Mali Patel chose to hide, fearing humiliation. His absconding further strengthened the case against him.

4

The case dragged on for three years. No one knew who the real murderer was, but Mali Patel was sentenced to two years in jail, and the ten fellows were sentenced to two to seven years in jail. Both the parties ended up spending nearly twenty thousand rupees. Mali Patel was finished.

---

177 Investigation at the crime scene – overseen/witnessed by five men (Panch = five). Similar to a coroner's inquest.

5

Years passed. Mali Patel and three of his men were released from jail. Vakil Yenkaiah's name struck terror – not just in his village but all nearby villages. He had a Midas touch when it came to his cases. One day, Balaiah – a thirty-year-old Boya from that village – married Yelli. Yelli was fifteen. She was beautiful, and no other girl in her caste matched her beauty. Her large eyes, silver armlets, coral necklace, nose pin, silver toe rings, anklets and pearl earrings amplified her beauty. About a month after she came to join Balaiah, Vakil Yenkaiah saw her when she was fetching water from the well. The same day, he called her to his house to clean rice. Then he started making advances towards her. Yelli didn't like his overtures. She scowled and scolded him. He held her hand. She shook him off. He pinched her cheek. Yelli was livid. She threw the sieve away and started to leave. "Who do you think I am? I am Vakil Yenkaiah." Saying this, Yenkaiah twisted his moustache (now grown to be very thick). Yelli was a little shaken. She kept looking back and went home and reported the matter to her husband. Balaiah was a well-built man with long hair and an exercised and toned body. He was furious. His neighbour Kurmanna arrived and inquired about the matter. "My dear fellow! Your strength and anger are no match to Vakil Yenkaiah's cunning. Didn't he send an innocent Mali Patel to jail for a crime he didn't commit? We need a clever plan to fix him," he advised Balaiah. They worked out a plan.

6

The next day, Yenkaiah called for Yelli again. Yelli went. He started his amorous advances again. "Many women in this village are at my beck and call. You are the only one I like. Ask for whatever you want, and you shall have it. You can live like a queen. Why these silver ornaments? I will get you gold jewellery by Saturday," it went on like this. Yelli smiled charmingly. Yenkaiah was emboldened. Immediately, he asked if she would come that night. Yelli looked at him from the corner of her eye and smiled again. Yenkaiah was entranced. Yelli said slowly, "Sir, I am not used to this. I am afraid of coming out in the darkness. My husband went to the market today. He will return tomorrow. There is no one at home. Why don't you come to my place? Will it be below your stature if you come to this poor woman's house?" Yenkaiah was by now wholly in her spell. He immediately agreed.

That night, Yenkaiah wore a fresh set of neatly starched clothes. He carried a silk handkerchief and applied perfume to his clothes. With a cigar in his hand, he made his way to Yelli's house. He gently knocked on the door. Yelli opened the door, invited him in and made him sit comfortably on the bed. She gave him a pillow to lean on and stood aside quietly. "Why are you so shy like a new bride? Close the door, bolt it and come here," said Yenkaiah. Yelli closed the door and stood afar. "Come closer," Yenkaiah kept saying. Yelli continued to dodge and didn't move. Finally, Yenkaiah got up and pulled her onto the bed. Suddenly, someone banged on the door. "Hey Yelli! Open the door!" shouts could be heard. Yelli started shivering. "Who is that? Your husband? You said he was not due until tomorrow. Why has the bastard come now?" asked Yenkaiah. "Sir, I beg your mercy. If my husband sees us, he will kill both of us. Hide in the granary house," Yelli locked up Yenkaiah in the granary house and opened the door. Balaiah entered. "Why, my dear! I can smell a nice perfume! Has any lover been here?" he asked in jest. "Enough of your jokes," said Yelli sternly. "Why are you upset with such a small joke, my dear Yelli? When I was going to the market today – I hope there is no one here – I found a box on the road. It had expensive jewels. Some rich folks had lost it. Here, keep it safe." Balaiah handed the box to Yelli. Yelli took it to the granary house and kept it in the notch. Yenkaiah heard the conversation and saw the box being kept there. He reached out, opened the box and searched inside with his fingers. There were two scorpion pricks on two fingers as if a hundred needles had pierced. "Oh My God!" he screamed in agony. Balaiah quickly said," I think we have some thieves in the house. Kurmanna! Thieves!" Kurmanna and his son arrived promptly. All three went inside the granary house with sticks and slippers. They caught Yenkaiah and thrashed him as if they didn't know who he was. Yenkaiah kept screaming, "I am Vakil Yenkaiah, stop beating me." They didn't listen to him, beat him black and blue, dragged him out and beat him again. Immediately, they went to Patel and Patwari and confessed their deed. Patel and Patwari promised to shield them. They didn't sleep that night. They alerted all the Boyas and their group of people.

7

Yenkaiah was bedridden for ten days. Everyone thought he would die. The entire village was abuzz with the talk of the humiliation Yenkaiah suffered. Balaiah became a hero, and Yelli a heroine. After about fifteen days, Yenkaiah stepped out again but could not show his face to anyone.

Plenty of wild pam trees were under government control in that village, possibly about two thousand in number. In these ten days, someone chopped them off without leaving a single tree. Mali Patel lodged a complaint against Vakil Yenkaiah. He had already met the Amin Saheb. Villagers collected two thousand rupees. Fifteen hundred went to Amin Saheb. As soon as Amin Saheb arrived, he handcuffed Yenkaiah. Yenkaiah managed to gather two thousand rupees. Mali Patel again called Amin Saheb and handed over an extra five hundred. Yenkaiah ran out of cash. Nothing could be done. About a hundred people in the village gave evidence. Folks in Venkaiah's group were terrified as soon as he was handcuffed. Surprisingly, not a single soul turned up to give evidence. Yenkaiah was sentenced to four years in jail.

8

Until then, life was smooth for Yenkaiah. He had a large farm ploughed by forty pairs of bulls, a big bungalow, plenty of milk and dairy produce, two sons, a wife and the daughter of the neighbouring village's Deshmukh – it was a dream run. When he was sentenced, people considered Yenkaiah's fortune to have overturned. Many even said, 'This fellow was a pest for the society. He destroyed several families, raped many women, had many houses burgled and murders done. This sentence is too lenient for him.' As soon as Yenkaiah went to jail, ten of his bulls disappeared. That day, there was a celebration in the Madiga community. After a month, the grain in his granary vanished. There was a wild party in the Boya locality that day. His granary was torched, and there was none to douse the fire. His house was robbed. There were no witnesses. Each day turned out to be a nightmare for Yenkaiah's family members. When Yenkaiah returned from jail, his bungalow was gone. His family was living in a small, old, thatched hut. Just one pair of bulls and a matching amount of land were left. The rest was gone. His wife was wearing coarse clothes. Parents were dead. When Vakil Yenkaiah saw this new picture unfold, he cried inconsolably and fainted with a "Ha!" When he regained consciousness, he said, "Oh My God! What has my Vakalat[178] led to?" and fainted again.

*****

178 Vakalat – Practice of Law or being a lawyer.

Justice

Original Author: Potlapalli Rama Rao. First Published in Telugu in 1945.

As if Madigas[179] were born only for vetti (bonded labour), the jawan started shouting at the vetti man even as the sun was yet to come up.

Although the officers, who follow propriety, had forgotten their duty (repaying the vettis for their services), the vetti madiga did not forget his duty. He had no other option for his livelihood. With the patience imbibed over generations, he slowly emerged near the front of chavadi (the public hall).

"Hey, you! Have you been sleeping with your wife?"

"Where do I have so much luxury, sir? She died long ago."

"Is it? You should also have gone with her, perhaps! Can government work wait?"

---

179 Madiga community was considered low in India's caste hierarchy and was treated as untouchable in the old days.

"When the time comes, I have no option. Until then, am I not at the government's service?"

"All that is fine. The officer is arriving today. I don't see any arrangements being made. Where the hell is the karanam[180]?"

"I will go and get him," Madiga said and went away. The jawan sat in the hall and lit a beedi. With the smoke swirling upwards, he was engrossed in thoughts of inspiring some fear in the karanam's head about the officer who was coming. He was busy in his mind, digging up anger and authority that didn't exist. The karanam arrived in the meantime and said –

"It looks like you've been asleep!" the jawan started and glared at the karanam.

"If *you* need more sleep, I suggest you sleep here."

"What's the matter? Looks like some nuisance again!"

"Why is it a nuisance to you?"

"If not to me, for others. So, what is it now?"

"That's better. I think you are still not done with sleep. Wipe your eyes. Tahsildar[181] sir is coming today to inspect the records. Will you sleep now? Call the komati[182]."

180 Karanam: Village accountant/record keeper. Typically, a brahmin.

181 Administrative head for a set of villages called Taluk or Taluq. Reports to the district collector.

182 Komati used to be the village merchant. Small villages typically had just one.

Before the karanam could reply, Madiga rushed off to get the komati.

With a bowed head, the karanam started writing a list.

"What are you writing?"

"The same thing that I write every time? What's new today?"

"You look like a new man today. Remember, there is a horse also coming."

"What do I have to lose by just writing?" Saying this, the karanam handed over the list – Chickpeas, rice, wheat, ghee, masala and salt – to the komati, who arrived just then.

The komati looked closely at the list.

"What do you want me to do with this?"

"Why are you asking me? Ask that gentleman?" the karanam snapped.

"Every fellow wants a free ride. How can I supply these items without money?"

"How have you been supplying all these days?" the jawan snarled.

"Do you mean that the same free ride should continue forever?"

"Go and complain to higher-ups."

"How much higher? If higher-ups themselves are eating – Oh God!"

"Or file a case!"

"Sure! Just as supplies appear at the sight of a list, justice will be done as soon as a case is filed!"

"So, what do you want to do? Waste time?"

"Be my guest and take whatever you can find in my house. I can show the house to the officer who is coming."

"What if any faulty weights and measures are found?"

"All the world's fraud and deceit are in a komati's house!"

"Pantulu![183] I leave it to you." Unable to argue with the komati, the jawan turned to the karanam.

"Nagaiah! Be reasonable! Why this sudden cry of poverty when we have been supplying all these years? Somehow manage. None of us is rich here," the karanam tried to reason it out.

"I don't know! One can take care of humans' needs. But what about horses? Even a grass-eating horse – when it sees a generous supplier - will start craving a variety of foods!"

"Tomorrow motor cars will come. What then?" asked the jawan.

"If they can run on castor oil, we can somehow manage."

---

183 Typically, Brahmins used to be addressed as Pantulu. In this case, he is addressing the Karanam. Karanams were normally Brahmins.

"No. You will need to supply petrol."

"It is better if you buy petrol and burn my house with it," saying this, a vexed komati left the place. As soon as the items arrived, the jawan demanded, "Chicken! Where is chicken!" It was common for the officers to fleece the villagers when they needed so much as a chicken egg. Whether it was the king who came for hunting, the minister who came for a holiday, or a party or entertainment, the villagers were the ones to bear the brunt of their demands. The treasury usually releases some money for the chickens, goats, butter, and ghee. No one knows where that money vanishes. Just as the water drops falling in a desert, it disappears into some officer's pocket.

The karanam started verifying who took the turn to supply chickens in the past and, unable to decide, asked the Madiga, "Whose turn is it today?"

"It was the Salees[184] last time, sir."

"Alright. Then go to the beggars today." Madiga obediently went on his way. Every officer who lands in the village goes after the beggars first. Usually, these beggars were criminal tribes. Their criminal background made them vulnerable to exploitation by the officers. Generations ago, their grandfathers or great-grandfathers would have been dacoits or robbers. For crimes committed by their forefathers, today's generation – that lived on selling mats, digging wells or tending to farms -remained branded as a criminal

184 Salee or Sale community are weavers.

tribe and always open to being exploited. The officers – who exploit them for their selfish gains – are treated as embodiments of justice by society.

Madiga, who went to fetch the beggars, returned saying they had all gone for work, and none could be seen. The jawan was livid. The anticipation for a chicken had now turned into anger. "What the hell?" he emerged outside the chavadi. Madiga was rattled completely. "What? If they went for work, have their chickens also accompanied them?" he smacked Madiga. Madiga lost his balance for a second, recovered his composure and was about to run.

"Stay there! I will kill you!" The jawan shouted. Madiga froze in his tracks. "Now, I want the truth. Where have the beggars gone?"

"They are very much at home, Sir." Madiga was trembling now.

"Then, why did you say no one was there?"

Madiga was about to touch the jawan's feet, pleading for mercy.

"Will you now go and return this moment with the chicken or not?"

"Of course, sir," Madiga nodded feebly. His hair was dishevelled, and he could barely control his anger. He dashed like a madman towards the beggars' huts.

When he arrived, the chickens were feeding on grain on the floor. He threw the stick randomly without knowing which chicken he would hit. Instantly, one rooster fell. When she heard the noise, an old lady—watching over the chickens—came running, fell on Madiga's feet, and started pleading.

"Is your chicken more important than a human life?" Madiga pushed her aside, grabbed the bird and left.

The cooking was done. Hearing that the Tahsildar was due to come, all the farmers gathered near the chavadi and waited for him. Hours passed, and the sun started setting in the west. The farmers remained there. They could neither go on their chores nor eat as none was sure when precisely the officer would come. Some instructed the others to wake them up when the officer arrived and settled under the tree for a nap. Some napped even while sitting. Some were into lazy conversation.

One farmer said, "Fellows, this jawan is already snoring. What if the officer comes now?"

"I doubt if any officer will come today. Look! He ate all that was cooked."

"If he comes, what will he feed him?"

"He knew that the officer wouldn't come. That's why he ate it all."

"So, just for his meal, would he torment so many people?"

"What can we do? We must believe even if it is unbelievable. How many such experiences didn't we have in the past?"

"Alright. There are so many things to take care of. Let us get moving now," one farmer said. Another and then more followed him, and soon, they were all gone.

The following day, the jawan started the theatrics again. "Where is the firewood?" he rushed at Madiga. "There," Madiga showed him the bundle of logs near his pillow. "Very good. This is how the government's work must be done. You fellows always complain about us. But why don't you complain when the komati doesn't supply the material to the officer? You cry when we beat you up. Why don't you cry when hungry? Only the crying baby gets the mother's milk. Go and fetch the komati quickly," He ranted. Madiga nodded and went.

The day progressed. "Yesterday, you gave a false alarm and wasted my material. The officer could have had his meal today if those items had not been spent yesterday. I am not giving the same supplies again," the komati remained adamant.

"Did anyone stop him yesterday from coming? Nagaiah, this will not look good. Look! Madigas already have a lot of complaints about you. If the officer hears..." the jawan didn't complete his sentence. Suddenly, all the farmers got up and spoke in a chorus, "There is the officer!" A tall horse could be seen galloping in on the horizon. Farmers started moving aside to let the horse in. The karanam adjusted his dress. The jawan checked if his badge was in place. The komati rushed to get the supplies. The horse came in panting and stopped in front of the chavadi. "Hey, is it you, Ali? So, you are the officer! Get off the horse and see how I will thrash you!" the jawan pulled the rider, Saisu, down from the horse.

"As long as I am riding the officer's horse, I am the officer!" quipped Saisu. The karanam's face went pale. He cursed himself for being tricked by the false alarm, readjusted his dress and felt relieved. Saisu handed the horse to Madiga and warned, "Before the officer comes, wipe the skin neat. Otherwise, he will skin you alive. Have you kept the fodder and water ready? What do I have to lose? When the officer comes, I will push you in front."

"So, tell me. Will the officer come today?"

"Who knows? They have a motor car. They can come whenever they want."

"I better get going then," the jawan said, collecting the supplies and getting busy with cooking. The farmers, who were downcast and feared today would also be a no-show day, felt a little cheered.

Just as they were anxious about their problems, the poor farmers assumed that the officer would also be equally anxious and he would fix all their problems. More than the good or bad of administration, the people believed in the office buildings, the officers' dresses and the dozens of files in their cupboards. They remained under the illusion that the officers had all the power and spirit of justice that they themselves lacked. It is always the vulnerability and ignorance in humans that leads to one becoming superior while the other remains inferior and dominated. The waiting was finally over, and the motor car arrived, making a loud whirring noise. The jawan dispersed the farmers as if the air that touched them might pollute the officer if it touched him. Farmers stayed away and waited for the officer's word. The officer signalled the karanam to come closer, handed a paper to him, and asked him to sign it.

The karanam didn't want to offend the officer by reading the note in detail. He just gave a cursory glance and signed it with a trembling hand. Even the brief look made his face ashen when he understood the import of the contents. When he recovered a bit, the car started. When the car started, the farmers, who were standing with folded hands, desperately followed the car as if the God who was supposed to deliver boons was flying away, and if they didn't catch hold of him, their hardships would never end. "Sir! What about us? Please, one minute!" These pleas were drowned in the sound of the engine. The car vanished, leaving a massive cloud of dust in its wake. As soon as the car disappeared, the karanam felt a big load on his chest and went to the jawan to try and get some relief.

"What, my dear fellow? Why did he make me sign the indent for chickens and sheep again? Who is coming this time?"

"Who needs to come? It appears you folks don't know..."

"Don't know what?"

"It is the officer sir's daughter's wedding!"

"It is the officer sir's daughter's wedding!" the words emerged reflexively from the mouths of all the shocked farmers gathered around the karanam.

*****

In Our Village Too?

Original Author: Kanchanapalli Chinavenkata Rama Rao. First Published in Telugu in 1945.

The midday sun was scorching the earth. The intense heat could pop a grain of paddy. The heat in the Nalgonda district topped them all. No other place comes close.

Despite the local fund being paid, the fate of the village road remained the same. The sandy road was gleaming in the bright sun, and the Vaisakha[185] month was burning at its peak.

The bullock cart was trying to maintain a speed of at least ten miles per hour. The sound of the jingling bells in the bulls' necks was in harmony with their footfalls. The dust thrown up by the cart was forming mini clouds.

Notwithstanding the dust clouds entering his eyes and nose, Madiga[186] Papaiah ran ahead of the cart as if a demonic force were driving him. The stick on his

185 Second month in the Indian calendar. Corresponds to April-May.

186 Madiga was a low caste as per India's old caste hierarchy.

shoulder, with the lantern hanging at one end, faithfully accompanied him.

With the bag of his master's clothes on his head, washerman Sarvaiah was running behind the cart, trying to catch his breath, sweat pouring out of his skin.

Papa Rao Dora[187] was dozing off in the cart, comfortably cocooned on a soft mattress and cushioned on all sides by pillows.

His massive frame was settled comfortably in the cart. His bulging cheeks, a moustache that could hold lemons, and shining black skin—having rarely been exposed to the sun—were a sight to behold.

"Why are you driving it slowly? Increase the speed!"

This little warning was enough for servant Venkanna to whip the bulls a couple of times.

The cart picked up speed. Papaiah and Sarvaiah had to increase their speed to keep up.

When the master was dozing, Papaiah and Sarvaiah reached an agreement with the dora's servant, Venkanna (they usually don't have any surnames). The result of the agreement was for Venkanna to get as much toddy as he could drink.

All he had to do was to reduce the speed of the cart. That would give some rest to the bodies of poor Papaiah and Sarvaiah, sweating it out under the hot sun.

---

187 Dora refers to a high-ranking officer (Indian or British), rich landlord or owner.

It would also save them from the thrashing they would receive in the Dora's hands for not keeping up with the cart.

But the agreement was broken, never mind who was responsible. The cart picked up speed in that blazing sun. And Papaiah and Sarvaiah were forced to keep pace. The Dora's limitless power, authority and violent temper – guarded by his servant Venkanna, with a stick in his hand – cast their brutal shadows on Papaiah and Sarvaiah.

I was going to meet my friend in the Dora's village. He was serving as a poor school teacher. I had set out with my old bicycle, whose tyre punctures were ready to open up anytime under the scorching heat.

The village was ten miles from the town. One needed a vehicle or to traverse it on foot. Since my legs could only go so far, I had no option but to use the old bicycle. On that terrible road, I couldn't keep pace with the cart. I was drenched in sweat. With the fear of humiliation—of lagging behind the cart—haunting me, I put all my energy into propelling the bicycle faster.

"Hey! Dora Garu is in the cart. You will be scaring the bulls by coming closer. Stay away!" Warned Venkanna sternly. This was when my dearest possession, the ten-year-old bicycle, was out of sight of the bulls behind the cart. In the kingdom of these carts, bicycles or cars had no option but to give way to the cart. I learned later that – if one encountered the Dora's cart – one must get off the bicycle and walk. Riding was forbidden.

Like an oasis in a desert, Dora's village, Kadapuram, appeared ahead of us. Everyone heaved a sigh of relief.

I went to my friend's house. He was staying close to where the washermen and barber community lived.

Behind me, Papaiah – with his shrunk stomach – and Narsaiah packed half-kilo maize and reached home.

We finished our lunch following the age-old tradition (now forgotten) of eating a meal with three portions of water and one portion of rice if one ventured out in the intense heat. I was on the veranda of my friend's house fixing my bicycle tyres, where punctures had come off.

A middle-aged man – with a sharp stick in hand and a badged belt around his waist – was calling out Sarvaiah's name, "Hey Sarva!"

"What, Kasim?" Sarvaiah stepped out.

"Patwari[188] Saheb is going to Nalgonda on official duty. It is your turn to carry his files. Come."

"You must be kidding! Isn't it just now that I carried the Dora's clothes bag? I haven't eaten yet! Don't you know Narsi? It is his turn now."

"He went to the Amin's office to hand over the commissions collected from the cowherds."

---

188 Patwari refers to village record keeper / accountant in the erstwhile Hyderabad / Telangana territory.

"What about other fellows like Seethi, Naari or others?"

"Some went to carry the palanquin, some went to grind the flour for the small Dora's event, and some went to draw rangolis. It is your turn now!"

"Kasim! Only yesterday, my turn came. Again, so soon?"

"What do you want me to do, brother? I have been running around since morning without a break to find someone. This is never-ending. If it is not the older Dora, it is the younger Dora. If it is neither of them, it will be the Patel, Patwari or the police inspectors who come to line their pockets. Where do I have time?"

I was busy with my work, lending an ear to this conversation. There was a puncture on top of an old puncture, and I was busy deciding whether to remove the old one or apply the new patch.

Suddenly, there were cries of "Oh God! Oh God!" from Narsaiah's house. My friend and I went to take a look. My friend commented that I had yet to get rid of the village habits and imbibe the town habits where one never cared about what was happening around him.

There was no time for us to indulge in criticism and counter-criticism.

We could see a pig-mouthed man beating up Narsaiah using the filthiest of abuses. His merciless blows were landing on Narsaiah's body without caring which vital organs would be hit. Narsaiah – worried about spilling the freshly mixed porridge – was trying to dodge Kasim's blows with the bronze bowl in hand.

"If it were me, I would slam the bowl on that pig and beat the daylights out of him. One must admire his patience! Why is Narsaiah so quiet?" I asked my friend.

"This is Kadapuram. Not your town. Why should we get entangled in this mess? Keep quiet. This is a routine affair," my friend said.

The neighbours gathered soon.

They started pleading with the man who was raining the blows, "Pantulu, stop now. He is an elderly man. We beg your mercy. Leave him alone." But there was no stopping the blows that were landing on Narsaiah. No one had the courage to intervene and stop the beating.

Suddenly, Kasim Saheb lunged forward. Blocking the stick with his stick, he asked, "What? Will you kill him, Maharaj?"

That was when we felt a little emboldened. We dragged Pantulu outside the hut. Pantulu was sweating profusely and shaking with anger. His dhoti knot came off. Speech eluded him, and he collapsed and sat down.

"Such a mad fury is not good, Pantulu!" the gathered farmers were trying to pacify him.

Pantulu Garu glared at Kasim and said, "If I don't get your piece of gifted land seized in the next survey, I am not born to my father! You Turk!" and rushed to his house.

"Do whatever, Maharaj! Is that land my only source of livelihood? I will live on my bullock cart in Nalgonda if my hands are in good shape." Kasim retorted.

Narsaiah kept the porridge bowl on the ground and started applying soil to his bleeding injuries – perhaps as first aid. He had a large injury on the head.

"Other than crying, this fellow is good for nothing. He couldn't even give it back verbally," I complained to my friend.

"These fellows are tough, so they have been putting up with this torture. Someone like you would have bolted long ago. Your town folks are as fast as a snake and timid as a centipede," My friend counter-attacked.

In the meantime, some young men and women arrived. With their muscular, Greek-statue-like bodies, they looked capable of shining in life if only they had freedom. Freedom would have helped their minds to develop along with their bodies. Injury marks were visible on their bodies, and many parts were swollen.

"What is this Sarvanna?" They asked. "What about the injury marks on your bodies?" Sarvayya countered.

"Dora beat us up with a cane because drops of paint fell on the mirror when we were whitewashing."

"Because we didn't grind the chilli powder soft enough, Dorasani[189] threw the powder in our eyes."

"Patel beat us up with a stick as the clothes were not delivered on time."

"Younger Dora threw a slipper at me, accusing me that the flour was coarse. It hit me on the breast. How can I feed my child now, Thatha[190]?" cried a woman.

A dazed Narsaiah could only say, "Our own sins are catching up with us."

"What virtues have these Doras amassed for them to torture us like this? Just because we are tolerating, they are taking us for granted," said one youth.

"There is no one we can turn to. They are the ruling class. What can we do?" sighed a despaired Narsaiah.

"We can't sit back and take it anymore, Thatha! Something must be done!" Emotions were running high among the gathered crowd.

"I heard that in some other village, they abolished vetti[191]. I believe when the workers united, even the Doras were helpless," said another.

"Your hot blood is making you say such things. There are some unions, I believe. We had never heard

---

189 Dorasani – Usually a Dora's wife or a female landlord / owner

190 Thatha – Grandfather or any elderly gentleman in the community.

191 Vetti – Bonded labour/slavery

such things before. Why do we want to play with that fire now?" Narsaiah said.

"Whatever it is, we must bring that 'fire' into our village," the youth said in one voice.

"The rest of our lives will be spent in police cases and jail. The entire government will land on us like a ton of bricks. I suggest we live quietly within our means," Sarvaiah tried to reason it out. Perhaps he could visualise the ramifications of any uprising.

"Thatha! We heard that you killed a tiger with just a stick in your youth. Why are you preaching this cowardice today? No jail will be worse than our lives," the youth retorted.

"I remember the proverb, *be a man and live just for three days*. I underestimated these folks. Each one has a volcano in their hearts!" I said to my friend.

"It is your turn to be fooled now," my friend quipped.

The mud sticking to a pensive Narsaiah's wounds was falling off. Other elders also gathered to debate the next course of action.

"Respecting your status as clan-elders, we asked for your opinion. This problem won't go away so easily. So far, we have gone by your ruling. Now, our word must prevail," the gathered youth said in one voice.

Soon, there was a clamour for the vetti to be eliminated and some drastic action to be taken.

Senior farmer Rangaiah came forward and said he would stand with the victims. Other farmers supported Rangaiah and joined him.

With the Dora's servant chasing him, Madiga Papaiah came running in, struggling to catch his breath.

"Rascal is refusing to clean the horse and get the plough ready," Dora's servant complained.

Papaiah joined the group. When he heard the united voice, he was reassured.

"Am I your servant to ready the plough?" he snapped.

"Scoundrel! How dare you say that?"

"Mind your tongue! These are *my* folks here. Be careful. If you want to retain your respect, get going. Leave! "

I couldn't hold myself back from saying, "Well done!" The hapless servant went back.

With the Tehsil peon on one side and the beat police jawan on the other side chasing them, potter Narsaiah and Kasim came running and joined the group.

Their crimes were not keeping water in the chavadi[192] and not bringing the chickens.

"Hey! Lisen carefully! One word against Kasim or Narsaiah, we will not tolerate anymore!" the group said in unison.

192 Chavadi – Community Hall.

"Is it so, my son? You seem to think you arrived from England just today! Come with me to the Dora. Patel and Patwari are also present there. Your bones will be smashed."

"Same treatment will be given right here and right now," came the strong reply.

The peon and jawan tried to bully. They didn't know the world had suddenly changed and had to beat the retreat.

"We will not do this bonded labour anymore. What can they do to us? Will they chop our heads off and hang them? Let us go and ask, come!" Sarvaiah, Papaiah, Narsaiah, Kasim and others started heading out. The entire village followed them.

"Down with vetti!" slogans rented the air. The crowd moved like an ocean.

With his lemon-holding moustache drooping down, Dora said to the Patel and Patwari – "This fire! In our village, too?"

*****

Narasanna's Daughter

Original Author: Adivi Bapiraju. First Published in Telugu in 1946.

My elder brother thrashed him when he tried to enter the Rudreswaram temple during the Shivaratri festival. My brother thrashed him! My brother clobbered him!

True. That boy was a Harijan[193]. But how did that give my brother a license to thrash him? What was his fault? He tried to enter the Rudreswaram temple on the Shivaratri day with the rest of us.

We took a dip in the tank, put on our silk clothes and set out to Rudreswaram carrying fruits, coconuts, flowers, incense sticks and camphor. Rudreswaram was about eight miles from our village. We started in the night on carts. We reached Rudreswaram early in the morning before sunrise. Our bullock cart doubled up as our tent. We tied screens all around for privacy. My mother made the preparations for cooking. After that, we stepped into the pond when the sun was rising.

193 Harijan was the name given to Dalits/untouchables in Indian society in order to give dignity to their lives.

That boy lived in our village's malapalle[194], and his father was a paleru[195] of our village's karanam[196].

His cries – when my brother was thrashing him – would melt even rocks. I wept inconsolably. Unable to bear the beating, he fainted. I ran to him and sprinkled water from my pitcher. He got up, wept in a heart-rending way and teetered off.

I continued to hear Narasanna's screams. The mantras being rendered by the temple priest resembled his cries. The bells tolling in the temple resembled his screams. I was eight then. Although I was young, when my brother was thrashing Narasanna, I felt as if he was thrashing me. I wondered if my brother would beat me up, too.

"Hey Ramana! Why are you still crying?" my mother asked severely.

"She needs a couple of blows to keep her quiet," Snapped my brother. So much anger! No wonder I was scared of my brother. We waded through the milling crowds and emerged from the temple.

Narasanna's shrieks, the swelling crowds, the sounds of drums and trumpets, the shouts 'Shivoham! Shivoham!' by the frenzied devotees, my silent tears, my brother's scolding, my mother's rebuke, Narasanna's

---

194 Malapalle: Hamlet outside the main village where Malas (untouchables) used to say.

195 Paleru: Subtenant who tilled the land for a land owner or tenant.

196 Karanam: Village accountant/record keeper.

crying! My brother thrashed him because he wanted to enter the temple.

Narasanna grew up. I, too, grew up. I got married. Narasanna also got married.

The image of that thrashing remained etched in my mind forever. In my marriage, the memories came back. When Narasanna's marriage was announced, I remembered it again!

Narasanna became the head-paleru for my in-laws and the head of the malas in the village. But the memory of his crying when my brother beat him up stayed with me as a loyal friend. That also formed a strange and sacred bond between me and Narasanna.

I never forgot the fact that my brother thrashed Narasanna. My brother forgot it, though. Even though they watched the beating along with me, my parents forgot about it, too. Finally, Narasanna also forgot.

"What Narasanna! I hear your wife is pregnant!"

"Yes, Khamandu[197] Garu[198]!" his face blossomed like a flower.

Narasanna grew up to be a tall and muscular man, like a well-sculpted figure from a black stone.

Narasanna remained illiterate. But his advice was as valuable as Thimmarusu's[199] advice!

197 Khamandu: Owner, Landlord.

198 Garu: Sir, Ji (Hindi), respectfully addressing someone.

199 Thimmarusu: Legendary minister in Emperor Krishnadeva Raya's court known for his sound political and strategic mind.

I took the lead in making Narasanna our paleru. We benefited immensely from his becoming our paleru. There was no other piece of land as fertile as ours in that village.

When Narasanna was about to enter the Rudreswaram temple on Shivaratri day, my brother thrashed him!

How many Malas and Madigas before and after him were not thrashed by upper-caste people?

How many Malas and Madigas didn't convert to Christianity?

Why should Malas and Madigas stay away from us? Do they pollute us with their touch? I used to ask Narasanna's wife to come closer and comb my hair when no one was watching. Rathalu initially dismissed my request with a peal of laughter. When I continued pleading and pretended anger, she finally yielded and combed my hair. I felt a thrill running through my body. It was as if Narasanna had entered the Rudreswaram temple. I, who entered the temple but wasn't there! Narasanna, who tried to enter but was beaten up by my brother! Narasanna's wife combed my hair! I combed Rathalu's hair!

It was election time. The fight was between the Congress party and the communists.

Among the Malas and Madigas –now called Harijans – there was a triangular contest among Congress, communists and some other federation.

My husband asked Narasanna to contest the elections. He belonged to the Congress. Narasanna didn't study when he was young, but my husband taught him later. His education was great. It began with the thrashing he received from my brother outside the Rudreswaram temple.

Each day, many Harijans are getting beaten up outside temples, in markets and fields!

Can they see any God? Do Lord Venkateswara, Chidambara Swamy, Ramalingeswara and Sri Ranga Sai manifest themselves in front of these Harijans? Our Rudreswara never appeared in front of Narasanna!

Narasanna's wife is pregnant. Will it be a boy or a girl? That child will never get to see Rudreswara!

"Rathalu, I will teach you. Will you study?" I asked her a few days after Narasanna became our paleru.

"Why do I need education, Khamandu Garu?" Rathalu guffawed. I didn't give up easily. I made her read 'Veera Valladu[200]'.

My parents educated me well. I studied English at home. My husband went to Bandar[201] to study Intermediate, failed the exam, and returned to pursue agriculture.

---

200 A famous drama written by the great Telugu poet Viswanatha Satyanarayana.

201 Bandar literally means a port. Another name for Machilipatnam, a port town in Andhra Pradesh.

He pulled me closer one day and said – as if talking to himself, "Ramana! Our Narasanna is a Harijan. They have been suffering for centuries. Aren't they humans like us, Ramana?"

"My brother thrashed Narasanna!"

"When?" He sounded anxious.

"In our childhood. He was about to enter the Rudreswara temple. My brother knew him. He thrashed him." Remembering that episode, tears flowed down my cheeks.

My husband hugged me and said, "Your heart is pure and soft, Ramana!" I blushed with deep happiness when he kissed me.

"I combed Narasanna's wife's hair." My eyes betrayed fear and a look of teasing.

My husband's embrace became tighter. Why would he care if my blouse knot came off or if I was coy? Naughty boy!

"Rathalu will hold a baby soon!" His gaze penetrated my eyes.

My eyelids dropped suddenly.

"Will that baby enter the Rudreswaram temple?" I asked.

"Rudreswaram? It is like entering Kashi Visweswara temple!"

"People like my brother will not beat up that baby, right?" I asked with my heart trembling.

Rathalu had a difficult delivery. An anxious Narasanna was not himself.

My husband called a senior doctor to assist with the delivery.

Rathalu was brought from the hut in her hamlet to our house. Our grain-pounding room became the delivery room.

After a three-hour effort by the doctor, Narasanna's daughter made her entry into this world and cried.

I ran inside to take a look. The baby was making a flutter, shaking her legs and arms.

Another Harijan baby arrived in this world. That, too, in a hamlet cut off from the village. She will have torn clothes and no oil to condition her hair. He will not have education! She will be malnourished! She would also end up getting beaten by someone like my brother if she tried to enter the Rudreswaram temple.

I was sweating profusely, and my heart was beating rapidly. Didn't my brother thrash Narasanna on a Shivaratri day when he tried to enter the Rudreswaram temple?

After a few days, the Harijan baby and her mother left for their hamlet. The baby morphed into a baby Krishna in fifteen days. With curly hair, a round nose and dark lips resembling ivy gourd, she was a sight to behold. It was beautiful to watch her rolling on the cotton bed with her tiny belly, small legs and arms and shell-like fingers. My husband and I used to visit Narasanna's house at night to see the baby.

I gave them my sarees and bedsheets. I stitched many frocks for the baby. Whenever I saw that baby, my husband appeared to be a small baby to me. My blouse used to stretch itself as if it would come off.

I heard that the villagers were accusing us of tainting our caste. Everyone revered and feared my husband, who embodied Lord Rama with his tall frame, handsome looks, golden hue and gentle demeanour. Still, it didn't stop them from accusing us.

They were the kind of people who would thrash a Harijan boy if he tried to enter a temple, just as my brother did long ago on a Shivaratri day. Ever since we brought Narasanna's wife to our house for delivery, my brother stopped visiting us. Now Narasanna is my brother! "Yes, Ramana! Born to that Rudreswara, he is your brother! He is feeding us!" my husband said with a gentle smile.

My husband is God himself!

Narasanna won the election. He became a member of the Chennapatna[202] Legislative Assembly.

That day, my husband hosted a feast for Congress leaders and other key people in the village. Narasanna sat next to my husband at the feast.

Our Narasanna, Narasanna Garu, is now an MLA. Will my brother beat him up even now, outside the Rudreswaram temple? Maybe! My brother is capable of anything!

---

202 Old name for Madras. Now called Chennai.

My husband spent five hundred rupees to convert the grain-pounding room into a house and accommodated Narasanna. His baby became the closest to me.

Narasanna's wife Rathalu—Ratnamma—and I started spinning Khadi. My husband had been doing it for a long time. My brother Narasanna, sister-in-law Ratnamma, niece Bharatamba, and I have started wearing Khadi.

Brother Narasanna and his family are now eating good food and wearing good clothes. The blows my brother landed on his body outside the Rudreswaram temple have become blessings for Brother Narasanna.

Should all the Harijans in India get beaten up by my brother outside the Rudreswaram temple?

Should all the Harijans in India become MLAs to earn a decent life?

I forgot to tell you. Narasanna's baby is under my care now. It is said that if childless people adopt others' babies, they will soon be blessed with a baby themselves. Bharatamba spends all her time with me. She calls me 'Athha[203]!' When she falls asleep next to me some days, her mother comes and takes her in the night.

One day that naughty Bharatamma did something that I had never experienced before! When my blouse knot came off, she grabbed my golden treasures, my milk pots, my hard projections and the beautiful pair that remained hitherto useless and started sucking the

203 Aunt

nipples. I woke up with a thrill that spread through my body and an ecstasy I had not known before! I saw her sucking away at my nipples in her sleep.

I quickly came to my senses, stopped her and checked if my husband was asleep. Once assured, I gave a gentle slap on her backside, called her mother and handed her over.

From that day onwards, I started having daily dreams! In two months, I missed my period. My baby, my Bharatam, blessed me.

Rathalu's joy was boundless. My husband – elated and glowing like a full moon - worshipped me like a Goddess!

Nine months later, I was blessed with a baby girl. It was like moonlight packaged into human form.

"May God bless her! She looks like her father fully, Vadina[204] Garu!" said Ratnamma while bathing the baby.

My baby girl is Bharatamba's sister-in-law. She is the embodiment of my husband's love and full of the compassion that was present in Narasanna's cries when my brother beat him up. We named her Poorna Swarajya Lakshmi[205].

*****

204 Vadina: Sister-in-law. Elder Brother's wife.
205 Poorna Swarajya Lakshmi: Goddess of total freedom.

To Whom?

Original Author: Madapati Hanumantha Rao. First Published in Telugu in 1912.

1

"We don't have a job at present that suits your qualifications. We want to keep you in our office, but there is not much we can do," Zamindar[206] Pratapa Varma Garu[207] told Mohan Rao in his royal splendour.

After leaving college, Mohan Rao was forced to find some suitable employment. His desire was to find a job where he could pursue the path of integrity, combine earning with social service, and work for the welfare of his fellow humans. He ruled out joining a government office as it didn't give him the opportunity to be in touch with common people. The legal profession would serve both purposes, but – despite one's best efforts – it was tough to remain uncorrupted. So, he ruled out being a lawyer.

---

206 Zamindar: A feudal landlord in British India who collects revenue from farmers and pays taxes to the Government.

207 Garu: Sir, Ji, suffix demoting respect in Telugu.

Police job gave the opportunity to be kind towards the poor. But the atmosphere in a police department doesn't lend itself to honesty and good behaviour. This, too, was ruled out. After exploring several options, he finally concluded that serving a zamindar was the best option. *If I join any zamindar in a key role – even at a lower salary – I will get the opportunity to mingle with the poor farmers all the time. I can work for their welfare. I can live a simple life without being flashy. This is the best course of action for me.* Having thus decided, he sought an audience with the famous zamindar Pratapa Varma and requested that he employ him in a suitable role. And the zamindar replied as above.

"There is no need for a special role for me," Mohan Rao said modestly. "I am ready to do any work. You can pay me as you wish. I have decided not to work anywhere other than in a zamindar's office."

"Consider working with a zamindar not as being a servant but as being a lord." Pratapa Varma Garu proudly proclaimed. "Look! I pay four rupees per month to a chaprasi[208]. He wears silk coats. There are horses in his house. My clerk earns eight rupees. They are building relationships with lawyers! I don't know what miracle exists in their earning. They never care to check how much salary they are earning even years after being employed. Many request me to employ them as chaprasis and clerks without salary! But that is not

208 Chaprasi: Office messenger or peon who runs all kinds of errands.

our culture. What do you think of our Mukhtyar[209] job? It is almost like being a second zamindar! Same splendour! Same opulence! Same grandeur! Someone who tastes this job will discard even a Tahsildar[210] job!"

Mohan Rao should have ideally nodded his head, saying, "Yes, sir." But he didn't do that. Not being worldly-wise, he said, "I never worked before in any zamindari[211]. I finished college recently. I am not seeking a job because of the reasons you mentioned. But I would like to make one thing clear. Such a small salary will not do for me. Your employees could be fleecing poor farmers and making their money. I will not be able to do that. If it is possible for a person of integrity to get encouragement, I believe I will soon be considered favourably."

Pratapa Varma: "Alright. But a higher salary is not possible!"

Mohan Rao: "In that case, please forgive me. Perhaps it is not possible to find a forthright person so cheap!"

Zamindar pondered. *There was always the work of filing documents in the courts. A lot of expenditure was anyway being incurred on translation to English. This fellow looks naive. And he knows English. There*

---

209 Mukhtyar: Administrative head of a set of villages reporting to the zamindar.

210 Tahsildar: Government employee who controls a few villages and reports to the district collector.

211 Zamindari: A zamindar's territory / office / estate.

is no harm in paying a slightly higher salary. But a response is due now. So, zamindar Garu said,

"Pantulu[212] Garu! A straightforward person never strays from this path, regardless of how low the salary is. Similarly, a dishonest fellow can never become straightforward, regardless of how high his salary is. Honesty and money don't have a correlation. I have seen many honest chaprasis. And I have seen many corrupt high court judges. Let it be. I can employ you as a Mukhtiyar for some of my villages. Your salary can go up depending on your performance."

Mohan Rao agreed to a salary of twenty rupees. He was appointed as the Mukhtiyar of Timmajipet Patti[213] on behalf of the zamindar.

2

To Mohan Rao, the job seemed like 'lordship' – just as the zamindar described. A lovely bungalow with plenty of tables, chairs and beds was provided. Many chaprasis, a horse cart for travel and plenty of other paraphernalia were at his disposal. But these luxuries didn't enthuse Mohan Rao. When there were countless thatched huts around him, the bungalow life didn't give him any comfort. When the people in the huts were using clay pots, the presence of expensive vessels in his house didn't appeal to him. When the poor around him lived with sagging cots, the four-poster beds in his bungalow

212 Pantulu: Teacher or Brahmin. In the past, brahmins and teachers were typically addressed this way.

213 Patti: Set of villages with Thimmajipet as headquarters.

didn't interest him. While the farmers lived in constant fear about small issues, the grand services provided by his team of servants didn't make him happy. He was constantly pained by the island of luxury in the ocean of poverty.

The day Mohan Rao joined the service and entered the bungalow, the farmers brought him gifts. He wouldn't touch anything—not even a penny! They were surprised and happy at his behaviour, but the chaprasis found it distasteful. The village barber came to massage his feet, but he was told his services were not required and sent back. The cowherds sent a potful of milk, but it was sent back. The gardener brought a bunch of betel leaves. Mohan Rao turned it away, saying he didn't have the habit of chewing them.

The farmers whispered among themselves, 'This man seems very righteous.' Regardless of who appreciated or rejoiced at his behaviour, the chaprasis couldn't tolerate it. They boldly told Mohan Rao, "Sir! It is alright if you don't want to accept these gifts. But stopping this tradition is not good. Any future officers may have difficulty in restarting the same."

Mohan Rao said nonchalantly, "Let the future fellows find their own ways. Why should I worry about their predicament?"

One chaprasi mustered courage and said, "Sir! These farmers are not as poor as you think. They are just pretending. That's all! They seem like horn-less cows. But each one is the equivalent of a high court lawyer!"

Mohan Rao wasn't moved by the chaprasis' argument. He began dealing with each farmer in a soft manner, showing a lot of kindness in matters that affected them. He would dispense medicines to them from seven to nine in the morning, and then he would get busy with his accounts.

With his behaviour, he conquered the hearts of the farmers. Previously, the zamindari was forced to attach the properties of the farmers due to non-payment of taxes. This year, the revenue came in effortlessly. The poor had direct access to Mohan Rao, where they could relate their woes any time of the day.

3

Our Pratapa Varma Garu also had a soft corner for the farmers. He gave them seeds to sow and money for oxen and labour. In return, he would collect one to one and a half times from the harvest! That's all!

Under this regime, the Thimmajipet farmers owed the zamindar. Some harvested grain was still on the grain-threshing floor, and some reached the farmers' homes. His lordship called the farmers and rushed them to repay the dues.

"Your lordship! We can't pay the entire amount now. Please take some. We will pay the balance later. Our lives are anyway at your mercy!" the farmers pleaded.

Pratapa Varma refused. "This won't do. Pay the last paisa and then leave. Otherwise, I will not let you out. This has become a routine with you fellows!" he said sternly.

Old Papireddy said, "Sir, have your way. Do we have a choice? What do we need? The porridge belongs to your lordship. The hungry stomachs are ours. Throw some bits at us, and we will keep eating and remain at your service. As a matter of fact, everything belongs to his lordship, isn't it? We are labourers who toil in the fields and fill our stomachs with a little porridge!"

These words infuriated Sri Sri Pratapa Varma Garu. He was the king. How dare anyone question him? He clattered his teeth, and his eyes reddened with anger. "What are you fellows waiting for? Squeeze the ears of the arrogant old fellow!" he ordered the chaprasis.

His lordship might have said this only to threaten, but the chaprasis didn't waste any time. They were already peeved with the Thimmajipet farmers! Abdullah chaprasi lunged forward immediately and pushed old Papireddy, holding him by his neck. The old man fell face down on the floor. Papireddy's two young sons–who stood patiently until then–attacked Abdullah. The saheb's[214] kurta was torn, and he fell down. But his tongue remained busy hurling abuses!

Experienced Papireddy quickly realised things were getting out of hand. He stood up and pulled Abdullah away. He started scolding his sons. The sons didn't relent. Suddenly, Reddy fell on Varma Garu's feet. But it was too late. Papireddy's clever move was

214 Saheb: Muslim.

wasted. Pratapa Varma's eyes were breathing fire. He yelled at Papireddy.

"Scoundrel! Get lost! Don't stand in front of me! If you stay here for another minute, I will drink your blood!"

The old man's body didn't have any blood for his lordship to drink. But there was heat. He was hoping justice would be done. Hearing such harsh words, he replied, "Sir! In my old age, in your palace, I stand humiliated. And you are abusing me!"

Pratapa Reddy said, "This is nowhere close to the humiliation you really deserve. There is more to come. Wait and see!"

Papireddy's sons came forward and said loudly, "Sir, will you take the rupees or our pride?"

Pratapa Varma: "Let us see. I will take your rupees later. Let us test how great your pride is!"

4

Thimmajipet farmers returned to their village and were narrating the incident to Mohan Rao when Pratapa Varma's servants arrived and told him, "His lordship wants to see you."

Mohan Rao calmed the farmers, mounted the horse, and went to the zamindar's office.

Pratap Varma, with his eyes blazing, was sitting in his hall of public audience. The clerks and chaprasis surrounded him and were adding fuel to the fire. When he saw Mohan Rao, Varma looked at him sharply and asked, "Have you seen the actions of Thimmajipet farmers?"

Mohan Rao lowered his head and said, "I heard about the episode, sir. I felt very sad. They were never this arrogant!"

Pratapa Varma: "Sir! You are right. They were not. But this is the result of your company. You are like a school student. What do you know about the affairs of the world? If your attitude towards the farmers continues the same way, my zamindari will be ruined! This is all your doing. Right in front of this compound door, I had people hung upside down using ropes! Are you getting me? Not one dared to protest! Today, they had the nerve to attack my servant!

Mohan Rao replied humbly, "Sir, what is my fault in this? I have been very sad ever since I heard about this incident."

Pratapa Varma: "Whose fault is it, if not yours? You gave them a lot of lenience. You ended bonded labour. You have been hobnobbing with them as comrades and given them unlimited access. Can these lowly fellows appreciate and understand your behaviour? Listen to me! The morals you learn in books, schools and colleges are good enough only in theory. Things work differently in the real world. Alright! Whatever has happened has happened. Let it be. We must teach a lesson to these farmer fellows for their arrogance. What do you say?

You have not yet given them receipts for the amount they paid towards malgujari[215], have you?"

A shaken Mohan Rao replied, "No, sir. Receipts are ready and waiting for your signature."

A pleased Pratapa Varma said, "Very good. This is good news. Burn those receipts. Understood? Let us file a case against them, claiming their malgujari payments are overdue. Let us get their produce attached and harass them. That's the only way these fellows will understand the value of the grain! Adjust the amount collected so far against seeds and oxen dues. In your evidence statement, say 'the amount paid by them was not against malgujari dues. They paid old dues.' That's all."

Mohan Rao pondered. *The same pain, to avoid which I opted for a peaceful job in this remote area, is now overwhelming me. How can I harass these poor farmers? Is this how I am supposed to earn my livelihood? I cannot do this!*

He asked weakly, "Sir! Can this not be managed without my evidence?"

Pratapa Varma asked calmly, "Can't you say so much? What is your objection?"

Mohan Rao replied calmly, "I am in your employment. I am ready to fulfil my obligations. But I have never given evidence before. I feel this task is beyond me. Please forgive me!"

215 Malgujari: Land revenue tax

Pratapa Varma said firmly, "You must do this. Don't waver. Who else can douse the fire that you started?"

Mohan Rao said, "I don't have the habit of lying. I cannot give such evidence."

Blending contempt and placation in his voice, Pratapa Varma preached, "My dear friend! This is not lying. I don't indulge in false business. I have not asked you to say, 'The money was not received at all.' As the farmers owe me even otherwise, I am entitled to adjust their payment against old dues. I have that right. If such a simple sentence sounds like a falsehood to you, then you are being unfair. You are not familiar with the ways of the world yet. Please know that there is no room in this world for your kind of truthful behaviour. You are my employee. Do you agree that you must demonstrate some loyalty or not? You are well-educated. You have a bright future ahead. You have a long life ahead, and there are so many achievements waiting for you. If you start behaving like this now, you will end up encountering only sorrow and despair. Truthful behaviour is good indeed! But one must exercise it in a limited manner. Too much of anything must be shunned. Don't think unnecessarily. Just go with the times!"

Pratapa Varma was an old, experienced hand in worldly matters. Mohan Rao remained speechless, listening to his discourse. He was drowned in a sea of sorrow and didn't know what to do.

5

In the next fifteen days, a case was filed in the Munsif court against Thimmajipet farmers, and the respondents were served the summons. Every household was gripped by sorrow, and womenfolk were cursing his lordship. Men blamed their fate. On the day of the trial, the farmers gathered and travelled as a group to the court. Women, carrying their children, followed them as if a large calamity had befallen them. Were they thinking they would never see their husbands again?

Imagine Mohan Rao's plight! On one side, he had to deal with the zamindar's prodding and, on the other, the wailing of the poor farmers. After three days of mental agony, he decided. *This is my first test in life. If I fail now, I will never succeed in other tests life will put me through! I will not put innocent farmers to hardship for my personal gain. I will not!*

The trial took place in court. Mohan Rao was the chief witness. He was made to stand in the dock, and his testimony was recorded. His responses caused some flutter in the court, and everyone's attention was focused on him.

Judge: "Do you know you are in the presence of a judge?"

Mohan Rao: "Yes. I do."

Judge: "If you lie, you can be charged with perjury. Do you understand?"

Mohan Rao: "Yes. I do. Only if I lie."

Judge: "Are you saying under oath that the farmers paid the amount in full?"

Mohan Rao: "Yes, sir. The farmers don't owe a single rupee towards this year's harvest revenue."

Judge: "In that case, why did you not give them the receipts?"

Mohan Rao: "It was the owner's order."

After he learned that the cases against the farmers had been dismissed, Pratapa Varma was livid. "Ungrateful fellow! Scoundrel! How much I had tried to take care of him! Will a dog's tail ever become straight? He ruined me! It is our good luck that he quit handing over keys and documents to the clerk as soon as the judge delivered the verdict. Or else, the damage would have been much more!" he vented his ire.

Our Varma Garu was sitting on old dues, running into thousands of rupees from the farmers. *It was tough to collect that money. Those dues looked in danger of being written off now. Mohan Rao had been too nice and lenient towards the farmers. What would they be afraid of now?* When he considered the situation, he was crestfallen. He huddled with a few of his senior employees. The unanimous opinion was, 'If we expose the papers to the court now, more complications may arise, but the collection will not be possible. If the true intricacies in the calculations get exposed, it will put the dues of farmers from other areas also at risk!' Govinda! Govinda![216]

6

On the morning of the third day, when the zamindar was seated in his public audience hall, Thimmajipet farmers arrived as a group. The zamindar became nervous, thinking they were coming to pick up a fight. But none of them was carrying any stick. Pulla Reddy was leading the group. He greeted the zamindar with folded hands. His lordship felt he was dreaming.

With folded hands, Pulla Reddy said, "Dora[217] Garu, please forgive our mistake. We are your servants. We live at your mercy. Please continue to shower your kindness in future, too."

Mohan Rao is gone, and these fellows have fallen in line. Who can they turn to for support now? That rogue was the one who incited them! zamindar screamed at the farmers,

"Where is your leader and sponsor, Mohan Rao? I am curious about his well-being. Why is he not coming forward?"

Tears swelled in Pulla Reddy's eyes.

He said, "Dora Garu, please don't say anything about him. He is not a human. He is an angel. He didn't incite us. I swear on your feet. He always warned us

216 Govinda: God's name. It is very often used to express frustration, helplessness and loss.

217 Dora: Feudal Lord.

not to fight with the owner. He had never consumed even a glass of water from us. While leaving, he told us sternly, 'Calculate your dues to the owner and pay every last paisa!' You are our benefactor, and we live under your patronage. These bodies have grown thanks to your feeding. Hence, we request you to calculate our dues and tell us. We will not drink even water without repaying the last paisa."

The clerk opened the books, and the farmers opened the money bags. Six thousand rupees stared at the Zamindar, and not one rupee remained due. This was the result of fair practices! What could not be achieved with pressure and coercion was achieved with goodness.

When the farmers returned from the court, they considered paying their dues. They treated Mohan Rao as God. Would they hesitate when such a person ordered payment of dues? Some sold grain, and others cattle. Some pawned jewellery. They were ready to endure any hardship, but they could not ignore Mohan Rao's orders.

Pratapa Varma's eyes opened. He concluded that Mohan Rao might have lacked tact and pragmatism, but he was righteous and fair.

He never faced any issues with Thimmajipet farmers from that day onwards. There was never any money due.

Pratapa Varma lived a luxurious life. His five daughters' marriages took place lavishly. Except for

Thimmajipet, other regions paid their obeisance as before. The daily clashes and court cases happened routinely. Threats, scoldings, making people sit in the hot sun and squeezing their ears were routine. If not, being a zamindar is of what use?

Zamindar Garu aged slowly. His yelling and screaming were reduced. His bodily faculties were getting weaker. His interest in court matters was reduced and was substituted by listening to the Bhagavad Gita and serving monks. In such old age, a son was born to Varma Garu.

Diseases slowly took over his body. The movement of doctors increased. Medicines stopped showing any effect. Two and a half years passed like this. Physical and mental abilities declined, and hopes of living a long life dwindled. He could sense that his end was near.

To whom do I leave this large estate? None of my desires could be fulfilled. I could not see my son marrying. To whom do I hand over this child? Who will nurture this sapling? The child's mother, being a woman, doesn't know anything. The load of estate affairs is huge. How can a woman manage? There are plenty of clerks and servants. But to what end? Everyone is a cheat, scoundrel and selfish. Not one of them can be trusted. Giving custody to the court of wards has its own complications. Those fellows would look to extract their pound of flesh!

I had discovered a gem, but I discarded it, thinking it to be a cheap stone. I could not comprehend its value. How wonderful it would be if I could find that gem again. All my problems would be resolved, and I don't have to look anywhere else. I can keep this unfortunate child at his feet and plead with him to pardon me for my mistakes and nurture this child. I could have handed over my entire estate to him. His heart was filled with kindness and compassion. He would certainly take pity on this fatherless child. Oh God! Will I ever see such a nobleman again? I would wash his feet and sprinkle the water on my head. I would wet his feet with my tears. I would stretch my arms and seek his protection. He is the only one who can steer this sinking ship to a safe shore. Is it in my destiny to see him again? Pratapa Varma lamented.

The final moments arrived. Whenever he looked at the child's face, he was heartbroken. He constantly mumbled, "Where would that angel be?" But Mohan Rao couldn't be found.

"Mohan Rao, I have been a fool! I lost a gem like you! I was completely blinded. Come and save me from this ocean of sorrow. Take care of this child and the would-be widow," he mumbled.

Relatives surrounded him. Pratapa Varma glanced at them all. He couldn't discern genuine kindness or honesty in anyone's face. He closed his eyes again.

Zamindar's wife stood crying. She was unable to control her emotions and the flowing tears. She slightly regained composure and asked, "To whom are you handing over me and this child?" And immediately started crying inconsolably.

Zamindar: "T-o-w-h-o-m? T-o---M-o-h-a-n-a-r-a-o," and closed his eyes and never opened them again.

*****

We Are Better Off

Original Author: Kaloji Narayana Rao. First Published in Telugu in 1943.

"Why is Yellaiah garlanding us, applying Kumkum on our forehead and gently stroking us on the back instead of lashing with the whip?" The black ox asked the white ox without Yellaiah's knowledge.

The white ox replied, "Be patient. Observe things as they happen. How do I know?"

That day, the local branch members of the SPCA (Society for Prevention of Cruelty towards Animals) decided to hold their annual event. They planned a procession that involved the city's important people and some well-built cows, horses, and oxen. The two oxen that pulled Mallanna Seth's[218] cart were chosen for the honour. That was why their keeper, Yellaiah, decked them for the occasion instead of tying them to the cart.

The procession started at three in the afternoon with much fanfare and a guard of honour by the volunteers. Government employees ranging from

218 Seth: Wealthy merchant.

chaprasi to subedar, millionaires, paupers, educated and illiterate, doctors, lawyers, and representatives from all castes, religions, and sections of society led the way. Cows, bulls, and horses followed. Many elites in the group (elite owing to their wealth) knew the importance of the occasion as much as our two friends at the story's beginning. The poor black ox was forced to participate due to Yellaiah's pressure. Many elites in the group were participating as they were ordered by their superior officers. That was the only difference.

With much hubbub, the procession of bipedals and quadrupeds reached the city hall. Arrangements were already in place for a meeting. A top bureaucrat from the government presided over the meeting. The secretary of the society presented the annual report. The report contained details such as – how many hundreds of sticks (used to beat the animals) were broken and how many jatkamen[219] and cartmen were dragged to court and fined for employing weak and injured horses and oxen to pull the carts. The report did not mention the killing of many such weak animals because they didn't have the money to feed them. This was followed by articulate speeches by some elites about the hardships faced by animals and how to mitigate them. Of course, none knew what was good or bad for any animal. After the meeting, the elites inspected the animals that participated in the procession. They were used to living in palatial houses and commuting in motor cars. For

219 Jatkamen: drivers who drive a single-horse carriage known as jatka.

them, it was very amusing to see the animals. Some didn't even know the difference between a horse and a bull. After this fun was over, the elites returned to their bungalows and the animals to their shelters. Our black and white oxen, who enjoyed the first day of their life without having to pull a cart, returned to their shelter, escorted by Yellaiah. The poor black ox remained gloomy, not having gotten any answer to its question in the morning. Then the white ox said,

"Did you not understand today's farce? Let me explain. Some of these humans, especially those who earn thousands without doing any labour, have formed a society for our welfare. There is no direct relation between them and us in daily life. They are of the opinion that those who directly employ us for their livelihood, those who produce thousands of measures of grain with our help, and those who ride on us and on carts pulled by us – all these folks illtreat us, make us toil even when we are injured or unwell without giving us any treatment. As a result, they think we are suffering a lot. So, these society members, after a lot of effort, snatched thousands of sticks from our keepers. I understand they are dragging folks to court and having them punished for making weak, injured and unwell from among us work. But these people have no mercy on animals that get slaughtered every day. Perhaps they believe one-time slaughtering is like liberating from life's labours! They have no objection when thousands of chickens, sheep, cows and oxen get slaughtered daily to provide for their food. Such animals meant for slaughtering must be healthy, brawny, young and strong. I wonder what kind of animal welfare this is! And how is cruelty towards animals being prevented? Only they know. And what is the great favour this society has bestowed upon us? Our chained life starts from the day we forget mother's milk and learn to chew a little fodder. Our daily routine is fixed. We don't know what liberty is. Humans are enslaving us and making our lives miserable. We have no option other than being tied to a pole, eating the little grass that he throws at us and then serving him by pulling a cart or driving a plough or whatever other task he makes us do. Any resistance will be met by bone-crushing blows. We have been toiling; we are toiling, and we will continue to toil until our final moment. The root cause of our hardships is this chained life. And the cause of that restraint is human. How can the same human uplift us? The same human who believes only in his comfort and selfish interests and doesn't hesitate to chain us to achieve his ends, how can he prevent atrocities on us? Disgusting! This is nothing but a farce and fraud! What do you say? Do you agree?"

The black ox, who was listening to the white ox's speech calmly until then, replied,

"Most of what you said is true. But how better are the lives of these humans who torture us so much? A majority of them live in conditions far worse than ours. Except for the small minority of the rich (the root cause of everyone's hardships), millions of others live in abhorrent conditions. Among the animals, those that are free are anyway happy. The remaining, like us, get some fodder, flour, drinking water and shelter after the hard work we put in. Many humans who put in bone-crushing work daily don't have a place to live, clothes to wear according to their customs, and even water to drink. They starve all the time and lead disgusting lives as if they were born only to serve the rich. They don't have a society like the SPCA that we have. And they don't have butcher shops that could slaughter them in one go and relieve them of their misery. So, we are better off than them!"

The white ox was left speechless.

*****

The Bet

Original Author: Nandagiri Indira Devi. First Published in Telugu in 1941.

That evening, the friend group assembled in Seth Rajaram's house. After eating a nice meal, they engaged in jovial conversation, discussing many topics. A cheerful Seth[220] Rajaram lay on a white mattress, leaning on white pillows and smoking hookah. He joined the conversation whenever he felt like it. Servant Laxman, standing nearby, was pouring wine into empty glasses. His friends were acting stiff and deliberately going easy on the wine, expecting Seth to push them to drink more. Seth said, "Laxman! Bring the special bottle that I recently ordered." Laxman brought the bottle and filled the glasses again. Friends glanced at each other meaningfully. One friend asked, "Seth! The business seems to be booming!" Another replied while taking the glass handed by Laxman, "Of course, it must be. Would it be possible to get such an expensive wine otherwise?" Seth also took two sips from the glass and smiled.

220 Seth: Refers to a wealthy businessman or merchant.

As the glasses became empty, the mood turned more cheerful. They resumed a topic that was being discussed earlier.

"Say whatever you want to! Life imprisonment is dreadful. Instead, it is better to quickly kill by hanging," said Ramlal firmly.

"It is better to live somehow rather than be dead," said Narottam Das.

"Is the death penalty not better than living in a jail for life without any freedom?" Seth joined the debate.

"Both these penalties are condemnable in civilised countries. Their intent is common—either slowly or quickly taking human lives. But eliminating wrongdoers from this society, instead of reforming them, is like chopping off an injured finger," said Lalita Prasad, flicking the ash from his cigarette.

"True! To me, life imprisonment seems to be the better option," said Narottam Das.

When he looked at Seth, Seth assumed it was a challenge to his argument and said, "Lifelong in prison? You will not be able to stay for five years! Living a full life in isolation is not a joke!" He jumped fully into the debate now. Both were adamant about winning the argument, and the friends were adding fuel to the fire while watching the fun.

"Why five? I will stay for ten years if you ask me to," said Narottam Das.

"Alright! The bet is on! Two lakhs!" said Seth, unable to control himself.

"I am ready! Are you ready with two lakhs?" challenged Narottam Das.

"Absolutely!" replied Seth.

What else? The matter became serious. The friends prepared an agreement between Seth and Narottam Das that said Narottam Das must live in isolation for ten years in Seth Rajaram's orchard, and at the end of that period, Seth must give two lakhs to Narottam Das.

When the deal was done and closed, Seth realised his folly. "What have I done? Why this pointless expense of two lakhs?" He lamented. Friends teased him as a miser backtracking on his promise to save two lakhs. The embarrassed Seth agreed to abide without another word.

Narottam Das was allotted a separate room in the orchard. Seth will have no obligation to pay if his stay falls short of ten years by even a few minutes. The inmate can order whatever he needs and have it delivered. These include books, clothes, food, etc. To prevent any contact with the external world, all these items would be supplied through a window. The inmate could write letters if he chose to.

The inmate spent the first year in gloom and frustration. The chowkidar could hear him crying many times. After two or three years, he got used to the lonely life. He used to read books day and night. Seth had a tough time getting books ordered by the inmate.

The inmate didn't even have time to worry about his situation.

One day, he wrote a letter to Seth in prisoner language. He asked the letter to be shown to people who knew the languages in that letter. If there were no errors, he asked for a conch to be blown. The conch was blown as he had hoped.

Seth Rajaram was surprised at these developments. He never imagined the inmate would complete ten years of isolation. Nor did he imagine paying two lakhs. He assumed the inmate would commit suicide in the first year itself. But when he saw that four years had passed and, more importantly, the inmate was not experiencing the 'pain' of isolation, he began to worry.

Ten years will be complete by tomorrow morning. I must pay him two lakhs as per the agreement, thought Seth. Times don't remain the same. Seth, earning five hundred daily ten years ago, is finding it tough to make fifty now. With the business in losses, he was spending two rupees as if it were two lakhs. *Tomorrow, I have no choice but to pay the two lakhs. If I do, I will become a pauper.* An agitated Seth paced the room restlessly. *How nice would it be if this fellow was dead, just as I hoped he would be?* He muttered under his breath. The clock struck twice. He looked out of the window. It was very dark and slightly drizzling. He quickly opened a trunk, pulled out a dagger in a velvet sheath, tucked it into his waist and set out with a bunch of keys in hand. He went to the orchard, shone the torch and called the chowkidar. There was no response. *Chowkidar will be the primary suspect. Later, I can somehow wriggle out.* He touched the dagger and felt assured. He approached the room slowly. He could see the light of the lantern on the table through the window. The inmate was sitting in the chair near the table with his back to the window. Five minutes passed, but the inmate didn't move. *Perhaps he got used to sitting still for the past ten years,* thought Seth. He gently knocked on the window shutter to make some noise. The inmate didn't move. Seth opened the lock on the door. The old lock made a creaking noise. Seth wondered whether the inmate would give a surprised look or say something when the door was being opened. But he didn't move an inch. His hair and beard were heavily grown. He looked emaciated. The lack of exposure to sunlight made his skin pale. On the table, there were dozens of open books. There was one book in his lap. Seth thought he must have slept while reading. *It is easy to kill him now.* With this thought, he was about to move forward when he noticed a paper with something written on it on the table.

He picked it up and began reading in the lamplight.

"I will be a free man tomorrow morning. I will be at liberty. But before I leave this room, I must share some of my thoughts with you.

As the learned say, this world is a myth. This liberty and life are worthless. The world shines only superficially. I don't want to live in such a world.

In the past ten years, I have experienced worldly pleasures through books, roamed in the orchards, rested in the gazebos, loved women, travelled extensively, seen many worthy sites, and heard many things worthy of hearing. I have experienced everything that was there to be experienced.

Through these books, I have gained wisdom. I am now confident I am wiser than all of you.

But these books and this knowledge are a waste. Death is inevitable for a human. Beauty, wealth, knowledge and greatness will all vanish when one dies.

The world calls a lie a truth. It believes the superficial glow to be the real beauty. It considers such a world as heaven.

I am tired of this world. None of these things attract me anymore. Some years ago, I dreamt a lot of two lakhs' wealth. I felt happy, as if I had experienced that wealth. But I don't need that wealth now. So, I am leaving ahead of time to quash our agreement. "

Seth read the note and whispered, "May you live a hundred years!" and quietly walked away. The next morning, chowkidar reported that the inmate was absconding.

Rajaram Seth looked at the two-lakh rupee agreement on this table and quietly dropped it in the drawer.

*****

The Verdict

Original Author: Krovvidi Lingaraju. First published in Telugu in 1945.

1

“Who is in charge here, sir?”

“What do you want?”

“Who will receive the case report?”

“Which case?”

“Murder.”

“What? Murder case? Hmm..”

“Yes, sir. I was the one who committed the murder.”

“Whom did you kill? Your wife?”

“No, sir. My son.”

“What? Your son?”

The sub-inspector was shocked. When a huge, burly man comes and admits his crime, why is the inspector shocked? Why is a police officer – who normally jumps with joy when he catches a criminal – so stunned? Instead of falling all over the criminal and grabbing him with all his energy, the police officer calmly stood up and said, "You are under arrest. Now sit down." Before he could ask any questions, the criminal said, "Don't hesitate. I killed him. You don't need to know the reason. Here is the blood-stained knife. The body was cremated."

Left with no option, the inspector started going through the due process, but his mind was plagued by doubt. When he was cuffing the criminal's hands, the handcuffs felt heavy. When he searched the criminal's body, he felt as if he was squashing a freshly bloomed rose without reason. When he was locking him up in the dark cell, he felt guilty, as if he was throwing the God of dharma in the lock-up. But duty, duty and the Indian penal code..it is a steamroller.

2

After recovering his composure, the inspector started questioning the criminal. He demonstrated all his interrogation skills. Suspecting that the dead man was the son of his dead wife, he rained questions. Next, he suspected that the father and son might have run into each other, chasing girls. For every question, the criminal had only one answer. "I committed the crime. I am the sinner who killed his son with his hands. I have neither the right nor the place to live in this world. Therefore, please punish me. I am not talking about a jail sentence. Please hang me to death," he said. Gajapati Rao Naidu found it tricky to deal with a criminal talking that way. Law is not a joke! Will it accept if a murderer claims he didn't commit the murder? Will it accept if an innocent person claims he committed the murder? There is so much ritual that needs to be followed, like in a marriage or death. Even when murder takes place in the presence of a hundred witnesses, the law demands so much process to be followed. If a man just walks in and claims he committed the murder, will it agree? Naidu, who never encountered such a case in his career, was surprised, though. When this was Naidu's condition, what about the jawans? They were happy about one thing, though. A big bird is trapped. Their belief has been that unless he committed a major crime, why would he walk in and confess?

3

The accused Ramanna's village, Vijayeswaram, was eight miles from Gopuru police station. The village was large and counted wealthy farmers among its inhabitants. But there was no connectivity to the village. Carts operated to the village only in summer. In other seasons, even a millionaire had no option but to walk. While the villagers suffered a lot, they apparently did not demand a better road because of less nuisance from government officials. Naidu, who was transferred to Gopuru station recently, started early in the morning and reached Vijayeswaram after traversing the eight miles with a lot of struggle. The villagers, not used to government officials, were perturbed when they saw a police officer. Gajapati Rai Naidu set up camp in the village chavadi[221] and sent for the Munsab[222]. When the Munsab arrived,

"Where is your Bakir[223]?" asked Naidu.

"What are you talking about, sir? Bakir?"

"Yes. Why are you pretending as if you don't know anything?"

"Inspector, sir! You are talking strangely!"

"My dear Munsab! Don't act too much. Just because someone is a big man in the village doesn't mean you can brush the case under the carpet. That, too, a murder case!"

"Murder case, sir! In our village! Are you serious?"

"Oh, wow! What a performance! So, his reputation is so great? Listen, Munsab! Stop this acting and get serious. Yesterday morning, there was a murder in your village. Isn't that Ramanna, the leader of this village? That doesn't mean the crime can be hidden. That Ramanna killed his son. And.."

"What are you saying, sir? Ramanna Dora[224] has killed his son!" The Munsab was stunned.

The inspector now began to suspect a larger plot in this affair.

221 Common village hall where meetings take place.

222 Munsab: Village administrative head.

223 I could not find the exact meaning of this word but it could be more like an FIR or first report that a Munsab is supposed to file when a crime takes place in his village.

224 Dora: Lord, Owner.

"Hey Munsab! There is nothing to hide in this. Ramanna came to the police station last night and confessed to having killed his son yesterday morning and got himself arrested voluntarily. I have come to investigate the case. If you don't write the Bakir, you will be in deep trouble."

Before the inspector could continue, Munsab interrupted him and said, "Sir, let me tell you the facts. Ramanna Dora is not such a man. He is a thorough gentleman. We look up to him as the epitome of righteousness. It is true that his son died yesterday. All of us went and cremated him. But how can you call it a murder? His son - that scoundrel - was infested with many diseases and finally succumbed. What do you mean he was murdered by an angel-like Ramanna Dora? There is something suspicious about this. Only yesterday, I recorded his death in the births and deaths register. But there is no murder! Please trust me!"

The inspector cut him short and said, "Munsab! This argument is of no use. The criminal himself confessed to the crime. What can you and I do? Do you know Ramanna is in the Gopuru lock-up?"

"Inspector, sir! I find it tough to believe. How can our Ramanna Dora be a prisoner? He is not such a loose character!"

"What's wrong with you? Why don't you understand despite me repeating so many times? If it continues this way, it will land you in trouble. Write the

Bakir as I dictate, without another word. Let us go to his house and investigate."

"What investigation, sir! How can we face that poor lady? Regardless of how much of a rascal he was, he was their only son. Did you consider the possibility of mental disturbance due to the loss of his only son?"

"There are no such signs. He appeared a little disturbed, that's all!"

4

Naidu, Munsab, and a few other village elders went to Ramanna's house. They informed Lachchamma (Lakshmidevamma in police records) about Ramanna's confession. Lachchamma, already deeply grieving her son's loss, collapsed like a banana tree that fell with a single blow. Her husband's plight, along with her son's death, suddenly plunged her life into a bottomless mire. More distressing than these two pains was the pain of answering the inspector's questions from behind the curtain. By then, Naidu's inquiry with villagers told him that Ramanna was a thorough gentleman and a man of virtue. He also learnt that even the residents of neighbouring four or five villages were bound by his decisions in matters of dispute. This made Gajapati Rao Naidu even more clueless as to Ramanna's crime. Why would such a gentleman kill a son – born late in life after so many prayers and reared with a lot of love and affection – regardless of how much he might have sinned? So, Naidu made sure to talk to Lachchamma in a very unlike-police soft tone.

"Why are you landing double blows on me, O God!" Lachchamma cried.

"Madam, it will help if you share whatever you know."

"The only help I need for this life is..... By the way, why would that great man kill his son? That fellow died his own death, paying for his sins."

"He came to the police station in person and confessed to the killing. Why would he do that?"

"I don't know, son. I can't say why he confessed like that. Is it a surprise that a man gets mentally disturbed when he loses an adult son? I am a tough nut, so I am still alive. As if this tragedy is not enough, now he has to do the rounds of courts perhaps, too!"

"Did the father and son have any quarrels?"

"Ayyo Rama[225]! Why would they? We brought him up so lovingly, having been blessed with him after a lot of prayers and very late in life. As our bad luck would have it, his behaviour was not good. But the father and son were not even on talking terms. Where was the question of any quarrel?"

"Did they have any specific fight that day?"

"I don't know. The previous night, at seven, Venkaiah Garu and some others came and complained

225 Expression of grief and frustration. Typical Telugu expression.

about him to my husband. I think it was about some molestation attempt on their girl! For a long time, our son got into bad company and strayed completely. My dear! I tried telling my husband several times but he didn't heed my words. Being busy with the village affairs, when did he have time to address family issues? After those people left, he was downcast and didn't come for dinner. I called him many times, but he didn't get up. Adding to his distress, I said foolishly, 'When it doesn't bend as a plant, would it bend as a tree? Not having controlled him when he was young, what is the point in feeling bad now? Please get up and come for dinner.' I don't know how he took those words. He had his meal and, like never before, sat in the veranda waiting for our son to come. That fellow came reeling at about ten in the night and was about to go to his room directly. Then he held his hand. That fellow shook off his father and went inside. He yelled from his room, saying he didn't want his meal. Father followed son into the room. When I tried to follow him, he asked me not to. Even though I wanted to be there, I turned back. Father scolded him and cajoled him. From what I could overhear, I understood our son abused his father once or twice in strong language. Just two days ago, there was a marriage match for him from Ramannapet. They offered twenty acres along with their girl. My husband didn't give any reply to them. As a woman, I said, 'If we marry him off, he will get better. Why don't you agree?' 'Should we destroy her life, too?' he retorted. I think he broached the marriage topic with his son that night again. All I could hear was, 'I don't want to marry!'

That's all I know. Around midnight, he got up, went to his son's room and then returned crying inconsolably. He woke me up and said, 'It is all over. Our son is dead.' When I went into the room crying, his face was already dark, and he was still. Then the neighbours gathered, and it was all crying and more crying! What is this, if not the influence of Kali[226]? A son, who is supposed to perform his father's final rites, is dead, and the father is now lighting his pyre. The much-awaited child became a short-lived pleasure." Lachchamma wept bitterly. The inspector was moved and didn't know what to do.

5

Gajapati Rao Nadu mentally summarised the story, which matched what he heard during his inquiry with the villagers. But he still had to contend with Ramanna's statement. He considered the possibility of suicide, *but why would Ramanna take the blame on himself? Love for one's son is great, but is the love for one's life any less? If a calm person gets angry, is it not like Dharmaraju's*[227] *anger? For a man who valued his prestige and public image a lot, it is possible that his honour weighed more than his love for his son. In a momentary rage about something wrong done by the son, he might have hit him, and that blow could*

226 Kali Yuga, the fourth of the yugas, when Dharma is supposed to be limping on just one leg.

227 Yudhishtira, eldest of the Pandavas in Maha Bharata. Known for his calm demeanour and adherence to Dharma at all times.

have landed in the wrong place and led to death. This explanation sounded plausible. While there are factors like momentary rage involved, the law is the law and has to take its course just as religious rituals, whether on a good occasion or a bad occasion. Involuntarily, Naidu felt for a second that Ramanna was innocent and he must be saved. But he quickly reminded himself of police duty, law and penal code and immediately returned to being a normal police officer. Ramanna's case became a tough one to crack for him. Ramanna would remain immersed in a deep thought and give only one answer to all his questions.

"Why are you hesitating so much? I am a callous murderer of my son. I don't deserve to live! Punish me according to the law and relieve me from this agony. Do whatever you want to do." These were Ramanna's standard words. He refused to meet his relatives and village folks who came to see him. How do you deal with such a person? The case has to move forward. Naidu stitched all the pieces together, consulted his superiors and filed a murder case against Ramanna.

6

The murder case moved forward. A statement was recorded in the magistrate's presence, and due process was followed in the magistrate court. Then, it was sent to the sessions court. How does it matter, even if there are many loopholes in the case? If the accused is confessing to his crime, where is the difficulty? Ramanna was lodged in the central prison.

7

It was almost time to receive his pension when sessions judge Giri Rao got promoted to district judge. He started as a district Munsab and rose through the ranks. The rumour has it that his promotion came just as calmly and slowly as his demeanour was calm and God-fearing. When sentencing an accused, he used to feel the pain and agony himself. Because of the limited service time left, the high court went easy on him and ignored his ways. Ramanna's trial reached his court. Public prosecutor Rao Saheb Venkaiah Naidu had been in that job for nine years, thanks to the blessings of the higher officials. He was desperately trying for an extension of three more years. He used to routinely argue police cases, assuming they were fool-proof as a rule. Even if there were minor exceptions and flaws, he believed it was the prosecutor's job to fix them. Whenever an accused was convicted, he used to believe it took him one step closer to his ideal of Diwan Bahadur[228]. That was the kind of unwavering faith he had in the tyranny of law. He was surprised when he noticed that Inspector Gajapati Rao Naidu did not show the same enthusiasm that police officers usually demonstrate in murder cases and was working mechanically and half-heartedly.

The prosecution witness testimony was over. Gajapati Rao Naidu was the main witness. His evidence was in line with Ramanna's confession statement. The accused refused to engage a lawyer. Why would he when

228 Honorary title bestowed by the British Government.

he didn't have any intention of being freed? On the judge's insistence, a lawyer was provided at government expense to defend the accused. What could he do? He could point out flaws in the prosecution argument, but could he make Ramanna change his mind? After the witness questioning was over, the judge asked the accused,

"What do you have to say? Have you committed the crime?"

"I am the criminal!"

"Have you voluntarily given the statement in the magistrate's presence?"

"Yes."

"Is that statement completely true?"

"There is nothing to change."

"What is the reason for killing?"

"When it is over, why do you care about the reason, sir?"

Ramanna's face showed sadness but no sign of fear. Giri Rao Pantulu studied human psychology but couldn't fathom this accused's attitude. Either this man must be the epitome of virtue or a cold-blooded criminal. When he correlated the evidence, the sadness in the face and the courage, he felt the second option must be ruled out.

The prosecutor presented his case strongly. The accused's confession, using his influence to cremate the body without sending it for post-mortem and the accused's wife's statement that mentioned an altercation between father and son were all used as sufficient proof to establish the guilt. He argued that there must have been a strong motive for the murder. It could even be a woman, but it is impossible to get evidence because of Ramanna's influence and status in society. When the prosecutor was arguing, Ramanna grimaced and felt distinctly uncomfortable as if ants were crawling over his body or it was being pierced with needles. How would Rao Saheb understand that discomfort? Can the bull's wound be a pain for the crow[229]? Whether the dead person was an old man or a youth, the priest conducting the rituals would treat them the same. His demands for Godanam[230] and Bhudanam[231] would remain the same. Law is no different. It must run its due course. Rao Saheb argued that the court can't take into consideration the accused's position in society and give weightage to the gaps in the evidence. If he is released on that basis, there would be no limit to the crimes in the region.

The government-provided defence lawyer did his job. His argument ran like this. Just because the accused had confessed to the crime, he can't be held guilty. It was highly likely that the accused -in a state of temporary mental disturbance after his son's death - might have decided to die and hence gave his confession statement accordingly. He further argued that the motive must be

229 A classic Telugu expression which originally says a Bull's wound is tasty for a crow.

230 Godanam: Donation of cows as part of rituals.

231 Bhudanam: Donation of land as part of rituals.

established for such crimes. Since the prosecution could not establish any motive, there was room for doubt. The British law calls for a not-guilty verdict in such cases. He eloquently argued that Ramanna could be taking this guilt upon himself due to moral and emotional reasons, but it was tough to fathom in the normal course. Hence, this case cannot be treated like a normal case, and the onus of a fair trial rests with the judge. With this, he concluded his argument.

Ramanna was baffled by this young lawyer's insistence on saving his life. When he heard the last sentence putting the onus on him, the judge felt an additional load on him. The public prosecutor mocked the defence argument. The case was adjourned.

8

Throughout the trial, the judge focused on the accused's face. He couldn't see any fear of death in that face. He remained calm like a pot full of water. Only God knows whether the pot was filled with true peace or sorrow. When the arguments were over, the judge's anxiety increased. Now, the accused's life was in his hands. While the prosecution's argument had gaps, the accused's confession remained a strong point. There was also scope for a strong moral reason, as argued by the defence lawyer. If he trusts only the accused's statement and sentences him, he would be responsible for taking the life of a man. He asked the jail officials about the accused's conduct in the jail. He got a response saying the accused always spent time in meditation, never discussed his case with other inmates and never troubled anyone. How could he discern the true motives of such an unfathomable person? Going only by the lifeless law books, if he sentences the accused, he would be responsible for taking a life. If he doesn't use his discretion in such a matter, what justice could he deliver? Who could help him in this regard? The judge was overwhelmed with anxiety.

The judgement day arrived. The accused was called into the judge's chamber. He stood alone, facing the judge. The judge asked him to take a seat. With folded hands, Ramanna declined the offer. The judge was impressed with his propriety.

Judge: "Ramanna, I have seen many cases and many criminals. But nothing comes close to this.

Ramanna: "Sir."

"Have you committed the crime?"

"I am guilty."

"That's not what I asked. Have you killed your son with your hands?"

"I am the guilty one, my lord!"

"Answer my question directly!"

"What is there to answer, sir? I am the criminal."

The judge could see the twist in Ramanna's answers. Finally, with some despair,

"Dear Ramanna! I am not asking these questions as a judge. If that was my intention, I could have asked you in the courtroom itself. Puzzled by your behaviour, I am asking like a gentleman. Also, if I don't find out the truth in your case, I will remain guilty."

The judge's cordiality and beseeching tone mellowed Ramanna. The dam holding back his sorrow broke, and tears flowed freely. Ramanna bowed. He said in a choking voice, "Sir, this poor man doesn't deserve so much respect."

"Ramanna, leave that aside. Tell me your story as it happened. Don't push me into the path of injustice. Don't let me sin."

The judge's words pierced Ramanna's heart. He felt like a long-lost friend returned. He couldn't hold himself back anymore.

"My lord! Please hear my story. When you ask with so much affection and with an intent of not straying from the path of virtue, it becomes my duty to tell you the complete facts. If I don't do it, this crime will become bigger than the one I have already committed."

The judge started listening quietly.

"It wouldn't be an exaggeration to say that I am counted amongst the well-to-do men in our region. What I inherited was a hundred acres, along with an orchard and a large house. There was never any shortage of anything. Our family comes from a traditional background. Through hard work, I increased the estate and also preserved the family traditions. Anything good or bad in that region happens on my watch."

"Yes. I heard about it. That made my task trickier."

"Yes, sir. I never had time to set right my own affairs. Each day would be spent mostly handling public matters. It was as if my word was law. But I had one lacuna at home. For a long time, we didn't have children. Two years after my wife joined me in the household, the void became very acute. The nagging started with my mother and then slowly spread to my wife. Immersed, as I was, in public matters, I neglected it initially. Eventually, I started feeling the gap, too, and it used to hurt a lot. Due to my reserved nature at home, I hid this pain within myself. Leaving my mother aside, my wife and I also started feeling the agony but never discussed it with anyone. Our lives became dull but they were going on mechanically. My wife prayed to several Gods and consumed countless drugs and tonics. To divert my mind from this pain, I spent more time on public affairs and religious matters. When I was about forty years of age, our long wait ended, and my wife became pregnant. I started showering her with more love. Thanks to God's grace, we were blessed with a male child. We celebrated in a big way and named him after my father, Ramaiah. We took every possible care in his upbringing and showered a lot of love and affection on him. The boy turned ten. He didn't show any keenness in education. I comforted myself, thinking character is more important than education. Day by day, his character became questionable. I am reticent by nature. I couldn't be tough with the boy who was the only son born after so many prayers.

He turned eighteen. I used to agonise internally at his lack of proficiency in studies. I consoled myself with the logic that *it was his fate. I gave him enough opportunities, and there was nothing more I could do.* My father was well-educated, and I was well-educated, but all my hopes were dashed. The one last hope about a good character was also dashed. "Ramanna's voice choked with emotion, and he paused for a while and continued.

"It came to my attention that my son started drinking and gambling and got into bad company. No one told me directly. His mother appealed to me a couple of times, 'Our boy is straying. Please scold him.' I ignored the warning, saying, ' If our gold is good, then why blame others?' I used to lightly scold him occasionally. Sometimes, I was more explicit. It was not my nature to go beyond that. I could not do it. Finally, people started talking in the open about his bad deeds. It affected my honour and prestige. When I was talking about public matters, I could hear some sarcastic comments, 'It is easy to preach to others. One would know when things are closer home.' Some people were more direct. They challenged me, 'You preach morals to the whole world. Why don't you set your son right?' On such days, except for showing my irritation at my son, I couldn't do much. Perhaps it was too late to do anything. My honour fell several notches by then. A few days ago, some village elders came home and warned me, 'You have let your son loose on the village. You must take responsibility for his actions.' I was dejected and couldn't speak. I accepted my guilt silently. I cursed my fate. It took just a fraction of a second for my love to turn into hatred towards my son. I strongly reprimanded him. But it was too late, and things went out of hand. He openly defied me. To cut the story short, I will come to the last day's events. That evening, when I came home, one of my neighbours approached me very agitatedly and spoke in strong language. He was entitled to use such language, and I deserved it. My son molested his daughter. Their family and friends gathered and thrashed him. They didn't stop there. They filed a police case, and came to inform me about the same. He was due to be arrested the next day. My honour, prestige and family tradition reached a nadir that day. When I tolerated their strong words silently, they misunderstood my silence. They accused me, saying my softness was the root cause of this state of affairs and it was also harmful to the welfare of the village. I felt humiliated. I somehow reasoned it out and sent them away. I then slumped in a chair on my veranda. I controlled my sorrow and emotions. My wife came to call me for dinner and noticed my position. When I told her what happened, she said, 'You didn't control him at the right time. Now we have to endure this.' She, too, transferred the onus onto me. That night, I waited until my son returned home. He came between nine and ten and was reeling under the influence of alcohol. His eyes were bloodshot. Without bothering to look at me, he vanished into his room. I waited for a second and followed him into the room.

'My son, what is this?'

'What?'

'What is your family background and tradition? What is your status in society? And what are you doing?'

"..........."

'Why are your eyes like that?'

'Drink...'

He was never so openly defiant before. Things were getting out of control.

'I understand there was some scuffle in the evening!'

'Yes. Routine matter. What's new in that?'

'I was told you will be arrested!'

'Nobody can arrest me!'

'Why?'

'No one can catch me. Humanly impossible!'

'My son! Why have you reached this terrible state?'

'Don't talk now! No use preaching anything now. You are the reason for my present state.'

'Me! How?'

'Absolutely you! Only you!'

His words rang out like thunderbolts.

'What did I do? I ensured you had everything you needed. It is just your fate...'

'My fate? Yes. Your fate is also like this. Your negligence brought me to this state.'

I was hurt. I asked him with a heavy heart, 'My son! Have I stopped you from being good?'

'Stop me! When I needed a father's help, you were busy. You had time to fix the village's matters, but you never had time for me. You already left me to my fate. In future, too, leave me to my fate.' He cried and turned away. I realised it was futile to continue the conversation in that state. Unable to control my crying, I came out. His words, 'You are responsible. Leave me to my fate,' kept ringing in my ears—even today. After three hours, I heard a light moaning sound. When I went inside to see, I was stunned. The boy was dying. There was a bottle on the bed. Struggling to speak, he said, 'Father, let me die peacefully. This is the last favour you can do for me. Don't call the public and disgrace me. Soon, the family will be stain-free.' Saying this, he passed away in my arms. What was there to hide? I called his mother. She collapsed on her son, crying. Honouring his wish, I arranged a quiet cremation the next morning." Ramanna wept, but his speech remained steady.

The tears that formed in the judge's eyes involuntarily swelled and flowed down his cheeks. He paused for a second and,

"Ramanna! So, why did you go to the police, and why this case?"

"Sir, after the cremation, my house seemed desolate, like a burial ground. His words, 'You are responsible! You took care of village matters, but you ignored your son's life,' kept piercing my heart. They sounded true. When he was young, I pampered him. Later, I was busy. After that, I was arrogant about my public image and didn't pay attention to his needs. I killed my son with my hands. My world became dark. I lost interest in living anymore. My ego and prestige stopped me from jumping into a well and taking my life. There is no need to narrate the story any further. I am guilty. Don't spare me. End my misery quickly." Ramanna prostrated himself in front of the judge.

9

The court, which was supposed to meet at eleven in the morning, was postponed to four in the afternoon. At four o'clock, the judge delivered a 'not guilty' verdict. He narrated the complete story along with his judgment and justified his verdict. Unlike other accused, Ramanna didn't jump with joy. Gloom and despair showed on his face. He walked unsteadily out of the dock like a blind man and entered an empty world like a destitute. There was a lot of commotion in the court, but Gajapati Rao heaved a sigh of relief.

10

No one knew when Ramanna went to his village. One morning, the house could be seen locked. Lachchamma, too, vanished. He formed a trust for his estate and appointed the soon-to-be-retired judge Giri Rao Pantulu as the trustee with full execution powers. He also decided to establish an orphanage for boys and girls and named it 'Srirama Orphanage' after his son. He handed over the required documents for the orphanage to Giri Rao Pantulu and made certain that his name wouldn't appear anywhere in that orphanage in future.

11

Ramanna and his wife remained untraceable, but the orphanage he founded continued in the village without any ostentation and serves orphan boys and girls.

*****

www.ingramcontent.com/pod-product-compliance
Lightning Source LLC
La Vergne TN
LVHW100249210926
848480LV00003B/869
* 9 7 9 8 8 9 3 6 3 6 2 4 6 *